PRAISE FOR RUTH RENDELL

"Unequivocally the most brilliant mystery writer of our time. Her stories are a lesson in a human nature as capable of the most exotic love as it is of the cruelest murder. She does not avert her gaze … she magnificently triumphs in a style that is uniquely hers and mesmerizing." – Patricia Cornwell

"Rendell's clear, shapely prose casts the mesmerizing spell of the confessional." – *The New Yorker*

"Superior writing by one of the best in the world."
– *Ottawa Citizen*

"Rendell writes with such elegance and restraint, with such a literate voice and an insightful mind, that she transcends the mystery genre and achieves something almost sublime."
– *Los Angeles Times*

"One of the finest practitioners of her craft in the English-speaking world … Even with the crowded, competitive and fecund world of career mystery writers, Ruth Rendell is recognized as a phenomenon." – *The New York Times Book Review*

"Ruth Rendell is the best mystery writer in the English-speaking world." – *Time*

"British crime at its best can be found in the fiction of Ruth Rendell, for whom no superlative is sufficient."
– *Chronicle-Herald* (Halifax)

"Ruth Rendell is surely one of the great novelists presently at work in our language…. She is a writer whose work should be read by anyone who either enjoys brilliant mystery or distinguished literature." – Scott Turow

ALSO BY RUTH RENDELL

Adam and Eve and
Pinch Me
Piranha to Scurfy
A Sight for Sore Eyes
The Keys to the Street
Blood Lines
The Crocodile Bird
Going Wrong
The Bridesmaid
Talking to Strange Men
Live Flesh

The Tree of Hands
The Killing Doll
Master of the Moor
The Lake of Darkness
Make Death Love Me
A Judgement in Stone
A Demon in My View
The Face of Trespass
One Across, Two Down
Vanity Dies Hard
To Fear a Painted Devil

CHIEF INSPECTOR WEXFORD NOVELS

Harm Done
Road Rage
Simisola
Kissing the Gunner's Daughter
The Veiled One
An Unkindness of Ravens
Speaker of Mandarin
Death Notes
A Sleeping Life
Shake Hands Forever

Some Lie and Some Die
Murder Being Once Done
No More Dying Then
A Guilty Thing Surprised
The Best Man to Die
Wolf to the Slaughter
Sins of the Fathers
A New Lease of Death
From Doon with Death

BY RUTH RENDELL WRITING AS BARBARA VINE

Grasshopper
The Chimney Sweeper's Boy
The Brimstone Wedding
No Night Is Too Long
Anna's Book

King Solomon's Carpet
Gallowglass
The House of Stairs
A Fatal Inversion
A Dark-Adapted Eye

THE BABES IN THE WOOD

RUTH RENDELL

SEAL BOOKS

Seal Books and colophon are trademarks of
Random House of Canada Limited.

THE BABES IN THE WOOD
Seal Books/published by arrangement with Doubleday Canada
Doubleday Canada edition published 2002
Seal Books edition published November 2003

ISBN 0–7704–2922–X

Cover image: Paul Mason/Photonica

Seal Books are published by Random House of Canada Limited.
"Seal Books" and the portrayal of a seal are the property of
Random House of Canada Limited.

Visit Random House of Canada Limited's website: www.randomhouse.ca

PRINTED AND BOUND IN THE USA

OPM 10 9 8 7 6 5 4 3

For Karl and Lilian Fredriksson
with love

BEFOREHAND

It was warm enough to be outdoors at ten and not feel a chill. The sky was all covered with stars and the moon had come up among them, a reddish harvest moon. Where they were was a wood with a clearing in it broad enough for a thousand people to dance on, but its springiness came from the dense green turf and its walls were a ring of tall forest trees, beech and ash and chestnut. Because the leaves hadn't yet begun to fall the house, which wasn't far away, couldn't be seen. Nor could its outbuildings and its gardens.

In the centre of the open space the people, a hundred or so, had formed a circle. Most of them had no idea the house was there. They had come in mini-buses and vans and some in their own cars, down a lane which debouched from another lane, which led from a rather narrow road. Nothing at the entrance to the lane indicated whether this was private land or not and nothing gave a clue to the presence of the house. Some of the people wore the ordinary clothes favoured by the young and middle-aged alike and both sexes, jeans, a shirt, a sweater or jacket, but others were enveloped in robes, black or brown. They held hands and waited, expectant, perhaps excited.

A man dressed in white – open-necked white shirt, white trousers, white shoes – strode into the middle of the ring. When he reached the centre the people began to sing. It was a rousing tune which might have been a hymn or a chorus from an opera or musical. When it was done they clapped their hands rhythmically. The clapping ceased when the man in white spoke.

He called out in ringing tones, 'Are there any evil spirits tormenting you? Is there anyone here possessed by a bad spirit?'

The silence was deep. No one stirred. A little breeze rose and flitted across the circle, lifting long hair and making draperies flutter. It fell again as someone appeared within the ring. None of those holding hands, the singers, those who had clapped, could have told where the newcomer came from. No observer, even from close to, could have told if this was a man or a woman and no living person could be seen immediately behind it, yet it stumbled a little as if given a push. It was draped from neck to feet in a black robe and its head covered by a black veil. A cry went up from the man who had asked about evil spirits.

'Send your fire down, Lord, burn the evil spirits!'

'Burn, burn, burn!' cried the ring.

The man in white and the figure in black met. From a distance they looked like a pair of lovers in disguise, masked and cloaked figures from the Venice Carnival perhaps. It was growing darker now, thin cloud passing across the face of the moon. The priest and supplicant, if that is what they were, were close enough to touch but no one could see if they touched or not. Seeing was less important than hearing and suddenly there was much to hear as the black figure let out a long low wail, a keening moan, but louder than a moan, and followed by a series of such cries. They sounded real, not staged, they sounded as if they came from a distressed and anguished heart, a soul in torment, and now they rose and fell, rose and fell.

The white figure kept quite still. The ring of people began to shiver and sway from side to side and soon they too were moaning while some beat at their bodies with their hands or, in several cases, with twigs they picked up from the ground. They swayed and wailed and the cloud passed so that the moon came out once more and blazed on this ritual, bathing it in white fire. Then the figure in black also began to move. Not slowly as the people did but with swift movements that became frenzied as it beat with its hands not on its own body but on the chest and arms of the man in white. Its moans became growls and you could hear its teeth chattering as it growled.

Apparently oblivious of the violent assault made on him, the man in white raised his arms above his head. In the voice of some ancient priest he called, 'Confess your sins and wickedness!'

Then it came, a catalogue of errors, of commission and omission, some of it murmured, some of it uttered so that all could hear, the voice rising to a shout of desperation. The people were quiet, listening avidly. The confession went on but in less impassioned tones, dwindling until the creature in black was stammering, growing limp and cringing. Then there was silence broken only by a soft, almost sensual, sigh which rose from the crowd.

The priest spoke. He laid one hand on the black-cloaked shoulder and said in a ringing voice, 'Now come out of him!' There was no absolution, only that assured command: 'Come out of him!'

A cloud drifted across the moon, an event which evoked another sigh from the people, more perhaps a gasp of wonderment. A shudder passed through them as if a gust of wind had ruffled a field of corn.

'See the evil spirits, my children! See them in the air flying across the moon! See Ashtaroth, the demon, she who dwells in the moon!'

'I see! I see!' came the cry from the ring of people. 'We see the demon Ashtaroth!'

'The creature that was their home has confessed to great sins of the flesh but she, the demon, the embodiment of fleshly sin, has come out, and with her those lesser spirits. See them high above us in the air now!'

'I see! I see!'

And at last the supplicant in black spoke. It was in a broken voice, weak and sexless. 'I see, I see . . .'

'Thanks be to the Lord God of Hosts!' cried the man in white. 'Thanks be to the Blessed Trinity and all angels!'

'Thanks be to the Lord!'

'Thanks be to the Lord and all angels,' said the figure in black.

Within moments it was in black no longer. Two women broke through the ring and came into the centre, bearing armfuls of white clothing. Then they dressed the black figure, covering it from head to foot until there were two in white.

The one who had been black called aloud but in misery no longer, 'Thanks be to the Lord who has delivered his servant from sin and restored purity once more.'

The words were scarcely uttered when the dance began. The two white figures were swallowed up in the crowd as someone made music, a tune coming from somewhere, a melody like a Scottish reel that at the same time, strangely, was a hymn. They danced and clapped. A woman had a tambourine and another a zither. The figure who had sinned and been redeemed and purified stood in the midst of them, laughing a merry laugh like someone enjoying himself at a children's party. There was nothing to eat, nothing to smoke and nothing to drink, but they were drunk on fervour, on excitement, on the hysteria which comes when many are gathered together in a single belief, a single passion. And the one who was absolved continued to laugh peal after peal, merry and joyful as a child.

The dance lasted for half an hour but ceased when the music was withdrawn. It was a signal for departure and everyone, suddenly subdued once more, moved back to the lane where vehicles were parked on the grass verge.

The priest figure, who had come alone, waited until the people had gone before stripping off his robes and emerging as an ordinary man in jeans and combat jacket. The robes he put into the boot of his car. Then he walked down the drive to the house. It was large by present-day standards, early Victorian, with two shallow flights of stairs mounting to a front door inside a modestly pillared portico, and a balustrade bordering its slate roof, a house that was pleasing to look at if rather dull. There are hundreds, if not thousands, like it all over England. Plainly, no one was at home, but no one would be on a week night. He mounted the steps on the left-hand side, took an envelope from his pocket and slipped it through the letter box. He lived in straitened circumstances like most of his flock and wanted to save the cost of postage.

The owner of the house and grounds had asked for a fee. Naturally, though he was a rich man. But the priest, if priest he was, had jibbed at two hundred pounds and they had finally agreed on a hundred. The envelope also held a note of thanks. The people might want to make use of the open space again, as they had done several times in the past. The priest always referred to it as 'the open space', though he had heard it called the dancing floor, a name he thought had an idolatrous ring to it.

He went back to his car.

CHAPTER 1

The Kingsbrook was not usually visible from his window. Not its course, nor its twisty meanders, nor the willows which made a double fringe along its banks. But he could see it now, or rather see what it had become, a river as wide as the Thames but flat and still, a broad lake that filled its own valley, submerging its water meadows in a smooth silver sheet. Of the few houses that stood in that valley, along a lane which had disappeared leading from a bridge which had disappeared, only their roofs and upper storeys showed above the waters. He thought of his own house, on the other side of that gently rising lake, as yet clear of the floods, only the end of his garden lapped by an encroaching tide.

It was raining. But as he had remarked to Burden some four hours before, rain was no longer news, it was tedious to remark on it. The exciting thing worthy of comment was when it wasn't raining. He picked up the phone and called his wife.

'Much the same as when you went out,' she said. 'The end of the garden's under water but it hasn't reached the mulberry tree. I don't think it's moved. That's what I'm measuring by, the mulberry tree.'

'Good thing we don't breed silkworms,' said Wexford, leaving his wife to decipher this cryptic remark.

There hadn't been anything like it in this part of Sussex in living memory – not, at least, in his memory. In spite of a double wall of sandbags the Kingsbrook had inundated the road at the High Street bridge, flooded the Job Centre and Sainsbury's but miraculously – so far – spared the Olive and Dove Hotel. It was a hilly place and most of the dwellings on higher ground had escaped. Not so the High Street, Glebe Road, Queen and York Streets with their ancient shopfronts and overhanging eaves. Here the water lay a foot, two feet, in places three feet, deep. In St Peter's churchyard the tops of tombstones pierced a grey, rain-punctured lake like rocks showing above the surface of the sea. And still it rained.

According to the Environment Agency, the land in the flood plains of England and Wales was saturated, was waterlogged, so that none of this latest onslaught could drain away. There were houses in Kingsmarkham, and even more in flatter low-lying Pomfret, which had been flooded in October and were flooded again now at the end of November. Newspapers helpfully informed their readers that such 'properties' would be unsaleable, worth nothing. Their owners had left them weeks ago, gone to stay with relatives or in temporarily rented flats. The local authority had used up all the ten thousand sandbags it had ordered, scoffing at the possibility of half of them being used. Now they were all under the waters and more had been sent for but not arrived.

Wexford tried not to think about what would happen if another inch of rain fell before nightfall and the water reached and passed Dora's gauge, the mulberry. On the house side of the tree, from that point, the land sloped very gradually downwards until it came to a low wall, quite useless as a flood defence, that separated lawn from terrace and french windows. He tried not to think about it but still he pictured the water reaching and then pouring over that wall . . . Once more he reached for the phone but this time he only touched the receiver and withdrew his hand as the door opened and Burden came in.

'Still raining,' he said.

Wexford just looked at him, the kind of look you'd give something you'd found at the back of the fridge with a sell-by date of three months before.

'I've just heard a crazy thing, thought it might amuse you. You look as if you need cheering up.' He seated himself on the corner of the desk, a favourite perch. Wexford thought he was thinner than ever and looked rather as if he'd just had a facelift, total body massage and three weeks at a health farm. 'Woman phoned to say she and her husband went to Paris for the weekend, leaving their children with a – well, a teen-sitter, I suppose, got back late last night to find the lot gone and naturally she assumes they've all drowned.'

'That's amusing?'

'It's pretty bizarre, isn't it? The teenagers are fifteen and thirteen, the sitter's in her thirties, they can all swim and the house is miles above the floods.'

'Where is it?'

'Lyndhurst Drive.'

'Not far from me then. But miles above the floods. The water's slowly creeping up my garden.'

Burden put one leg across the other and swung his elegantly shod foot in negligent fashion. 'Cheer up. It's worse in the Brede Valley. Not a single house has escaped.' Wexford had a vision of buildings growing legs and running, pursued by an angry tide. 'Jim Pemberton has gone up there. Lyndhurst Drive, I mean. And he's alerted the Subaqua Task Force.'

'The *what*?'

'You must have heard of it.' Burden just avoided saying 'even you'. 'It's the joint enterprise of Kingsmarkham

Council and the Fire Brigade. Mostly volunteers in wetsuits.'

'If it's amusing,' said Wexford, 'that is to say, if we aren't taking it seriously, why such extreme measures?'

'No harm in being on the safe side,' said Burden comfortably.

'All right, let me get this straight. These children – what are they, by the way? Boy and girl? And what's their name?'

'Dade. They're called Giles and Sophie Dade. I don't know the sitter's name. They can both swim. In fact, the boy's got some sort of silver medal for life-saving and the girl just missed getting into the county junior swimming team. God knows why the mother thinks they've drowned. They'd no reason to go near the floods as far as I know. Jim'll get it sorted.'

Wexford said no more. The rain had begun beating against the glass. He got up and went to the window but by the time he got there it was raining so hard that there was nothing to see, just a white fog and, near at hand, raindrops exploding on the sill. 'Where are you going to eat?' he said to Burden.

'Canteen, I suppose. I'm not going out in this.'

Pemberton came back at three to say that a couple of volunteer frogmen had begun searching for Giles and Sophie Dade but it was more a formality, an allaying of Mrs Dade's fears, than a genuine anxiety. None of the water lying in the Kingsmarkham area had reached a depth of four feet. It was over in the Brede Valley that things were more serious. A woman who couldn't swim had been drowned there a month before when she fell from the temporary walkway that had been built from one of her upper windows to the higher ground. She had tried to cling to the walkway struts but the floods came over her head and the rain and wind swept her

away. Nothing like that could have happened to the
Dade children, competent swimmers to whom twice
the present depth of water would have presented no
problems.

More a cause for concern in everyone's view was the
looting currently going on from shops in the flooded
High Street. A good many shopkeepers had removed
their goods, clothes, books, magazines and stationery,
china and glass, kitchen equipment to an upper floor
and then removed themselves. Looters waded through
the water by night – some of them carrying ladders –
smashed upper windows and helped themselves to
what they fancied. One thief, arrested by Detective
Sergeant Vine, protested that the iron and microwave
oven he had stolen were his by right. In his view, the
goods were compensation for his ground-floor flat
being inundated, he was sure he would get no other.
Vine suspected that a bunch of teenagers, still at
school, were responsible for stealing the entire CD and
cassette stock from the York Audio Centre.

Wexford would have liked to check with his wife
every half-hour but he controlled himself and didn't
phone again until half past four. By then the heavy rain
had given place to a thin relentless drizzle. The phone
rang and rang, and he had almost decided she must be
out when she picked up the receiver.

'I was outside. I heard it ringing but I had to get my
boots off and try not to make too much mess. Rain and
mud make the simplest outdoor tasks take twice as long.'

'How's the mulberry tree?'

'The water's reached it, Reg. It's sort of lapping
against the trunk. Well, it was bound to, the way it's
been raining. I was wondering if there was anything we
could do to stop it, the water coming up, I mean, not
the rain. They haven't found a way to stop that yet. I

was thinking about sandbags, only the council haven't any, I phoned them and this woman said they're waiting for them to come in. Like a shop assistant, I thought.'

He laughed, though not very cheerfully. 'We can't stop the water but we can start thinking about moving our furniture upstairs.' Get Neil over to help, he nearly said, and then he remembered his son-in-law was gone out of their lives since he and Sylvia split up. Instead he told Dora he'd be home by six.

That morning he hadn't brought the car. Lately he'd been walking a lot more. The almost endless downpours stimulated his need to walk – there was human nature for you! – because the chance to do so in comfort and in the dry came so seldom. At first light no rain had been falling and the sky was a wet pearly blue. It was still dry at eight thirty and he'd begun to walk. Huge heavy clouds were gathering, covering up the blue and the pale, milky sun. By the time he reached the station the first drops were falling. Now he thought he would have to make it home through this wet mist that inter-mittently became drizzle, but when he came out of the newly installed automatic doors the rain had lifted and for the first time for a long while he felt a marked chill in the air. It *smelt* drier. It smelt like a change in the weather. Better not be too optimistic, he told himself.

It was dark. Already dark as midnight. From this level, on foot, he could see nothing of the floods, only that the pavements and roadways were wet and puddles lay deep in the gutters. He crossed the High Street and began the slightly uphill walk to home. The Dades he had forgotten and wouldn't have recalled them even then but for passing the end of Kingston Gardens and reading the street name in the yellow light from a lamp. Lyndhurst Drive met it at its highest point and those living there could have looked down from their windows on to his roof and his garden. They were safe. Someone had told him that for the floods to reach such a height they would have had first to rise above the cupola on Kingsmarkham Town Hall.

Yes, the Dades were safe up there. And the chance of their children being drowned practically nil. Before he left, a message had come through from the Subaqua Task Force to say that no living people or bodies had been found. Wexford stared up the hill, wondering exactly where they lived. And then he stopped dead. What was the matter with him? Was he losing his grip on things? Those children might not have drowned but they were missing, weren't they? Their parents had come home from a weekend away and found them gone. Last night. All this nonsense about floods and drowning had obscured for him the central issue. Two children, aged fifteen and thirteen, were *missing*.

He walked on fast, thinking fast. Of course, the chances were that they were back by now. They had been, according to Burden, in the care of an older person, and they were all three missing. That surely meant that the sitter, presumably a woman, had taken them somewhere. Probably she had told the mother on the previous Friday or whenever it was the parents went away, that she intended to take them on some outing and the mother had forgotten. A woman who would assume that her children had drowned, just because they weren't there and part of the town was flooded, had to be – well, to put it charitably, somewhat scatterbrained.

Dora wasn't in the house. He found her down the garden, directing the beam from a torch on to the roots of the mulberry tree. 'I don't think it's come up any more since I spoke to you at four thirty,' she said. 'Do we really have to move the furniture?'

They went indoors. 'We could shift some of the stuff we value most. Books. Favourite pictures. That console table that was your mother's. We could make a start with that and listen to the weather forecast at ten.'

He gave her a drink and poured one for himself. With the much-diluted whisky on the table beside him, he phoned Burden. The inspector said, 'I was about to call you. It just struck me. The Dade kids, they must be missing.'

'I had the same thought. Still, correction: they *may* be missing. Who knows but that their sitter's just brought them back from an educational trip to Leeds Castle?'

'Which started yesterday, Reg?'

'No, you're right. Look, we have to find out. The last thing they'd do is let us know if they've turned up safe. We're strictly reserved for disasters. If these children still haven't turned up the parents, or one of them, will have to come down to the station and fill in a missing persons form and give us a bit more information. No need for you to do it. Get Karen on to it, she hasn't been exactly crushed with toil lately.'

'I'd like to call the Dades before I do anything,' Burden said.

'And ring me back, would you?'

He sat at the table and he and Dora had their dinner. The letter box flapped as the evening paper, the *Kingsmarkham Evening Courier*, arrived.

'It's too bad,' Dora said. 'It's nearly eight o'clock, two hours late.'

'Understandable in the circumstances, don't you think?'

'Oh, I suppose so. I shouldn't complain. I expect the poor newsagent had to bring it himself. Surely he wouldn't let that girl go out in this.'

'Girl?'

'It's his daughter delivers the papers. Didn't you know? I suppose she does look rather like a boy in those jeans and that woolly cap.'

They kept the curtains at the french windows drawn back so that they could see if the rain started again and see too the tide of flood which had crept perhaps six feet across the lawn since last night. One of the neighbours, his garden elevated a few inches above the Wexfords', but enough, enough, had an Edwardian street lamp at the bottom of his lawn and tonight the light was on, a powerful white radiance that revealed the water lying gleaming and still. It was a shining grey colour, like a sheet of slate and the little river, somewhere down there, was lost in the broad shallow lake. It was weeks since Wexford had seen the stars and he couldn't see them now, only the bright but hazy lamplight below and a scurrying clotted mass across the sky where the rising wind agitated the clouds. Black leafless tree branches bowed and swayed. One swept the surface of the water, sending up spray like a car driving through a puddle.

'Do you want to start moving stuff now?' Dora asked when they had finished their coffee. 'Or do you want to see this?'

He shook his head, rejecting the paper which seemed to hold nothing but photographs of floods. 'We'll move the books and that cabinet. No more till we've seen the weather forecast.'

The phone rang as he was carrying the sixth and last cardboard box of books upstairs. Luckily, most of his books were already on the upper floor, in the little room they had once called his study and now was more like a mini-library. Dora took the call while he set the box down on the top stair.

'It's Mike.'

Wexford took the receiver from her. 'I've a feeling they haven't turned up.'

'No. The Subaqua Task Force want to resume the search tomorrow. They've got some idea of going under the deep water in the Brede Valley. They've not much to do and I think they like the excitement.'

'And Mr and Mrs Dade?'

'I didn't phone, Reg, I went up there,' said Burden. 'They're a funny pair. She cries.'

'She what?'

'She cries all the time. It's weird. It's pathological.'

'Is that right, doctor? And what does he do?'

'He's just rude. Oh, and he seems to be a workaholic, never an idle moment. He said he was going back to work while I was there. The kids are definitely missing. Their dad says it's all rubbish about them drowning. Why would they go near floodwater in the depths of winter? Who got hold of this ridiculous idea? His wife said she did and started crying. Jim Pemberton suggested maybe they went in the water to rescue someone else but in that case, who? The only other person to go missing is this Joanna Troy . . .'

'Who?'

'She's the friend of Mrs Dade who was spending the weekend in their house to keep an eye on the two kids. Dade's doing the missing persons forms now.' Burden's voice took on a hesitant tone. Perhaps he was remembering the heartfelt note in Wexford's voice when he expressed a wish not to get involved. 'As it happens, things are a bit more serious than they seemed at first. The Dades got home from Paris – they came in through Gatwick – a little while after midnight. The house was in darkness, the children's bedroom doors were shut, and the parents just went to bed without checking. Well, I suppose they wouldn't check. After all, Giles is fifteen and Sophie is thirteen. It wasn't till mid-morning that Mrs Dade found the kids weren't there. And that means not only that they've been missing since Sunday midnight but possibly since Friday evening when the parents left.'

'And this Joanna Whatever?'

'Troy. Mrs Dade's been phoning her home number all day without getting a reply and Dade went round there this afternoon but no one was there.'

'It doesn't seem to matter whether I sincerely hope or don't bother,' said Wexford wearily. 'But we'll leave it all till tomorrow.'

Burden, who could be sententious, said cheerfully that tomorrow was another day.

'You're right there, Scarlett. Tomorrow will be another day, always providing Dora and I haven't been drowned during the night. But I dare say we'll be able to get out of the bedroom windows.'

He had been watching for more rain as he was speaking and the first drops had splashed against the glass midway through his last sentence. He put the receiver back and opened the front door. It was milder out there than he could ever remember for the time of year. Even the wind was warm. It had brought with it the next downpour and the rain increased in intensity as he watched, straight-down rain like glass or steel rods crashing on to the stone flags and splashing into the waterlogged gullies between them. The down-flow pipe from the roof gutters began to pour out water like a tap turned full on and the drain, unable to cope with so great a volume, was soon lost under an eddying flood of its own.

Dora was watching the news. It ended as he came in and the weather forecast began with its typical irritating preamble: a kind of improbably glamorous creature in the guise of a water sprite and a silver lamé designer gown, sitting on top of a fountain while a concealed fan blew her hair and draperies about. The meteorologist, an altogether more normal sort of woman, pointing with a ferrule at her map, told them of flood warnings out on four new rivers and an area of low pressure rushing across the Atlantic in pursuit of the one presently affecting the United Kingdom. By morning, she said, as if this wasn't true already, heavy rain would be falling across southern England.

Wexford turned it off. He and Dora stood at the french windows looking at the water which now, as in the front garden, filled the paved area immediately outside. The rain made little waves on its surface where a twig bobbed about like a boat on a choppy sea. The trunk of the mulberry tree was half submerged and it was now a lilac bush which had become the criterion. The rising water lapped its roots. A few yards of dry land remained before the incoming tide would reach the wall. As he watched, the light at the end of the garden next door went out and the whole scene was plunged into darkness.

He went up the stairs to bed. The possibility of two young proficient swimmers being drowned no longer seemed to him so absurd. You didn't need too much imagination to fancy the whole country sinking and vanishing under this vast superfluity of water. Everyone overcome by it like shipwrecked men, their raft inadequate, their strength gone, the young and the old alike, the strong and the weak.

CHAPTER 2

So much for not getting involved. He was on his way there now, heading up Kingston Gardens towards Lyndhurst Drive, with Vine who was driving. Vine seemed to think drowning in the Brede Valley, particularly in the very deep water now filling Savesbury Deeps, where the frogmen had begun searching again, a real possibility. The night before he had thought so himself. Now, with the sun shining on wet pavements and glittering dripping branches, he wasn't so sure.

Three hours earlier, when he got up, the rain had apparently just stopped. It was still dark but light enough to see what had happened during the night. He didn't look out of the window. Not then. He was afraid of what he might see, and even more afraid, when he went down to make Dora's tea, of the water waiting for him at the foot of the stairs or lying, still and placid, across the kitchen floor. But the house was dry and when he had put the kettle on and at last made himself pull back the curtains and look out of the french windows, he saw that the silvery grey lake still stopped some ten feet from the little wall that divided lawn from paving.

Since then there had been no more rain. The weather forecast had been right as far as the coming of a further downpour but wrong in its timing. There was still the second approaching area of low pressure to look forward to. As he got out of the car at the point where

Kingston Gardens met Lyndhurst Drive, a large drop of water fell on to his head, on to his bald spot, from a hollybush by the gate.

The house on the corner was called 'Antrim', a name neither pretentious nor apparently appropriate. Unlike any other in Lyndhurst Drive, where neo-Georgian sat side by side with nineteen thirties art deco, nineteen sixties functional, eighteen nineties Gothic and late-twentieth-century 'Victorian', the Dades' house was Tudor, so well done that the undiscerning might have mistaken it for the real thing. Beams of stripped oak criss-crossed slightly darker plaster, the windows were diamond-paned and the front door heavily studded. The knocker was the ubiquitous lion's head and the bellpull a twisty wrought-iron rod. Wexford pulled it.

The woman who came to the door was very obviously the anxious mother, her face tear-stained. She was thin, wispy and breathless. Early forties, he thought. Rather pretty, her face unpainted, her hair a mass of untidy brown curls. But it was one of those faces on which years of stress and yielding to that stress show in its lines and tensions. As she led them into a living room a man came out. He was very tall, a couple of inches taller than Wexford, which would make him six feet five, his head too small for his body.

'Roger Dade,' he said brusquely and in a public school accent which sounded as if he purposely exaggerated it. 'My wife.'

Wexford introduced himself and Vine. The Tudor style was sustained inside the house where there was a great deal of carved woodwork, gargoyles on the stone fireplace (containing a modern, unlit gas fire), paisley pattern wallpaper and lamps of wrought iron and parchment painted with indecipherable ancient glyphs.

The top of the coffee table round which they sat held,
under glass, a map of the world as it was known in, say,
fifteen fifty, with dragons and tossing galleons. Its
choppy seas reminded Wexford of his back garden. He
asked the Dades to tell him about the weekend and to
begin at the beginning.

The children's mother began, making much use of
her hands. 'We hadn't been away on our own, my husband and I, since our honeymoon. Can you believe
that? We were desperate just to get away without the
children. When I think of that now, I feel just so guilty
I can't tell you. A hundred times since then I've bitterly
regretted even thinking like that.'

Her husband, looking as if going away with her was
the last thing he had been desperate to do, sighed and
cast up his eyes. 'You've nothing to be guilty about,
Katrina. Give it a rest, for God's sake.'

At this the tears had come into her eyes and she made
no effort to restrain them. Like the water outside, they
welled and burst their banks, trickling down her cheeks
as she gulped and swallowed. As if it were a gesture
which he was more than accustomed to perform, as
automatic as turning off a tap or closing a door, Roger
Dade pulled a handful of tissues from a box on the table
and passed them to her. The box was contained in
another of polished wood with brass fittings, evidently
as essential a part of the furnishings as a magazine or
CD rack might be in another household. Katrina Dade
wore a blue crossover garment. A skimpy dressing gown
or something a fashionable woman would wear in the
daytime? To his amusement, he could see Vine doing
his best to avert his eyes from the bare expanse of thigh
she showed when the front of the blue thing parted.

'But what's the use?' The tears roughened her voice
and half choked it. 'We can't put the clock back, can we?

What time did we leave on Friday, Roger? You know how hopeless I am about things like that.'

Roger Dade indeed looked as if, with varying degrees of impatience and exasperation, he had borne years of unpunctuality, forgetfulness and a sublime indifference to time. 'About half past two,' he said. 'Our flight was four thirty from Gatwick.'

'You went by car?' Vine asked.

'Oh, yes, I drove.'

'Where were the children at this time?' Wexford had directed his eyes on to Dade and hoped he would answer but he was to be disappointed.

'At school, of course. Where else? They're quite used to letting themselves into the house. They wouldn't have to be on their own for long. Joanna was coming over at five.'

'Yes. Joanna. Who exactly is she?'

'My absolutely dearest closest friend. That's what makes all this so awful, that she's missing too. And I don't even know if she can swim. I've never had any reason to know. Perhaps she never learned. Suppose she couldn't and she fell into the water, and Giles and Sophie plunged into the water to save her and they all . . .'

'Don't get in a state,' said Dade as the tears bubbled up afresh. 'You're not helping with all this blubbing.' Wexford had never actually heard the word used before, only seen it in print years before in boys' school stories, old-fashioned even when he read them. Dade looked from one police officer to the other. 'I'll take over,' he said. 'I'd better if we're to get anywhere.'

She shouted at him, 'I want to do the talking! I can't help crying. Isn't it natural for a woman whose children have drowned to be crying? What do you expect?'

'Your children haven't drowned, Katrina. You're being hysterical as usual. If you want to tell them what happened, just do it. Get on with it.'

'Where was I? Oh, yes, in Paris.' Her voice had steadied a little. She pulled down the blue garment and sat up straight. 'We phoned them from Paris, from the hotel. It was eight thirty. I mean, it was eight thirty French time, seven thirty for them. I just don't understand why Europe has to be a whole hour ahead of us. Why do they have to be different?' No one supplied her with an answer. 'I mean we're all in the Common Market or the Union or whatever they call it, the name's always changing. We're supposed to be all the same.' She caught her husband's eye. 'Yes, all right, all right. We phoned them, like I said, and Giles answered. He said everything was fine, he and Sophie had been doing their homework. Joanna was there and they were going to have their supper and watch TV. I wasn't worried – why should I be?'

This too was obviously a rhetorical question. To Wexford, although he had been in her company only half an hour, it seemed inconceivable that she would ever be free from worry. She was one of those people who manufacture anxieties if none naturally occur. Her face puckered once more and he was afraid she was going to begin crying but she went on with her account.

'I phoned again next day at the same sort of time but nobody answered. I mean not a real person. The answering machine did. I thought maybe they were all watching something on television or that Giles had gone out and Joanna and Sophie weren't expecting me to call. I hadn't *said* I'd call. I left the number of the hotel – not that they didn't have that already – and I thought they might have called me back but they never did.'

Vine intervened. 'You said you thought your son might have gone out, Mrs Dade. Where would he go? Somewhere with his mates? Cinema? Too young for clubbing, I expect.'

A glance passed between husband and wife. Wexford couldn't interpret it. Katrina Dade said, as if she were skirting round the subject, avoiding a direct reply, 'He wouldn't go to the cinema or a club. He isn't that sort of boy. Besides, my husband wouldn't allow it. Absolutely not.'

Dade put in swiftly, 'Children have too much free-dom these days. They've had too much for years now. I did myself and I know it had an adverse effect on me for a long time. Until I dealt with it, that is, until I disciplined myself. If Giles went out he'd have gone to church. They sometimes have a service on Saturday evening. But in fact, last weekend it was on the Sunday morning. I checked before we left.'

Most parents in these degenerate times, thought Wexford, who was an atheist, would be gratified to know that their fifteen-year-old son had been to a church service rather than to some kind of popular entertainment. Never mind the religious aspect. No drugs in church, no AIDS, no predatory girls. But Dade was looking unhappy, his expression at best resigned.

'What church would that be?' Wexford asked. 'St Peter's? The Roman Catholics?'

'They call themselves the Church of the Good Gospel,' said Dade. 'They use the old hall in York Street, the one the Catholics used to have before their new church was built. God knows, I'd rather he went to the C of E but any church is better than none.' He hesitated, said almost aggressively, 'Why do you want to know?'

Vine spoke in an equable calming tone. 'It might be

a good idea to find out if Giles did actually go there on Sunday, don't you think?'

'Oh, possibly.' Dade was a man who liked to provide ideas, not receive them from some other source. He glanced at his watch, frowning. 'All this is making me late,' he said.

'Shall we hear about the rest of the weekend?' Wexford glanced from Dade to his wife and back again.

This time, Katrina Dade was silent, making only a petulant gesture and sniffing. Roger said, 'We didn't phone on the Sunday because we were going back in the evening.'

'That night, rather,' said Vine. 'You were very late.' He probably didn't mean to sound severe.

'Are you trying to insinuate something? Because if you are I'd like to know what it is. May I remind you that you're to *find my missing children*, not find fault with my conduct.'

Soothingly, Wexford said, 'No one is insinuating anything, Mr Dade. Will you go on, please?'

Dade looked at him, curling his lip. 'The flight was delayed nearly three hours. Something to do with water on the runways at Gatwick. And then they took half an hour getting the bags off. It was just after midnight when we got home.'

'And you took it for granted everyone was in bed and asleep?'

'Not everyone,' said Katrina. 'Joanna wasn't staying that night. She was due to go home on Sunday evening. They could be alone for a little while. Giles is nearly sixteen. We all thought – everyone thought – we'd be home by nine.'

'But you didn't phone home from the airport?'

'I'd have told you if we had,' snapped Dade. 'It would have been after ten thirty and I like my children to be in bed at a reasonable hour. They need their sleep if they're to do their school work.'

'What difference would it have made if we had phoned?' This was Katrina, sniffling. 'The answerphone was still on. Roger checked yesterday morning.'

'You went straight to bed?'

'We were exhausted. The children's bedroom doors were shut. We didn't look inside if that's what you mean. They're not babies to be checked up on every moment. In the morning I had a lie-in. My husband went off to the office at the crack of dawn, of course. I woke up and it was gone nine. It was unbelievable, I haven't overslept like that for years, not since I was a teenager myself, it was incredible.' Katrina's speech quickened in pace, the words tumbling over one another. 'Of course, my first thought was that the children had to go to school. I hadn't heard them, I'd been so deeply asleep. I thought, they'll have got up, they'll have gone, but as soon as I got up myself I knew they hadn't. You could tell no one had used the bathroom, their beds were made, something they never do, and it looked as if someone who knew what she was doing had made them. Joanna, obviously. There was no mess, everything was tidy – I mean, it was *unknown*.'

'You must have tried to find out where they were,' Wexford said. 'Phoned round friends and relatives? Did you phone the school?'

'I phoned my husband and he did, though we knew they weren't there. And they weren't. Of course they weren't. Then he phoned his mother. God knows why. For some unaccountable reason that's quite beyond me the children seem fond of her. But he drew a complete blank. The same with the children's friends' parents – those we could get hold of, that is.

So many mothers aren't content to be homemakers, are they? They must have careers as well. Anyway, none of them knew a thing.'

Vine said, 'Did you try to get in touch with Ms Troy?'

Katrina Dade stared at him as if he'd uttered some extreme obscenity. 'Well, of course we did. *Of course.* That was the first thing we did. Before we even phoned the school. There was no answer – well, her answerphone was on.'

'I was obliged to come home,' Dade said, implying it was the last place he wanted to be. 'I went over to her house. No one was there. I went next door and the woman there said she hadn't seen Joanna since Friday.'

That meant very little. A neighbour isn't always aware of the comings and goings of the people next door. Wexford said, 'And then?'

Katrina had assumed the vacant look and glazed eyes of a member of the local drama group playing Lady Macbeth in the sleepwalking scene. 'It was while my husband was out that I looked out of the window. I hadn't looked out before. I saw a devastating sight. You can see all the floods from here, like a great sea, an *ocean.* I could hardly believe my eyes but I had to, I had to. That was when I knew my children must be out there somewhere.'

In the calmest, steadiest voice he could muster, Wexford said, 'The frogmen have resumed their search, Mrs Dade, but what you suggest is very unlikely. The floods are quite a distance from here and nowhere in Kingsmarkham are they more than four feet deep. The search has moved to the Brede Valley, three miles away at the nearest point. Unless Giles and Sophie are great walkers or Ms Troy is, I find it hard to see why they should go near the Brede.'

'None of them would walk anywhere if they could help it,' said Dade.

Katrina looked as if he had betrayed her and she withdrew her hand. 'Then where are they?' she appealed to the two policemen. 'What has become of them?' Then came the question Wexford had been anticipating, the question that always came from a parent in this sort of situation, and came early, 'What are you doing about it?'

'First we'll need some help from you, Mrs Dade,' said Vine. 'Photographs of Giles and Sophie for a start. And a description. Some background – what sort of people they are.' He glanced at Wexford.

'A photograph of Ms Troy as well, if possible,' the Chief Inspector said. 'And we have a few more questions. How did Ms Troy get here on Friday evening? By car?'

'Of course.' Dade was looking at him as if he'd questioned Joanna Troy's possession of legs or as if every normal person knew human beings were born with motor vehicles attached, as it might be hair or noses. 'Naturally, she came by car. Look, is this going to go on much longer? I'm late as it is.'

'Where is her car now? Has she a garage at home?'

'No. She leaves it parked on a kind of drive or pad in front of the house.'

'And was it there?'

'No, it wasn't.' Dade began to look a little ashamed of his recent scorn. 'Would you like her address? I don't know if we have a photograph?'

'Of course we have a photograph.' His wife was shaking her head in apparent wonder. 'Not have a photograph of my very dearest friend? Darling, how could you think that?'

How he could Dade didn't explain. He went into another room and came back with two photographs

which he removed from their silver frames. They were
of the children, not their sitter. The girl looked like neither parent. Her features were classical, almost sharp,
her nose Roman, her eyes very dark, her hair nearly
black. The boy was better-looking than Roger Dade, his
features more nearly corresponding to a classical ideal,
but he looked as if he also might be tall.

'Just topping six feet,' said Dade proudly as if reading Wexford's thoughts. Katrina had fallen silent. Her
husband glanced at her, went on, 'You can see they've
both got dark eyes. Giles has fairer hair. I don't know
what else I can tell you.'

Some time, thought Wexford, you can explain
what makes a good-looking, tall and far from deprived
fifteen-year-old join something called the Good Gospel
Church. But perhaps you won't have to, perhaps we'll
have found them before that's necessary. 'Do you know',
he said to Katrina Dade, 'the names of any close relatives of Ms Troy?'

She was speaking dully now, though still far from naturally. 'Her father. Her mother's dead and he's married
again.' She got up, moving like a woman recovering
from a long and serious illness. She opened a drawer in
a desk designed to look as if made for a contemporary of
Shakespeare, lifted out a thick leather-bound album and
extracted from one of its grey, gilt-ornamented pages a
photograph of a young woman. Still slow and somnam-
bulant, she handed it to Wexford. 'Her father lives at 28
Forest Road, if you know where that is.'

The last street in the district to bear the postal
address Kingsmarkham. It turned directly off the
Pomfret road and the houses in it would very likely have
a pleasant view of Cheriton Forest. Katrina Dade was
sitting down again but on a buttoned and swagged sofa,
beside her husband, who was making an exasperated

face. Wexford concentrated on the picture of Joanna Troy. The first thing that struck him was her youth. He had assumed she would be the same sort of age as Katrina but this woman looked years younger, a girl still.

'When was this taken?'

'Last year.'

Well. Of course it was true that many people had friends a lot older or a lot younger than themselves. He wondered how these women had met. Joanna Troy looked confident and in control rather than handsome. Her short straight hair was fair, her eyes perhaps grey, it was hard to tell. Her skin was the fresh pink and white that used to be called a 'real English complexion'. Somehow he could tell she would never be very clothes-conscious, but rather a jeans and sweater woman when she could get away with it, though the photograph showed nothing of her below the shoulders. He was asking himself if there were any more questions he need put to the Dades at this stage when a shattering scream brought him to his feet. Vine also leapt up. Katrina Dade, her head back and her neck stretched, her fists pumping the air, was shrieking and yelling at the top of her lungs.

Dade tried to put his arms round her. She fought him off and continued to make some of the loudest screams Wexford had ever heard, as loud as children in supermarket aisles, as loud as his granddaughter Amulet at her most wilful. Seldom at a loss as to what to do, he was almost flummoxed. Perhaps the woman's face should be slapped – that used to be the sovereign remedy – but if so, if that wasn't about as politically incorrect as could be, he wasn't going to be the one to do it. He beckoned to Vine and they moved as far from the screaming Katrina and her ineffectual husband as they could get, standing by a pair of french

windows that gave on to a terraced garden and then to
the floods below.

Katrina having subsided into sobs, Dade said,
'Would you get me a glass of water, please?'

Vine shrugged but went to fetch it. He watched
Katrina choke over the water, dodged out of the way
before she hurled the remaining contents in his direction. This action seemed to relieve her feelings and she
laid her head back against a cushion. Wexford took
advantage of the silence to tell Dade they would like to
have a look at the children's rooms.

'I can't leave her, can I? You'll have to find them yourselves. Look, as soon as she shuts up I have to get off to
work. All right with you, is it? I have your permission?'

'Rude bugger, isn't he?' Vine said when they were on
the stairs.

'He's got a lot to put up with.' Wexford grinned.
'You have to make allowances. I can't really believe anything much has happened to these kids. Maybe I
should, maybe it's their mother's behaviour making me
think none of this is quite real. I could be entirely
wrong and we have to act as if I am.'

'Isn't it because there are three of them, sir? It's
harder to believe in three people disappearing. Unless
they're hostages, of course.' Vine was remembering
that Wexford's wife had been one of the hostages in
the Kingsmarkham bypass affair. 'But these three
aren't, are they?'

'I doubt it.'

It was probably mention of the bypass abductions
which reminded Wexford that sooner or later the
media were going to have to know about this. He
remembered last time with a shudder, the intrusion
into his own privacy, the continued onslaughts of Brian
St George, editor of the *Kingsmarkham Courier*, the

embargoes he could barely enforce. Then there had been the furore over that one-time paedophile and poor Hennessy's death . . .

'This is the boy's room, sir,' Vine was saying. 'Someone certainly tidied it and it wasn't a fifteen-year-old, not even a religious maniac.'

'I'm not sure we should brand him like that, Barry. Not at this stage. You might feel like going along to the old Catholic Church after we've left here and get some background on these Good Gospel people, not to mention whether the boy went to church on Sunday or not.'

If there are any two features which distinguish a teenager's bedroom from anyone else's, it must be the presence of posters on the walls and a means of playing music. These days, too, a computer with Internet access and a printer, and these last Giles Dade had, though the posters and player were absent. Almost absent. Instead of a recommendation for a pop group, endangered species rescue or soccer star, the wall facing Giles's bed had tacked to it an unframed life-size reproduction Wexford recognised as Constable's painting of *Christ Blessing the Bread and Wine.*

Perhaps it was only because he didn't, couldn't, believe that he found this distasteful. Not because of what it was, though Constable's genius found its best expression in landscape, but *where* it was and who had put it there. He wondered what Dora, a churchgoer, would say. He'd ask her. Vine was looking inside a clothes cupboard at what both of them would have expected to find there, jeans, shirts, T-shirts, a pea jacket and a school blazer, dark-brown, bordered in gold braid. One of the T-shirts, on a hanger and probably valued, was red and printed in black and white with a photograph of Giles Dade's face, 'Giles' lettered underneath it.

'You see he had some elements of normal adolescence,' said Wexford.

They must ask Dade, or if it had to be, his wife, which particular clothes were missing from the children's wardrobes. Football boots were there, trainers, a single pair of black leather shoes. For going to church in, no doubt.

A shelf of books held a Bible, *Chambers Dictionary*, Orwell's *Animal Farm* – a GCSE set book? – some Zola in French – surprisingly – Daudet's *Lettres de mon Moulin*, Maupassant's short stories, Bunyan's *Grace Abounding to the Chief of Sinners* and something called *Purity as a Life Goal* by Parker T. Ziegler. Wexford took it down and looked inside. It had been published in the United States by a company named the Creationist Foundation and sold there for the hefty sum of $35. On the shelf below, plugged in for recharging, was a mobile phone.

Drawers below held underpants, shorts, T-shirts – or one did. In the middle drawer was a mêlée of papers, some of them apparently a homework essay Giles was writing, a paperback on trees and another on the early church, ballpoints, a comb, a used light bulb, shoelaces, a ball of string. The top one was much the same but out of the confusion Vine extracted the small dark-red booklet that is a British passport. It had been issued three years before to Giles Benedict Dade.

'At least we know he hasn't left the country,' said Wexford.

The girl's room had far more books and posters enough. Just what you'd expect, including one of David Beckham, Posh Spice and their child, apparently off on a shopping spree. In the bookcase were the works of J. K. Rowling and Philip Pullman, the two *Alice* volumes, a lot of poetry, some of it just what you would not

expect, notably the *Complete Works* of T. S. Eliot and a
selection from Gerard Manley Hopkins. The girl, after
all, was only thirteen. A photograph of a handsome but
very old woman and one she resembled stood on top of
the bookcase but the one of her brother, identical to
that which they had been given, was on the bedside cabinet. A rack of CDs held hip-hop and Britney Spears,
showing Sophie to be more normal than her brother.
Her clothes contributed nothing in the way of enlightenment except that things to wear didn't much interest
her. From the brown-and-gold blazer and brown
pleated skirt, they saw that she went to the same school
as her brother. There was a hockey stick and a tennis
racquet in the wardrobe as well. Sophie's computer was
a humbler version of Giles's with Internet access but no
printer. No doubt, she shared his. She also had a com-
bined radio and cassette player, and a CD Walkman.

Wexford and Vine went downstairs and put a few
more questions to the parents. Katrina Dade was lying
down. Her husband was on his knees picking up broken
glass, having made her a cup of coffee. None was offered
to the two police officers. Wexford asked about clothes
and Dade said they had looked, this had seemed
important to his wife, but they had been unable to say
what had gone. So many of the clothes their children
wore looked just the same, blue jeans and black jeans,
plain T-shirts and T-shirts with logos, black, grey and
white trainers.

'How about coats?' Vine asked. 'Where do you keep
coats? When they went out they must have worn something more than a sweater at this time of the year.'

Wexford wasn't so sure. It had become a sign of a
kind of macho strength and youthful stamina not to
wear a coat outdoors, not even in snow, not even when
the temperature fell below freezing. And it hadn't been

cold for the time of year. But was Giles Dade that sort of boy? The boastful swaggering sort who would strut about in a sleeveless vest while others wore padded jackets? He followed Vine and Giles's father out into the hall, and the inside of a large and rather ornate clothes cupboard was examined.

A fur coat hung there, mink probably, very likely Roger Dade's gift to his wife in happier days before disillusionment set in, but very politically incorrect just the same. Wexford wondered when and where she dared wear it. In Italy, on a winter holiday? There were two other winter coats, both belonging to the parents, a man's raincoat, a padded jacket, a fleece, a reinforced red garment that looked as if designed for ski-ing in and a striped cagoule with hood.

'Giles has got an army surplus greatcoat,' said Dade. 'It's hideous but he likes it. It should be here but it's not. And Sophie has a brown padded jacket like that one but that's not hers. That's Giles's.'

Then it looks likely they at least went of their own volition, Wexford thought. Roger Dade took his own raincoat out of the cupboard, hung it over his arm, said, 'I'm going. I just hope this will all have blown over before I get back tonight.'

Wexford didn't answer. 'You say you phoned parents of the children's friends. We'd like names and addresses, please. As soon as possible. Have you cleared the messages from your answerphone?'

'We've listened to them, not cleared them.'

'Good. We'll take the tape.'

He walked back into the living room to say goodbye to Katrina. They would keep in touch. They would want to see her and her husband very soon. Lying on her back, she kept her eyes closed and her breathing steady. He knew she was awake.

'Mrs Dade?' Vine said. She didn't stir. 'We're leaving.'

'I suppose it's understandable,' said Wexford in the car. 'All the many times I've talked to parents whose children are missing I've never been able to understand why they don't scream the place down with rage and fear. And when I come across one who does I pass judgement on her.'

'It's because we don't believe anything serious has happened to them, sir.'

'Don't we? It's far too soon to make up our minds.'

CHAPTER 3

Kingsmarkham's new Roman Catholic church of Christ the King was a handsome modern building designed by Alexander Dix and built with donations from the town's growing Catholic population, including Dix himself. Foreign tourists might not immediately have recognised it as a sacred building, it looked more like a villa on some Mediterranean promontory, but there was nothing secular about its interior, white and gold and precious hardwoods, a stained-glass window depicting a contemporary version of the Stations of the Cross and, above the black marble altar, a huge crucifix in ivory and gold. A far cry, as members of the congregation often remarked, from 'the hut' where they had heard mass from 1911 till two years ago.

It was this humble building which Barry Vine was approaching now. Its appearance aroused no curiosity in him and not much interest. He had seen several like it in every country town he had ever visited in the United Kingdom, was so accustomed to these single-storey century-old (or more) brick edifices with double wooden doors and windows high up in the walls that he had scarcely noticed this one before. Nevertheless, it was instantly recognisable. What else could it be but a church hall or a church itself, most likely in use by an obscure sect?

No fence or gate protected it. The small area of broken paving which separated it from the York Street pavement held pools of water that seemed to have no means of escape. Someone signing himself Fang had decorated the brickwork on either side of the doors with incomprehensible graffiti, black and red. For some reason, perhaps a taboo born of superstition, he hadn't touched the oblong plaque attached to the left side on which was printed in large letters: CHURCH OF THE GOOD GOSPEL, and in small ones, THE LORD LOVES PURITY OF LIFE. There followed a list of the times of services and various weekly meetings. Underneath this: *Pastor, the Rev. Jashub Wright, 42 Carlyle Villas, Forest Road, Kingsmarkham.*

Jashub, thought Vine, just where do you get a name like that? I bet he was christened John. Then he noticed the coincidence, if coincidence it was, that this pastor lived in the same street as Joanna Troy's father. He tried the church door and found to his surprise that it was unlocked. This, he saw as soon as he was inside, was plainly because there was nothing inside worth stealing. It was almost empty, rather dark and very cold. Decades must have passed since the walls had been painted. The congregation was expected to sit on wooden benches without backs, and these were bolted to the wooden floor. On a dais at the far end stood a desk, such a desk as Vine hadn't seen since he left his primary school thirty years before. Even then parents had pronounced the school furniture a disgrace. This one, he saw as he bent over it, had been operated on with penknives by several generations of children, and when cutting and carving palled, scribbled over, initialled and generally decorated with ink, crayon and paint. There was a cavity for an inkwell but the inkwell was missing and someone had cut a hole of corresponding size in the middle of the lid. A stool, presumably for the officiating priest to sit on, looked so uncomfortable that Vine supposed Mr Wright preferred to stand.

Jashub . . . 'Where do you reckon it comes from, sir?'
Vine said to Wexford when he got back.

'God knows. You could try the Book of Numbers.
"Take ye the sum of all the congregation of the children
of Israel after their families, by the house of their fathers
. . ." You know the sort of thing.'

Vine didn't look as though he knew.

'Or you could ask the man himself. Mike Burden
wants to see this Troy chap and since they live practically
next door to each other you might as well go together.'

Wexford himself was off to Savesbury Deeps, or as
near as he could get, to see how the Subaqua frogmen
were getting on. But as soon as Pemberton had driven
half a mile out of Myfleet it was clear that the only way
to get an overview was to take a circular route round
what had become a lake. Lakes, of course, usually have
a road encircling them and this had nothing but soggy
meadows and a few houses whose owners, like himself,
watched the lapping waters with apprehension.

'Go back the way we've come,' he said, 'and try
approaching it from Framhurst.' He noticed for the first
time that the windscreen wipers weren't on.

Once they were returning, splashing through a
ford where no ford had been before, he dialled his
own number on the car phone. Dora answered after the
second ring.

'It's just the same as it was when you left. It may even
have gone down a bit. I thought I might bring some of
those books down.'

'I wouldn't,' he said, remembering how he'd humped
the boxes up those stairs.

Framhurst looked as on a summer's day, apart from
the puddles. The clouds had gone while Wexford was
on the phone, the sky was blue and everything glittered
in the sun. Pemberton took the Kingsmarkham road

until he could see ahead of him something very like the seashore with the tide coming in. Reversing for a dozen yards, he took a right-hand turn along what was usually a country lane but which now skirted the lake. The sun on the water was so bright, turning the surface to blazing silver, that at first they could see nothing. The River Brede had disappeared under the waters. A little way ahead on the road, Wexford spotted a van, a fire engine and a private car parked as near to the water's edge as was safe. A motor boat could be seen slowly circling. They drove up and parked. As Wexford got out he saw a black gleaming amphibian break the surface, rise a little into the brightness and then begin the swim to shore. He waded the last part.

'Ah, the Loch Brede Monster,' he said.

The frogman peeled himself out of some of his gear. 'There's nothing down there. You can be positive about that. My mate's yet to come up but he'll tell you the same.'

'Anyway, thanks for your help.'

'My pleasure. We do enjoy it, you know. Though, if I may say so, it was a pretty crazy idea in the first place, thinking anyone might be down there. I mean, why would they go in?'

'You may say so. I feel the same,' said Wexford. 'The mother got it into her head they'd been drowned.'

'It's not as if there'd been ice on it and they'd been skating, is it?' the frogman persisted, creating unlikely options. 'It's not as if it's hot and they'd felt like swimming. Or that anyone could fall in and need rescuing, it's as shallow as a kids' paddling pool round the edges. Ah, here's my mate, getting in the boat. He'll tell you the same.'

He did. Wexford wondered whether to return to Lyndhurst Drive and 'Antrim' but, recalling details of Katrina Dade's hysteria, decided to phone instead.

*

George Troy lived in the only house of any architectural interest in Forest Road. It had once been the lodge of a mansion, demolished at the start of the previous century, whose parkland filled the area bounded by Kingsmarkham, Pomfret, Cheriton Forest and the Pomfret road. All this was since changed out of recognition but the lodge still stood, an awkwardly shaped small Gothic house with a pinnacle and two castellated turrets, separated from the road by an incongruously suburban garden of lawn and flowerbeds bounded by a white wooden fence and gate.

A lot of explaining and production of warrant cards was needed before the woman who came to the door would let them in. The second Mrs Troy seemed unwilling to understand that two police officers could actually come to her house, wish to enter it and talk to her husband about the whereabouts of his daughter. She said, 'She's at home. In her own home. She doesn't live here.'

Burden repeated that at home Joanna Troy was not, that he and Vine had checked and checked thoroughly before coming here. 'May we come in, Mrs Troy?'

She remained suspicious. 'I must ask my husband. Please wait there . . .'

A voice from the staircase cut her short. 'Who is it, Effie?'

Burden answered for her. 'Detective Inspector Burden and Detective Sergeant Vine, Kingsmarkham Crime Management, sir.'

'*Crime* management?' The voice had become incredulous and Burden thought, not for the first time, what an unfortunate effect this new title had on the law-abiding. 'Crime? I don't believe it. What's this about?'

'If we could come in, sir . . .'

The owner of the voice appeared, Effie Troy whispered to him and stepped aside. He was a stout, upright man who had had the good fortune to keep his hair and its fair sandy colour into, Burden guessed, his sixties. Vine, who had seen Joanna Troy's photograph, thought how very like her father she must be. Here were the same high forehead, longish nose, blue eyes and fresh-coloured skin, in George Troy's case rather reddened especially about the high cheekbones.

Burden had to repeat his request and now Troy nodded and exclaimed, 'Of course, of course, I can't think what we were doing, keeping you out there. On the doorstep in the wet. Come in, come in. Welcome to our humble abode. What was it you wanted Joanna for?'

Before answering that, they waited until they were in a small rather dark sitting room. At the best of times, not much light would have penetrated the two narrow arched windows, and this was far from the best of times, the sun fast disappearing and rainclouds gathering once more. Effie Troy switched on a table lamp and sat down, looking inscrutable. 'When did you last speak to your daughter, Mr Troy?'

'Well, I . . .' Anxiety was beginning to show in the drawing together of George Troy's eyebrows. 'She's all right, isn't she? I mean, she's all *right*?'

'As far as we know, sir. Would you mind telling me when you last spoke to her?'

'It would have been – let me see – last Friday afternoon. Or was it Thursday? No, Friday, I'm almost positive. In the afternoon. About four. Or maybe four thirty, was it, Effie?'

'About that,' said his wife in a guarded tone.

'You phoned her?'

'She phoned me. Yes, Joanna made the call. She phoned me – us –' here a reassuring smile at his wife '–

somewhere between four and four thirty.' This was going
to be slow work, Burden thought, largely due to George
Troy's habit of saying everything two or three times over.
'I'm retired, you see,' he went on. 'Yes, I've given up
gainful employment, a bit of an old has-been, that's me.
No longer the breadwinner. I'm always at home. She
could be sure of getting me any old time. She *is* all right?'

'As far as we know. What did she say, Mr Troy?'

'Now let me see. I wonder what she actually *did* say.
Nothing much, I'm sure it didn't amount to much.
Not that I'm saying she wasn't a well-informed, highly
educated young woman with plenty to say for herself,
oh, yes, but on that particular occasion . . .'

To general surprise except perhaps on her husband's
part, Effie Troy suddenly butted in, a cool and crisp
contrast to him, 'She said she was going to her friend
Katrina Dade for the weekend. She was going to keep
the children company while their parents were away.
Paris, I think. She'd be back home on Sunday night.
Another thing was that she'd come round on Wednesday,
that's tomorrow, and drive George and me over to
Tonbridge to see my sister who's not been well. The
car's George's but he lets her use it because he's given
up driving.'

Troy smiled, proud of his wife. Burden spoke to her.
'What kind of car, Mrs Troy? Would you know the
index number?'

'I would,' she said. 'But first I'd like you to tell
Joanna's father what's brought all this on.'

Vine glanced from one to the other, the man who
looked young for his age and acted old, and the woman
whose initial suspiciousness had changed to a thoughtful alertness. She was good-looking in a strange way,
perhaps ten years her husband's junior, as thin as he
was fat and as dark as he was fair, with a mass of black

hair, grey-threaded, and thick black eyebrows, the swarthy effect heightened by the glasses she wore in heavy black frames.

His eyes on Troy, he said, 'Ms Troy appears to be missing, sir. She and the Dade children were not in the house when Mr and Mrs Dade returned and their present whereabouts aren't known. The car – *your* car – also appears to be gone.'

Troy sat, shaking his head. But he was plainly an optimist, one to take as cheerful a view as possible. 'Surely she's only taken them on some trip, hasn't she? Some outing somewhere? She's done that before. That's all it is, isn't it?'

'Hardly, Mr Troy. The children should have gone to school yesterday morning. And wouldn't your daughter have to go to work? What does she do for a living?'

Possibly fearing a ten-minute-long disquisition from her husband on work, jobs, retirement and employment in general, Effie Dade said in her practised way, 'Joanna used to be a teacher. She trained as a teacher and taught at Haldon Finch School. But now she's self-employed and works as a translator and editor. She has a degree in modern languages and a Master's Degree, and she teaches a French course on the Internet.' She glanced at Burden. 'I don't know if it's relevant –' irrelevance was something she must know plenty about, he thought '– but that's how she and Katrina met. She taught at the school and Katrina was the head teacher's secretary. I'll find the car number for you.'

'My wife is a marvel,' said Troy while she was away. 'I'm a bit of a dreamer myself, a bit vague they tell me, find it hard to stick to the point. But she – well, she has such grasp, she has such ability to *manage* things, organise, you know, get everything straight – well, shipshape and Bristol fashion. She'll find that number,' he said, as if his wife would be obliged to use differential calculus to do so, 'nothing's beyond her. Don't know why she married me, never have understood, thank God every day of my life, of course, but the "why" of it's a mystery. She says I'm a nice man, how about that? She says I'm kind. Funny old reason for marrying someone, eh? Funny old thing to . . .'

'The number's LC02 YMY,' said Effie Troy as she came back into the room. 'The car is a VW Golf, dark-blue with four doors.'

Only a couple of years old then, Burden thought, with a L registration. What had happened to George Troy just after buying a new car to make him decide to give up driving? At the moment it wasn't important. 'I would like to enter your daughter's house, Mr Troy. Do you by any chance have a key?'

He addressed the father but hoped the reply would come from the stepmother. It did but only after Troy had bumbled on for a couple of minutes about types of keys, Yale and Banham locks, the danger of losing keys and the paramount need to lock all one's doors at night.

'We have a key,' said Effie Troy. Suspicion returned. 'I'm not at all sure she'd like the idea of your having it.'

'That's all right, my darling. That's quite OK. They're police officers, they're OK. They won't do anything they shouldn't. Let them have it, it'll be all right.'

'Very well.' The wife had evidently decided long ago that, notwithstanding her superior intellect and grasp, her husband must make the decisions. She fetched the key but not before Troy had told them what a marvel she was and how there was no doubt she would run that key to earth.

'In Ms Troy's absence you personally would have no objection to our taking a look inside the house?'

The fact that his daughter had disappeared and had been gone for two days, and possibly more, at last seemed to penetrate the father's cheerful bonhomie. Repetition, apparently for the sake of it, was abruptly forgotten. He said with slow deliberation, 'Joanna is actually missing, then? No one knows where she is?'

'We've only just begun our enquiries, sir. We've no reason to think any harm has come to her.'

Hadn't they? The very fact that she had vanished without leaving a note or a message for the Dades was close to a reason. But his reply seemed to have gone some way to allaying Troy's fears.

'One more question, Mrs Troy. Did your step-daughter have a good relationship with Giles and Sophie Dade? Did they get on?' God, he was doing it himself now . . .

'Oh, yes. She was a great favourite with both of them. She'd known them since they were nine and seven, that was when Katrina started working at the school.'

'Anything you want to ask, Barry?' he said to Vine.

'Just one thing. Can she swim?'

'Joanna?' For the first time Effie Troy smiled. The smile transformed her almost into a beauty. 'She's a top-class swimmer. When the woman who taught PE was off sick for a whole term Joanna took the students to swimming and gave lessons to the first and second years. That was a year before she gave up.' She hesitated, then said, 'If you're thinking of the floods – that is, that there could have been an accident, don't. Joanna was always saying how terrible the last lot we had were, the damage they'd do, she wished she could hibernate till all this was over. She had quite a thing about it. And the upshot was that in October she never went out except in the car. When she talked to us on Friday she said to me that once she got to the Dades she wasn't going to set foot outside till she drove home on Sunday evening.'

No outings then, no trips. And the rain had come down more heavily on Friday night and most of Saturday than it had on any single two days in the October floods. Joanna Troy wouldn't have gone near Savesbury Deeps. She wouldn't have taken Giles and Sophie for a nice Sunday afternoon walk in macs and wellies to see the water rising over the top of the Kingsbrook Bridge. When she went out, as she must have done, she went by car and the children with her. Because, Burden thought suddenly, she had to. Something happened to make it paramount for them all to leave the house at some time during the weekend . . .

'You mentioned a course she teaches on the Internet. Would you happen to know . . .?' He was certain she wouldn't. Neither of them would.

George Troy didn't but that didn't stop him beginning a lecture on the intricacies and obscurity of cyberspace, his own total inability to understand any of it and his position as an 'absolute fool when it comes to things like that'. Effie waited for him to finish his sentence before saying quietly, 'www.langlearn.com.'

'By the way, the media have been told,' Wexford said. At the look on Burden's face he added, 'Yes, I know. But it was a directive from Freeborn.' Mention of the Assistant Chief Constable's name evoked a groan. 'He says it's the best way to find them and maybe he's right.'

'The best way to get calls and no doubt e-mails from all the nuts.'

'I quite agree. We know in advance they'll have been seen in Rio and Jakarta, and going over Niagara Falls in a barrel. But they may be in a hotel somewhere. She may be renting a flat for the three of them.'

'Why would she?'

'I'm not saying she is, Mike. It's a possibility. We know so little about her. For instance, you say she has a good relationship with the Dade kids. Suppose it's more than that, suppose she's so fond of them she wants them for herself.'

'Adopt them, you mean? They're not exactly the babes in the wood. The boy's *fifteen*. She'd have to be mad.'

'So? The very fact that she's disappeared and with two children makes her a bit out of the ordinary, doesn't it? Did you get to see the shepherd of the gospel flock?'

Burden had. He and Barry Vine had walked up the road a hundred yards or so to a house very different from the Troys', a semi-detached bungalow, plain and unprepossessing. The Rev. Mr Wright had been a surprise. Burden had a preconceived idea of what he would be like, an image which derived from television drama and newspaper stories of American fundamentalists. He would be a fanatic with burning eyes, a fixed stare and an orator's voice, a tall, thin ascetic in a shabby suit and constricting collar. The reality was different. Jashub Wright was thin certainly but rather small, no more than thirty, quiet-voiced and with a pleasant manner. He invited the two officers in without hesitation and introduced them to a fair-haired young girl with a baby in her arms. 'My wife, Thekla.'

Seated in an armchair and given a cup of strong hot tea, Burden had asked the most important question. 'Did Giles Dade attend church last Sunday morning?'

'No, he didn't,' the pastor answered promptly. No beating about the bush, no wanting to know why Burden wanted to know. 'Nor the service in the afternoon. We have a young people's service on a Sunday afternoon once a month. I remarked to my wife that his not coming was odd and I hoped he wasn't unwell.'

'That's right.' Thekla Wright was now holding the baby in the crook of her left arm while passing the sugar basin to Vine with her right hand. Vine helped himself freely. 'It was so unusual that I rang up to ask if he was all right,' she said. 'We were both anxious.'

Burden leant forward in his chair. 'Would you tell me what time you phoned, Mrs Wright?'

She sat down, placing the baby, now fast asleep, on her lap. 'It was after afternoon service. I didn't go in the morning, I can't go to every service because of the baby, but I did go in the afternoon and when I got home – it was about five – I phoned the Dades' house.'

'Did you get a reply?'

'Only the answerphone. It just said no one was available, the usual thing.' Thekla Wright said very politely, 'Would you mind telling us why you want to know all this?'

Vine explained. Both Wrights looked deeply concerned. 'I *am* sorry,' Jashub Wright said. 'That must be deeply distressing for Mr and Mrs Dade. Is there anything we can do?'

'I doubt if there's anything you could do for them personally, sir, but it would help if you'd answer one more question.'

'Of course.'

Burden had found himself in a fix. These people were so *nice*, so helpful, so unlike what he had expected. And now he had to ask a question which, unless he phrased it with the greatest care, must sound insulting. He made the attempt. 'I've been wondering, Mr Wright, what attracts a teenager to your church. Forgive me if that sounds rude, I don't mean it to. But your, er, slogan, "The Lord loves purity of life" sounds – again, forgive me – sounds something more likely to arouse – well, derision in a boy of fifteen than a desire to belong to it.'

In spite of his apologies, Wright looked rather offended. His voice had stiffened. 'We practise a simple faith, Inspector. Love your neighbour, be kind, tell the truth and keep your sexual activities for within marriage. I won't go into our ritual and liturgy, you don't want that and anyway it too is simple. Giles was a confirmed member of the Church of England, he'd sung in the choir at St Peter's. Apparently, he decided one day that it was all too complicated and confused for him. All these different prayer books in use, all these Bibles. You couldn't be sure if you were getting the RC mass or matins of 1928 or happy-clappy or the Alternative Service Book. It might be smells and bells or it might be tambourines and soul. So he came over to us.'

'His parents aren't members of your church? Are any of his friends or relatives?'

'Not so far as I know.'

Thekla Wright cut in, 'We're simple, you see. That's what people like. We're direct and we don't compromise. That's the – well, the essence of us. The rules don't change and the principles don't, they haven't changed much in a hundred and forty years.'

This intervention provoked a glance from her husband. Burden couldn't interpret it until she said, rather humbly, 'I'm sorry, dear. I know it's not for me to talk about matters of doctrine.'

A smile from Wright brought a little flush to her pretty face. What did it mean? That she mustn't intervene because she was a *woman*? 'We welcome new people, Inspector, though we don't make a song and dance about it. Youngsters, as I'm sure you know, often have much more enthusiasm than older people. They put their hearts and souls into worship.'

To this neither Burden nor Vine had any response to make.

Thekla Wright nodded. 'Would you like another cup of tea?'

The experience he had related to Wexford. 'He wasn't particularly fanatical. Seems quite a decent chap and his church is simple and straightforward, nothing suspicious about it.'

'Sounds as if you'll be their next convert,' said the Chief Inspector. 'You'll be popping along there next Sunday morning.'

'Of course I won't. For one thing, I don't like their attitude to women. They're as bad as the Taleban.'

'Anyway, the main thing is that Giles Dade didn't go to church on Sunday morning and it seems that if he was at home he would have gone, come what might. Nor did he go in the afternoon. On Friday evening when Mrs Dade phoned from Paris the answerphone was not on but it was on Saturday evening and again on Sunday evening. All this makes it look as if the three of them left the house some time on Saturday. On the other hand, the answerphone may have been on on Saturday evening for no better reason than that they all wanted to watch something on television without being disturbed.

'Now on Saturday evening, as the whole country knows, the last ever episode of *Jacob's Ladder,* in which Inspector Martin Jacob dies, was shown on ITV. It's said to have had twelve million viewers and it may well be that Giles and Sophie Dade and Joanna Troy were among them. To put the answerphone on would be the obvious way of assuring peace and quiet. Giles's failure to go to church next day is much more indicative of when they left the house.'

'Early on Sunday morning,' said Burden, 'or possibly around lunchtime. But why did they leave? What for?'

CHAPTER 4

The water had advanced during the morning and was now within inches of the wall. Dora had been taking photographs of it, first when it was approaching but not touching the mulberry tree, later of the point it had reached by four o'clock. Dusk had come and now darkness, a merciful veiling of that sight. The camera had been put away until the morning.

'I couldn't do it,' said Wexford, half horrified, half admiring.

'No, Reg, but you've never been much of a photographer, have you?'

'You know I don't mean that. We're about to be engulfed and you're taking *pictures*.'

'Like Nero fiddling while Rome burned?'

'More like Sheridan sitting in a coffee house opposite the burning Drury Lane Theatre and saying that surely a man could have a drink by his own fireside.'

That made Sylvia laugh. Not so her new man whom she had brought round for a drink. It wasn't the first time Wexford had met him and he was no more impressed than on the last occasion. Callum Chapman was good-looking but neither clever nor a conversationalist. Did good looks in a man really mean so much to a woman? He had always supposed not but unless his daughter was the exception he must be wrong. Charm too was lacking. The man seldom smiled. Wexford had never heard him laugh. Perhaps he was like Diane de Poitiers whose good looks meant so much to her that she never smiled lest the movement wrinkle her face.

Now Chapman was looking puzzled by Wexford's anecdote. He said in his nasal Birmingham tones, 'I don't see the point of that. What does it mean?'

Wexford tried to tell him. He explained how the theatre was virtually the playwright's own, that his plays had all been performed there, he had put his heart and soul into it and now, before his eyes, it was being destroyed.

'Is that supposed to be funny?'

'It's an example of panache, light-hearted bravado in the face of tragedy.'

'I just don't see it.'

Sylvia laughed again, quite unfazed. 'Maybe by tomorrow Dad'll be having a drink beside his own pond. Let's go, Cal. The sitter will be fidgeting.'

'Cal,' said Wexford when they had gone. 'Cal.'

'She calls him "darling" too,' said Dora mischievously. 'Oh, don't look so gloomy. I don't suppose she'll marry him. They're not even living together, not really.'

'What does "not really" mean?'

She didn't deign to answer. He knew she wouldn't. 'She says he's kind. When he stays the night he makes her morning tea and gets the breakfast.'

'That won't last,' said Wexford. 'That New Men stuff never does. He reminds me of that Augustine Casey Sheila once brought here. The Booker shortlist bloke. Oh, I know he's not in the least like him. I admit he's not so obnoxious and he's got a pretty face. But he's not clever either or entertaining or . . .'

'Or rude,' said Dora.

'No, it's not that he's like Casey, it's just that I don't understand why my daughters take up with these sorts of men. Ghastly men. Sheila's Paul's not ghastly, I'll grant you that. He's just so handsome and charming I can't believe he won't be off chasing some other woman. It's not natural to look like him and be neither gay nor unfaithful to your wife or partner or whatever. I can't help suspecting him of having a secret life.'

'You're impossible.'

She sounded cross, not teasing or indulgent any more. He went to the window to look at the water, illuminated now by his neighbour's lamp, and at the steadily falling insistent rain. Not long now. Another half-inch or whatever that was in millimetres and it would be at the wall. Another inch . . .

'You said you wanted to see the news.'

'I'm coming.'

Just the bare facts coming after another rail crash, chaos on the railways, congestion on the roads, another child murdered in the north, another newborn baby left in a phone box. Just an announcement that the three were missing, then their photographs much magnified. A phone number was given for the public to call if they had information. Wexford sighed, thinking he knew well the kind of information they would have.

'Tell me something. Why would a bright, good-looking, middle-class teenage boy, a boy with a comfortable home who goes to a good school, why would he join a fundamentalist church? His parents don't go there. His friends don't.'

'Perhaps it provides him with answers, Reg. Teenagers want answers. Lots of them find modern life revolts them. They think that if everything became more simple and straightforward, more fundamentalist, in fact, the world would be a better place. Maybe it would. Mostly they don't care for ritual and facts that ought to be plain covered up in archaic words they can't

understand. He'll grow out of it and I don't know if
that's a shame or something to be thankful about.'

He woke up in the night. It was just after three and
rain was still falling. He went downstairs, into the dining room and over to the french windows. The lamp
was out but when he turned out the light behind him
and his eyes grew used to the dark he could see out well
enough. The water had moved up to lap the wall.

Two men were unloading sacks of something on to the
police station forecourt. For a moment Wexford couldn't
think what. Then he understood. He parked the car,
went inside and asked Sergeant Camb at the desk,
'What do we want sandbags for? There's no possible
chance of the floods reaching here.'

No one could answer him. The driver of the truck
came in with a note acknowledging receipt of the sandbags and Sergeant Peach came out from the back to sign
it. 'Though what we're to do with them I don't know.'
He looked at Wexford. 'You're not far from the river, are
you, sir?' He spoke in a wheedling tone, though half
jokingly. 'I don't suppose you'd like a few. Take them off
our hands?'

In the same style, Wexford said, 'I wouldn't mind
helping you out, Sergeant.'

Ten minutes later four dozen had been loaded into a
van Pemberton drove to Wexford's home. He phoned
his wife. 'I can't get home to put up the fortifications till
this evening.'

'Don't worry, darling. Cal and Sylvia are here and
Cal's going to do it.'

Cal . . . He didn't know what to say and came up
with an ineffectual, 'That's good.'

It was. Especially as it was once more pouring with
rain. Wexford checked on the calls they had received as

a result of the media publicity but there was nothing helpful, not even anything that seemed the suggestion of a sane person. Burden came in and told him the outcome of calls on the various friends and relatives of the missing children. In the main, negative. Giles's and Sophie's maternal grandparents lived at Berningham on the Suffolk coast, where in the seventies and eighties had been a large United States Air Force base. They seemed to get on well with their grandchildren but they hadn't seen either of them since September when they came to stay in Berningham for a week.

Roger Dade's mother, remarried since her divorce from his father, was apparently a favourite with the children. Her home was a village in the Cotswolds and she lived alone. The last time she had seen them was at their half-term in October when she had stayed for three nights with the Dades, leaving under some sort of cloud. A quarrel, Burden had gathered, though no details had been given. Katrina Dade was an only child.

'How about Joanna Troy?'

'No siblings,' said Burden. 'The present Mrs Troy has two children by a previous marriage. Joanna's been married and divorced. The marriage lasted less than a year. We haven't traced her ex-husband yet.'

Wexford said thoughtfully, 'The answer to all this is with Joanna Troy, don't you think? I don't see how it can be otherwise. A boy of fifteen isn't going to be able to persuade a woman of thirty-one to take him and his sister off somewhere without telling their parents or leaving any clue to where they were going. It has to be her plan and her decision. Nor can I see how she could have taken them away without criminal intent.'

'That's a bit sweeping.'

'Is it? All right, give me a scenario that covers everything and in which Joanna Troy is innocent.'

'Drowning would be.'

'They didn't drown, Mike. Even if it remained a possibility, what became of her car? Or, rather, her dad's car.
Who fell in and who rescued whom? If by a huge stretch
of the imagination you can get that far, isn't it a bit odd
they all drowned? Wouldn't one have survived, especially in four feet of water?'

'You can make anything sound ridiculous,' Burden said
peevishly. 'You're always doing it. I'm not sure it's a virtue.'

Wexford laughed. 'You and Barry went to her house.
Where's your report on that?'

'On your desk. Under a mountain of stuff. You haven't
penetrated to it yet. I'll tell you about it if you like.'

It was a very small house, a living room and kitchen
on the ground floor, two bedrooms and a bathroom
above, part of a row of eight called Kingsbridge Mews
put up by a speculative builder in the eighties.

'As Dade said, the car was kept outside in the front,'
said Burden. 'Needless to say, it's not there now.'

Inside the house it was cold. Joanna Troy had apparently switched off the central heating before she left on
Friday. She was either naturally frugal or obliged to
make economies. Vine found her passport too. It was
inside a desk which held little else of interest. There
were no letters, no vehicle registration document, no
certificate of insurance, though these of course would
have been with her father, nothing pertaining to a mort-
gage. Insurance policies for the house itself and for its
contents were also in the drawer. A large envelope contained certificates acknowledging a degree in French
from the University of Warwick, a Master's Degree in
European Literature from the University of Birmingham
and a diploma Burden said was the Postgraduate
Certificate in Education. Upstairs one of the bedrooms
had been turned into an office with computer and

printer, a photocopier, a sophisticated recording device and two large filing cabinets. The walls were lined with books, in this room mostly French and German fiction and dictionaries.

'Vine says she has all those French books you found in Giles's bedroom. *Lettres de mon* something and Emile Zola and whatever the other one was. Mind you, she's got about a hundred others in French too.'

On the desk, to the left of the PC had lain a set of page proofs of a novel in French. To the right were pages in English, fresh from Joanna Troy's printer. She had apparently been engaged in the work of translation on the day she left for Lyndhurst Drive and her weekend with the Dade children. In the bedroom Burden had looked with interest at her clothes.

'You would,' said Wexford nastily, eyeing Burden's slate-blue suit, lighter blue shirt and deep-purple slub silk tie. Not for a moment would anyone have taken him for a policeman.

'To my mind,' Burden said in a distant tone, 'dressing decently is one of the markers of civilisation.'

'OK, OK, depends what you mean by "decently". You found something funny about her clothes, I can see it in your beady eye.'

'Well, yes, I did. I think so. Everything in her wardrobe was casual, *everything*. And I mean really casual. Not a single skirt or dress, for instance. Jeans, chinos, Dockers . . .'

'I haven't the faintest idea what these things are,' Wexford interrupted.

'Then leave it to me. I have. T-shirts, shirts, sweaters, jackets, pea coats, padded coats, a fleece . . . All right, I know you don't know what that is either. Take it from me, it's not something a woman would wear to a party. The point is she'd nothing she could wear to a party, nothing dress-up, except possibly one pair of black trousers. What did she do if someone asked her out to dinner or a theatre?'

'I've been to theatres, even to the National when my daughter Sheila's been in something, and there've been women dressed as if about to muck out the pigpen. For all you being such a fashionista you don't seem to realise this isn't the nineteen thirties. But you'll say that's beside the point. I agree it's odd. It just adds to what I've been thinking already. We need to go back to the Dades, search the place, get a team in there if necessary. Those children have been missing four days by now, Mike.'

It was a short drive to the house called 'Antrim' but Wexford asked Donaldson the driver to make a detour and take in some of the flooded areas. Heavy rain was falling, the water was still rising and of the Kingsbrook Bridge only the parapet rails still showed above the water.

'It's a good deal more than four feet deep there,' said Burden.

'It is now. Wherever they are and whatever they've been doing, they haven't been hanging about waiting for the water to get deep enough to drown themselves in.'

Burden made an inarticulate noise indicative of finding a remark in bad taste, and DC Lynn Fancourt, who was sitting in front next to Donaldson, cleared her throat. There were mysteries about the Chief Inspector she hadn't yet solved in her two years attached to Kingsmarkham Crime Management. How was it possible, for instance, to find such irreconcilables bunched together in one man's character? How could one man be liberal, compassionate, sensitive, well-read and at the same time ribald, derisive, sardonic and flippant about serious things? Wexford had never been nasty to her, not the way he could be to some people, but she was afraid of him just the same. In awe of him, might be a better way to put it.

Not that she'd have admitted it to a soul. Sitting there in the front of the car, trying to see out of the passenger window down which rain was streaming, she knew it was wisest for her to keep silent unless spoken to, and no one spoke to her. Donaldson made the detour required of all vehicles when they approached the bridge, splashing up York Street and then following the one-way system.

Wexford was a stickler for duty. And exacting obedience from his subordinates. Lynn had once been disobedient, it was during the investigation of the Devenish murder that somehow got mixed up with the paedophile demos, and Wexford had spoken to her in a way that made her shiver. It was only justice, not nastiness, she admitted that, and it had taught her something. About a police officer's duty, for one thing, and it was because of this that she was all the more astonished when Wexford told Donaldson to drive first up the road where his own house was and drop him off for two minutes.

Wexford let himself in with his key, called out but got no reply. He went through to the dining room. Outside the french window, in driving rain, Dora, Sylvia and Callum Chapman were raising the height of the two little walls with sandbags, evidently working as fast as they could, for the water was creeping up the walls. The sandbags had arrived just in time. Wexford tapped on the glass, then opened one of the side windows.

'Thanks for what you're doing,' he called to Callum. 'My pleasure.'

That it could hardly be. Sylvia, who had been much nicer and easier to get on with since her divorce, held on to her boyfriend's shoulder and, standing on one leg, took off her boot, pouring water out of it. 'Speak for yourself,' she said. 'I'm hating every minute of it and so is Mother.'

'It could be worse. Just think, if the ground floor floods we shall have to come and stay with you.'

He shut the window, went back to the car. He wondered if his daughter was still doing voluntary work for that women's refuge in addition to her job with the local authority. She must be or Dora would have told him, but he must ask. It would be a relief to know she wasn't, that she was removed from a situation where being assaulted by other women's rejected husbands or partners was always a risk. He got in next to Burden and within two minutes they were at 'Antrim'.

A creature of moods, Katrina Dade seemed quite different today, girlish but quiet, withdrawn, her eyes wide and staring. She was sensibly dressed too, wearing trousers and a jumper. Her husband, by contrast, was more expansive and more polite. What was he doing home from work at this hour? They looked as if neither of them had slept much.

'I suppose it's really come home to us. It wasn't real before, it was like a bad dream.' Katrina added wistfully, 'That drowning business, that was nonsense, wasn't it? I don't know what made me think they'd drowned.'

'Quite understandable, Mrs Dade,' said Burden, earning himself a frown from Wexford. 'Later on, we'd like to talk to you in greater depth.' He hoped no one noticed the unintentional pun. Wexford would have, of course. 'First we should take a look at the room where Ms Troy spent the night or the two nights.'

'She didn't leave anything behind,' said Katrina when they were on the stairs. 'She must have brought a bag but if she did she took it away with her.'

The room was under one of the steep-roofed gables of the house. Its ceiling was beamed and sharply sloping above the single bed. If you sat up unexpectedly during the night, thought Wexford, you could give your head a nasty bang. What Katrina had said appeared to be true and Joanna had indeed left nothing behind but he watched with approval as Lynn got down on her knees and scanned the floor. There was no en suite bathroom and the built-in clothes cupboard was empty. The drawers in a chest were also empty but for an ear-ring in the top one on the left-hand side.

'That isn't hers,' Katrina said in her new little girl voice. 'Joanna *never* wore earrings.' Where anyone else might have talked of 'pierced' ears, she said, 'She didn't have holes in her ears for them to go through.' She held the single pearl in the palm of her hand, said mischie-vously as if she hadn't a care in the world, 'It must belong to my horrible old ma-in-law. She stayed here in October, the old bat. Shall I throw it away? I bet it's valuable.'

No one answered her. Lynn got up from the floor, plainly disappointed, and they all went down the stairs. There the old Katrina returned. She subsided on to a chair in the hall and began to cry. She sobbed that she was ashamed of herself. Why did she talk like that? Her children leaving her was a judgement on her for saying the things she did. Roger Dade came out from the liv-ing room with a handful of tissues and put a not very enthusiastic arm round her.

'She's in such a state,' he said, 'she doesn't know what she's saying.'

Wexford thought the opposite, that while *in vino veritas* might be true, *in miseria veritas*, or 'in grief truth', certainly was. He didn't say so. He was watching Lynn who had once more got down on hands and knees, but not in mere speculation this time – she had spotted something. She knelt up and said, like the promising young officer she was, 'Could I have a new plastic bag, please, sir, and a pair of sterile tweezers?'

'Call Archbold,' said Wexford. 'That's the best way. He'll bring what's necessary. It'll be more efficient than anything we can do without him.'

'But what is it?' said Dade, gaping, when they were in the living room.

'Let's wait and see, shall we?' Burden had a pretty good idea but he wasn't going to say. Not yet. 'Now, Mrs Dade, do you feel able to tell us something about Ms Troy? We know she's a translator who's been a teacher, that she's thirty-one and been married and divorced. I believe you met her when you were a school secretary and she was teaching at Haldon Finch School?'

'I only did it for a year,' said Katrina. 'My husband didn't like me doing it. I got so tired.'

'You were exhausted, you know you were. Other women may be able to juggle a job and the home but you're not one of them. Regularly every Friday night you'd have a nervous collapse.'

He said it lightly but Wexford could imagine those nervous collapses. He very nearly shuddered. 'When was this, Mrs Dade?'

'Let me think. Sophie was six when I started. It must be seven years. Oh, my darling little Sophie! Where is she? What's happened to her?'

Everyone would have liked to answer that. Burden said, 'We're doing our best to find her and her brother, Mrs Dade. Telling us whatever you can about Ms Troy is the best way to help us find them. So you met and became friends.' He added bluntly, 'She was a good deal your junior.'

Katrina Dade's expression was one of a woman who has just been not so much insulted as deeply wounded. If he had unjustly accused her of child cruelty, selling her country's secrets to a foreign power or breaking and entering her neighbour's property, she couldn't have looked more appalled. She countered it with a stammered-out, half-broken, 'Do you think it's fair to speak to me like that? Considering what I'm going through? Do you?'

'I'd no intention of upsetting you, Mrs Dade,' Burden said stiffly. 'We'll leave it.' I know there was a good thirteen years between them, anyway, he thought. 'Ms Troy gave up teaching some time after that – do you know when?'

It was a reply sulkily given. 'Three years ago.'

'Why was that? Why did she give up?'

Dade broke in. 'I'm surprised you have to ask. Isn't the way kids behave at these comprehensives reason enough? The noise, the foul language, the violence. The way no one can keep discipline. A teacher who dares to give a child a little tap gets up before the Human Rights Court. Isn't that reason enough?'

'I take it Giles and Sophie attend a private school?' Wexford said.

'You take it right. I believe in the best education for my children and I don't believe in letting them take it easy. They'll thank me one day. I'm a stickler for home-work promptly done. Both of them have private tutors as well as school.'

'But Ms Troy isn't one of them?'

'Absolutely not.'

Before Dade could say any more there came a shrill ringing at the doorbell as if Archbold clutched the bell pull and hung on – as he probably had. Lynn went to let him in.

Burden resumed, 'Had Ms Troy come to look after your children on previous occasions?'

'I *told* you. Roger and I had never been away together all the time we were married. Not till last weekend. If you mean for an evening sometimes while we went out – it didn't happen often, mind – she'd done that. The last time would have been a month ago, something like that. Oh, and there was one night we went to a dinner-dance in London and she stayed then.'

'I'd hoped this weekend away would be the very last time they'd need a sitter. Giles would have been – *will* be – sixteen very shortly.' Roger Dade flushed deeply at what he had said, made it worse: 'I mean – what I meant to say was . . .'

'That you think he's dead!' Katrina's tears began afresh.

Her husband put his head in his hands, muttered from between his fingers, 'I don't know what I think. I can't think straight. This is driving me mad.' He looked up. 'How much time am I going to have to take off work over this?'

Wexford had almost decided he must give up for the day, try some other tack, when Archbold tapped on the door and came in. He had a small sterile pack in his hand, which he held up for Wexford's inspection. Peering through the transparent stuff of which the envelope was made, he saw something that looked like a small fragment of whitish porcelain, backed with a strip of gold.

'What is it?'

'It looks to me like the crown or cap off a tooth, sir.'

This fetched Dade out of his despair. He sat up. Katrina scrubbed at her eyes with a tissue. The sealed pack was passed to them, then to Burden and Lynn.

'Did either of your children have crowns in their mouths?' Burden asked.

Katrina shook her head. 'No, but Joanna did. She had two of her teeth crowned. It was years ago. She had a fall in the gym, something like that, and broke her teeth. Then one of the crowns came off when she was eating a caramel. The dentist put it back and Joanna told me he'd said she ought to have them both replaced. He said meantime not to chew gum but she did sometimes.'

Wexford had never heard her speak so lucidly. He wondered if it was because what they were discussing was something not so much physical and personal as pertaining to the appearance. She would probably talk as informatively on such subjects as diet and exercise, cosmetic surgery and minor ailments, subjects dear to her heart.

'Wouldn't she notice it had fallen out?'

'She might not,' Katrina said in the same earnest tone. 'Not at once. She mightn't until she sort of wiggled her tongue round her mouth and felt a rough bit.'

'We'd like to come back this afternoon,' Wexford said, 'and find out more about the children, their tastes and interests and their friends, and anything more you can tell us about Ms Troy.'

Dade said in his unpleasantly harsh and scathing voice, 'Have you never heard that actions speak louder than words?'

'We are acting, Mr Dade.' Wexford controlled his rising anger. 'We have all available resources working on the disappearance of your children.' He hated the terms he was obliged to use. For him they made things worse. What did this man expect? That he and Burden would help matters by personally digging up his back garden or poking into the lakes of water with sticks? 'You'd surely agree that the best way of discovering where Ms Troy and your children have gone is to find out what they are most likely to do and where they are most likely to go.'

Dade gave one of his shrugs, more an indication of contempt than helplessness. 'I shan't be here, anyway. You'll have to make do with her.'

Wexford and Burden got up to go. Archbold and Lynn Fancourt had already left. He meant to say something to Katrina but she had so profoundly retreated into herself that it was as if a shell sat there, the outer carapace of a woman with staring but sightless eyes. Her transformation into a rational being had not lasted long.

*

The inevitable house-to-house enquiries in Lyndhurst Drive elicited very little. Every householder questioned about the previous weekend spoke of the rain, the torrential, relentless rain. Water may be see-through but rain nevertheless, when descending heavily, creates a grey wall that is no longer transparent but like a thick ever-moving, constantly shifting veil. Moreover, human beings in our climate take a different attitude to weather from those who live in arid countries, being conditioned not to welcome rain but to dislike and turn away from it. That is what those neighbours of the Dades had done once the rain began on the Saturday afternoon. The more it fell, the more they retreated, closing their curtains. It was noisy too. When at its heaviest it made a continuous low roar that masked other sounds. So the Fowlers who lived on one side of the Dades and the Holloways next door to them had heard and seen nothing. Both families heard their letter boxes open and close when their evening paper, the Evening Courier, was delivered at about six, and both assumed a copy was delivered as usual to Antrim. The neighbours on the other side of the Dades, the first house, in fact, in Kingston Drive, were away for the weekend.

However, Rita Fowler had seen Giles leave the house on Saturday afternoon before the rain began.

'I can't remember the time. We'd had our lunch and cleared up. My husband was watching the rugby on TV. It wasn't raining then.'

Lynn Fancourt told her it had begun raining just before four but she knew she had seen Giles earlier than that. By four it would have started to get dark and it wasn't dark when she saw him. Maybe half past two? Or three? Giles had been on his own. She hadn't seen him return. She hadn't returned to the front of the house until she went to pick up the evening paper off the doormat.

'Did you see a dark-blue car parked on the Dades' driveway during the weekend?'

She had and was proud of her memory. 'I saw her come – she was the children's sitter – I saw her come on the Friday evening. And I can tell you that car was there when I saw Giles go out.'

But had it still been there when she picked up the evening paper? She hadn't noticed, it had been raining so hard. Was it still there next morning? She couldn't answer that but she knew it hadn't been there on Sunday afternoon.

If someone had entered the house in order to abduct Joanna Troy and Giles and Sophie Dade, or somehow to entice them away, it began to look as if this must have happened after the rain began. Or else they had all gone for a drive on Saturday evening, a very unlikely time to go out at all. The teeming rain had kept everyone who didn't have to leave his or her house firmly indoors. Wexford was turning all this over in his mind and noting how it made the drowning theory less and less probable when Vine came in and held out to him something soaking wet and mud-stained on a tray.

'What is it?'

'It's a T-shirt, sir. A woman found it in the water in her back garden and brought it in here. It's got a name printed on it, you see, and that's what alerted her.'

Wexford took the garment by the shoulders and lifted it an inch or two out of the muddy water in which it lay. The background was blue and it was smaller but otherwise it was the twin to the red one they had seen in Giles Dade's cupboard. Only the face was a girl's and the name on it was 'Sophie'.

CHAPTER 5

The river floods were at their widest here. The woman who had found the T-shirt said ruefully that when she and her partner had been looking for a home in the neighbourhood, they almost rejected this house because it was so far from the Kingsbrook. 'Not far enough, evidently.'

But a good deal further away than Wexford's. Still, it was also lower-lying and in spite of the rain which had been falling steadily since nine, the tide had reached only about a third of the way up the garden, bringing with it a scummy detritus of plastic bottles, a carrier bag, a Coke can, broken twigs, dead leaves, used condoms, a toothbrush . . .

'And that T-shirt.'

'You found it here?'

'That's right. Among all this lot. I saw the name and it rang a bell.'

Wexford went on home. He was meeting Burden for a 'quick' lunch but he wanted to see the new wall first. It wasn't necessary to go outside. No one would go outside today if he didn't have to. Four tiers of sandbags on each side raised the height of the walls by two feet but the swirling water hadn't yet quite reached the bottom of the lowest tier.

'It was very kind of Cal,' Dora said.

'Yes.'

'He's taking me out to lunch.'

'What, just you? Where's Sylvia?'

'Gone to work. It's her day off but she offered to do the helpline at The Hide. One of the other women is off sick.'

Wexford said no more. It struck him that a man doesn't take his girlfriend's mother out to a meal on her own unless he is very serious about that girlfriend, unless, in fact, he contemplates making her mother his mother-in-law or something very near it. Why did he mind so much? Callum Chapman was suitable enough. He had been married but his wife had died. There were no children. He had a reasonable job as an actuary (whatever that was), a flat of his own in Stowerton. At his last birthday he had become forty. According to Sylvia, her children liked him. Dora apparently liked him. He had been eager to do a good deed by volunteering as a sandbag shifter in the water crisis.

'He's dull,' Wexford said to himself as he drove down the hill through the rain to meet Burden at the Moonflower Takeaway's new restaurant. 'Abysmally dull and dreary.' But was that important? Wexford wasn't going to have to live with him, see his handsome face on the pillow beside him – he grinned at the thought of that – watch his deadpan look when anything amusing was said. But, wait a minute, maybe this last was more than a possibility if Sylvia got into some permanent arrangement with him . . . How much of a New Man was he? These days, he thought, women seemed to like best a man who'd do the housework and mind the kids and iron his own shirts, and never mind if he was boring as hell. In much the same way, men had once preferred and many still did, housewifely women with empty heads and pretty faces. It didn't say much for human discernment.

Burden was already seated at one of the Moonflower's twelve tables. Famous in the district for their Chinese takeaway, this restaurant had been opened a year before by Mark Ling and his brother Pete. It was already popular and with visitors not only local but from further afield, not least because of its (self-styled) head waiter, Raffy Johnson, the Lings' nephew. Raffy was young, black, handsome and in Wexford's opinion the most courteous server of food in mid-Sussex. No one could spread a napkin over a customer's lap with a more graceful flourish than Raffy, no one be more prompt with the menu or more assiduous to check that the single red or purple anemone in its cut glass vase was placed on the table where it neither blocked diners' sight of each other nor got in the way of the dishes of lemon chicken and black bean squid. He was engaged now in pouring for Burden a glass of sparkling water. He set the bottle down, smiled and drew back Wexford's chair.

'Good morning, Mr Wexford. How are you? Not liking all this rain, I dare say.'

If ever there was a success story . . . Wexford remembered Raffy a few years back when he had been a hopeless seventeen-year-old layabout, a feckless boy whose only virtue seemed to be his love for his mother, and whom his aunt Mhonum Ling had called a hopeless case, one who would never find work his life long. But his mother Oni had had a win on the Lottery and much of the money had gone on Raffy's training. There had been hotel work in London, in Switzerland and Jordan, and now he was a partner with his uncles and aunt in this prosperous business.

'I comfort myself with thoughts of Raffy when I'm feeling low,' said Wexford.

'Good. I must try it. I reckon we're all feeling low at the moment. I'm going to have the dragon's eggs and cherry blossom noodles.'

'You're joking. You made that up.'

'I did not. It's on page four. Raffy recommended it. It's not real dragon's eggs.'

Wexford looked up from the menu. 'I don't suppose it is since there aren't any real dragons. I may as well have the same. We have the unenviable task of showing that T-shirt to the Dades this afternoon and the sooner we get it over with the better.'

Their order was taken and Raffy, agreeing that perhaps 'dragon's eggs' was an unfortunate name, assured them it was a delicious seafood concoction. He'd tell his uncle and they'd find something that sounded more suitable. Could Mr Wexford suggest somehing? Wexford said he'd think about it.

'What I'm thinking at the moment', he said to Burden, 'is that we ought to be sure just when these floods began. I mean, when the Kingsbrook first burst its banks, that sort of thing. When I got home last Friday it was raining, but not heavily and there weren't any floods. I didn't go out at all on Saturday and I didn't know about the flood warning till I saw the television news at five fifteen.'

'Yes, well, I heard the flood warning on Radio Four on Saturday morning early but I guessed we'd be OK, we're too high up and too far from the Brede or the Kingsbrook. But on Saturday afternoon – well, early evening – Jenny and I and Mark went round to her parents to see how it was affecting them. As you know they've got a river frontage, their house backs on to the Kingsbrook, and as it happens, they moved out and went to Jenny's sister Candy on Sunday afternoon. But to get to their place we crossed the Kingsbrook Bridge and you could do it at six with ease. The height of the river wasn't anywhere near the bridge and it wasn't at seven thirty when we came back.

'But it wasn't raining very heavily then. The really heavy rain didn't start until about ten or later, nearer eleven. You know I've got that skylight in my house? Well, I heard it starting to crash on there as I was going to bed. I thought for a bit the water would come in and Jenny found an old enamel bath to put underneath it in case. Skylights are a menace. Anyway, the water didn't come in but we both lay awake a long time listening to the rain. I don't know when I've heard it heavier. It woke Mark and we had to take him in with us. I did go to sleep at last but I woke up at five and the crashing was still going on. I can tell you, I was scared to look out of the window.'

The dragon's eggs came. It was a prettily coloured dish, mostly butterfly prawns and shrimps and lobster claws with beansprouts and shredded carrot in a primrose-coloured sauce. Wexford, who had forgotten to take the linen napkin printed with anemones and birds of paradise out of its silver clip, had it graciously spread across his knees by Raffy.

'And the water went on rising all day,' he said.

'Absolutely. The Dade kids and Joanna Troy could have gone out at any time on the Sunday to take a look and that's when they possibly all went in.'

'Impossible,' said Wexford.

As he spoke, the street door opened and Dora entered with Callum Chapman. At first they didn't see him and Burden. Raffy was showing them to a table when Dora looked round and spotted him. Both came over and Wexford was starting to thank Chapman for his morning's work when, glancing from one to the other of them, he smiled – at last he smiled – and interrupted in his slow monotone, 'Skiving off, eh? So this is how you fritter away our taxes.'

Wexford was suddenly so angry he couldn't speak. He turned his back while Dora attempted to laugh it off. There was no introducing Burden now and Sylvia's mother and Sylvia's lover went back to their table. Whether his wife had much appetite for her lunch Wexford couldn't tell but his had gone. Burden glanced over his shoulder.

'Who *was* that?'

'Obviously my daughters don't get their taste in men from their mother.' Wexford had tried a joke but it failed miserably. 'Sylvia's new bloke.'

'You're kidding.'

'If only I were.'

'It takes all sorts, I suppose.'

'Yes, but I wish it didn't, don't you? I wish it took two or three sorts. Funny people, kind and thoughtful, sensitive people with imagination, tolerant and forbearing with good conversation, those sorts. No room for pompous, mean-spirited bastards like him.'

They ate as much as they were going to and Burden paid the bill. 'What he said, it wasn't that bad, you know,' he said as they were leaving. 'Haven't you got it a bit out of proportion? People are always saying that sort of thing to us.'

'They aren't all sleeping with my daughter.'

Burden shrugged. 'You were going to tell me why you didn't think finding the T-shirt was evidence of those three being in the water.'

Wexford got into the car.

'I don't know about not being in the water. I mean not being drowned. If she'd been wearing the T-shirt, why would it come off? I looked at it quite carefully. It's got a fairly tight round neck – do they call that a crew neck?' Burden nodded. 'It might be dragged off if she'd gone over Niagara but not in the flooded Kingsbrook. Another thing is, wouldn't she have had a coat over it? At least something rainproof. And if so, where's that? You'll say it's still to come to light. Maybe. This afternoon we have to find out positively what topcoats are missing.'

'If it didn't come off Sophie Dade what was it doing there?'

'It was put there to make us think she drowned. A red herring. It was to distract us, at least for a while, from looking further.'

Katrina Dade identified the T-shirt, though there had never been any doubt about its ownership. Once again she became rational and calm when anything connected with outward appearance was involved. 'Sophie and Giles both had these done. It was when we were all on holiday in Florida last April. You can have a look at his, it's in his room.'

'We've seen it, thank you, Mrs Dade.'

'Now maybe you'll accept that they've drowned.' Once more she had changed her tack. They had drowned. From reproaching herself for even considering the possibility, she had returned to believing it. 'Oh, I wish my husband was here. I want him. Why is he always working when I need him?' No one could answer that. 'I want my children's bodies. I want to give them a dignified burial.'

'It hasn't come to that, Mrs Dade,' said Burden. He assured her truthfully that the frogmen had begun searching again as soon as the T-shirt had been found. 'But it's a precaution,' he said, denying his own private belief. 'We don't accept the drowning theory, we still don't. While we're here we want to establish positively what topcoats or jackets Giles and Sophie were wearing when they left this house. They must have been wearing coats.'

'I was quite surprised Sophie was wearing that brown anorak,' she said. 'I can't think why. Not when she had a brand-new jacket in canary yellow with a plaid lining. She chose it herself. She loved that jacket.'

I can think why, Wexford said to himself. So that she wouldn't be easily identified, so that she wouldn't stand out a mile. That, too, may be a better reason for getting rid of the T-shirt. Or someone else getting rid of it and someone else persuading her not to wear the bright yellow jacket . . .

'Did Ms Troy see much of her former husband, Mrs Dade?'

'She never saw him.'

'His name is Ralph Jennings, I believe, and he lives in Reading.'

'I don't know where he lives.' Katrina, for whom acting naturally was impossible, whose posturing was almost pathological, seemed uncertain how to proceed with regard to Joanna Troy. Was her former friend still her friend or had she become an enemy? 'I said to her once that she wouldn't know about something, I don't remember what it was, because she'd never been married, I said, and she said, oh, yes, she had. "Believe it or not," she said, "but I was once a Mrs Ralph Jennings," and she laughed. The name just stuck in my mind. She isn't suited to marriage, you can tell that.'

'Why would that be?' Burden asked.

'My husband says it's because she's a lesbian. He says you can see that with half an eye.' Her sudden coyness and eyelid-batting was an embarrassment. 'He knows a dyke when he sees one, he says.'

Wexford thought he had seldom come across a more unpleasant man. Chapman was a pussy cat beside him.

'I'm innocent, he says, and he's glad I didn't know because it proves she never tried anything on.' Katrina achieved a convincing shudder. Then she said, 'Joanna's done this, hasn't she? Whatever it is. Taken them where they shouldn't go, got them into trouble. Maybe it's her that's drowned them, is that it?'

Before Wexford could come up with an answer the front door closed with a slam and Dade came striding in. 'You wanted me home,' he said to his wife, 'and I've come. For ten minutes.' He gave Wexford an exasperated glare.

Wexford said, 'I'd like a list of names of Giles's and Sophie's friends. I expect they'd be school friends. Their names and addresses, please.'

Katrina got up and went to the french windows where she stood, holding on to the curtain with one hand and looking out. With a show of impatience her husband began writing, in a large backward-sloping hand, on the sheet of paper Wexford had given him. He crossed the room to fetch a telephone directory.

'What do you do for a living, Mr Dade?'

The ballpoint was flung down. 'What can my profession possibly have to do with this inquiry? Can you tell me that?'

'You never know. But probably nothing. Nevertheless, I would like to know.'

The writing was resumed. 'I'm a domestic property broker.'

'Is that what I'd call an estate agent?' asked Burden.

Dade didn't answer. He handed Wexford the list. Katrina turned round and said thrillingly, 'Look, the sun has come out!'

It had, in a watery blaze. The Dades' garden, trees, shrubs, the last of waterlogged autumn flowers, sparkled with a million water drops. Curving across slatey clouds and blue patches the arc of a rainbow had one foot in the flooded Brede Valley and the other in Forby.

'May I keep my little girl's T-shirt?'

'I'm afraid not, Mrs Dade. Not at present. It will be returned to you later, of course.'

Wexford disliked the way he had to put this but he couldn't think of a better phrasing. It smacked to him, inescapably, of post-mortems. Then, as he and Burden moved towards the door, she threw herself at his feet and clasped her arms round his knees. Such a thing had never happened to him before and, unusually for him, he felt deeply awkward.

'Find my children, Mr Wexford! You will find my darling children?'

Afterwards, as he told Dora, he didn't know how he and Burden managed to escape. They heard the domestic property broker snarling at his wife for 'making an exhibition of herself' as he strained to raise her from the carpet.

'I'd like to go down and see how Subaqua are getting on,' Wexford said when he had recovered from his embarrassment. 'Where are they now?'

'Back at the bridge. They were going to have another look in the weir pool. It's the deepest part. Apparently they've turned the weir off. Did you know they could do that?'

'No, but seeing they can turn off Niagara Falls I'm not surprised.'

'I supposed we've checked on the whereabouts of Joanna Troy's car? Or, rather, checked it's not parked anywhere around here?'

'That was done yesterday. No dark-blue Golf with that index number anywhere in the area. The, er, tooth's gone off to the lab at Stowerton for something or other, I'm not sure what. Maybe only to establish that it's what we think it is.'

Wearing rubber boots and raincapes, they were standing on the temporary wooden bridge which had been put up during a pause in Tuesday's downpour to carry river frontage dwellers up to the comparatively dry land of the High Street. Wednesday's lull was still going

on and, as always, everyone was hoping it was less a lull
than a cessation. But the clouds were too massy and dark
for that, the wind too brisk and the temperature too
mild. Upstream the frogmen were in the weir pool. It was
always deep water there, a favourite place for the local
children to swim in until a new council member created
alarm about it in a national newspaper – 'there will be a
fatality sooner rather than later . . .' The water was deeper
now and widening into an inland sea, the furthest reaches
of which were creeping up Wexford's garden. That this
might be the fatality, happening in the here and now, was
taking shape in everyone's mind but his.

A boat on this water was something he had thought
he would never see. The frogman surfaced and hung on
to the gunwale. Wexford didn't know if he was the one
he'd talked to on the Brede or someone different.
Everything was so wet, everything dripping and spray-
ing, that he couldn't tell if the cold drop he felt on his
cheek was renewed rain or a splash from a stone
Burden had kicked into the water. But it was soon followed by another and another, a shower of splashes,
and the rain began in earnest, threatening to drench
them. They waded back to the car. Wexford's cellphone
was ringing.

'Freeborn wants to see me.' Sir James Freeborn was
the Assistant Chief Constable. 'He sounded thrilled to
bits that we were down here "watching the operations",
as he put it. I wonder why.'

He was soon told. Freeborn was waiting for him in
Wexford's office. This was what he always did when he
came to Kingsmarkham rather than summoning the
Chief Inspector to Headquarters at Myringham. There
was nothing private in the office and Wexford wasn't
one of those men who keep photographs of his wife and
children on his desk, yet Freeborn was always to be

found seated in Wexford's chair, looking into Wexford's computer and once, when the Chief Inspector returned rather sooner than expected, with his nose and a hand in one of the desk drawers. This time he wasn't sitting down but standing at the window, contemplating in the dying light and through the fine misty rain, the sheets of water that lay this side of Cheriton Forest.

'Makes it look like Switzerland,' he remarked, still gazing.

Coniferous forest and a lake . . . Well, perhaps, a little. 'Does it, sir? What did you want to see me about?'

In order to see him, Freeborn was obliged to turn round, which he did ponderously. 'Sit,' he said, and took Wexford's own seat himself. The chair on this side wasn't quite big enough for Wexford's bulk but he had no choice and settled himself uneasily. 'Those children and that woman are somewhere under all that.' Freeborn waved impatiently at the window. 'Here or in the Brede Valley. They have to be. Finding that, er, garment, clinched things, didn't it?'

'I don't think so. That, I believe, is what Joanna Troy wants us to think.'

'Really? You've evidence to show that Miss Troy is an abductor of children, have you? Possibly a child murderer?'

'No, sir, I haven't. But there's absolutely no evidence of any of the three of them entering the water, still less drowning. And in any case, where's the car?'

'Under the water too,' said Freeborn. 'I've been to Framhurst myself, I've seen how the floods have engulfed the road there. There's a steep drop from that road into the valley – or there was. They were all out in the car, the water was rising and she tried to drive through it. The car went over and down the incline with them all in it. Straightforward.'

Then how did the T-shirt find its way into the water between the Kingsbrook Bridge and the weir, a distance of at least three miles? If it's a possibility the bodies are still there, that Subaqua haven't yet found them, they could hardly have failed to find a car. And the water didn't begin to rise until late Saturday night, so this trip in the car, presumably to view the floods, couldn't have taken place until Sunday morning, more probably Sunday afternoon. In that case why didn't Giles Dade go to church *as he always did*? Why did his sister wear a dark, anonymous-looking jacket when she had a new yellow one she loved?

Wexford knew it would be useless to say any of this. 'I still think there's some point in trying to trace these people, sir. I believe they all left the house on Saturday evening before the floods started.'

'On what grounds?'

He could imagine Freeborn's face if he said, 'Because Giles didn't go to church.' He wasn't going to say it but, anyway, Freeborn didn't give him a chance. 'I want you to call off the search, Reg. Call off this "tracing", as you put it. Leave it to Subaqua. They're highly competent and they've reinforcements coming in from Myringham. I'm assured by their boss – incidentally, a fellow Rotarian – that they won't rest until they've found them. If they're there – and they are – they'll find them.'

If they're there . . . Since they weren't, couldn't be, time was going by, anything could have happened. He went home, asked Dora, who had been taking and apparently excelled at a computer course, if she could get into a website on the Internet for him.

'I should think so.'

'It's called www.langlearn.com. And when you've found it perhaps you'd give me a call so I can look at it.'

'Darling,' she said indulgently, 'I don't have to do that. I can print it out.' She sought for language he would understand. 'It will be like a book or a newspaper. You'll see.'

It was. 'Page 1 of 2' it said at the top and, in Times New Roman type, thirty-six point: 'Fantastic French with Joanna Troy.' The portrait photograph was smudgy. It might have been almost any young woman. There was a page of text, most of it incomprehensible to Wexford, not because it was in French, it wasn't, but because of the cyber-speak which he couldn't follow. A column down the left-hand side, extending on to page 2, offered twenty or thirty options including All the Words You Want, Verbs Made Easy, Books You Need and Instant Chat. You highlighted the one you wanted. Dora had apparently highlighted All the Words You Want for him and downloaded page 1 (of 51). It held an eye-opening vocabulary but not a word he could ever imagine using. Here the student could learn the French for pop music, 'house' and 'garage', the kind of drinks teenagers like, types of cigarette and, he suspected, types of cannabis, the translation of 'miniskirt', 'tank top', 'distressed leather' and 'kitten heels', the when, where and how of buying condoms and how a French girl would ask for the morning-after pill.

Did it tell him anything about Joanna Troy? Maybe it did. That, for instance, she had a grasp of what people of the age of her former students required from the Internet, that she was uninhibited, unshocked by drug-taking and the free availability of contraceptive measures. That she was what, in his day, used to be called 'with it' and in his father's 'on the ball'. She might not be a fashionable dresser herself but she knew about teenagers' clothes. And it was hardly part of his self-imposed brief to enquire why she assumed that everyone who wanted to learn French must be under eighteen and conversant with a language far more obscure than that she was aiming to teach.

But how very different from Katrina Dade she must be showed in all the words of this text he could understand and perhaps even more in those he couldn't. Did it also show that, her own age more or less halfway between theirs and that of their children, she had common ground with those children? Far more in common than with Katrina who would have defined 'garage', he was sure, as somewhere you kept a car and 'spliff' as an expostulatory noise made by a character in a comic strip.

And why did he feel, now more than ever, that the answer to all this would lie in the reason for the friendship between Katrina Dade and Joanna Troy? Whatever that might be. Katrina's motives were obvious enough. She was flattered by the attentions of a woman younger and cleverer than herself. Besides, she was what the psychotherapists, what Wexford's Sylvia, would call 'needy'. But what about Joanna's purpose? Perhaps it will emerge, he thought, as he put the printout into his pocket.

CHAPTER 6

According to the Environment Agency, all the ground in mid-Sussex, all the south of England, come to that, was waterlogged. Even when the rain stopped there would be nowhere for the accumulated water to go. Sheila Wexford, flying into Gatwick from the west of the United States, came to stay a night with her parents and told them the aircraft's descent had felt like a sea-plane landing, the floods spread across thousands of acres and the downs rising out of it like islands.

The days passed, damp days, wet days, but the rain lessening, downpours giving place to showers, torrents to drizzle. The weekend was cloudy, the sky threatening, but what the Met Office had once called 'precipitation', an absurd name they had dropped recently, that had stopped. Joanna Troy and Giles and Sophie Dade had been missing for a week. On Monday a feeble watery sun came out. Instead of churning it into billows, the wind merely ruffled the gleaming grey surface of the floods. And contrary to what had been gloomily fore-told, the water began to recede.

Its level had never reached the topmost sandbags in Wexford's garden but had lapped the walls and lain there, a menacing stagnant pool, unchanging for days. As Monday passed it started to sink and by the evening the whole of the highest sandbags were exposed. That evening Wexford brought his books downstairs and Dora's favourite small items of furniture.

Subaqua, whose headquarters were in Myringham, had opened a temporary office in Kingsmarkham. Since they had found nothing, its only use, as far as Wexford could tell, was as somewhere to send Roger and Katrina Dade when their demands on him became peremptory. They were quite natural, these demands. More and more he was begining to feel deep sympathy for these parents. Katrina's tears and Dade's brusqueness were forgotten in an overwhelming pity for a couple whose children had disappeared and who must feel total impotence in the face of an investigating officer temporarily warned off investigating. She at least probably spent long hours in the Subaqua trailer parked on the dry side of Brook Road next to the Nationwide Building Society and waited for the news that never came. Roger Dade's snatching time off work was very likely an agony to him. Neither of them looked as if they had eaten for a week.

George and Effie Troy, as anxious now as those other parents, called to see him and them he sent to Subaqua too. Not that he had entirely obeyed Freeborn's injunction. Rather he had interpreted it as applying to activity on his part and that of his officers. Passivity was another matter. He couldn't (or wouldn't) stop people coming to *him* or even, if they phoned first, forbid them to air their fears in his presence. Of course, he could send them to Subaqua as well but surely that was no reason not to hear them out first?

The first of them arrived while he was reading the lab report on the little object Lynn Fancourt had found in the Dades' hall. A tooth it was, or rather, the crown of a tooth, constructed of porcelain and gold. There was no reason to suppose violence had contributed to its separation from the root and base of the natural tooth to which it had been attached. An interesting factor, in the opinion of the forensic examiner, was that a small amount of an adhesive was found on the crown and this was of the type which Joanna Troy might have bought over the counter in a pharmacy temporarily to reattach the crown if, say, she had been unable to visit her dentist. Wexford wasn't sure it was particularly interesting. While having no crowns on his own teeth, he felt that if he had and one came out he might, especially if pain resulted, buy and use such an adhesive. Surely anyone would as a temporary measure. Patch up your tooth and ring your dentist for an appointment.

But now she might be in pain. Would she seek a dentist wherever she was? And should he do something about this? Alert dentists nationwide . . . Only he couldn't because Freeborn had banned any further action. While he was thinking about this Vine came in and said there was a Mrs Carrish wanted to see him. Matilda Carrish.

'She said it as if I was expected to have heard of her. Perhaps you have.'

Wexford had. 'She's a photographer or used to be. Famous for taking pictures of eyesores, blots on the countryside, that sort of thing.' Wexford had been going to add that Matilda Carrish had also been much praised some five years back for her exhibition of street people's portraits in the National Portrait Gallery, but one look at Vine's expression of apprehensive distaste stopped him. 'She must be getting on a bit now. What does she want?'

'You, sir. She's the Dade kids' grandmother. Roger Dade's mum.'

'Really?' How unlikely, he thought. Could she be a hoaxer? Frauds and con-people turned up in hordes when they had cases like this. Yet she was called Carrish, he recalled, and it was an unusual name. If he had had to conjecture the sort of woman Dade's mother would be, also taking into account the pearl earring and Katrina's crushing put-down of her as an 'old bat', he would have come up with a meretricious interfering creature, never a professional woman, but someone who had too little to occupy her or allay her chronic frustration. 'You'd better bring her up here,' he said, curious now to see what she was like, hoaxer or not.

That Matilda Carrish was indeed 'getting on a bit' showed in her lined face and her bright silver hair but not in her step, her carriage and her general agility. She was very thin and springy, though without the nervous energy that showed in so many of her daughter-in-law's movements. The hand she held out to him was dry and cool, ringless, the nails filed short. Sometimes he ignored extended hands but hers he took and was oddly surprised by the fragile bones. Remembering the photograph in Sophie Dade's bedroom told him at once she was who she said she was.

The black trouser suit she wore had been designed for a woman half her age, yet it was entirely suitable, it fitted as if it had been made for her, as perhaps it had. Aquiline though her face was, her lips thin and her cheekbones sharp, he could see Roger Dade in her and realised that only a little padding out and smoothing, a little lifting and plumping, would make mother and son as alike as twins.

She came straight to the point, no preamble, no excuses. 'What are you doing to find my missing grandchildren?'

This was the question Wexford dreaded. It was he who had to answer it, not Freeborn, and he was aware that by now any response he gave must sound feeble and as if the police simply weren't bothering. But he tried.

From the first Mrs Dade had believed her children had drowned and that was now the police belief. Today or at the latest tomorrow the waters would have receded sufficiently to put the matter beyond doubt.

'I understood that frogmen had been down and there had been a comprehensive search.'

'That is so and –' he could use these words to a grandparent, not a parent '– no bodies have been found.'

'Then – if I'm not being naïve – why haven't you widened the search? Have ports and airports been alerted? What of other police authorities? I understand we now have a national missing persons register. Are they on that register?'

She sounded more like an investigative journalist than a photographer. Her voice was crisp and direct, her turquoise-blue eyes piercing. When she started speaking they had fixed themselves on his face and never left it, never blinked. He wanted to tell her she wasn't being naïve. Instead he said lamely, 'The children's passports are here. Ms Troy can't, for instance, have taken them out of the country.'

She shrugged, the way her son did. For the first time she expressed an opinion. 'I was staying at my son's home in October. For three nights. I found those children exceptionally mature for their ages. Mature and particularly intelligent. I don't know if you're aware that Giles took a French GCSE last spring and got an A star.' I wonder if he managed to get the French for 'miniskirt' and 'garage' into his essay, Wexford thought. 'Sophie will be a scientist one day,' Matilda Carrish said. 'It is beyond me why they had to have a sitter at all. Sophie is a responsible thirteen and her brother is nearly sixteen. Let me correct that, he *is* sixteen. His birthday was two days ago.'

'Young to be left.'

'You think so? A boy or girl may marry at sixteen, Chief Inspector. If what I read in the newspapers is true, a large proportion of the female population of this country have babies at thirteen, fourteen and fifteen, and are set up in flats with their child by their local authority. No one babysits them, they are babysitters themselves.'

'It was Mr and Mrs Dade's decision,' Wexford said, thinking that whatever had been the guiding principle behind Roger Dade's choice of a wife, he hadn't married his mother. 'We have no reason –' he nearly said 'as yet' but suppressed it '– to associate Ms Troy with any criminal activity. Whatever has happened to these three people, she may be as much an innocent victim as the children.'

Matilda Carrish smiled. There was no humour in that smile, it was the stretching of the lips of someone who has superior knowledge and knows it, a facial expression of triumph. 'You think so? What you don't know, I can see, is the reason Joanna Troy gave up her teaching job at Haldon Finch. I will tell you. She was dismissed for stealing a twenty-pound note from one of her own students.'

Wexford nodded. There was nothing else he could do. He remembered this woman's son telling him Joanna Troy had left her job because she had been unable to put up with the behaviour of class members. 'If we need to widen our search,' he said, 'you may be sure Ms Troy's antecedents will be investigated. Now, if there is nothing else, Mrs Carrish . . .'

'Oh, but there is. I must tell you that first thing this morning, before I came down here – I live in Gloucestershire – I got in touch with a private investigation agency. Search and Find Limited of Bedford Square. I'll give you their telephone number.'

'Bedford Square, London?' Wexford asked.

'Is there another?'

Wexford sighed. She would make an excellent witness, he thought, as he showed her to the door and closed it behind her. A drift of her perfume had wafted past him as for a moment she stood close by him, perfume and some other scent as well. It was – it *couldn't* be – cannabis? It couldn't be. Not at her age, in her position. The cologne she used must have some pot-like ingredient in it and his sometimes too-acute sense of smell had picked it out.

He dismissed it from his mind. He hadn't asked her how well she got on with her grandchildren and it was too late now. It was hard to imagine small children liking her, but Sophie and Giles were of course small no longer. Yet he couldn't picture her being drawn to teenagers, making concessions to them, entering in any way into their interests. Would she, for instance, know what hip-hop was? Or gangsta rap? Or the identity and nature of Eminem? Would the availability of the morning-after pill mean anything to her and, if it did, would she censure it out of hand? She had, he thought, spoken of teenage mothers as of some alien species permitted to exist only by the dispensation of a merciful authority.

But what of this story of hers accounting for Joanna Troy's abandonment of her profession? If it were true, why hadn't the Dades revealed it? Why had Roger Dade been at some pains to cover it up? Wexford couldn't fit Matilda Carrish into the Dade ménage at all. She seemed to have nothing in common with Roger except a physical resemblance. It was possible, of course, that she was a fantasist, that she had invented her account of Joanna's stealing from a pupil. He knew better than to believe that because a woman or man seemed straightforward, direct, was articulate, avoided circumlocution and evasiveness, they must also be truthful and beyond deceit. One had only to think of successful conmen. He went to the window and looked out across the landscape. Waterlogged or not, the solid ground could still absorb more, was absorbing more. He could see the floods receding, the water sinking into somewhere still enough of a sponge to receive it, meadows reappearing, willows rising, their trunks free and their fine trailing branches swaying once more in the wind.

Suppose, when the Brede became a river again and not a lake, a mud-coated blue four-door saloon VW Golf was revealed lying in what had been the deepest part. And suppose three bodies had failed to come to the surface when gases inflated them because the three people had all this time been *inside* the car. Reason told him this was impossible, that there was no way the car could have got into the deepest part unless it had been parked on the river bank and everyone inside it unconscious for the time it took for the water to rise to its highest level. Suppose this was so and they had been overcome by carbon monoxide fumes . . . Impossible, though this must be something like what Freeborn and Burden had in mind. And if so, when had Joanna Troy parked there? On Sunday morning? In heavy rain with a flood warning out? In any case, Giles wouldn't have gone. He had to go to church . . .

All this went round and round in Wexford's head. He put on his raincoat from force of habit rather than because he needed it and went out to get himself a sandwich for his lunch. He could have sent someone but he wanted to look at the water levels at the same time. For the first time for nearly a fortnight the pavements were dry. He walked along the High Street and noted that St Peter's churchyard was no longer flooded. Gravestones looked like what they were, markers of burial sites. They had ceased to be rocks protruding from the sea. The parapet of the Kingsbrook Bridge was clear, its roadway awash with mud drifts. As stonework and walls, lamp standards, bollards, signposts emerged from the receding flood, everything had a sodden look, not washed clean but soiled with tidemarks, mud-stained and draped with dirty waterweed. What was it going to cost, putting all this to rights? And what of the flooded houses, some of them twice engulfed since September? Would insurance companies pay up and would their owners ever be able to sell them?

Going back, he made a detour up York Street to buy his sandwich. Kingsmarkham's finest were to be obtained at the Savoy Sandwich Bar where they made them for you while you waited. He chose brown bread and smoked salmon, no spread. Dr Akande had forbidden butter except in minuscule amounts, had forbidden so many kinds of substitutes that Wexford couldn't remember which. It was easier to do without but he asked for some watercress on the salmon, not because he liked it but because Akande did. The next customer, a small man wearing a clerical collar, asked for cheese and pickle, the cheapest kind they did. It was this which made Wexford linger, his suspicion confirmed when the man behind the counter called out to someone in the kitchen, 'The usual for Mr Wright!'

'You won't know me,' Wexford said when the sandwiches had been packaged and handed over. 'Two of my officers interviewed you. Chief Inspector Wexford, Kingsmarkham Crime Management.'

Wright gave him an uncertain look. Many people did when they first met him, Wexford was used to it. They wondered what it was they had done and what he wanted them for. Wright's wary expression gave way to a faint smile.

'Giles Dade and his sister are still missing, I believe?'

'Still missing.'

They left the shop. Because Jashub Wright turned right and began walking in the direction of 'the hut' Wexford went that way too. The pastor of the Church of the Good Gospel talked about the floods. Everyone in Kingsmarkham and the villages talked constantly about the floods and would for weeks, months, to come. As he was speaking a pale sun, a mere pool of light, appeared among the clouds.

'What sort of purity of life?' Wexford asked when they paused in front of the church and its signboard with the sub-title.

'All sorts really. Purity of mind and conduct. A sort of inward cleanness, if that doesn't sound too much like the fashionable vogue for clearing the body of toxins.' Wright laughed heartily at his joke. 'You might say our aim is actually to clear mind, body *and* spirit of toxins.'

Wexford had always had difficulty in establishing the difference between mind and spirit. Which was which and where were they? As for the soul . . . He said none of this but instead, very simply, 'How do you do it?'

'That's a pretty big question to ask at midday out on the pavement.' More hearty laughter.

'Briefly.'

'If new members want to join the congregation they must make confession before they can be accepted. We hold a cleansing for them and they undertake not to commit the sin again. We understand about temptation and if they are tempted they have only to come to us – that is, to me and the church elders – and we give them all the help we can to resist whatever it is. Now if you'll excuse me . . .'

Wexford watched him enter the church by a side door. He wondered what on earth Burden had been thinking of to describe Wright as 'decent'. That creepy laugh had made him shiver. The cleansing sounded ominous – how could you get in and witness it? Only by applying to join, he supposed, and he wasn't as interested as that.

'I've been away,' the woman said. 'I've been away for a fortnight. When I got home yesterday someone down the street told me Joanna had disappeared.'

This was his second uninvited guest, a short dumpy woman of forty dressed in red. She had been waiting a long time and he had to bolt his sandwich to prevent her waiting any longer. Grumblings of heartburn troubled him. 'And you are?'

They had told him but only her Christian name, Yvonne, had stayed with him. 'Yvonne Moody. I live next door to Joanna. There's something I think you ought to know. I don't know what those Dades have told you and Joanna's father but if they've said she was fond of those kids and they were fond of her, they couldn't be more wrong.'

'What do you mean, Mrs Moody?'

'Miss,' she said. 'I'm not married. I'll tell you what I mean. First, you shouldn't run away with the idea she and Katrina were best friends. Joanna may have been Katrina's but Katrina wasn't hers. Far from it. They'd nothing in common. I don't know what brought them together in the first place, though I have my ideas. One day Joanna said she wasn't going to have any more to do with the family. But she did, though she'd come home and tell me that was the last time she'd babysit – well, not babysit but you know what I mean – she only did it for Katrina's sake, she was sorry for Katrina, and the next week there she was, up there again.'

'What did you mean, you have your ideas?'

'It's obvious, isn't it? She liked Roger Dade – liked
him too well, I mean. The way no one should let herself
think about a married man. I don't know him, I've only
come across the son, but whatever he's like it was wrong
what she was doing. She's said to me once or twice that
if Katrina went on the way she did, all those scenes and
tears and drama, she'd lose him. If that doesn't tell you
she meant she'd step into her shoes I don't know what
does. I told her she was heading for trouble besides
behaving immorally. You can commit adultery in your
heart just as much as in the flesh. I said that but she
laughed and refused to discuss it.'

Wexford wasn't surprised. He certainly wouldn't have
wanted to expose his private life to this woman. Just as
Burden came into the room his phone rang and he was
told the Assistant Chief Constable was on the line.

'You can go ahead now, Reg. Tomorrow we can be
certain.' Freeborn sounded mildly embarrassed. 'There's,
er, nothing down there.' Would he have preferred to
find three corpses and a waterlogged car?

Burden had been over to Framhurst where the floods
were disappearing fast. 'As if someone had pulled the
plug out,' he said. 'By this time tomorrow you'll be able
to see the fields again.'

Wexford thought this a bit over-optimistic. 'What do
we make of the sanctimonious Yvonne Moody? If it's
true what she says, why would abducting the Dade kids
help Joanna? Surely it would be more likely to put the
Dades against her for ever, both of them. Or is everything Ms Moody says a lie?'

'Who knows? You have to admit there are some funny
aspects about this case. I mean, what on earth did Katrina
have in common with a highly educated single woman
fourteen or fifteen years younger than herself? Katrina
may have admired her greatly, which one can imagine,

but Joanna? What this Moody woman says does provide a reason for Joanna's friendship with Katrina, it would account for her going over there to look after the children. But there's so much about the lot of them we don't know. For instance, that weekend seems to have been the first time she'd stayed in the house . . .'

'No, I asked. Back last April or May, they couldn't remember which, she stayed overnight while the Dades went off to some estate agents' bunfight in London. Roger didn't want to drive back in case he was over the limit.'

Burden nodded. 'OK. The other occasions she'd only have been there for the evening, but there may have been times when she sat in so that Katrina could go out while Roger was working late. Only he got home earlier than he expected or earlier than he'd told Katrina. Other times she may have deliberately come without her car so that he had to drive her home.'

'I'd never have suspected you were such an expert on seduction, not to say adultery.'

The once-widowed, twice-married Burden said frankly, 'Well, as you know, I've committed what they used to call fornication but never adultery. Still, you pick up this stuff in our line of business.'

'True. Your solution is ingenious but it doesn't help with why she took the kids, if she did. Stealing a twenty-pound note is hardly a rehearsal for stealing two people. However, when your weather forecast comes true tomorrow or whenever and we know for sure the car and those three were never down there, we can proceed to find out more.'

'Better start by asking all the dentists in the United Kingdom to be on the watch for a young woman coming to them with a missing tooth crown. Or asking them if any young woman has already come to them.'

'We can try,' said Wexford, 'but if she's as intelligent as you say, and I dare say she is, though that website could have fooled me, she'd guess we'd check up on dentists and instead of getting the crown professionally fixed she'll have been back to the pharmacist and bought another pack of that adhesive stuff.'

CHAPTER 7

As the floods subsided, among the detritus left behind were a bicycle, two supermarket trolleys, an umbrella with spokes but no cover, the usual crisp packets, Coke cans, condoms, single trainers, miscellaneous clothes as well as a wicker chair, a prototype video recorder and a Turkey carpet.

Wexford expected a further directive from Freeborn but none came. He phoned headquarters and was told the Assistant Chief Constable had started on a week of his annual leave. 'We proceed, I think, don't you?' he said to Burden.

'Is there any point in checking on where all these sweatshirts and jeans come from? Some of them are barely recognisable, they're in shreds.'

'Get Lynn on it. It can't do any harm. Our priorities are the parents and a further investigation of Joanna Troy's background.'

Early that morning, as soon as it began to be light, he had carried out a survey of his garden. A depressing business. It wasn't that he was much of a gardener himself. He didn't know the names of many plants, knew nothing of their Latin or Linnaean names, had never understood what needs sunshine, what shade, what plenty of water, what very little. But he liked to look at it. He liked to sit in it of a summer evening, enjoying the scents and the quiet and the beauty as pale flowers closed their petals for the night. Although Browning's poem itself revolted him, the awful adjectives like 'lovesome' – God walks in gardens indeed! – he agreed with the sentiment. His garden was the veriest seat of peace. Now it looked like a swamp and worse, the kind of marsh that has been irresponsibly drained and abandoned as a waste land. Things which had grown there and which he had known as 'that lovely red thing' or 'the one with the wonderful scent' had either disappeared entirely or survived as a bunch of wet sticks. It was Dora he felt sorrier for than himself. She had done it, chosen the plants and shrubs, tended them, loved the place. Only the lawn seemed to have come out of the water unscathed, a brilliant, yellowish, evil green.

He went indoors, took off his boots and searched for the shoes he'd left somewhere. Dora was on the phone. She said, 'That's for you to decide, isn't it?' and he knew it must be something unpleasant, something he wouldn't want to know.

She said goodbye and put the receiver down. Only one person apart from Burden ever phoned at eight in the morning, and she'd never speak in that crushing tone to Mike.

'You'd better tell me what Sylvia's up to now.'

'Cal's moving in with her. Apparently, it's been suggested before but Neil made a fuss. On account of the boys, I suppose.'

'I'm not surprised. So would I.'

'He seems to have withdrawn his objections now he's got someone of his own.'

He thought about these things now as he had himself driven to Forest Road. Had he and Dora been exceptionally lucky in that their marriage had endured? Or was it rather that in their day people worked harder at marriage, divorce if not actually disgraceful was a distant last resort, you married and you stayed married? If his first wife had lived would Burden's marriage have endured? He couldn't recall any child in his class at his own school whose natural mother and father weren't together. Among his parents' friends and neighbours no one was divorced. So were half those marriages deeply and secretly unhappy? Did their homes ring with frequent bitter quarrels conducted in the presence of their children, his classmates? No one would ever know. He disliked even thinking of the feelings of his son-in-law Neil, whom he was fond of and who loved his children. Now he would see these boys in the care of what amounted to a new father of whom they would perhaps grow fonder. Would he also give them a new step-mother? And all because he bored Sylvia and hadn't talked to her much. Maybe that was unfair but wasn't this Cal the most awful crashing bore? With time his looks would fade and his sexual prowess, if that was also part of the attraction, would wane . . .

Banish it from your mind, he told himself as he and Vine made their way to the last street in Kingsmarkham. This would be his first meeting with George and Effie Troy, though Vine had met and talked to them before. He noted the girth of George, fatter than he, Wexford, had been at the worst of his overeating, and a lot less tall. His wife had an interesting face and manner, a woman of character. These little Gothic houses, of which there were a number scattered around Kingsmarkham and Pomfret, looked quaint but were poky and dark, comfort, even when they were first built, sacrificed to some mistaken idea – the Oxford Movement and then Ruskin, he thought vaguely – that England would be a better place if mediaevalised. He seated himself in a chair far too small for him.

Already, after having only exchanged a few words with the Troys, he knew that Effie would speak for them both. Effie would be the coherent one, the less emotional one, and the question he had to ask was highly emotive.

'I'm sorry I have to ask you about this and I wouldn't if I didn't think it necessary.' The dark-browed face, the dark eyes, were turned on him inscrutably. 'I've learned that your daughter gave up teaching because she was accused of stealing money from one of the students.'

'Who told you such a thing?' It was the father who asked, not the stepmother.

'That I'm not at liberty to tell you. Is it true?'

Effie Troy spoke slowly, in measured tones. Wexford suddenly thought that if you had to have a stepmother, the way his grandsons would, this might not be such a bad one to have. 'It's true that Joanna was accused by a boy of sixteen of taking a twenty-pound note out of his back-pack. He later, er, recanted. This is some few years ago. You're right when you say she "gave up" teaching because of this. She did, of her own volition. She wasn't sacked or asked to resign. She was never charged with stealing.'

This last Wexford already knew. He was about to ask why she gave up when she had apparently been exonerated when the father, unable to contain himself any longer, burst into a harangue. Joanna was victimised, the boy was a psychopath, he accused her purely to make trouble and make himself the centre of attention, he hated her because she expected him to do too much homework. Effie listened to all this with an indulgent smile, finally patting her husband's hand and whispering to him as to a child, 'All right, darling. Don't get in a state.'

Obedient but still looking mutinous, George Troy fell silent. Vine said, 'Do you know the boy's name?'

'Damian or Damon, one of those fashionable names. I don't remember the surname.'

'Mr Troy?'

'Don't ask me. All I wanted was to put it out of my head. The monstrous behaviour of the modern child is beyond my comprehension. I don't understand and I don't want to. Joanna may have told us his surname but I don't recall. I don't want to. No one has surnames any more, do they? She brought one of her pupils here once – I'm not calling them students, students are in colleges – I forget why, she called in and this pupil was with her. Called me George if you please. Because my wife did. No, they don't have surnames any more. They all of them called my daughter Joanna at that school. When I was a child we called our teachers "sir" or "miss", we were respectful . . .'

'Tell me about your daughter,' Wexford said. 'What sort of a person is she? What's she like.' He seemed to address both of them but he looked at Effie.

She said, to his astonishment, because he thought her husband about to ask this of her, 'Would you like to make us all a cup of coffee, darling?'

He went. He seemed not to suspect Effie wanted him briefly out of the way. But did she?

'Her mother died when she was sixteen,' Effie began. 'I married her father three years later. It wasn't difficult for me, being her stepmother, I'd known her all her life. She was never rebellious, she was never resentful. She's very bright, you know, won all the scholarships, went to Warwick University and Birmingham. I expect she worked hard but she managed to give the impression she never worked at all. This is the kind of thing you want to know?'

Wexford nodded. The old man was slow and he was thankful for it.

'I was surprised when she went in for teaching. That sort of teaching, anyway. But she loved it. It was her life, she said.'

'She got married?'

'She met her husband when they were both in graduate school in Birmingham and lived together for a while. Ralph's some sort of computer buff. His father died and left him quite a lot of money, enough to buy a house. Joanna wanted to live around here and Ralph bought quite a big house. She got her job at Haldon Finch School, a very good job for someone so young, but of course her qualifications were marvellous. She and Ralph seemed to be a case of two people who got on fine while they lived together but just couldn't handle being married. They split up after a year, he sold the place and she bought that little house of hers with her share.'

Effie smiled sweetly at her husband as he lumbered in with a tray on the surface of which coffee had slopped. Their drinks were in mugs, milk in whether desired or not, no spoons, no sugar. 'Thank you, George, darling.'

She hadn't said a word her husband might not hear, Wexford thought. Perhaps she would have if he had taken longer. Since he had heard her last words, George launched into criticism of the Kingbridge Mews house. It was too small, badly planned, the windows too narrow, the staircase perilous. A psychiatrist would call this projection, thought Wexford, who had noticed the stairs in this house, as steep and narrow as a ladder. He addressed the father.

'Your daughter uses your car, I understand.'

Wexford guessed this question might result in a long and intricate explanation from George as to why he bought a new car and passed it on to his daughter instead of driving it himself, so he wasn't surprised by the fresh flow of words. Effie interrupted smoothly when he paused to take a sip of coffee.

'My husband wasn't confident at the wheel any longer, I'm afraid. He'd suddenly become rather nervous of causing an accident.' Or *you* had, Wexford thought. 'His eyesight was letting him down. Of course, I ought to have taken over the driving but the fact is I can't drive. I never learned. Absurd, isn't it? Joanna said she was thinking of buying a car and George said, don't do that, you can have mine on permanent loan.'

Far from being offended at his wife's taking over the conversation, George Troy looked pleased and proud. He patted her hand in a congratulatory way. Effie went on, 'Joanna set up as a freelance translator and editor. And of course she did private teaching – coaching, I suppose you'd call it. French and German. The students, er, pupils mostly came to her house but sometimes she went to them. Then she landed this job writing French lessons for the Internet. I'm sure I haven't put that well but perhaps you know what I mean. The company had a website and she put these lessons on it, first of all an elementary course, now an intermediate one, and she's doing a third for advanced students. I don't really know what more I can tell you.'

What a pity the old man had come back! 'Boyfriends since the break-up of her marriage, Mrs Troy?'

'There haven't been any,' said George. 'She was too busy for that sort of thing. She had a new career to establish, didn't she? No room for men and any of that nonsense.'

The stepmother said, 'Joanna wasn't fond of children, she told me that. Not small children, that is. Of course she liked them when they were old enough for her to teach them. She liked *bright* children. She wouldn't have wanted to marry again for the sake of having children.'

According to their grandmother, the Dade children were very bright indeed. 'Mr Troy, Mrs Troy, have you ever heard of the Church of the Good Gospel? Their slogan is "God loves purity of life".'

Both looked blank.

'Giles Dade is a member of it. Ms Troy never mentioned that to you?'

'Never,' Effie said. 'Joanna isn't religious herself. I don't think she was very interested in religion.'

'Lot of mumbo-jumbo,' said her husband. 'I feel the same.'

'Finally,' Wexford said, 'did Joanna have crowned teeth?'

'Crowned teeth?'

'We have found what we believe to be a crown off one of her teeth in the Dades' house. It looks as if it fell out and she had temporarily – and obviously not effectively – secured it with some kind of adhesive.'

Effie knew exactly what he was talking about. 'Oh, yes, she had two teeth that were crowned. She had them done years ago because they were discoloured. She said they aged her, which of course wasn't true. She can't have been more than twenty-one when they were done. The crown you're talking about came off two or three weeks back, it actually came off while she was eating a chocolate caramel in this house. She said she'd have to go to the dentist but she hadn't the time, she couldn't make it that week. I was just going to the shops and she said while I was out would I get her a tube of that stuff from the pharmacy. And I did.'

Of the other parents only the mother was at home. Roger Dade was, as usual, at work. Katrina had her own mother with her, a woman very unlike her and very different from Matilda Carrish, plump and sturdy, maternal, wearing what are usually called 'sensible' clothes, a skirt, blouse and cardigan, and lace-up walking shoes. The house looked as if she had taken charge. It had never been dirty, just rather too untidy for comfort, but Mrs Bruce had transformed it like the housewifely woman she was. All those diamond panes had been polished, ornaments washed and on a coffee table, as in the lounge of a country house hotel, magazines were stacked, their corners perfectly aligned with the angle of the table. A bowl that had looked as if it could serve no useful purpose had been filled with red and yellow chrysanthemums and a sleek black cat with a coat like satin, presumably owned by the Bruces, lay stretched out on the mantelpiece.

The only unkempt and wretched object (animate or inanimate) in the room was Katrina who sat huddled, a blanket round her shoulders, her once pretty brown hair hanging in rats' tails, her face gaunt. Wexford sensed there would be no more acting, no more posing, striking of attitudes, scene-setting. In the face of reality all that faded. She no longer cared how she looked or what impression she might make.

No tea or coffee or even water had ever been offered them in that house. Doreen Bruce now offered all three. Wexford was sure that if drinks had been accepted, they would have appeared in matching china on a lace cloth. He asked the children's grandmother when she had last seen Giles and Sophie or spoken to them on the phone.

She looked like a woman who would have a low, comfortable sort of voice but hers was high and rather shrill. 'I never spoke to them, dear. I'm not keen on phones, never know what to talk about. I can say what I've got to say or pass on a message but as to conversation, never have been able to and never shall.'

'They came to stay with you in the school holidays, I believe.'

'Oh, yes, dear, that's a different thing altogether. We like having them with us, that's quite different. They've always come to stay with us in the holidays, Easter as well as the summer sometimes. There's lots to do round where we live, you see. It's lovely country, quite isolated, plenty of things for young people.'

Not much, as far as Wexford could see. Nothing for the kind who used Joanna's website. Of course, he hadn't been there but he knew that parts of the Suffolk coast, though only seventy miles from London, had a remoteness scarcely felt here. What would there be to do? The seaside perhaps no more than ten miles away but no seaside resort, fields all strictly fenced in with barbed wire, fast traffic making the roads difficult to walk along. No facilities for young people, no youth club, no cinema, no shops, and probably one bus a day with luck.

'Where do you think Giles and Sophie are, Mrs Bruce?'

She glanced at her daughter. 'Well, I don't know, dear. They didn't come near us. I'm sure they were happy at home, they had everything they wanted, their parents couldn't do enough for them. They weren't one of those – what-d'you-call-it – dysfunctional families.'

He noticed the past tense. So, perhaps, did Katrina, for she turned to look at him and, still cowering under her blanket, shouted, 'When are you going to find them? When? Have you looked? Has anybody been looking?'

With perfect truth he said, 'Mrs Dade, every police force in the United Kingdom knows they are missing. Everyone is looking for them. We have made a television appeal. The media know. We shall continue to do everything we can to find them. I assure you of that.'

It sounded impotent to him, it sounded feeble. Two teenagers and a woman of thirty-one had vanished off the face of the earth. The muffled face emerged and tears began to wash it so that it was as wet as if put under the tap.

Later that day he discussed it with Burden. 'It's almost two weeks now, Mike.'

'What do you think happened to them? You must have a theory, you always do.'

Wexford didn't say that it was Burden's theory of drowning, influencing Freeborn, which had delayed the investigation for eight days. 'Joanna Troy has no criminal record. That we know for sure. But what's the truth about that allegedly stolen note? And are there any more such incidents in her past?'

'Her ex-husband's been found. He doesn't live in Brighton any more. He's moved to Southampton, got himself a new girlfriend who comes from there. Anything like that he may be able to tell us.'

'I feel about her that she's a bit of mystery. She's a young woman who's been married but she's apparently had no boyfriends since. She's a teacher who loves teaching but dislikes children, yet she minds two children quite regularly while their parents go out. If she has friends apart from Katrina and up to a point the woman next door, we haven't found any. When she's challenged about a possible affair with Roger Dade she laughs but she doesn't deny it. We need to know more.'

'You haven't said what your theory is.'

'Mike, I suppose I think, on the slight evidence we've got, that Joanna has killed those children. I don't know her motive. I don't know where – certainly not in the

Dades' house. I don't know how she's disposed of the bodies or what she's done with her car. But if all this happened on Saturday evening, she had time to dispose of them and time to leave the country before anyone knew they were missing.'

'Only she didn't leave the country. Her passport's in her house.'

'Exactly,' said Wexford. 'And we don't believe in false passports, do we? Except for spies and gangsters and international crooks, especially fictional ones. Not unless the killing was carefully premeditated and I'm sure it wasn't. Improbable as it sounds, she took those children out somewhere and killed them on an impulse because she's a psychopath with a hatred of teenagers. And if you think that's rubbish, can you come up with anything better?'

CHAPTER 8

Toxborough lies north-east of Kingsmarkham, just over the Kentish border, but the Sussex side of the M20. Once a small town of great beauty and antiquity, its spoliation began in the 1970s with the coming of industry to its environs and its ruin was complete when an approach road was built from it to the motorway. But several villages in its vicinity, yet in remote countryside, have retained their isolation and unspoilt prettiness. One of these is Passingham St John (pronounced, for reasons unknown, 'Passam Sinjen') which, being no more than two miles from Passingham Park station, is a favourite with wealthier commuters. Such a one was Peter Buxton who, two years before, had bought Passingham Hall as a weekend retreat.

Originally intending to retreat there every Friday evening and return to London on Monday morning, Buxton soon found that escape to rural Kent was not so easy as it had at first appeared. For one thing the traffic on Fridays after four in the afternoon and before nine at night was appalling. Going back on Monday morning was just as bad. Moreover, most of the invitations he and his wife received to London functions it was prudent for an up-and-coming media tycoon like himself to accept were for Friday or Saturday evenings, while Sunday lunchtime parties were not unknown. Especially in the winter these invitations came thick and fast, and thus it was that the first weekend of December was the first he and his wife had been to Passingham Hall in more than a month.

The house stood on the side of a shallow hill, so Buxton knew there was little danger of its flooding. In any case Pauline, who came in two or three times a week and kept an eye on things, had reported to Sharonne Buxton that all was well. Her husband had also worked for the Buxtons as handyman and gardener but had given up in October, offering the excuse of a bad back. Urban Buxton, originally from Greenwich, was learning how common this disability is in the countryside. Unless you are prepared to pay extravagantly for basic services, bad backs explain why it is so hard to find anyone to work for you.

He and Sharonne arrived very late on the night of Friday, 1 December, drove along the gravel drive through the eight-acre wood and up to the front door. The exterior lights were on, the heating was on and the bed linen had been changed. Pauline, at any rate, hadn't a bad back. It was long past midnight and the Buxtons went straight to bed. The weather forecast had been good, no more rain was predicted, and Peter was awakened at eight thirty by sunshine streaming through his bedroom window. This was early by his weekend standards but mid-morning in rural Kent.

He thought of taking Sharonne a cup of tea but decided not to wake her. Instead, he put on the Barbour jacket he had recently acquired and a pair of green wellies, requisite wear for a country landowner, and went outdoors. The sun shone brightly and it wasn't particularly cold. Peter was intensely proud of owning his twenty acres of land but his pride he kept secret. Not even Sharonne knew of it. As far as she was concerned this garden, paddock, green slopes and wood were only what a woman like her could expect to possess. They were her due as a star of the catwalk and one of those few models to be known – and known nation- if not worldwide – by her (somewhat enhanced) given name alone. But Peter, secretly, gloried in his land. He intended adding to it and was already in negotiation with the farmer to buy an adjoining field. He dreamed of the huge garden party he planned for the following summer with a marquee on the lawn and picnic tables in the sunny flower-sprinkled clearing, the open space in the centre of the wood.

It was towards this clearing that he was walking now, along the lane to where a track wound its way through the hornbeam plantation. In the absence of Pauline's husband, the grass verge wasn't as overgrown as he expected – Peter still didn't know that grass grows hardly at all between November and March – but still he must find another gardener and woodsman, and soon. Sharonne hated untidiness, mess, neglect. She liked to make a good first impression on visitors. He turned on to the track and wondered why no birds were singing. The only sound he could hear was the buzz and rattle of a drill, which he assumed to be the farmer doing something to a fence. It was, in fact, a wood-pecker whose presence would have thrilled him had he known what it was.

The track continued up to the old quarry, but a path branched off it to the left. Peter meant to take this path, for the quarry, an ancient and now overgrown chalk deposit, was of no interest to him, but at the turn-off he noticed something a more observant man would have seen as soon as he left the lane. The ruts a car's tyres make were deeply etched into the gravelly earth of the track. They were not new, these ruts. Water still lay in the bottom of them, though it hadn't rained for days. Peter looked back the way he had come and saw that they began at the lane. Someone had been in here since he was last at Passingham Hall. Pauline's husband, according to Pauline, had been forbidden to drive on account of his back and she had never learned. It wasn't them. The farmer might come into the wood but would certainly do so on foot. Some trespasser had been in here. Sharonne would be furious . . .

Peter followed the rutted track up to the edge of the quarry. It was plain to see that the vehicle, whatever it was, had gone over, taking part of the quarry's grassy lip with it as well as two young trees. Down there it was full of small trees and bushes, and among them was the car, a dark-blue car which lay on its side but hadn't fully turned over. Stouter trees had prevented its taking a somersault on to its roof. Then, in the dappled sunshine, the stillness and the silence but for the woodpecker's drilling, he smelt the smell. It must have been there from the first but the sight before him had temporarily dulled his other senses. He had smelt something like it before, when he was very young and poor, and had a Saturday job cleaning the kitchens in a restaurant. The restaurant had been closed down by the food hygiene people but before that happened he'd one night opened up a plastic bag leaning against the wall. He had a dustpan of floor sweepings to get rid of but as soon as the bag was open a dreadful smell wafted out and in the bottom he saw decaying offal running with white maggots.

Much the same smell was coming from the car in his quarry. He wasn't going to look inside, he didn't want to know. He didn't want to continue up to the clearing either. What he must do was go back to the house and call the police. If he had been carrying his mobile, as he always did when in London, he would have made that call on the spot. Dialled nine-nine-nine for want of knowing the local police number. But a country gentleman in a Barbour doesn't carry a mobile, he hardly knows what it is. Peter walked back the way he had come, feeling a bit weak at the knees. If he had eaten breakfast before he came out he would probably have been sick.

Sharonne had got up and was sitting at the kitchen table with a cup of instant coffee and a glass of orange juice in front of her. Though nothing could detract from the beauty of her figure and her facial structure, she was one of those women who look completely different, and hugely improved, by good dressing, make-up and a hairdo. Now, as usual in the mornings, she was in her natural state, wrapped in his old Jaeger dressing gown, her feet in feathery mules, her face pale, greasy and anaemic-looking, and her ash-blonde hair in uneven spikes. Such a style may be fashionable but not when the spikes stand out at right angles on the sides of the head and lie flat on the crown like a wind-ravaged cornfield. Sharonne was so confident of her good looks at all times that she bothered only when an impression was called for.

'What's the matter with you?' she said. 'You look like you've seen a corpse.'

Peter sat down at the table. 'I have. Well, I think I have. I need a drink.'

To Sharonne these last alarming words were triggers of danger, annulling the sentence which had preceded them. 'No, you don't. Not at nine in the morning, you don't. You'd better remember what Dr Klein said.'

'Sharonne,' said Peter, helping himself to her orange juice as a poor substitute, 'there's a car in the quarry. I think there's someone in it, someone dead. The smell's ghastly, like rotten meat.'

She stared at him. 'What are you talking about?'

'I said there's a dead person in a car in the quarry. In our quarry. Up in the wood.'

She stood up. She was twelve years younger but much tougher than he, he had always known it. If he was ever in danger of forgetting, she reminded him. 'This car, did you look inside?'

'I couldn't. I thought I'd throw up. I've got to call the police.'

'You didn't look inside, you just smelt a smell. How d'you know it was a body? How d'you know it wasn't rotten meat?'

'God, I could do with a drink. Why would a car have meat in it? It'd have a driver in it and maybe passengers. I have to get on to the police now.'

'Pete,' said Sharon in a voice more suited to an animal rights or anti-capitalism activist than a model, 'you can't do that. That's crazy. What business is it of yours? If you'd not gone up there – God knows why you did – you'd never have seen a car in there. You're probably imagining the smell – you do imagine things.'

'I didn't imagine it, Sharonne. And I know whose car it is. It's that blue VW Golf that's missing, the one that belongs to that woman who's kidnapped those kids. It's been on telly, it's been in the papers.'

'How d'you know that? Did you go down and look? No, you didn't. You couldn't tell it was a Golf, it was just a blue car.'

'I'm getting on to the police now.'

'No, you're not, Pete. We're lunching with the Warrens at one and this evening we've got the Gilberts' drinks party. I'm not missing out on those. You get the police here and we'll not be able to go anywhere. We'll be stuck here and all for something that's not our business. If there is a body in that car, which I doubt, they'll suspect you. They'll think you did it. They always think the person who found the body did it. They'll have you down here next week talking to them and then they'll have you in court. Is that what you want, Pete?'

'We can't just leave it there.'

When her husband uttered those words, Sharonne knew the battle was won. 'If you mean leave the car there, why not? We needn't go near the place.' She never did, so this wouldn't be difficult. 'Come the spring there'll be leaves on the trees and everything overgrown, and you won't even be able to see it. I don't see why it shouldn't stay there for years.'

'Suppose someone else finds it?'

'Great. Let them. It won't affect us then, will it?'

Secure in her conviction that she had brought Peter round to her point of view, she went off upstairs to begin the two-hour-long process that would make her fit to attend the Warrens' lunch party. Peter took himself into the dining room where, safe from her hectoring, he helped himself to a generous tot of Bushmills. Very soon the stench was dispelled from his nostrils. It was several hours later before the subject was again raised. They were returning from Trollfield Farm where they had lunched and Sharonne, who never touched anything stronger than sparkling water, was driving, Peter being rather the worse for wear.

'I'll have to call the police tomorrow,' he said, slurring his words. 'I'll tell them I've only just found it.'

'You won't call them, Pete.'

'It's probably against the law to consheal – I mean conceal – a body.'

'There's no body. You imagined it.'

In spite of overdoing it at lunchtime, Peter overdid it again at the Gilberts'. In normal circumstances, he more or less kept within the limits laid down by Dr Klein because he wanted to keep his liver for a few more years, but normal circumstances didn't include his finding abandoned cars which stank of rotting flesh. Next day he felt as if he were rotting himself and he didn't call the police, only heaving his racked body out of bed at three in the afternoon to drive them back to London.

'Out of sight, out of mind' is a truism of remarkable soundness. Once back in the South Kensington mews house where the only cars were his own and those on the residents' parking in the street, and the only trees those planted in the pavement, the memory of his discovery became hazy and dreamlike. Perhaps he *had* imagined the smell. Perhaps it wasn't from a decaying body, or not a human body, but a dead deer or badger lying concealed in the undergrowth. What did he know of such country matters? Sharonne was right when she said he couldn't have said from where he stood if the car was a VW Golf or some other make of small saloon. He hadn't seen its grid or read the name on its boot lid.

He was a busy man, he always was. There was a possible takeover to avert, a new merger to accelerate. Such things become very real in a mirror-façaded tower just off Trafalgar Square while events in rural Kent take on a peculiar remoteness. But Friday always comes. Unless you die or the world ends, Friday will come.

His way of continuing to avoid the issue would be not to go to Passingham St John until – well, after Christmas. But something strange had happened, displacing his detachment. The blue car began to prey on his mind. He knew it was there and he knew the smell came from inside it. Sharonne was right when she said he imagined things. He was gifted, or burdened, with a powerful imagination, and now it magnified the car to twice its size, clearing away the bushes and trees which partly concealed it, while it strengthened and worsened the smell, spreading it from its source in the quarry up into the wood, along the track and all the way up to the house. He began to fancy that next time he drove to his country home, whenever that might be, the smell would meet him as he turned into the lane. Inexorably, Friday came. He both wanted to go to Kent and he didn't, and now he was beginning to fear that the presence of that car in the quarry would alienate him from his beautiful house and grounds, and make them repulsive to him. Suppose he never wanted to go there again?

Sharonne had no intention of going to Passingham Hall two weekends in succession. Owning a country place was great so long as you seldom went there. It was useful for mentioning idly to people you sat next to at dining tables. She had a new dress which she meant to wear at a charity gala dinner at the Dorchester on Saturday night, and on Sunday she'd got her mother and her sister and four other people coming to lunch and caterers were booked. None of that was going to be put off so that they could go to Passingham. Peter dared not go without her. Such a thing had never happened. He must study to banish that car from his mind and restore himself to what now seemed the carefree state he was in before he went walking in the wood last Saturday morning.

CHAPTER 9

Once he had cleared it with the Hampshire police, Wexford phoned Ralph Jennings for an appointment. As soon as possible, please. He had to leave this message with an answering service. On the desk in front of him was a stack of reports and messages from other police authorities, and as he went through them he soon saw that most were negative. The same with the collated list, the huge protracted list, of sightings of the three by members of the public. To fail to follow them up would be negligent even though he knew the idea that Joanna Troy had advertised both children for sale on the Internet and that she and Giles Dade had been married at Gretna Green was gross nonsense. Barry Vine, Karen Malahyde, Lynn Fancourt and the rest of them would get on with the weary work.

Several hours passed, during which he had dialled the Southampton number twice more, before Ralph Jennings called him back. The voice was cautious, almost fearful. What was it about? What could Kingsmarkham Crime Management have to do with him? He hadn't lived in the neighbourhood for six years.

'You've read the newspapers, Mr Jennings? You've seen television? Your former wife is missing and has been now for a fortnight.'

'Maybe but it's got nothing to do with me. She's my *ex*-wife.'

He made the term sound not as if it referred to a no longer extant relationship but rather as if Joanna Troy were X-rated.

'Nevertheless I would like to see you. There are questions it's important I ask you. When would it be convenient for me and another officer to call on you?'

'At my *home*?'

'Where else, Mr Jennings? I'm not asking you to come here. The interview wouldn't take long, probably an hour at most.' The silence was long. Wexford thought they had been cut off. 'Mr Jennings, are you there?'

In an abstracted, not to say *dis*tracted, voice, Jennings muttered, 'Yes, yes . . .' Then, as if making a decision that would radically change the whole course of his life, 'Look, you can't come to my home. It won't do. It's not on. Too much — explanation would be involved and then . . . You really do need to see me?'

'I thought I'd made that clear, sir,' said Wexford patiently.

'We can fix something. We could, er, meet outside. In a pub — no. In a — a restaurant and have a coffee. How's that?'

He couldn't exactly insist on visiting the man's home, though his curiosity had been aroused. Probably Jennings was capable of not answering the door or being out at the crucial time or answering the door and refusing them entry. It wasn't a situation in which he could get a warrant. 'Very well,' he said, much as it went against the grain.

Jennings named a time on the following day and the meeting place as a café. There was plenty of parking 'around there', he said, speaking now in a helpful, even cheerful, voice. And the coffee was very good, you could get ninety-nine different varieties. That was their gimmick, that was why the place was called the Ninety-Nine Café. Wexford thanked him and rang off.

What could be the reason behind Jennings's refusal to let them call on him? The sinister possibility was that Joanna Troy was there. Even more sinister that the bodies of Giles and Sophie Dade were concealed there. Wexford didn't believe either was true. Jennings would have got Joanna out of the way during the interview. As for the bodies, if they were, say, buried in his garden, far from refusing the visit he would have put on a show of welcoming the police with open arms. So what was it? He intended to find out.

When his phone rang again almost immediately he thought it was Jennings calling back with some fresh excuse or change of venue. But it was his daughter Sylvia at The Hide, the women's refuge where she currently worked two evenings and one morning a week.

'You may know already, Dad, but a guy's just been arrested outside this building for attacking his wife with a hammer. I saw it. From this window. It's shaken me up a bit.'

'I'm not surprised. You don't mean she was killed, do you?'

'Not as bad as that. He's shorter than her. He aimed at her head but he got her in the shoulder and the back. She fell down screaming and then – then she stopped screaming. Someone phoned for the police and they came. He was sitting beside his wife on the path by then, crying and still holding the hammer. There was blood everywhere.'

'D'you want me to come?'

'No, it's all right. I think I just wanted to talk about it. Cal's got the car today, he's said he'll come over and fetch me. I'll be OK.'

Wexford ground his teeth, but not until after she'd put the phone down. Did she mean that on the days she was at The Hide she let Chapman have her car and went to work on the bus? Perhaps only some days, but that was bad enough. Hadn't he a car of his own? He'd done pretty well for himself, thought the father, a fine big house, the Old Rectory that Neil had refurbished, a ready-made family, the use of a car, and all because he'd made himself pleasant – or something – to a lonely woman.

He looked out of the window. It was raining again, the fine light rain that once it had started seemed to find no reason to stop. A car came in from the High Street, windscreen wipers on to the fast speed, parked close up to the doors and Vine and Lynn Fancourt got out of it, hustling into the station a man who had his head covered with a coat. The wielder of the hammer, that would very likely be.

And what of Sylvia? Perhaps he and Dora should go over to what everyone had got into the habit of called 'the Old Rectory' and see how she was. He was always pleased to see his grandsons. Chapman would be there, though. Wexford was cursed with a too-volatile imagination and now the horrid thought came to him that Sylvia *might have another child*. Why not? It was what women wanted to do when they embarked on a new and presumably intended to be a steady – and what was the current politically correct word? Ah, yes, *stable* – relationship. The nauseating phrase was 'I want to have his child'. No reasonable person could want to have Chapman's child. He might be good-looking but he was stupid too and lack of brains was as likely to be inherited as beauty – perhaps more likely, but Sylvia's father had often thought Sylvia very unreasonable.

Still, they would go. She was his daughter, whomsoever she took up with, and she had had a bad shock.

Not for the first time he wished she would work for a less worthy cause.

'I picture a handsome wimp,' said Wexford when he and Burden were being driven down the M3, his mind still on Callum Chapman. 'And yet I don't know why. Joanna Troy doesn't seem to have been very conscious of appearance.'

'Those clothes.' Burden uttered the two words in a monotone that expressed more of his feelings than an impassioned outburst would have done. He himself was wearing the slate-blue suit once more with a white shirt this time and a blue, emerald and white patterned tie. Wexford fancied he had been reluctant to cover all this with his raincoat, but he conceded that this aspersion might be unfounded. 'If you want to know how I picture him, I see a skinny little pipsqueak with big teeth.'

'Nice word, pipsqueak,' said Wexford. 'Old-fashioned now. In the First World War it's what they called a shell distinguished for the sound it made in flight.'

'I don't see why that should apply to an insignificant sort of person.'

'Nor do I.'

'Anyway, it's useless speculating about what someone's going to be like. People never are the way we expect. The law of averages ought to make us right sometimes but we never are.'

'I don't believe in the law of averages,' said Wexford.

The café was indistinguishable from thousands like it all over the country. Vaguely hi-tech with a lot of chrome, red vinyl floor and black leather seating, it had booths for hiding or taking refuge in, circular tables for sitting round and circular tables at chest height for standing at. They were early and Jennings wasn't. There were no men on their own in the Ninety-Nine Café.

'Why would anyone want coffee with walnuts?'
Wexford asked after he and Burden had seated themselves in a booth and ordered respectively a large filter
and a cappuccino.

'Or almonds or cinnamon, come to that? God
knows. It's a gimmick.'

Their coffee came. Wexford faced the door to spot
Jennings when he came in. He wondered if it was obvious to the man behind the counter and the woman who
served them that they were police officers. Probably in
his case, if not in sartorially elegant Burden's. It couldn't
be helped. Jennings had chosen to meet them here and
not at his home. 'Where is he, anyway?' Wexford said,
looking at his watch. 'It's ten past and he was due here
at eleven.'

'Time doesn't mean as much to people as it used.
Haven't you noticed? Especially the young. They put a
sort of mental "about" in front of an appointment time,
so it's "about ten" or "about eleven" and that can easily
be half past, though you notice it's never a quarter to.'

Wexford nodded. 'The trouble is we can't stalk off in
high dudgeon. We need him a good deal more than he
needs us. "Dudgeon", by the way, is a dagger hilt, so
why it should mean resentment is something else I don't
know.' He finished his coffee, sighed and said, 'You
remember that pain in the arse Callum Chapman? Well,
he's . . . But here's our reluctant witness, unless I'm
much mistaken.'

As Burden had forecast, he was very different from
the way either of them had imagined him. Wexford had
been right, though, in his belief that they were easily
recognisable as policemen, for Jennings homed in on
them immediately. It was a tallish thin man who sat
down next to Burden and opposite Wexford. Joanna's
father had told them Jennings was thirty-two. Apart

from a bald patch he had tried to conceal by combing his hair over it, he looked much younger than that age. His was one of those puckish or Peter Pan faces, almost babyish, large-eyed, the nose small and tip-tilted, the mouth not quite but nearly a rosebud. Fair hair, slightly wavy and copious in front, clustered round his temples and grew in little fringes above his ears.

'What kept you, Mr Jennings?' Wexford's tone was pleasanter than his words.

'I'm sorry I'm late. I couldn't get away.' The voice by contrast was rather deep and, though Jennings looked as if no razor had ever passed across those rosy cheeks, unmistakeably masculine. 'I had a bit of a tussle, actually. My, er, story wasn't believed.'

'Your story?' said Burden.

'Yes, that's what I said.' The waitress came. 'I'll have one of your lattes with cinnamon, please. Look, I've decided I have to explain to you. I know it looks odd. The fact is – Oh God, this is so embarrassing – the fact is my partner – she's called Virginia – she's madly jealous. I mean, pathologically jealous, though maybe it's unkind to say so.'

'We shan't tell her,' said Wexford gravely.

'No. No, I'm sure not. The fact is she can't bear it that I've been married. I mean, if my wife had died I don't suppose it would be so bad. But I was divorced, as you know, and I've been forbidden even to mention, er, Joanna's name. Just to show you how bad it is, she can't bear it if she reads the name Joanna in some other context and if she meets a Joanna . . . I suppose it's flattering in a way – well, it is. I'm very lucky to be – well, loved like that.'

'I was adored once,' mumured Wexford. 'What you're saying, if I understand you, Mr Jennings, is that you stopped us coming to your home because your girlfriend would be there and would take exception to the subject of our conversation?'

Jennings said admiringly, 'You *do* put it well.'

'And in order to come at all, you had to construct a cast-iron excuse for, er, going out on your own for an hour at eleven in the morning? Yes? Well, no doubt you know your own business best, Mr Jennings.' A sensible man would run a mile from this Virginia, Wexford thought to himself. 'And now perhaps we can get down to the purpose of our meeting. Tell us about your ex-wife, would you? What kind of a person she is, her interests, pursuits, her habits.' He added in the same grave tone, 'Don't worry. There is no one to over-hear you.'

Jennings wasn't a sensible man. His prevarications and failure to stand up to tyranny proved that. But he didn't make a bad job of character analysis, even though he sometimes looked over his shoulder while he talked, presumably fearing Virginia might materialise from the street door. Wexford, who had anticipated a 'Well, she's just like anyone else' approach, was pleasantly surprised.

'We met at university. She was doing a postgraduate modern languages degree and I was doing one in business studies. I guess a lot of people would say we were too young to settle down together but that's what we did. We were both twenty-three. She was after a job at a school in Kingsmarkham. Her father lives there. Her mother was dead.

'Joanna's very bright. She wouldn't have got that job before she was twenty-four if she hadn't been. Very, er, positive. I mean she's got strong opinions about almost everything. Impulsive too, I'd say. If she wants some-thing she's got to have it and she's got to have it *now*. I suppose I was in love, whatever that may mean – Aren't I quoting some famous person?'

'The Prince of Wales,' said Burden.

'Oh, was it? Well, I must have been in love with
Joanna because she's not . . . What I'm trying to say is,
I never actually liked her, she's not very *likeable*. She can
make herself pleasant if she wants something but alone
with the person she'd chosen – well, presumably to
spend her life with, she can be a bit of a pain. Nasty, if
you know what I mean. When I first met her I noticed
she hadn't any friends. No, that's not quite true. She had
one or two but after we split up I realised they were
both very weak types of people, they'd be the sort to let
Joanna push them around. It's like she can't have an
equal relationship.'

Now he had embarked on his ex-wife's nature and
proclivities, Jennings was in full swing. He had even
stopped starting each time anyone came into the
Ninety-Nine Café. Wexford let him talk. Any questions
could come later.

'We decided to get married. I don't know why.
Looking back, I can't imagine. I mean, I knew by then
I'd be in serious trouble if I disagreed with her over anything. Her views were right and everyone else had to
have them too, especially me. I suppose I thought, I'll
never find anyone else as clever and as dynamic as
Joanna. I'd never find anyone with so much energy and
– well, drive. She's on the go all day and she's an early
riser, I mean like six thirty a.m., weekends and all,
showered, dressed, but – well, you don't want to hear
all this. The upshot was I thought that no one else
would do for me after her. Well, I was wrong but I
thought I was right.' That would make a good epitaph
for a lot of people, Wexford thought, maybe most people. He was wrong but he thought he was right. 'My
dad bought us a house in Pomfret. He was dying but
he said I might as well have it then and there while he

was still alive. He died about two months after we were married. Joanna had a job at a school in Kingsmarkham – Haldon Finch it was – and I was with a London firm. I used to commute.'

'D'you want some more coffee? I think I will.' Wexford and Burden both nodded. Each was afraid that if they didn't choose this way to prolong things, Jennings might notice the time and be off. He waved to the waitress. 'Where was I? Yes, right. I've heard people say you can get on perfectly well with someone you're living with but as soon as you get married it starts to go wrong. Maybe, but Joanna and I only really got on if I was a yes-man and she called the tune. Then there was the sex.' He broke off as the waitress came to take their order, glanced at his watch, said, 'I told Virginia I'd not be more than an hour and a half, so I've still got a bit of time. Yes, the sex. You do want to hear this?' Wexford nodded. 'Right. It had been quite good at first, I mean when we first met but it went off long before we got married. By the time we'd been married six months it was almost non-existent. Don't think I just took this lying down.' An unfortunate phrase in the circumstances, Wexford thought, but Jennings didn't seem aware of what he had said. 'No, I tried to tell her what I thought. I did tell her. I mean, I was twenty-six years old, a normal healthy man. I will say for Joanna she didn't pretend. She never did. She came straight out with it. "I don't fancy you any more," she said. "You're going bald." I said she must be mad. I mean, premature baldness runs in my family. So what? Apparently, my father was bald before he even met my mother and he was only thirty. They still had three kids.'

Their coffee came. Jennings sniffed his, presumably to detect if it contained the appropriate amount of cinnamon. 'To resume,' he said. 'I thought there must be someone else. She'd just met this Katrina, the mother of those missing kids. They were always together. Now don't get any ideas Joanna's a lesbian. For one thing, I noticed she'd never let any woman touch her, she wouldn't even let her stepmother kiss her and there's nothing repulsive about Effie, far from it. Once or twice Katrina would put her hand on her arm or something but Joanna always retreated or actually took it off. Besides, I wasn't the first man in her life, far from it. She'd had a lot of relationships before me, started at school. But they were all of the male sex. I did wonder if she was so keen on Katrina because she fancied her husband. He's nothing to look at and a bit of a shit but you never know with women, do you? I couldn't think of any other reason for her going about with Katrina – well, yes, I suppose I could. She just agreed with everything Joanna said and did, and she was always telling her how clever and gifted she was. Joanna liked that, she *basked* in it. I still don't know the answer. Anyway, soon after the arrival of the Dades on the scene she said she'd decided there'd be no more sex. Our marriage was to be a partnership, I quote, "for convenience and companionship".'

'It was you who left, Mr Jennings?'

'You bet it was and don't let anyone tell you different. I sold the house and gave her half the proceeds. Anything to get clear of all that. I haven't seen her since.'

Burden said, 'Was Ms Troy ever violent towards you? In these arguments you had, if you disagreed with her, would she have struck you? And do you know of any incidents of violence in her past, perhaps before you met her but that she told you about?'

'There was nothing like that. It was all verbal. Joanna's very verbal. There's only one . . .'

'Yes, Mr Jennings?'

'I was going to say one incident of – well, what you mean. Not to me. It was long before we met. She didn't tell me, someone else did, someone I knew at university. I don't know whether I ought to tell you, though I can't say this chap told me in confidence, not really.'

'I think you had better tell us, Mr Jennings,' Wexford said firmly.

'Well, yes. I will. When this chap heard I was going about with Joanna he said she'd been at school – Kingsmarkham Comprehensive, that was – with his cousin. They were both in their teens but she was older, three years older, I think. She beat this kid up, blacked both his eyes, actually knocked a tooth out. He was all over bruises but nothing was actually broken. It was all hushed up because his cousin recovered and no harm done but also because Joanna's mother had just died and some counsellor said that accounted for it. Of course, I asked Joanna about it and she said the same, her mum had died and she was in shock, she didn't know what she was doing. The cousin denied it, by the way, but she said he'd said something rude about her mother. That's what she told me, that he'd insulted her mother's memory.

'But there was a funny thing. Not really funny but you know what I mean. The kid died. Years later, leukaemia, I think it was. He must have been twenty-one or twenty-two. It was Joanna who told me. It was before we were married, we were still doing our MAs. She said, "You know that Ludovic Brown –" funny I remember the name but it's a peculiar one, isn't it? "– you know that Ludovic Brown," she said. "He's dead. Some sort of cancer." And then she said, "Some people do get what they deserve, don't they?" That was typical of her. The poor kid maybe said something rude and for that he deserved to die of leukaemia. But that was

Joanna. That's what I meant when I said she wasn't very likeable.'

Ludovic Brown, thought Wexford. Kingsmarkham, I suppose, or environs. He went to Kingsmarkham Comprehensive, died young, his family shouldn't be hard to find. 'You've been very helpful, Mr Jennings. Thank you.'

'Better not say my pleasure, had I?' Again the watch was glanced at, to alarming effect. 'My God, I've got five minutes to get back in. A cab, I think, if I can get one.'

He ran. The waitress watched him go, a faint smile on her lips. Did he come in here with Virginia and she give public examples of her possessiveness?

'Some people', said Burden, when Wexford had paid the bill, 'don't seem to have a clue about self-preservation. Talk about out of the frying pan into the fire.'

'He's weak and he's attracted by strong women. Unfortunately, he's so far picked two with the kind of strength that's malevolent. You could persuade him into anything, sell his grandmother into slavery, swallow cyanide, I dare say. Still, from our point of view he's an improvement on everyone else we've questioned in this case, isn't he? He's given us some good stuff.'

CHAPTER 10

Burden fell asleep in the car and Donaldson never spoke unless he was spoken to or felt obliged to intervene, so Wexford retreated into his own thoughts, mainly concentrated on Sylvia and their encounter the evening before. He and Dora had gone over to the Old Rectory after supper, ostensibly to check on their daughter's condition after what she had witnessed at The Hide that morning. Chapman came to the door and seemed less than pleased to see them.

'Sylvia didn't say she was expecting you.'

Dora had cautioned him to watch his tongue so Wexford remained silent. She asked how Sylvia was.

'She's OK. Why shouldn't she be?'

They found the boys occupied with their homework in what was known as the family room where the television was on, albeit turned very low, and where by the look of the half-full wineglass on the side table, the dent in the seat cushion of an armchair and the *Radio Times* on its arm, Chapman had been relaxing before their arrival. Wexford, who had put his head round the door and quickly absorbed all this, said hello to Robin and Ben, and followed Dora to the kitchen. There they found Sylvia cooking the evening meal, pasta boiling in a saucepan, mushrooms, tomatoes and herbs in another pan, the materials for a salad spread on the counter.

'I've only just got home,' she said, as if self-defence or excuse was necessary. 'Cal was going to do it but there was this programme on TV it was important for him to watch and now he's helping the boys with their homework.'

Again Wexford was silent – on that subject, at least. 'How are you?'

'I'm fine. I ought to be used to that kind of thing by now. I've seen enough of it. Only usually I've not witnessed the actual attack, just heard about it afterwards. But I'm fine, had to be. Life goes on.'

Any sort of man who called himself a man – Wexford was amazed at himself, using such an expression even in his thoughts – any decent sort of man would have sat her down with a drink, moved the kids elsewhere, got her to talk while he listened and sympathised.

'It's terribly late to eat but I couldn't get away. D'you want anything? Drink?'

'We only came in for a minute,' Dora said soothingly. 'We'll go.'

In the car, driving home, he'd said, 'Wasn't he supposed to be the New Man? I thought that was the point. What other point is there to him?'

And Dora, who usually put a curb on his excesses, had agreed with him. He'd often heard it said that it wasn't a man's appearance or character that kept a woman with him but his sexual performance, but he'd never believed it. Surely the sex was fine if you loved the other person or were powerfully attracted to them. Otherwise it made men and women into machines with buttons to press and switches to turn on. He'd ask Burden's view if the man weren't so prudish about things like this. Besides, he was asleep. Pondering on Sylvia and Chapman and Sylvia's jobs and Neil, he let Burden sleep for another ten minutes and then woke him up.

'I wasn't asleep,' said Burden like an old fogey in a club armchair.

'No, you were in a cataleptic trance. What's the name of the head teacher of Kingsmarkham Comprehensive?'

'Don't ask me. Jenny would know.'

'Yes, but Jenny's not here. No doubt she's at work in that very school.'

Donaldson, though he hadn't been addressed, said, 'Dame Flora Gregg, sir.'

'*Dame*?'

'That's right,' said Burden. 'She got it in the Birthday Honours.'

'For rescuing the school from the mess it was in. My fourteen-year-old's a student there, sir.'

'Then she must be relatively new,' said Wexford. 'This business with Joanna Troy happened – when? Fifteen years ago. Who came before Dame Flora?'

Donaldson didn't know. 'A man,' Burden said. 'Let me think. He was there when I first met Jenny and she was teaching there. She used to say he was lazy, I particularly remember that, lazy and fussy about the wrong things. It's coming back to me – Lockhart, that was his name. Brendon Lockhart.'

'I don't suppose you know where we can find him.'

'You don't suppose right, as Roger Dade would say. Wait a minute, though. It's going to be five or six years since he retired and Flora Gregg took over. He'd have been sixty-five then. He may be dead.'

'Any of us might be dead at any old time. Where did he retire *to*?'

'He stayed in the district, that I do know.'

Wexford considered. 'So who do we see first? Lockhart or the parents of poor Ludovic Brown?'

'First we've got to find them.'

Tracing Lockhart was the easier and done through the phone book. Wexford left Lynn Fancourt with the unenviable task of phoning every one of the fifty-eight Browns in the local directory and asking as gently and tactfully as she could which one of them had lost a son to leukaemia at the age of twenty-one. He reflected, as he and Barry Vine were driven to Camelford Road, Pomfret, that the two possibly criminal incidents in Joanna Troy's life were both school-related. First there was the assault on the fourteen-year-old, then the alleged theft. Was the school aspect significant? Or was it merely coincidence?

Brendon Lockhart was a widower. He told Wexford this within two minutes of the policemen entering the house. Perhaps it was only to account for his living alone, yet in almost chilling order and neatness. It was a cottage he had, Victorian, detached, surrounded by what would very likely be a calendar candidate garden in the summer. He showed them into a living room entirely free of clutter, a characterless place rather like the kind of photograph seen in Sunday supplements advertising loose covers. Instinctively, Wexford knew no tea would be offered. He sat down gingerly on pristine floral chintz. Vine perched on the edge of an upright chair, its arms polished like glass.

'The school, yes,' said Lockhart. 'A woman took over from me, you know. I don't usually care for new importations into our vocabulary but I make an exception for "pushy". A very good word "pushy". It perfectly describes *Dame* Flora Gregg. What a farce, wasn't it, giving a woman like that a title? I only met her once but I found her overbearing, didactic, distressingly left-wing and *pushy*. But women rule the world now, don't they? How they have taken over our schools! Haldon Finch also have a woman head now, I hear. In an amazingly short time women have completely taken over, they have *pushed* themselves into every sphere once prohibited to them. I am very glad to see two police*men* calling on me.'

'In that case, Mr Lockhart,' said Wexford, 'perhaps you won't mind answering some questions about two former pupils of yours, Joanna Troy and Ludovic Brown.'

Lockhart was a small man, thin and spry, his face pink and smooth for his age, his white hair more evenly distributed than Ralph Jennings's. But as he spoke that face contorted and stretched, taking on a skull-like look. 'So glad to hear you use that word. "Pupil", I mean. "Student" would be favoured by the good *Dame*, no doubt.'

How very much Wexford would have liked to ask him if he'd thought of seeing someone about his paranoia. Of course he couldn't. 'Joanna Troy, sir. And Ludovic Brown.'

'That was the young lady who mounted a savage attack on the boy, wasn't it? Yes. In the cloakroom, if I remember rightly. After the Drama Group, as I was expected to call the Dramatic Society. I believe she alleged afterwards that he'd done something to annoy her while they were rehearsing some play. Yes, I recall. *Androcles and the Lion*, it was. A choice much favoured by school dramatic societies, largely, I believe, because it has such a large cast.'

'He was quite badly injured, wasn't he, though no bones were broken?'

'He had two black eyes. He had a lot of bruises.'

'But the police weren't called, nor an ambulance? I've been told it was hushed up.'

Lockhart looked a little uncomfortable. He twisted up his face into a gargoyle mask before answering. 'The boy wanted it that way. We sent for the parents – well, the mother. I believe there was a divorce in the offing. There usually is these days, isn't there? She agreed with her son. Let's not have any fuss, she said.'

The boy had been only fourteen. Wexford tried to remember something about *Androcles and the Lion* but could only recall Ancient Rome and Christians thrown to wild beasts. 'Ludovic would have been an extra, would he? A slave or minor Christian?'

'Oh, yes, something like that. I believe she said he tripped her up or made a face at her or something. I do know it was totally trivial. By the by, it wasn't leukaemia he died of. I think you said leukaemia?'

Wexford nodded.

'No, no, no. He *had* leukaemia, that part is true, but it was controlled by some drug or other. My dear late wife knew the boy's grandmother. She was charwoman or some kind of servant to a friend. My wife told me what this woman told her. No, what happened was that he fell to his death off a cliff.'

Vine said, 'Where was this, sir?'

'I'm coming to that. Let me finish. His mother and – well, stepfather, I suppose. He may have been Mrs Brown's paramour, I know nothing of these things. They took him on a holiday to somewhere on the south coast, not all that far. He went out alone one afternoon and fell off a cliff. It was really a very tragic business. There was an inquest but no suspicious circumstances, as you would put it. He was weak, he wasn't able to walk far, and the suggestion was that he was too near the edge and he collapsed.'

Wexford got up. 'Thank you, Mr Lockhart. You've been very helpful.'

'I heard Joanna Troy had become a teacher. Can that be right? She was a most unsuitable woman to be in charge of children.'

'So where was Joanna while Ludovic Brown was in Eastbourne or Hastings or whatever?'

Wexford asked this rhetorical question of Burden while they shared a pot of tea in his office. 'And how are we going to find that out?' said Burden. 'It must have been – let's see – eight years ago. I suppose she was teaching at Haldon Finch. Shacked up with Jennings, though not yet married to him. No reason why she shouldn't have popped down to the south coast for a couple of hours. It wouldn't be much of a drive.'

'There seems to be some doubt as to what Brown did to annoy her. Insulted her mother, says Jennings. Tripped her up or made a face, says Lockhart. Which is it? Or is it both? Did she still know Ludovic Brown? Had she ever really known him beyond being somehow insulted or affronted by him at a play rehearsal? When they were both teenagers?'

'There's a possible yes to all that if she's a criminal psychopath.'

'We've no evidence that she is. If you don't want another cup we'll make our way *chez* Brown. Lynn found her in a flat at Stowerton and she's still called Brown in spite of the paramour.'

'The *what*?'

'It's what that old dinosaur Lockhart called him.'

It looked as if Jacqueline Brown had done far less well out of her divorce than Joanna Troy had from hers. Her home was half a house in Rhombus Road, Stowerton, and the house had been small to start with. The front window overlooked the one-way traffic system. Thumps, a heavy beat and the voice of Eminem penetrated the wall that divided this flat from next door. Jacqueline Brown thumped on it with her fist and the volume was very slightly reduced.

'I don't know why she attacked Ludo.' Her voice was weary, greyish, like her appearance. Life had drained her of colour and joy and energy, and it showed. 'Silly name, isn't it? It was his father's choice. That girl Joanna, he didn't even know her, she was a lot older than him. Well, it's a lot older when you're in your teens. She'd never done it before to anyone, or so they said. And all he'd done was make a face at her when she was acting that part. He put out his tongue, that's all.'

'I'm sorry to have to ask you these questions, Mrs Brown,' said Wexford. 'I will try to make them as pain-less as possible. You took your son on holiday in 1993 — to where exactly?'

'Me and my partner it was. He's called Mr Wilkins. It was his idea, he's always kind. We went to Eastbourne, stayed with his sister.'

Burden intervened. 'Neither you nor your son had ever encountered Ms Troy since her assault on Ludovic?'

'No, never. Why would we? Ludo went for a walk most afternoons. The doctor said it was good for him. Mr Wilkins usually went too but that day he'd got a bad foot, couldn't hardly put it to the ground, we don't know what it was, never did know, but the upshot was he couldn't walk so Ludo went alone. Most times he was only out twenty minutes at the most. This time he never came back.'

Foosteps sounded on the stairs, the door opened and a man came in. He was short and round, and he had several chins. He was introduced as 'Mr Wilkins'. Wexford wished Lockhart could see him. That might stop him describing this unromantic man as a 'paramour'. 'We were discussing Ludovic's unfortunate death.'

'Oh, yes?'

At the arrival of her partner, Jacqueline Brown had brightened. Now she repeated what she had said earlier but in a far more cheerful voice. 'Silly name, isn't it? It was my husband's choice.'

'You want to know where he got it from?' Wilkins sat down and took Jacqueline's hand. 'He'd been read-ing a book.' He spoke as if this was an esoteric activity, comparable perhaps to collecting sigmodonts or studying metaplasm. 'A book called *Ten Rillington Place* by Ludovic Kennedy – see? Funny thing, that, calling your only child after the author of a book about a serial killer.'

Jacqueline achieved a tiny smile, shaking her head. 'Poor Ludo. But it may have been all for the best. He wouldn't have lasted long anyway, never have made old bones.'

'People don't cease to amaze me,' said Wexford as they went down the steep dark staircase.

'Me too. I mean, me neither. There's another set of parents to see and maybe the boy too. The one she may or may not have stolen the twenty-pound note from.'

'Not today. He'll keep. I have to pay my usual visit to the Dades. You can come if you want. And while I'm there I want to look in on those Holloways. There's been something niggling at the back of my mind for days, something the boy's mother said and he denied.'

Roger Dade was at home. He answered the door, saying nothing but looking at them the way one might look at a couple of teenagers come to ask for their ball back for the fifth time. Katrina was lying down, her face buried in cushions.

'How are you?'

'How d'you expect?' said Dade. 'Bloody miserable and out of our minds with worry.'

'I'm not worried,' came the muffled voice of Katrina. 'I'm past that. I'm *mourning*.'

'Oh, shut up,' said Dade.

'Mr Dade,' said Wexford. 'We have been trying to reconstruct the events of that Saturday. Your son appears to have gone out in the afternoon on his own. Do you know where he might have gone?'

'How should I know? Shopping, probably. Taking advantage of my absence. These kids are always shopping when they get the chance. They don't get much chance when I'm home, I can tell you. I can hardly think of a more time-wasting empty occupation.'

Wexford nodded. He fancied Burden looked a little awkward, shopping being a pastime he rather enjoyed. If Giles Dade had been to the shops, what had he bought? This was almost impossible to say. One didn't know which of the objects in his room were old, newish or brand-new and he was sure Dade wouldn't.

'One of his friends, Scott Holloway, your neighbours' son, left a message on your phone and phoned several times after that without getting a reply. He intended to come round and take Giles back to hear some new CDs. Was he a frequent visitor?'

Dade looked exasperated. 'I thought I'd made it clear my children don't have frequent visitors or go to other people's houses. They don't have time.'

Suddenly Katrina sat up. She seemed to have forgotten that she had recently called her 'best and dearest friend' a murderer. 'I was able to do Joanna a good turn there. I recommended her when Peter wanted someone to tutor Scott in French.'

'Peter?' said Burden.

'Holloway,' said Dade. 'Giles, needless to say, didn't need help with his French.'

'And she did tutor him?'

'For a while.' Katrina put on a *schadenfreude* face. 'I felt so sorry for those poor Holloways. Joanna said Scott was hopeless.'

Dade's insults, on the lines of how ineffectual and unprofessional they were, accompanied them to the door.

'Funny, really,' said Wexford as they walked the fifty yards to the Holloways, 'I don't mind what he says nearly as much as a milder jibe from Callum Chapman.

It seems an inseparable part of his character, I suppose, the way', he added mischievously, 'shopping and natty dressing is of yours.'

'Thanks very much.'

The Holloways' doorbell was virtually unreachable owing to the garland of red poinsettias, green leaves and gold ribbon hanging in front of it. They were well in advance of others in the street with their Christmas decorations. A wreath of holly hung over the cast-iron door knocker but Burden managed to insert his fingers under it and give it a double bang.

'Goodness,' Mrs Holloway looked severe. 'What a noise that makes!' As if they were responsible for the poinsettias. 'Did you want Scott again?'

The boy was coming down the stairs, ducking his head under a bunch of mistletoe, hung there no doubt to catch kissable callers. They all went into a living room as glittery and bauble-hung as the Christmas section of a department store.

'Doesn't it look lovely?' said Mrs Holloway. 'Scott and his sisters did it all themselves.'

'Very nice,' said Wexford. It surely wasn't his imagination that the boy appeared terrified. His hands were actually shaking and, to control them, he pressed the palms into his knees. 'Now, Scott, there's no need to be nervous. You only have to tell us the simple truth.'

Scott's mother interrupted. 'What on earth do you mean? Of course he'll tell the truth. He always does. All my children are truthful.'

What a paragon he must be, thought Wexford, more than that, a superhuman being. Did anyone *always* tell the truth? 'Did you call at Giles's house that Saturday afternoon, Scott?' Scott shook his head and Mrs Holloway fired up. 'If he said he didn't go he didn't and that's all there is to it.'

'I didn't,' whispered Scott and, rather more loudly, 'I didn't.'

Burden nodded. He said in a gentle tone, 'It is only that we are trying to reconstruct what happened that day at the Dades' house, who called, who came and went and so on. If you had been there you might have been able to help us but since you say you didn't . . .'

'I didn't.'

'I expect you know that Miss Troy, Joanna Troy, is also missing. She gave you private coaching –' did they use that term any more? '– in French?'

'Scott and my daughter Kerry.' Mrs Holloway had evidently decided, with some justification, that Scott was unfit to answer any more questions. 'Scott only had three sessions with her, he couldn't get on with her. Kerry didn't like her – no one seemed to like her – but she got something from what she was taught. At any rate, she passed her exam.'

There was no more to be done. 'I know the boy is lying,' Wexford said as they got back into the car. 'I just wonder why. And what's he so afraid of? We'll go home now. What I want to do tonight is think about it all and see if I can come up with some reasonable idea of where that car can be. It's been our stumbling block all the way. And yet, apart from every force in the country looking for it, we haven't done much to construct a workable theory for its whereabouts.'

'We've heard about a boy falling off a cliff into the sea. Maybe she pushed him and later on maybe she pushed her car over.'

'Not on the south coast she didn't,' said Wexford. 'It's not like the west coast of Scotland where you might drive a car right up to the edge. Can you imagine doing that somewhere around Eastbourne? I'll think about it.

I'm going to go home and think about it. Drop me off, will you, Jim?'

It is, in fact, very difficult to sit down in a chair, even if it's quiet and you're alone, and concentrate on one particular subject. As men and women trying to pray or meditate have found, there is much to distract your thoughts, a human voice from outside the room or in the street, traffic noise, 'the buzzing of a fly', as John Donne said. Wexford wasn't trying to pray, only to find the solution to a problem, but after he had sat for half an hour, had once dozed off, once forced himself to stay awake, and twice felt his thoughts drift off towards Sylvia and the possibility of more flooding, he acknowledged his failure. Concentration is more easily achieved while going for a long walk. But it was raining, sometimes only lightly and sometimes lashing down, and the vagaries of the rain had been another factor in disrupting his train of thought. He had no more idea of what had happened to George Troy's dark-blue VW Golf four-door saloon, index number LC02 YMY, than when he first sat down.

In the night he dreamed of it, one of those mad chaotic dreams in which bizarre metamorphosis is the rule. The car, driven by a vaguely male driver, was ahead of him on some arterial road but when it moved into a lay-by and parked it changed into an elephant which stood placidly chomping the leaves of an apple tree. The driver had disappeared. He had some idea of climbing on to the elephant's back but again it had changed, wriggling its outlines into a Trojan Horse of dark-blue shiny coachwork, and as he stared, one of the four doors in its side opened and a woman and two children climbed out. Before he could see their faces he woke up.

It wasn't the kind of wakefulness you know will soon give place to sleep once more. He would lie there sleepless for at least an hour. So he got up, found the *Complete Plays* of George Bernard Shaw and turned to *Androcles and the Lion*. More whimsical than he remembered – it was thirty-five years since he had read it – deeply dated and the sentiments, which may have seemed new when it was written, now stale. There were only two women's parts, Megaera, Androcles's wife, and Lavinia, the beautiful Christian. This latter must have been played by Joanna Troy. What then of Ludovic Brown? The only young boy's part was that of the Call Boy who had six or seven lines to speak. That surely would have been Ludovic's.

At some point, perhaps when Lavinia was flirting with the Captain, a scene likely to make fourteen-year-old boys snigger, he had made a face and stuck out his tongue. Or he had done so on one of the occasions when he had to come on to call a gladiator or lion's victim into the arena. And for this Joanna had beaten him mercilessly? Where did the story of insulting Joanna's mother come from? It was pretty obvious this was just the version Joanna had given her husband. It made the attack on Ludovic more justifiable. All he had really done was stick out his tongue at her.

Wexford went back to bed, slept, woke at seven. The first words that came into his mind were: the car is somewhere on private land. It is on an estate, the parkland of a great house, the wild untended grounds of some neglected demesne. Somewhere no one goes for long months in the winter. She drove it there and abandoned it. Because there were ineradicable things inside, stains, damage, incriminating evidence – or the children's bodies.

CHAPTER 11

George Troy tried to supply an answer and failed, diverting from the central enquiry into all kinds of irrelevant by-paths. These threaded their way through properties he had visited owned by the National Trust, great houses such as Chatsworth and Blenheim he had always wanted to see but never had the time for and a stretch of Scottish moorland where a distant cousin, long-dead, had been shot in the leg while injudiciously walking there during a shoot. His wife, not Vine, finally cut him short with a, 'That's very interesting, darling, but not quite what the sergeant wants just at present.'

'This moorland,' said Vine, 'where your cousin was, was it family-owned? I mean, did someone he knew or was related to own it?'

'Good heavens, no,' said Effie Troy, who had evidently heard the story before, perhaps many times before. 'The Troys aren't in that sort of league. This cousin came from Morecambe and, anyway, it was in nineteen twenty-six.'

Vine wasn't surprised. 'So Joanna –' he had graduated to calling her Joanna since no one seemed to object '– didn't know anyone who owned a large country property?'

'Not to say "know". The nearest she ever came to anyone like that was when she was giving GCSE candidates extra coaching for their exams. There was a girl, I can't remember what she was called –' Mrs Troy looked

as if she would like to have asked her husband for help
but knew what the result would be '– Julia something,
Judith something. Joanna didn't care for her, said she
was rude. Her parents owned Saltram House, probably
still do. You know that big house that was completely
refurbished ten or fifteen years back in about twenty
acres? It's on the Forby road. What was their name?'

'Greenwell,' said Vine. As part of a general search of
estates in the neighbourhood, Saltram House and
grounds had already been visited and the Greenwells
interviewed. 'There's nowhere Joanna herself liked to go
to? She wouldn't necessarily have to know the owners
and it wouldn't have to be around here. A place where
she went walking where there were public footpaths?'

'She isn't much for walking,' said George Troy, no
longer suppressible. 'She'd go running, or jogging as
they call it nowadays, or race-walking I think some
would say. Not that she or anyone else would go a distance to a footpath on private land to do that. No, you
can't imagine anyone doing that, not if they had ample
jogging or running space at home. When she wanted
exercise she'd go to the gym, as they call it, short for
"gymnasium" of course. She told me it comes from a
Greek word meaning "to strip naked". Not that she did
strip naked, of course not. Joanna is always decently
dressed, isn't she, Effie? We've seen her in shorts, in hot
weather that is, and possibly she wears shorts for this
gym. Whatever she does wear, there's no doubt that's
where she gets her exercise, at the gym.'

He paused to draw breath and Effie cut in swiftly,
'We really can't help you, I'm afraid. Joanna was born in
the country and most of her life she'd lived in it but I
wouldn't call her a country person, not really. The environment, farming, wildlife, that sort of thing didn't
much interest her.'

'You'll let us know when you find her, won't you?' George Troy, who seemed to have abandoned worrying about his daughter, spoke as if Kingsmarkham Police and forces all over the country were looking for an umbrella he had mislaid on a bus. 'When she turns up, wherever she is? We'd like to know.'

'You may be sure of that, sir,' said Vine, trying to keep the grimness out of his voice.

'That's good to know, isn't it, Effie? It's good to know they'll keep us informed. I was worried at first, we were both worried. My wife was as worried as I was. She's not your typical stepmother, you know, no, not at all. She was a family friend while my poor dear first wife was alive, she was in fact Joanna's godmother. Godmother and stepmother, that can't be a very usual combination, what do you think? Effie's both, you see, godmother and stepmother. Poor Joanna was only sixteen when her mother died, terrible thing for a young girl, she was disturbed by it, very badly disturbed, and there was nothing I could do. Effie did everything. Along came Effie like an angel, completely saved Joanna, she was mother as well as godmother and stepmother, all three she was, and I'm not exaggerating when I say she saved Joanna's sanity . . .'

But at this point Barry Vine, feeling as if he had been hit over the head with something large and heavy, shut off his hearing. He sat, as Wexford might have para-phrased it, like patience on a monument smiling at these streams of pointless drivel, until Effie released him by springing to her feet and repeating her last words, 'We really can't help you, I'm afraid.'

She accompanied him to the door, paused before opening it and said, 'I'm still worried. Should I be?'

Vine said truthfully, 'I don't know, Mrs Troy. I really don't know.'

*

Not a single dentist had come forward to report a young woman coming to him or her with a missing tooth crown. Wexford was sure some would have claimed to have seen her and worked on her mouth, even if these patients had obviously been incorrectly identified. But there had been none at all. Because it was so unusual he even had a call put through to a police headquarters, selected at random in a remote part of Scotland, and checked with the Detective Superintendent in charge there that his officers actually had alerted dentists. No doubt about it, every dentist in the large sprawling area had been told and every one had been anxious to help.

If a crown fell off your tooth wouldn't you be in pain? He didn't know. He phoned his own dentist and was told that it depended what the crown was attached to. If the nerve in the tooth whose root was still there was dead or if the crown were attached to an implant there would be no pain. From a cosmetic point of view, the broken tooth wouldn't show if it were a molar as it very likely was. But when he rang off Wexford remembered what Effie Troy had said, that Joanna had her teeth crowned because she thought them unsightly and they aged her . . .

The tooth would be even more unsightly now. If she hadn't been to a dentist, why hadn't she? Because she no longer cared about this aspect of her appearance and wasn't in pain? Because she guessed dentists would be alerted and didn't want to attract attention to herself? Or for a more sinister reason?

While the searches went on at Savesbury House and Mynford New Hall, both properties with extensive grounds easily accessible from the road, he walked to his appointment at Haldon Finch School. This too was a large comprehensive but generally considered – at least before the coming of Philippa Sikorski – as far more upmarket than the former Kingsmarkham County High School. It was where you sent your children if you could. Education-conscious parents had been known to move into the Haldon Finch catchment area with this purpose in mind. Joanna Troy must have obtained very good degrees and made an unusual impression to have got a job there at so young an age.

It was the last day of term. Haldon Finch would break up at lunchtime and go home for the Christmas holiday. After today, no one would be there to look at the Chrismas tree, decorated in austere white and silver, which stood on a shallow plinth in the entrance hall. A man came out of the lift who looked neither like a teacher, a parent nor a schools inspector, but might have been any of these. He was small, thin and sandy-haired, dressed in jeans and a brown leather jacket. Wexford was escorted upstairs to the head teacher's room. She was not at all his idea of what he had to stop himself calling a 'headmistress'. She had dark-red fingernails and dark-red lipstick, and if her skirt wasn't quite a mini it reached only to her kneecaps. Pale-blonde hair curled closely round her well-shaped head: She looked about forty, was tall and willowy, and smelt of a scent Wexford – who was good on perfumes – recognised as Laura Biagiotti's Roma. Like many successful women in the newly turned century, Philippa Sikorski's appearance, manner and way of speaking were quite different from her stereotype.

'Naturally, I've read about Joanna's disappearance, Chief Inspector. I imagine you want to ask me about the circumstances that led up to her resignation.' The voice he expected to be patrician held a strong intonation of Lancashire. Another surprise. 'By the way, you may care to know that a man called Colman has just been here.

He said he was a private investigator. Of course I couldn't
see him, I had my appointment with you.'

'I think I saw him downstairs. His firm has been
engaged by the missing children's grandmother.'

'I see. But you'll want me to get back to Joanna Troy
now. I had only been here six months at the time she
resigned and though it's five years ago I still haven't got
over the shock.'

'Why is that, Miss Sikorski?'

'It was so *unnecessary*,' she said. 'She hadn't done anything. The silly boy imagined it or invented or whatever. I don't know why. Some counsellor said he was on
the verge of a breakdown. Nonsense, I said, I don't
believe in these breakdowns.' Wexford heartily agreed
but didn't say so. 'You'll want to know what happened.
Have you heard the Wimbornes' side of the story?'

'The Wimbornes?'

'Oh, I'm sorry. They're Damon's parents. He's called
Damon Wimborne. Obviously, you haven't heard it. It's
briefly like this. Joanna had been substituting for the PE
teacher who was ill. She'd been out with the students on
the courts where the girls were playing netball and the
boys, about eight of them, tennis. It was a double
period in the afternoon. She came back with them into
the cloakroom but she didn't stay more than a couple of
minutes. Next day Mr and Mrs Wimborne turned up
here in a fine old rage and told me Damon said Joanna
had stolen a twenty-pound note out of his backpack. It
was hanging on his peg and when he came into the
cloakroom with the other boys – all the girls were
already there – and Miss Troy was doing something to
his bag. She had her hand inside it, he said.

'Well, it was all very awkward. I questioned Damon
and he stuck to his story. He hadn't realised till he got
home, he said. Then he looked for his money and it was

gone. I asked him what on earth he thought he was doing leaving a twenty-pound note in a bag hanging up in the cloakroom, but of course that wasn't really the point. I questioned the girls who were there but none of them had seen a thing. The next thing was that I had to ask Joanna.'

'Not a pleasant task,' said Wexford.

'No. But it was rather odd. I'd anticipated outrage, disbelief, shock. But she didn't seem all that surprised. No, that's the wrong way to put it. She seemed to accept it the way – well, the way you'd accept hearing something bad had happened when there was a strong probability of its happening. You'll wonder how I can remember after so long.' She smiled as Wexford shook his head. 'I just can. I remember everything about those interviews, they made such an impression on me. Joanna said something very strange. I could hardly believe what I was hearing. She said, "I didn't steal his money but I'll give him twenty pounds if that will make him feel better." She spoke absolutely steadily, in a very cool and calm voice. Then she said, "I shall resign anyway. You'll get my resignation this afternoon." She didn't say anything about the police, didn't ask me not to call the police in. I said, "I can't stop Mr and Mrs Wimborne calling in the police if they want to," and she said, "Of course you can't. I know that."'

'What happened?'

'The Wimbornes didn't call the police, as I expect you know. I don't know why not but my guess is they knew more about their precious boy than they were letting on. Perhaps he'd made unfounded accusations of this sort before. But as I say, I don't know. Joanna was adamant, there was no turning her. I was very sorry. She was an excellent teacher and I can't help feeling it's rather a waste when you can teach and you're as good at it as she was, it's a pity to waste that talent on translations and lessons on the Net or whatever it is she does now.'

Philippa Sikorski had become very animated. A faint flush had mounted into her face. Here was someone else who appeared to be or have been fond of Joanna Troy, the woman her ex-husband had described as not like-able. 'Have you kept in touch with her?' Wexford asked.

'It's strange you should ask in the circumstances. I tried to but she didn't seem keen. I had the impression she wanted to cut all connection with Haldon Finch School, put it behind her and try to forget. Damon, by the way, left school with just two GCSEs and the last I heard of him he was wandering about the world doing odd jobs to pay his way.' She smiled. 'The incident in the cloakroom, whatever that really was, evidently hasn't put him off backpacks.'

Thanking her and leaving, Wexford wondered if it would be much good talking to the Wimborne family if Damon, now aged twenty-two, was away in some dis-tant place. On the other hand, the parents might know as much or more about it than he did. Why would a boy of sixteen accuse a teacher of stealing from him? Perhaps because he really had seen, or thought he had seen, her searching through his bag. So what happened to make him change his mind? Or he hadn't seen her and knew he hadn't but wished for some reason to get her into trouble and so injure her. Again, why later change his mind? Mrs Wimborne or her husband might be able to enlighten him. Their home wasn't far from the school. As he walked along the street where their house was, he thought about the protective and defensive mechanisms that were usually switched on when a parent was called upon to listen to accusations against his or her child. Especially *her* child. Women could be tigerish when they perceived their offspring as threatened. Even the most reasonable were unlikely to agree with anyone that their child had behaved badly.

Rosemary Wimborne wasn't among the most reasonable. As soon as he had told her what he wanted, seated opposite her in her very small and untidy living room, she broke into shrill denials that Damon's conduct had been anything less than exemplary. All he'd done was make a genuine mistake. Anyone could make a mistake, couldn't they? He thought he'd seen 'that woman' stealing his money. He was so upset he didn't know what he was saying. But when he found his twenty-pound note was missing . . . Twenty pounds was a lot of money to poor Damon, a small fortune. They weren't wealthy people, they had enough to get by on but that was all. Damon had earned that money working for the greengrocer on his stall on Saturdays.

'But Miss Troy hadn't stolen it, had she, Mrs Wimborne?'

'No one had stolen it, like I said. Anyone can make a mistake, though, can't they?' She was a virago of a woman, sharp-featured, her face prematurely furrowed. 'There was no call for her to leave like that. Damon admitted he'd made a mistake. She was proud of herself, that was what it was, she thought such a lot of herself that she couldn't take it when an innocent boy made a genuine mistake. She just went off in a huff.'

'Did Damon like Miss Troy?'

'Like her? What's that got to do with it? She was just a teacher to him. I'm not saying he didn't prefer the real PE teacher. That was a man anyway, he didn't need a woman supervising him, he said.'

Wexford said mildly, 'Where did Damon eventually find the note?'

'It was in his bag all the time, folded up and stuck inside his book to keep the place.'

A pointless exercise, a fruitless enquiry, Wexford thought as he walked back. It was quite a long way to the police station and now he couldn't understand what had possessed him to make the journey on foot. Good for him it might be but he hadn't at the time faced the fact that he would have to walk back again. The rain had begun once more, was now falling steadily.

Stocking up for Christmas? said the bad pun on a winking neon sign spanning the Kingsbrook Bridge. Once it would have said *Five Shopping Days to Christmas* but all days were shopping days now. Had the sign been there earlier and he hadn't noticed? Probably he hadn't noticed the decorations in the High Street either, the customary symbols, angels, fir trees, bells, old men with beards in funny hats. This lot, executed in red, green and white lights, seemed more than usually tasteless. What hadn't been there earlier was the poster headed 'Missing from Home' with two colour photographs of Giles and Sophie under it. He didn't recognise the phone number. It wasn't a local one but probably belonged to a dedicated line opened by Search and Find Limited. For some reason it made him cross, exacerbating his anger with himself for so far failing to buy any presents. Would he and Dora be expected to buy something for Callum Chapman? The usual Christmas panic seized him. But, really, it was only for Dora he had to buy. All the rest she would have seen to, had probably bought them already and wrapped them as exquisitely as usual. He felt a pang of guilt, hoping she *liked* doing this, hadn't been only pretending to like it all these years.

The film showing at the cinema was too appropriate: *What Women Want.* They never seemed to want anything he bought them. He went into the Kingsbrook Centre, walking slowly, catching sight of more 'Missing from Home' posters, then staring bemusedly at displays of clothes, handbags, small ridiculous bric-a-brac 'for the woman who has everything', at bottles of perfume, tights, absurd, mind-boggling underwear. Into this boutique he went. Burden was standing at the counter, making what looked like a knowledgeable choice.

'Snap,' said Wexford, but he felt better. Mike would *know*. He would probably know more than Wexford himself what other men's wives liked or wore. He might even know what size other men's wives were. With a sigh of relief he gave himself into the inspector's keeping.

CHAPTER 12

Peter Buxton's idea of marriage had never been that the two people in question should live in one another's pockets. He had been married before. His first wife and he hadn't exactly lived separate lives but they had individually had their own interests and pursuits, and often went out without the other. That was where the rot started, Sharonne said, that was what went wrong. Her beliefs were quite different.

Her husband needed her support and counsel, an ever-present voice in his ear uttering words of wisdom and prudence. Without her he would be lost. She didn't even care to have him sit next to someone else at a dinner party lest his indiscreet behaviour and unwise words landed him in trouble. It wasn't that she was jealous or even particularly possessive. Her absolute confidence in her appearance, sexual attractions and personality saw to that. In her own eyes, she was there to look after him every minute of the day except when he was in Trafalgar Square, and then she phoned frequently. Her power over him consisted in a need for her which she had largely manufactured herself. She had set out to mould him into the pattern of the man she wanted and all she had failed to do was stop him drinking.

Almost all. Such is human nature that few people are willing prisoners for long. Peter didn't want to escape from his marriage. He was pleased with his marriage and proud of his wife. When she had two or three babies she would transfer her bossiness and need to be needed to them. He didn't want permanent escape, only the chance to get away for a few hours. To be by himself, an individual, not one of a pair, half of the entity that is marriage, and he only wanted it for a little while.

Another weekend had gone by and another. Sharonne shopped for Christmas and he shopped for Sharonne. As well as her 'big' present she liked him to prepare a stocking full of goodies: perfume, expensive little make-up gimmicks, an eighteen-carat gold key ring, pearl ear studs. She appeared to have forgotten all about the blue car in the quarry, what was inside it and the smell. They never discussed it, not a word had been said about it by either of them since they left Passingham Hall that Sunday afternoon. Sharonne no doubt believed he had taken her advice to heart and, as she had, decided to forget the car, let it remain where it was until branches and brambles and ferns grew over it, rust corroded its bodywork, and the things inside decayed and dissolved until bones only remained. Until time absorbed and neutralised that terrible smell.

He hadn't forgotten it. By now he was thinking about the car almost all the time. He thought about it at meetings, at conferences, while Christmas shopping, while viewing new productions, when he was on-line and when he was signing contracts. The only way to rid himself of the monstrous fantasy that the car was the size of a bus, filling the quarry, and that the smell was wafting across the countryside like poison gas, was to go down there, see for himself and maybe – maybe – do something about it. But how, without Sharonne knowing?

He was, after all, the boss. If he didn't want to go to the midweek conference, no one could reproach him.

Certainly – unless the threatened takeover happened – no one could fire him. He had only to say he had another, more important, engagement. But Sharonne would phone. His assistant wouldn't disturb him in conference unless the message was urgent but he *wouldn't be in conference*, he'd be on the way to the M2. If Sharonne asked where the other engagement was, the assistant could say she didn't know, she *wouldn't* know because it didn't exist, but Sharonne would play merry hell. In the event, things turned out quite differently from what he expected. They usually do. He told his wife he had a meeting with an important investor in Basingstoke and he'd be out of London most of the morning and over lunchtime. She didn't even ask who it was or for a phone number. She was having her hair done at ten and afterwards going to a fashion show.

The company, or those he bothered to tell, got a different story. A funeral in Surrey. His driver got quite pushy and insistent when Peter said he wouldn't be needing him or the Bentley but would drive himself. Such a thing was unheard-of. When Peter said his own car needed the run, it hadn't been out of the garage for three weeks, Antonio offered to drive it down to Godalming. His employer, forced into a corner, was obliged to say weakly that he wanted to be alone to think.

He hadn't been alone in the Mercedes since he bought it eighteen months before. At first, being alone and at the wheel was quite pleasant but after a time, when there were queues and hold-ups and roadworks, he began to miss someone to talk to about the traffic, someone to tell him how much worse it was than last year and that she blamed the government. But at last he had a clear run ahead of him, he left the main road, entered the lane and just before midday the narrower one that was the approach to Passingham Hall.

Although it was a chilly day, he lowered the car window and sniffed the air. No smell, nothing. Had he really thought there would be? Up here? Of course he had, his fears had troubled his days and horribly haunted his nights. Now, because there was no smell and none as he ascended the lane towards the house, hope seized him, a hope he knew was absurd and irrational, that the car had gone, had sunk into the wet ground or been towed away into the field. He even half convinced himself that he had imagined it all. After all, no one else had seen it, this whole terror depended on something that might be a hallucination . . .

Although he could have parked at the point where the track turned off, he went on all the way down to the house. Now he was here he felt a craven need to put off investigating the quarry. For of course it hadn't been a hallucination, nor had he imagined it. He got slowly out of the car, sniffed the air. If he didn't do something about that car he would spend his time down here sniffing the air, it would become an indispensable part of life at Passingham Hall. Arrive, park, sniff. Get up in the morning, go outside, sniff. . . . He changed his shoes for rubber boots and began to walk along the lane. And then a very awkward thing happened. He had forgotten all about the farmer's shed in the field but there the farmer was, standing on its roof, lopping off overhanging tree branches with a chainsaw. Avoiding him was impossible. Rick Mitchell saw Peter, raised one hand and called out, 'Long time no see. You OK, then?' Peter nodded, waved vaguely. At the turn-off to the track, out of the farmer's sight, he once more lifted his head, breathed in through his nose, and again. Nothing. If it really wasn't there he would have to see a psychiatrist, for this was serious stuff. Behind him, the chainsaw began to rattle and whine.

Of course it was there. A small, dark-blue car lying on its side, emitting through its open window that terrible stench. He could smell it here all right and he was twenty feet above it. Should he go down a bit, go nearer, *take a look inside*?

The sides of the quarry were a cliff of small landslides, tree roots, brambles, dead bracken and loose broken sticks. Treacherous sticks you might mistake for a root, step on and be sent flying. Peter began to climb down gingerly. The timber was slippery with wet, blackened moss. Once he made a mistake and grabbed on to what looked like a root but turned out to be a lopped-off branch. He slid, let out a sound halfway between a cry and a curse, but seized on to a growing root this time and came to a halt. From there he looked down once more. Inside the car he could see something blue which might have been a denim garment and he could see a hand, a pale, long-fingered hand.

That was it. He wasn't going any nearer. That was one of those children. He began to climb back. Going up was easier than getting down. He was more aware of the pitfalls and dangers now. At the top he tried to wipe his muddy hands on damp grass, withdrew them sharply when his finger came into contact with a three-inch-long slug. Standing up, looking up, he saw something which made him catch his breath. Rick Mitchell was coming towards him along the path from the lane.

'You OK?' called Mitchell when he was within earshot. It was a favourite phrase of his. 'I heard you shout out. You're all over mud.'

Peter cursed that involuntary cry. He knew it was all up now. He could no longer pretend there was nothing down there. Mitchell was sniffing now, approaching the quarry edge. 'What's that stink?'

Coming clean at last, Peter said, 'You see that car? There's a body in it – well, two, I think.'

'It's those missing kids.' Mitchell was awe-stricken. He took a step backwards, then two steps. 'What made you look? You haven't been down here for weeks, have you?' He answered his own question. 'The smell, I suppose. Good thing you came down. Piece of luck.'

Peter turned and began to walk back along the path. Mitchell beside him asked if he was OK and began offering helpful advice. Phone the police. Get on to them now. Did he have a mobile on him? If not he, Mitchell, did. He'd stay with him, give him some support. Peter said he'd prefer to make the phone call from the house. 'Don't let me keep you,' he said. 'I can handle it. There's no need for you to get involved.'

Mitchell shook his head. 'My pleasure. I wouldn't leave you to handle this alone.' He was evidently dying to play a part in the unfolding drama. It would beat messing about with a chainsaw any day. Incredibly, as they came into the lane, he said chattily, 'What you doing for Christmas? You and Mrs Buxton coming down for a day or two or have you got plans for living it up in London?'

Resisting the temptation to say that he felt like never setting foot in Passingham St John again, Peter said they'd be in London. He stared at the house. It looked unkempt, untended, even neglected, the way a place will when no one goes near it for weeks on end but a cleaner longing to get the job done and go home. No Christmas tree in the drawing room window, no lights, though it was a gloomy day. Followed by Mitchell, he went up the shallow flight of steps on the right-hand side, unlocked the front door on its three locks and let them in.

Cold inside. Very cold. What had happened to the efficient central heating, set to come on daily at 9 a.m. and go off at 9 p.m.

'I'd have thought you'd keep the heating on,' said Mitchell.

'We do. It must have gone wrong.'

Ostentatiously, to set an example to Mitchell, he took off his boots on the doormat, but the farmer who wore trainers by now caked with mud, kept them on. He tramped across the hall floor. Peter tried not to look at the footmarks. Trapped as he was, he knew the best thing was to do it and get it over. Sharonne's Christmas would be ruined and therefore his. Why hadn't he thought more carefully before coming down today? But he had thought, he had done nothing but think about that bloody car for weeks, he had thought to the exclusion of everything that should more usefully and profitably have occupied his mind. He picked up the phone receiver, realised he had no idea of the number of the local police and he turned to his helper.

'Zero-one-eight-nine-two . . .' Mitchell began. He knew it off by heart. He would.

They came, two uniformed officers, both men, and they asked Peter to show them where the car was. The sergeant knew Rick Mitchell and was very matey with him, asking after his family and what he was going to do for Christmas. Neither officer seemed to find the farmer's presence irksome. When the car had been pointed out to them they suggested that Peter go back to the house to 'avoid a repetition of your unpleasant experience, sir'.

Peter felt he had no choice. He sat at the table in the icy kitchen and asked himself what he would have done if Mitchell hadn't turned up. Nothing, he thought now, nothing. He'd have left the car where it was and gone home. After a moment or two he got up, switched on the oven to its fullest heat and opened its door. This reminded him of his early days when he'd lived in a bedsitter with 'kitchen area' and putting on the oven had sometimes been the only way to heat the place. Sitting down again, he tried to phone Pauline and then the central-heating engineer. Both had switched their phones on to an answering service. Conveniently forgetting his own roots, Peter thought things had come to a pretty pass in this country when cleaning women had cars and answerphones.

Half an hour had passed before the police – and Mitchell – came back. All three commented on the cold and the fact that his oven was on, but neither officer seemed to see this as a reason for Peter not to hold himself in readiness indefinitely at Passingham Hall for phone calls and for more police to come.

'I have to go back to London.'

'I'm sure there's no reason why you shouldn't go back this evening, sir,' said the sergeant.

His subordinate suggested it would give Peter the chance, 'hopefully', to get his heating seen to. 'I want to go back now,' said Peter.

'Afraid not. This is a case for the CID. Very likely the pathologist will want to see the, er, on the site. Then equipment will have to be brought in to remove the vehicle.'

'What's in it?' Peter asked.

'That I'm not at liberty to tell you at this stage,' said the sergeant.

He asked Mitchell the same question when the police had gone. It struck him as ludicrous that this busybody of a neighbour might know more about a car with bodies in it *on his land* than he did. 'Better leave that to the police, don't you think?' said Mitchell officiously, a smug look on his face. 'It's down to them to tell you when they think fit.' This made Peter believe they hadn't let Mitchell get near the car. 'Perishing in here, isn't it? I'll get off home for my dinner. Now can I get the wife to bring you down something? Maybe a pizza or a slice of her quiche?'

'I shall be fine.' Peter spoke through clenched teeth. Like cleaners with answerphones, the world was turned upside down when peasants like this one were eating pizza and quiche. 'Please don't bother.'

'Thanks for all your help, Rick,' said Mitchell, taking his leave. 'Have to say it yourself when no one else will, don't you?'

Muddy footprints were all over the kitchen floor. Like most householders today who employ a limited staff, Peter was always afraid of losing Pauline. She wouldn't like cleaning up mud two days before Christmas. He almost got down on his hands and knees to wipe it up. He would have done but for hearing a mechanical tune tinkling out. Such was his nervous state that for a moment he didn't know why someone was playing 'Sur le pont d'Avignon' in his kitchen at ten past noon. Then he realised and took the mobile out of his jacket pocket. It was Sharonne.

'Where have you been, Peter? I've been trying all over, the office, some place where they thought you'd be. They said you'd gone to a funeral. Where are you?'

He didn't answer. 'Is it important, er, darling?'

'That depends on whether you want the pipes at Passingham to freeze if we get a cold snap. Pauline's been on to say the heating's gone off and she can't start it. Where *are* you?'

It was a let-out. He could say . . . Ideas for what he could say came thronging. 'I'm in Guildford. Look, why don't I get over to the Hall and see what I can do? I've got an hour or two to spare.' He'd say the smell was so bad he'd had to tell the police . . . 'I may be able to fix the heating myself.'

'Promise to call me back, Peter.'

'Of course I will.'

He had recourse to the drinks cupboard and, indulging in something he knew was a step down the road to ruin, gulped down quite a lot of neat whisky out of the bottle. Then he went upstairs and opened the cupboard where the boiler lived. The front cover lifted off, a switch pressed, a flame struck and maintained and the heating was on again. This is the kind of thing that cheers one up, going a long way to show that one merits a degree in gas engineering. The radiators chugged and bubbled, and the place began to warm up. He wouldn't phone Sharonne back yet. Better let her think he'd had to work on the system for an hour or two. The front doorbell and the phone rang simultaneously as he was coming downstairs. Phone first. It was a man called Vine from Kingsmarkham Crime Management.

'Hold on a minute,' said Peter.

At the front door were two uniformed police officers. In their car, on the forecourt, sat a silver-haired man in a camel coat.

'Lord Tremlett is here, sir.'

Harassed, Peter said, 'Who the hell is Lord Tremlett?'

'The pathologist. He's here to examine the body *in situ.*'

'You mean the *bodies*, don't you?'

'That I can't say, sir.'

Perhaps the chap on the phone could. Peter asked him, but he didn't answer. 'We'd like to see you, Mr Buxton. As soon as possible.'

CHAPTER 13

By the time Burden and Barry Vine got to Passingham
Hall the pathologist had gone but the car was still
where Peter Buxton said he had first seen it. Scene-of-
crime officers had been busy measuring and taking
samples, and the fingerprint people were still there. A
truck with a crane on it followed them down the drive,
prepared to haul the VW Golf and its contents out of
the quarry, and behind the truck a car driven by
Pauline Pearson's husband Ted, his back and the doctor's injunction forgotten. It was half past five and dark
but powerful lamps had been brought to the scene and
these could be seen between the trees, lighting up the
wood. Two cars and a van were parked on the grass
verge that bordered the lane.

A single exterior light showed Burden the façade of
the hall, the two flights of steps leading up to the portico
and front door, and the two cars on the forecourt, a
staid-looking Mercedes and a dashing Porsche. Lights
appeared to be on in several rooms. Vine rang the bell
and the door was answered by a spectacularly beautiful
woman of about twenty-seven. She looked less than
pleased to see them. Yet, thought Burden, the expert on
all things sartorial and cosmetic, the effect of casual
carelessness – apparently no make-up, pale-blonde hair
spikily untidy, blue jeans, white sweater, no jewellery –
must have been achieved for their benefit or that of the
scenes-of-crime men.

'My husband's in the drawing room,' were the only words she was to utter for some time. She opened double doors and walked in ahead of them.

Peter Buxton was thirty-nine and looked fifteen years older. The skin of his face was a dull greyish red. He was one of those men who are very thin with narrow shoulders and spindly legs but wear their belly as if it were a cushion hung on them in a bag. They have the problem too of arranging it to bulge above the trouser belt or below it. Buxton had opted for the former. He was sitting in an armchair with a drink that looked like whisky and water on a small table beside him. The room contained a great many such small tables, piecrust-edged and with lamps on them, consoles and a couple of chaise longues, bunchy flounced curtains at the windows. It had the air of having been put together by an interior decorator recovering from a nervous breakdown.

'When can I go back to London?' said Peter Buxton.

Burden knew a little about him, where he lived and what he did for a living. 'Chief Inspector Wexford will want to see you tomorrow, Mr Buxton . . .'

'Here?'

'You can come to the police station in Kingsmarkham if you prefer that.'

'Of course I don't. I want to go back to London. It's Christmas. Sharonne – my wife, that is – and I have to get ready for Christmas. She kindly came down here this afternoon to support me but now we want to go home.'

'Why don't you tell me about your discovery of this car on your property, sir? You drove down here this morning, I believe. You came because your central heating wasn't functioning, is that right?'

Before Peter Buxton could answer, the door opened and a woman walked in, followed by a rather stout man who, as soon as he saw the company, pressed his hand into the small of his back. The woman was solid, upright, middle-aged and, from her newly set hair to her lace-up ankle boots, might have been an actress playing a farmer's wife in some rustic soap opera. A flood of words poured out of her. 'Sorry to come bursting in like this, Mrs Buxton, but having a key I thought I wouldn't trouble you to answer the door. I heard about your spot of bother in the village, you know what village gossip is, and I thought you might be in need of some help. I see the heating's on again. I feel it, rather. Nice and warm, isn't it? And it's turning quite cold out, I wouldn't be surprised if we had a white Christmas. Oh, whoops, I'm sorry, I didn't realise you'd got company.'

'They are police officers,' said Buxton in a voice as cold as the weather.

'In that case, I'll sit down a minute if you've no objection. I might be able to contribute. You sit on that hard chair, Ted, you have to think of your back.'

Apparently, Buxton baulked at actually telling them to go. He tried to catch his wife's eye but she kept her head averted, determined not to be caught.

'You were saying, Mr Buxton,' said Burden, 'about coming down to see to your central heating.' Something in Buxton's face told him all was not well. The man was more uneasy than he should have been. 'What time was that?'

It was the right question to ask. 'I don't know. I don't remember.'

Sharonne Buxton spoke at last. 'Yes, you do, Peter. Let me jog your memory. The first time I tried to get hold of you at the office was just after ten. That was on my mobile at the hairdresser's and you'd already left. They said you'd gone on your own instead of having Antonio drive you. I wanted to tell you Jason's asked us to dine at the Ivy the day after Boxing Day. Then I'd planned on going to Amerigo's new collection but I went home first and that was when Pauline phoned to tell me about the heating.'

Quick on the uptake, Vine said, 'But you already knew about the heating, Mr Buxton, because that was the reason for your coming down here.'

'No, he didn't.' Pauline Pearson seized her opportunity. 'He couldn't have known. I didn't know till I came in to have a tidy up and dust round. That was at half past ten. I kept trying to phone Mrs Buxton to tell her and I thought she must be out. I thought she'd be home for lunch so I kept on trying and I finally got hold of her just after eleven.'

'You'd left long before that, darling. Don't you remember? And when I got hold of you at last you weren't here. You were in Guildford. You said so.'

Interesting, thought Vine. Very interesting. Peter Buxton had driven himself to Passingham Hall, had unusually dispensed with his driver and had used the central-heating failure as an excuse for his visit. So what was his true purpose? Something to do with a woman? Possible but, according to Vine's information, the man had been married less than three years and Sharonne Buxton was very beautiful. Moreover, he spoke of her and looked at her with admiration bordering on idolatry. And what was he doing in Guildford? Leave it for now, Vine thought. Think about it. And who the devil was Amerigo and what did he collect?

'You went up into the wood,' Burden said. 'Why was that?' He glanced at the notes he'd made earlier. 'A Mr Mitchell who farms nearby told the local police he encountered you at about eleven by the quarry. You told him about the car and the, er, smell was very strong. He went back to the house with you and gave you the number of the nearest police station. Is that right? But what made you go into the wood?'

'You couldn't have smelt it from down here,' said Vine.

Pauline Pearson intervened. 'You certainly could not. I've got a very good sense of smell, haven't I, Ted? I was here earlier and I couldn't smell it. Thank God. Makes you feel sick to your stomach, doesn't it?'

'Nasty,' said Ted. 'Very nasty.'

'If it wasn't that made you go into the wood, what did?'

'Look, I found the bloody car and told you people. What does it matter why or how?'

'This is a suspicious death, sir,' said Burden. 'All the circumstances may be very important.'

'Not to me. Nobody has told me anything. I don't even know how many people were in the car. I don't know if it was those kids and that woman who was with them. I'm told nothing.'

'There's very little to tell, sir,' said Vine. 'The body in the car hasn't yet been identified.'

'What else do you want to know?' Peter Buxton reached for his glass, realised it was empty and looked longingly at his wife.

Her reaction amused Burden. 'No, darling,' she said firmly, 'no more. Not yet. I'll make you a nice cup of tea in a minute.' She turned her head, as exquisite as a flower on a stalk, towards the policemen. 'I hope you won't be long. My husband should go to bed early. He's had a shock.'

It was ten past six. 'I'll make the tea, Mrs Buxton,' said Pauline, 'when they've gone.'

'When did you last come down to Passingham Hall?' Burden addressed the wife this time.

It was a question, he inferred from her suddenly wavering manner, that she wasn't entirely happy to answer. 'I can't say offhand. Some weeks ago. When was it, darling? Maybe the last weekend in November or the first in December. Something like that. It's not exactly a fun place in winter, you know.'

This piqued Pauline Pearson, the native, who showed her displeasure in a tightening of the lips and a stiffening of the shoulders. Ted gave a loud sniff. The Buxtons would be lucky if they got their tea, Burden thought, reflecting how he'd have liked a cup himself.

'Did you go to Guildford *after* you found the car in the quarry, Mr Buxton?' Vine looked at his notes. 'I don't quite understand the time sequence here. You found the car at about eleven, phoned the local police station at about a quarter past, they got here just before twelve, talked to you and went up into the wood with Mr Mitchell. At ten past twelve Mrs Buxton phoned you on your mobile and you were in Guildford. But *I* phoned you on your home number here at twelve twenty and you answered.'

Burden's lips twitched. He put on a serious expression. 'How do you manage to be in two places at once, sir? It must be a useful accomplishment.'

Peter Buxton looked at his wife and this time their eyes met. 'My wife made a mistake. I never said I was in Guildford. I'd no reason to go there.'

'But you'd a reason to come here? Did you make a mistake, Mrs Buxton?'

She said sulkily, 'I must have.'

'All right.' Burden got up. 'I think we'll leave it there. Chief Inspector Wexford will want to interview you in the morning. Will ten a.m. be convenient?'

'I want to go home,' said Peter Buxton like a child on his first day at primary school.

'No doubt you may – after the Chief Inspector has talked to you.'

Outside in the car Burden started laughing. Vine joined in. They were still laughing when the Pearsons came down the steps and got into their car. Pauline gave them a glare and muttered something to her husband. 'I shouldn't laugh,' Burden said. 'God knows what he's been up to. Now they're alone the showdown will start.'

'The divine Sharonne is very easy on the eye,' said Vine.

'True. I dare say he'll forgive her for spilling the beans or whatever she did. Funny they didn't arrange things better before we got there, wasn't it?'

'I reckon she'd only just arrived. He didn't have the chance.'

The lamps were gone, the truck with the crane was gone and all that showed it had ever been there were double lines of ruts in the soft soil revealed by their car headlights.

'Who'll identify the body?' Vine asked.

'God knows. It'll be a grim task, whoever it is. His *Lordship* seemed to think she'd been there getting on for a month. It's probable she's been there since that weekend the Dades were in Paris. She won't be a pleasant sight.'

Too unpleasant a sight for a father to see, Wexford had decided. For this must be Joanna Troy. They had marked her down as perpetrator, quite a reasonable assumption, but she was the victim and quite possibly the missing children were victims too. The grounds of Passingham Hall and the whole area of open country-side surrounding it would have to be searched for their bodies. Meanwhile, this morning, Tremlett would begin on the post-mortem. Her dentist, whoever that was, to identify her? To match the broken-off piece of crown to her dentition? Then, if they could do some sort of make-over on her face, restore it to a semblance of the human, ask the stepmother to look at it? Wexford shuddered.

A nice Christmas present, to be shown the decaying face of your husband's only child. Perhaps they could avoid it. How had she died? It wasn't immediately apparent, according to Tremlett. No obvious wounds. Taking Vine with him – 'They won't be over the moon seeing me again.' The sergeant grinned – Wexford had himself driven to Passingham Hall for ten o'clock and arrived as Peter Buxton was carrying a suitcase out to the open boot of the Porsche.

'Anticipating an early departure, Mr Buxton?' said Vine.

'You said I could go home once I've talked to who-ever it is.'

'Chief Inspector Wexford. And we'll have to see about that.' Being, like God, no respector of persons, Wexford looked at him reflectively. 'Can we go inside?'

Buxton shrugged, then nodded. They followed him in. 'The divine Sharonne', as Barry Vine had called her, was nowhere to be seen. Too early in the morning for a high-maintenance woman, Wexford decided. They went into a smallish room with leather chairs, a desk and a few books, the kind that, while they have hand-somely tooled spines, look hollow and as if no pages are behind those morocco and gilt façades. A window afforded a view of Passingham Hall woods. Peter Buxton jumped, starting violently when a pheasant rose out of the undergrowth, flapping and squawking.

'So when did you *first* see this car in the quarry, Mr Buxton?' Wexford was acting on intuition and what Burden and Vine had told him. He was rewarded by the dark flush that mounted into Buxton's face.

'Yesterday morning. Haven't they told you that?'

'*They* have told me what you said. What they haven't told me, because they don't know, is why you came down here yesterday. Not because there was something wrong with your heating, you didn't know that. At your London office you told Mr Antonio Bellini you were going to a funeral in Godalming. Your wife seems to think you were in Guildford when she phoned you.'

'She's already said she made a mistake about that.'

'Did Mr Bellini make a mistake too? When Inspector Burden spoke to him on his home phone at nine last evening, he seemed very sure of what you'd told him.'

Peter Buxton affected to sigh impatiently. 'What does all this matter? I came down here. To my own house. Is there something unusual in that? I wasn't trespassing, I wasn't breaking and entering. *This is my house.* I've a perfect right to be here. I found a car in the woods and told the police. What's wrong with that?'

'On the face of it, nothing. It sounds very public-spirited. But when did you *first* see the car in the quarry? Was it the last time you came here? Was it the weekend of Saturday, December the second, just under three weeks ago?'

'I don't know what you're insinuating.' Buxton jumped to his feet and pointed out of the window. 'What are all those people doing on my land? Who are they? What are they looking for?'

'First of all, they are not on your land. They are on Mr Mitchell's land. They are police officers and conscientious members of the public helping them in the search for two missing children. We should like to search your land also. I've no doubt there'll be no objection on your part.'

'I don't know about that,' said Buxton. 'I don't know at all. Here's my wife. We're of one mind on this. We resent being kept here, we want to go home.'

Sharonne Buxton was of a type Wexford had never found attractive, belonging as he did to the class of men who admire sweeter-faced, darker, livelier women with hour-glass figures, but he acknowledged her beauty. A less sullen and contemptuous expression would have improved her. Instead of a 'Good morning', 'hello' or even 'hi', she said in a voice and with an accent that required but hadn't received the same honing and polishing as her face and body, 'You don't need us here. We've engagements in London. It's Christmas or hadn't you noticed?'

Wexford ignored her. He said to her husband, 'Thank you for your permission. The search is very important and the searchers will be as careful of your property as possible'

'I didn't give permission. And I shan't. Not unless you let us go. That's a fair exchange, isn't it? Let us return to London and you can search the place until the New Year for all I care.'

Wexford, who had been looking at his notes, snapped the book shut. He felt like paraphrasing *Through the Looking Glass* with a, 'Police officers don't make bargains.' Instead he said, 'In that case I shall apply for a warrant. I have no powers to force you to stay here but I think I should remind you that obstructing the police in the course of their enquiries is an offence.'

'We'll stay,' said Sharonne Buxton, 'But we'd like it to go on record that we didn't want the place searched or any of you here.'

It was Burden who attended the post-mortem. For a man of such fastidious tastes and sleek appearance, he was surprisingly unmoved by the sight of an autopsy. He watched it impassively with much the same attitude as anyone else viewing a hospital sitcom on television.

Wexford, who felt differently, but was accustomed by now to hiding those feelings, arrived when it was nearly over. Hilary, Lord Tremlett, whose macabre sense of humour had increased with his elevation to the peerage, was at the stage of talking about bagging up the dead mutton and doing a 'quickie facelift' for the benefit of the relatives. He seemed to find it hugely amusing that the dentist who had looked in to check the dentition against his chart and to match the crown, unused to such sights, had retched and required a glass of water before he could look inside the cadaver's mouth.

'It's her, though,' said Burden, as callous as Tremlett in his attitude to the poor dentist. 'It's Joanna Troy.'

'I shall get Effie Troy to look just the same,' Wexford said, remembering certain mis-identifications in the past. 'She's a sensible woman and Lord Tremlett's tidied up the face. So what did she die of?'

Tremlett began stripping off his gloves. 'A blow to the head. Death would have been instantaneous. Could have been inflicted with that dear old standby, the blunt instrument, but I think not. I favour a fall and a striking of her head against something hard, possibly the ground, but not soft ground. Not that famous wood of yours, that wouldn't have killed her, more likely sucked her in, like the quagmire in *The Hound of the Baskervilles.*'

'Could it have been the car itself?' Wexford asked. 'I mean, when the car went over the quarry could she have struck her head on the windscreen with sufficient force to kill her?'

'Your people can tell you more about that. Marks on the screen and whatever. But I doubt it. I doubt if she was driving the car. I doubt it very much. It's a crying shame I didn't get to see her sooner, she's been dead a month.'

'You would have done if I'd had a say in it,' said Wexford. But thanks to that clown . . . 'Did the fall or the blow knock the crown off her tooth?'

'How do I know? I'm not an orthodontist. A common butcher, that's me. It might have. I can't say. There was nothing else wrong with her and she wasn't pregnant. You'll get it all in appropriate language you won't understand a word of when I've done my report.'

'I can't stand that man,' said Burden when they were back in Wexford's office. 'Give me the other one – what's he called? Mavrikiev – any time.'

'You're not alone in that. What was she doing in Passingham Hall woods, Mike, why was she there? I had a look around after that fool Buxton had tried to make a bargain with me. I went up to the quarry and walked about in the wood. There's a great rather beautiful – well, it'd be beautiful in the spring – kind of open space in the middle, all ringed by treees, but there's nothing else except the quarry and more trees. If she wasn't driving, who was? And where are Giles and Sophie Dade?'

'The search is well under way. And we'll have that warrant by this afternoon to search Buxton's grounds.'

'By which time it'll be getting dark. I'm glad I kept Buxton there, I'll keep him over Christmas, I'll keep him till the New Year if I can. I'm not usually vindictive but I'd like to lock him up.'

'The divine Sharonne will have to drive to the nearest supermarket and buy herself a frozen turkey,' said Burden, 'and a Christmas pud in a packet *and* cook it all herself.'

'If I were a religious man I'd say God is not mocked.'

That afternoon it began to snow. This was the first snow to fall on Kingsmarkham and points eastward for seven years. The search of Rick Mitchell's land was called off at three thirty and the searchers, Kent police, mid-Sussex police and Passingham St John villagers, all adjourned to the Mitchells' large farmhouse kitchen. There Rick regaled them with mugs of tea (whisky-laced), newly baked scones and Dundee cake, and a spiteful account of his treatment at the hands of Peter Buxton the previous morning. It was a tale of ingratitude, snobbery and the contempt of the town dweller for honest country yeomen. If Buxton thought he, Rick, was going to sell him even half an acre of his land he had another think coming. As for Sharonne, according to Mrs Mitchell, a large woman in leggings and shocking-pink sweatshirt, she was 'common as dirt' and only in it for the money. She'd give that marriage another year at most.

It was still snowing when they left, the world was glowing white in the dusk, any bodies or newly dug graves obscured. During the evening, according to the meteorologist doing the weather forecast after the ten o'clock news, 12.7 centimetres of snow fell. This was a figure understood by only that segment of the population under sixteen. Wexford looked it up and found it was five inches. He waited until Dora had gone to bed and then he wrapped up the scent he'd bought her, the silver-framed photograph of her four grandchildren, the two boys and the two girls, and the pink silk jacket Burden had promised him would fit her. Gift-wrapping wasn't his forte and he didn't make much of a job of it. Dora was asleep when he got upstairs. He hid the presents in the back of his wardrobe and went to bed, lying there sleepless for a while, wondering if there would be more floods when the thaw came.

George Troy's car yielded a harvest of information. Fingerprints were all over its interior, most of them

Joanna's. But if you had relied on prints to show you who had been driving it you would have concluded no one had, for the steering wheel, automatic shift rod and windscreen showed nothing. All had been carefully wiped. The car was untidy, books on the back seat, books and papers on the floor, chocolate papers, a half-drunk bottle of water in one of the rear door pockets, screwed-up credit card chits from petrol sales. The glove compartment held sunglasses, two ballpoint pens, a notepad, a comb and two paper-wrapped barley sugar sweets. Hairs from those back seats belonged to Joanna, the rest possibly to George Troy and his wife. A hair on the floor in the front was dark brown, a fine young hair, that could have come from the head of Sophie Dade. It had gone to the lab with hairs from her own hairbrush for comparison.

In the boot was an overnight bag, small, dark-blue in colour, with the intials 'JRT' in white on one side. Inside it were a pair of clean black jeans, a clean white T-shirt, a clean white bra and pants, a pair of grey socks, a grey wool cardigan, and two used bras with two used pairs of pants and two used pairs of socks in a Marks and Spencer's carrier bag. The sponge bag in the bottom held a toothbrush, a tin of baby powder, a sachet of shampoo and a spray bottle of very expensive perfumed cologne, Dior's Forever and Ever. That cologne surprised Wexford. Unless the bag had contained a couture evening gown, it was the last thing he had expected to find there.

The clothing of the body itself had puzzled him. A pair of black trainers were on the feet but only a barely knee-length pale-blue T-shirt covered it and this was of the kind made for a very large man. Nothing else, no underwear, no socks. If she had sprayed herself with Forever and Ever, no trace of its scent remained.

Effie Troy went to the mortuary two days before Christmas and identified the body as that of her step-daughter, Joanna Rachel Troy. She did it calmly, without flinching, but when she turned away and the face was covered once more, she was very pale. Wexford accompanied her home to Forest Road and spent half an hour with the bereaved father. Apparently, it hadn't occurred to George Troy that something as seriously terrible as this, the worst thing, might have happened to his daughter. He had never contemplated it. She'd be all right, she was a sensible girl, she knew what she was doing. At first he was disbelieving, then shocked beyond words, literally beyond them for the founts and streams of speech so characteristic of him were dried up by horror. He could only stare at Wexford, his mouth open, his head shaking. His wife had tried to prepare him but he had taken her caution and her warning as referring to her being in some sort of trouble with the law or having left the country for some suspect reason. That she might be dead, and dead by violence, he had refused to confront, and the news had blasted him.

Wexford saw him as being in the best hands and he left, telling Effie Troy of the counselling available to her and her husband, and of other sources of help, though he had little faith in this himself. Next to the Dades, up to Lyndhurst Drive, past houses with cypress trees in front gardens hung with fairy lights, Christmas trees in windows, paper chains, angels and cribs just visible in interiors. Nothing in the windows of Antrim, not a light showing on this gloomy overcast morning. He had to tell the Dades there was still nothing known of the whereabouts of their son and daughter, though the body of Joanna Troy had been found. But no news is good news and this was better than what he had had to tell Joanna's father.

They bombarded him with queries, Katrina pleadingly, Roger rudely. His question as to why the police had made the effort to find Joanna but not his children was one Wexford had never been asked before in comparable circumstances. He didn't want to stress that the search at Passingham St John was continuing because it sounded as if it was bodies they searched for, as indeed it was, but he had to say it, reducing Katrina to weeping. Her departure from the room in tears was a cue he couldn't afford to miss but he braced himself for the storm which must inevitably follow. He came out with it bluntly.

'Have you ever had reason to believe Joanna Troy was in love with you?'

'*What?*'

'What' is easy to say, Wexford thought. 'You heard me, Mr Dade. Have you? Did you have any interest in her yourself? Were you attracted?'

Dade began roaring like a lion, his actual words indecipherable, his articulation entirely lost. Katrina could be heard, sobbing in the kitchen.

'Good morning,' Wexford said, and added more gently, 'I shall want to talk to you again soon.'

On Christmas Eve more snow fell and the hunt for the children was temporarily suspended. As yet there was no sign of them, nothing of theirs that might have given a clue as to where they were.

Late that day Wexford was told from the lab that the hair was not Sophie Dade's but had come from the head of some unknown child. He wondered why the perpetrator had brought Joanna's bag in the car but nothing for the children.

CHAPTER 14

It was less the enjoyment of their own festivities in peace that kept Wexford and his officers from pursuing their enquiries on Christmas Day than a sense of the wrongness of such action, the outrage of intruding even on the Troys and the Dades at that time. To him Christmas had never afforded much pleasure and he took no joy in a white one. But Dora did and the sight of their garden blanketed and gleaming seemed to inspire her in all those inescapable tasks of cooking and table setting and finding places to put things.

'I hate the way it covers everything up,' said Wexford. 'You talk about a blanket of snow and that's what I dislike. As if it's all been put to bed for the – the duration.'

'The duration of what? What are you talking about?'

'Oh, I don't know. I don't like hibernation, suspension, everyone having to stop doing things.'

'You don't have to stop doing things,' said Dora. 'You should be doing things now like opening the red wine to let it breathe and seeing we've got enough ice – oh, and you might check on the liqueur glasses in case anyone wants apricot brandy or Cointreau after dinner.'

The 'anyone' who might want liqueurs were Sylvia and Callum and Sheila and Paul. All would be accompanied by children – 'Check the orange juice and Coke, would you, darling,' said Dora – Sylvia's Ben and Robin, and Sheila's Amulet and the new one, Annoushka, Amy and Annie to most people.

'Have you got a present for Chapman?'

'Cal, Reg. You'll have to get used to it. Yes, of course I have.'

Pauline Pearson had treated as ludicrous the suggestion that she should cook the Buxtons' Christmas dinner. 'You won't find a soul who'll do that, Mrs Buxton. Not on Christmas Day. They'll all be cooking their own, won't they? It was different in my grandma's time but them days are gone when they put everything on the back burner to wait on the gentry. Not that there's any gentry left, not in our classless society, and thank God for it. You want to get that bird you've bought thoroughly defrosted, at least twenty-four hours, and that you haven't got. You leave a bit of ice inside there and you'll get salmonella or worse. A lady my auntie knew went down with that stuff women stick in their faces – what's it called? Bot-something – from a half-defrosted turkey.'

It was something of a revelation to Peter that Sharonne couldn't cook. He hadn't left his roots as far behind as he thought and he still took it for granted that all women could cook a straightforward dinner, it was part of them, in their genes. Sharonne couldn't. Hopelessly, she watched the frost slowly slipping off the turkey and asked Peter why they couldn't go out to lunch.

'Because every place you'd set foot in and a lot you wouldn't have been booked up for Christmas dinner for months.'

'Don't say dinner when you mean lunch, Peter, it's common.'

'Everybody says Christmas *dinner*. Never mind what time of day it is, it's *dinner*.'

Peter cooked the turkey. He smothered it with butter, stuck it in the oven and left it for six hours. He could have done worse. There were tinned potatoes and frozen peas and Bisto gravy and he was rather proud of what he'd achieved. His cooking had been helped on by liberal tots of single malt and by the time the meal was ready he was unsteady on his feet and glad to sit down.

Drink helped him forget about past police visits and, worse, possible future police visits. But along with the dry mouth, raging thirst and banging head which ensued during the evening came the suspicion that they knew he had found the car weeks before he said he had. Now he couldn't understand his own behaviour. Why hadn't he told the police then? Surely it wasn't because if he had done so he would have had to cancel two local engagements that, in any case, held no particular charm for him. Surely it couldn't have been that. No, it was Sharonne. She had stopped him.

He looked at her through bleary eyes that intermittently afforded him double vision. She was curled up in an armchair, her shoes kicked off, her face calm, serene, unsmiling, watching a Christmas comedy show on television. The inevitable glass of sparkling water was beside her. Why had he let her stop him do what was manifestly his duty as a good citizen? The events of the first weekend in December had become inexplicable. He, a sensible man who would be forty next birthday, had let his wife, twelve years his junior, a model but by no means a *super*-model, a woman who had never done a thing beyond walk up and down catwalks in that third-class designer Amerigo's clothes, *tell him what to do*. And now God knew what would happen to him. He hadn't liked that jibe about obstructing the police being an offence. If he appeared in court it would get into the papers.

'Sharonne?' he said.

She didn't turn her head. 'What? I'm watching this.'

'Is there a bed made up in one of the spare rooms?'

'I suppose so. Why? Are you feeling ill?' Now she did turn, perhaps remembering her role as his carer. 'You've only yourself to blame, Peter. I'm sure I don't know what's the attraction of all that hard liquor. Stay where you are and I'll get you a big glass of water and some Nurofen.'

Why didn't she know if a bed was made up? It was her job to know if not do it herself. He couldn't see why she didn't do it herself, she did nothing else. She hadn't even supported him when he tried to explain why he'd come down here. Nobody asked her to intervene when that detective inspector was questioning him. She'd done it off her own bat, almost spitefully. There was no call for her to tell the *whole* truth. She could have kept quiet. As for that ridiculous Pauline, she wouldn't have said all that about the heating if Sharonne hadn't set her an example.

He drank the water and swallowed the painkiller. Sharonne returned to her television programme and this time a smile disturbed her flawless features. Peter looked at her with something bordering on dislike. Then, without a word, he got up and went off to find himself a bed with blankets on it if not sheets as far from the master bedroom as possible.

Callum Chapman played with the two boys and the two-year-old girl, thus vindicating his reputation as a man who was 'good with children'. He was rather rough with them, though, Wexford thought, disliking the manhandling of little Amy. It mattered less with the boys who were big and could take care of themselves. But it was for Amy's parents to intervene, not a grandfather.

A woman living with the lover of her choice ought to be serene and revitalised but Sylvia looked unhappy. Of course they were all on edge, all trying too hard to enjoy this 'family' Christmas, Sheila worn out with breast-feeding and rehearsing for a new play, and Paul worried

about her. Dora was piqued with him because he'd forgotten her injunction about the ice and he couldn't relax,
his thoughts turning to the missing Dade children, the
discovery of Joanna Troy's body and the inexplicable
behaviour of Peter Buxton.

Whoever had driven the blue VW into the
Passingham Hall woods must have known the place, at
least known the woods were there and there was a way in
for a vehicle. But not known it well enough to avoid driving it over the edge of the quarry? Or known it well and
driven the car into the quarry on purpose? No, not driven it. Got out of it and pushed it over. With Joanna
passively agreeing to sit in the driving seat? That wasn't
possible. She must have been dead or at least uncon-
scious before the car went over. Dead most probably.
And what of the children? Were they dead at the time or
hidden somewhere? If he, whoever he was, had killed the
children and buried them why not kill and bury Joanna
too? He saw no purpose in putting her body in the car.
The blue VW could just as well have been pushed over
the quarry edge empty. Whoever it was must have
known the Hall and its grounds were seldom visited, so
was he known to Peter Buxton? The perpetrator could
have *been* Peter Buxton. Wexford was convinced he
would never have reported finding that car if Rick
Mitchell hadn't come into the wood at that moment . . .

'Reg,' said Dora, 'wake up. I've made tea.'

Sylvia set cup and saucer in front of him. 'Do you
want anything to eat, Dad?'

'Good God, no. Not after that dinner.'

He looked up and as she drew back her arm saw a
mark like a burn, a dark-red abrasion, encircling her
wrist. Later on, he was to wonder why he had failed to
ask her what it was.

*

On Boxing Day they resumed the search. They weren't looking for living people but for graves. Teaching himself the metric system, Wexford calculated there were now about 7.6 centimetres of snow on the ground. Whatever it was – and three inches meant much more to him and always would – it made searching pointless, confirming his opinion that snow was a nuisance, covering everything up. His thoughts returned to the day before, Callum Chapman throwing Amy up into the air and feigning not to catch her, Sheila falling asleep the moment she sat down in a chair, Dora edgy, and all the time the spectre at the feast, the one who wasn't there and never would be again, Neil Fairfax, Sylvia's ex-husband.

Grandparents – who would be one? You couldn't interfere, you couldn't even advise. You had to shut up and smile, pretend that everything your daughters did and provided for their children was perfect parenting. Grandparents . . . Had he paid sufficient attention to the grandparents in the Dade case? To the Bruces and Matilda Carrish? It might perhaps be a good idea to call on these people in their own homes, make it all right with the Suffolk and the Gloucestershire police, and take a drive out there before the thaw. The roadways were clear and if no more snow fell . . .

If they didn't know more about their children's children than the parents themselves, they sometimes had insights denied to the mothers and fathers. Look how *he* knew Amy didn't like being thrown around by Chapman, he could tell from her stoical little face, her determination to be polite as she'd been taught, while Paul seemed to notice nothing. Sylvia was convincing herself her lover was good with children, but Wexford sometimes saw a look in Robin's eyes expressive of contempt. He would follow through this idea of his to see the Dade grandparents in their own environment, make appointments for soon, maybe as soon as possible.

But for now, the Dades themselves. He went alone. Theirs was the only house he was likely to enter at this time in which no decorations had been put up, yet he fancied the place would be shimmering with glitter and sylvan with green branches at a normal Christmas. Katrina opened the door to him, her face as the woman's in *The Scream* must have been just before Munch started painting it.

'No, Mrs Dade, no,' he said quickly. 'I'm not bringing you news, bad or otherwise. I only want to have a talk now the situation has changed.'

'Changed?'

'In that Ms Troy's body has been found.'

'Oh, yes. Yes. You'd better come in.' It was ungracious but less so than Roger Dade's behaviour who, when he saw Wexford, cast up his eyes in silence and retreated into the living room.

'I thought maybe you'd found my children,' Katrina said miserably, tears never far away. 'I thought maybe you'd found them dead.'

'Please sit down, Mrs Dade. I must tell you both that an extensive search is being carried out in the neighbourhood of Passingham Hall but so far nothing has been found.'

'What's the point of searching when the place is under snow?' said Dade.

'Apart from it's being a more than usually unpleasant task for the searchers, the snow isn't deep and the thaw has begun. Now I'd like you to tell me if either Giles or Sophie had ever been to Passingham St John? Did they ever mention the place?'

'Never. Why would they? We don't know anyone there.'

Katrina was less brusque. 'I'd never heard of Passingham St John till we were told they'd found – Joanna. And found her car. I've been to Toxborough but that was years ago and the children weren't with me.' At the emotive word she began to cry noisily.

'The car was found in the woods at Passingham Hall. It's the property of a man called Peter Buxton. Do you know him?'

'Never heard of him,' said Dade. 'You heard my wife say we don't know this Passingham place. What are you, deaf?'

The hardest thing, Wexford sometimes thought, was to keep your cool when spoken to like this by a member of the public, especially when you were quick-tempered yourself. But it had to be. He had to remember – and remember all the time – that this man's two children had disappeared, his only children, and were very likely dead.

Katrina, through her tears, gave her husband the sharpest look he had ever seen from her but said, instead of something helpful, 'Do you know when Joanna's funeral will be?'

'I'm afraid I don't.'

'I'd like to go. She was my very dearest friend, poor Joanna.'

After that, he thought another call on Peter Buxton might be helpful. He took Vine with him. This time they walked down the lane in the hope of seeing just how clear the entry to the woods was, the path the blue VW had taken, but the snow masked everything, all that could be observed in these conditions was that at the point where the path probably started and deep into the woods, the trees stood further apart, far enough apart to allow the passage of a car.

Buxton opened the door himself. Again it was too early in the morning for his wife. He looked like a sick man, destined for some coronary or arteriosclerosis crisis, his face the mottled grey and red of pink granite and as rough-surfaced. Blood-red veins made a lacework across his eyeballs. There was a faint tremor in his hands and his breath, which peppermint toothpaste hadn't much disguised, was a mixture of stale whisky fumes and some indefinable digestive enzyme, enough to make Wexford step back. He felt an unaccustomed urge to warn the man he was killing himself but of course he didn't. Newspapers and magazines were stuffed with articles about what happened when you ate rubbish and overdid the booze. He'd had Moses and the prophets. Let him hear them.

'Seems a good time to have a word, Mr Buxton,' said Vine breezily.

Buxton glowered. For him there had never been a worse time. He led them down passages to the kitchen, making Wexford think the drawing room, no doubt littered with yesterday's plates and glasses, might be unfit for morning entertaining. But this can't have been the case, for the kitchen was possibly worse, Christmas dinner cooking utensils, pots and pans and empty tins lying about. For some reason Buxton offered them a drink.

'Water, orange juice, Coke or something stronger?'

The reason was obviously so that he could have something stronger too. Wexford and Vine would have accepted tea if it had been available but it wasn't.

'Hair of the dog,' said Buxton with a ghostly snigger, pouring Scotch. He gave the policemen fizzy water with a perceptible sneer. 'What was the word it was a good time to have, then?'

'Who knows this place apart from you and your wife?' Wexford asked. 'Who visits you here?'

'Our friends. The people who work for us.' Buxton uttered the first two words loftily, the second six with scarcely disguised contempt. 'You can't expect me to tell you the names of my friends.'

Vine was looking incredulous. 'Why not, sir? They've no reason to object if they've done nothing wrong.'

'Of course they've done nothing wrong. Chris Warren is a County Councillor and his wife Marion, well she's a . . .' Buxton seemed to have encountered some difficulty in defining exactly what Marion Warren was '. . . a very well-known lady in these parts.'

'And where might Mr and Mrs Warren live?' Vine wrote down the Trollfield Farm address Buxton reluctantly gave. 'And who else, sir?'

Their neighbours, the Gilberts, said Buxton. Perhaps he meant 'neighbour' in the biblical sense, thought Wexford, for there was no house within sight of Passingham Hall. 'They live in a very lovely mansion in the heart of the village.' Buxton sounded like a second-rate travel brochure. He didn't know the name or number of the house, he just knew it by sight, no one could miss it. More names were dragged out of him by Vine's persistence: village acquaintances, met on the Chardonnay party circuit, a couple of Londoners who had once been weekend guests. On the subject of those he apparently considered his social inferiors he was more expansive and, in the case of Rick Mitchell and his wife, vindictive. They were nosy, interfering people who probably snooped about all over his land in his absence. Suddenly he seemed to see that police enquiries, far from intruding on his privacy, gave him opportunities he was unlikely to find elsewhere.

'The same with that Pauline and her husband. She comes down here whenever she feels like it. Never mind keeping to a routine. I was here up in the wood – I don't think these people realise I enjoy walking on my own land – when who do I come upon but Pauline's husband strolling about with a very undesirable-looking fellow he introduces as a Mr Colman. A private detective. On my land. And that's just one instance. For all I know the whole neighbourhood's trespassing on my land when I'm not here.'

'Where is Mr Colman now?'

'How should I know? This was yesterday. Christmas Day, if you've ever heard of such a thing.'

Wexford nodded. It proved only that Search and Find Limited were keen as mustard. 'How long have you owned Passingham Hall, Mr Buxton?'

'Getting on for three years. I bought it from a man called Shand-Gibb, if that interests you.'

Buxton turned round – nervously, Wexford thought – as his wife came in. Today she was wearing a tracksuit, as white as the snow outside. Was she planning to go running, to find herself a local gym or was it just the day's preferred costume? He said good morning to her and she asked sharply what they wanted. He didn't think himself called upon to answer that. Buxton answered for him in a sulky voice while Sharonne pounced on the whisky, replaced the cap and carried the bottle away. She acted exactly as Wexford had once seen Sylvia respond to Ben's excessive consumption of mint humbugs from a jar and the expression on Buxton's face was, as far as he could remember, identical to Ben's. He looked both furious and mutinous.

'Is there anyone else you can think of, Mr Buxton?'

'No, there isn't. Are they still searching those fields? And when can we go back to London?'

'Yes to your first question,' said Wexford, 'and tomorrow morning to your second. But I'm not satisfied with your explanation about the discovery of the car, Mr Buxton, and I shall want to talk to you again.'

He and Vine didn't wait for protest. Outside the sun had come out and the thaw begun. Water dripped from the eaves of the house and the snow had begun to turn transparent. 'If an English heatwave is two fine days and a thunderstorm,' he remarked, 'a cold snap must be twelve hours of snow and forty-eight of muddy meltdown.'

The lane, which an hour before had been under its crisp covering, was in parts like a running stream. Halfway up they met a party of searchers who had found nothing. Wexford had an uneasy sense of frustration. Logically, the Dade children should be somewhere within a reasonable distance, they had to be there, where else would they be? He tried to imagine a scenario in which all three of them were brought here by the perpetrator – by perhaps more than one perpetrator – all killed and Joanna left in the car which was then pushed over the quarry edge. What then became of the other bodies? There was no sense in taking them away while Joanna's body was left behind. Perhaps it wasn't bodies he had to think of but two living people. Had there then been two cars? One to be left behind as tomb for Joanna, the other to be driven away. The children taken away – where?

It was all too unreasonable to allow for the working out of a sequel. Who, for instance, were these two people, possibly a man and a woman, who had driven here in two cars? What was their motive? How, above all, did they know of Passingham Hall grounds and the quarry in its heart. Suddenly he found himself thinking of the open space, the clearing in the wood, and he suggested to Vine that they go up there again before leaving.

This would be one of the areas from which the snow would take longest to clear, for nothing broke its smooth untouched whiteness and no foot had trodden it. From where they stood it looked like a lake of snow surrounded by a wall of leafless dark-grey trees of uniform size. There was no wind and nothing stirred their branches.

'Maybe this Shand-Gibb can help us,' said Vine.

CHAPTER 15

He had no memory for recent events. And in his case 'recent' meant the past two or three decades. Before that, his early and middle years, he could readily recollect. Wexford, of course, had come across this in old people before but seldom to this extent. Bernard Shand-Gibb could scarcely remember the name of his housekeeper, a woman not much younger than himself, whom he addressed as 'Polly – Pansy – Myra – Penny,' before getting it right and coming out with 'Betty!' on a shout of triumph.

It was a long time since Wexford had heard that accent. His was the speech of the old gentry, spoken by an upper class when he was a boy and liable to strike awe into those lower down the social scale, but now almost dead and gone. Actors had to learn how to do it, he had read somewhere, before playing on television in a drama of the nineteen twenties, learn to say 'awf' for 'off' and 'crawss' for 'cross'. Such an accent would have prevailed, he thought, when his own grandfather was young and the local rector, riding past him and his friends, cracked his whip and called out, 'Take your hats off to a gentleman!'

Shand-Gibb was a gentleman but a very gentle one, puzzled by his inability to remember his last years at Passingham Hall. 'I do wish I could recall something or someone, my dear chap,' he said in that incomparable voice, 'but it's all gawne.'

'Perhaps your housekeeper . . .?'

Mrs Shand-Gibb had been alive then and Betty had tended on them both. But she was a servant of the old school, not one to know or wish to know her employer's business. Wexford thought that if she had to refer to him it would be as 'the master'. She sat down in his company because Wexford had asked her to stay and asked her to sit down too, but she sat uneasily and on the edge of the chair.

'Can you recollect anything?' Shand-Gibb asked her in his mild, courteous way. He was not the sort of man to omit names or styles or titles when he addressed someone and he had made an effort to remember what she was called, had tried and failed, had struggled with it, mouthing names, but had failed.

'I'm sure I don't know, sir,' she said. 'I could try. There was the Scouts came to camp in the springtime and in the autumn too. They was good lads, never made any trouble, never left a mess behind them.'

'Did anyone else camp in the wood?' asked Vine. 'Friends? Relations?'

Shand-Gibb listened courteously, occasionally nodding or giving a puzzled smile. He was like someone who has tentatively claimed to understand a foreign language but when addressed in it by natives finds it beyond his comprehension. Betty said, 'There was never anything like that, sir. Not to *sleep*, there wasn't. The village had their summer fête there. Is that the kind of thing you mean? Regular they did that. In June it was and they put up a marquee in case of rain, sir, as it mostly did rain. They was clean too, never left a scrap of litter.' She considered. 'Then there was those folks that did their singing and dancing up there. On the Dancing Floor, sir.'

A smile of nostalgia spread across Shand-Gibb's face. A light seemed to come into his faded blue eyes, half

lost as they were in a maze of wrinkles. 'The Dancing
Floor,' he said. 'We used to have fine hot summers then,
Mr Er – . I don't believe it ever rained in June. The
whole village came to dance on Midsummer's Eve and
made their own music too, none of your gramophones
then.' The tape and CD revolutions had passed him by.
A long-playing record was probably the last innovation
he could recall. 'We danced on the Dancing Floor, the
loveliest spot in Kent, high up but as flat as a pancake
and as green as an emerald. We should go up there
when the summer comes, Polly, er, Daisy, never mind.
We should ask young Mitchell to wheel me up in my
chair, what?'

Betty looked at him. It was a look of infinite sweet
tenderness. She spoke very softly, 'You don't live at the
Hall any more, sir. You moved away three years since.
Another gentleman and lady live there now. You
remember, don't you?'

'I do for a moment,' he said, 'when you tell me I do,'
and he passed one shaky, veined hand across his brow as
if the stroking movement might wipe away the mist that
descended on his memory. 'I take your word for it.'

Wexford could imagine a maypole set up between
the greening trees, a young girl, plump, fair, rustic, not
beautiful by today's standards, not a Sharonne Buxton,
brought to be crowned Queen of the May. 'These were
people Mr Shand-Gibb gave permission to use the
ground?' he asked.

'Not just anyone who asked,' Betty said quickly. 'If
they was the sort that made a mess they never was
allowed back. There was a couple wanted their wedding
reception there. Mr Shand-Gibb said yes on account of
him not being too well and Mrs Shand-Gibb –' she lowered her voice, though ineffectively '– in her last illness.'
The old man winced, tried to smile. 'Ooh, the state they

left the place in. Litter everywhere, tin cans and I don't know what. They had the cheek to want to come back for some party or other they was giving but Mr Shand-Gibb said no, he was very sorry, but not this time, and they took it badly. It was shocking how rude they was.'

Wexford took down these people's names but they were the only names he was destined to get. Betty could remember other applicants for the use of the dancing floor but not what they were called. Mr Shand-Gibb knew but she hadn't been told, it wasn't her place to be told, she incredibly said. She only knew the name of the bridal couple because Mrs Mitchell had talked about them, the whole village had talked about them.

'When you mentioned singing and dancing,' said Vine, 'were you referring to the people who got married?'

'That was another lot,' said Betty. 'These folks never made no mess. After they'd gone you wouldn't know they'd been there. Mind you, they made a lot of noise, singing you could call it but some would call it screaming and shouting. Didn't bother Mr Shand-Gibb, he let them come back the next year.' Her employer had fallen asleep. 'I don't reckon he could hear it from the house, poor old gentleman.'

Screaming and shouting, Wexford thought, as they drove back to Passingham Hall with the Kent police DC who was accompanying them. No doubt an elderly woman of old-fashioned ideas meant no more than that the gathering danced to the kind of music habitually heard in discos or reverberating from cars with their windows open. The Mitchells at the farm might know, would almost certainly be more helpful than a servant of the old school who knew her place and an aged man with a memory irretrievably gone.

Rick Mitchell and his wife Julie knew everything. That, at least, was the impression they liked to give.

They knew everything and they were 'good people', the kind that swamp you with offers of food and drink, comfort and their time, when you come to call. That the three policeman would be calling they had been told in advance and Julie Mitchell had prepared a mid-morning spread, coffee and orange squash, scones, mincepies and a bakewell tart. Vine and the young DC tucked in. Wexford would have liked to but dared not. Rick Mitchell moved swiftly into a lecture on Passingham St John village life from the Middle Ages to the present day. Or that was what it seemed like to Wexford who found himself powerless to cut the man short, as one is when the speaker ignores one's interruptions and continues relentlessly on. He wondered if Mitchell had learned this technique from listening to interviews with Cabinet ministers on Radio Four.

But at last the man paused to draw breath and Wexford put in swiftly, 'How about this couple –' he referred to his notes '– a Mr and Mrs Croft who had their wedding reception in the wood? Where do they live?'

Mitchell was looking affronted. It was easy to tell what he was thinking. You come here and eat my food, the good home-baked cakes my wife has sweated over a hot stove for hours to make, and you can't even have the courtesy to let me finish my sentence . . . 'Down in the village,' he said sulkily. 'Cottage called something daft. What's it called, Julie?'

'I don't know if I'm pronouncing it right. It used to be called Ivy Cottage but now it's got some funny Indian name. Kerala or however you pronounce it.'

'She's Indian, the one that got married.' Rick Mitchell seemed to forget his grievance in the pleasure of imparting information. 'Got a funny Indian name. Narinder, if I've got my tongue round it right. The husband's as English as you or me.' He glanced uneasily at the Kent DC, an olive-skinned man with jet-black hair and dark-brown eyes. 'They've got a baby now, what they call mixed-race, it must be. I reckon it takes all sorts to make a world.'

'Mr Shand-Gibb's housekeeper has told us there were some people who used the wood, apparently several years in succession, and who made a lot of screaming and shouting. Does that mean anything to you?'

Whether it did or not Wexford was not to learn for some minutes. Both Mitchells broke into extravagant praise and regrets for the departure of the former owners of Passingham Hall. They were lovely people, of the old gentry, but not a scrap of 'side' to them.

'That was a sad day for Passingham when dear old Mr Shand-Gibb sold up,' said Julie Mitchell in the kind of lugubrious voice television newscasters use when they segue from an England soccer victory to the death of a pop singer. 'He was one in a million. A far cry from those new folks, those Buxtons, newvo rich yuppies they are.'

'You can say that again,' said her husband and for a moment Wexford was afraid she would. But she only shook her head more in sorrow than in anger and Mitchell went on, 'It's my belief he'd known that car had been there for weeks. Maybe put it there himself *and* what was inside it, I wouldn't put it past him. What was he doing there mid-week in the middle of December, that's what I'd like to know. Revisiting the scene of his crime, there is no other explanation. He knew it was there all right.'

Wexford was inclined to agree, not that he did so aloud. 'Let's get back to the visitors who made the music, shall we? The "screaming and shouting". Have you any idea who they were?'

The worst question you can ask a man like Rick Mitchell is one to which he doesn't know the answer.

Far less bad is one which, if he answered truthfully, might incriminate him. Plainly he had no reply to make but that didn't stop him replying. 'Not exactly *who* they were, if it's names you're meaning. I know *what* they were, a bunch of vandals, if the way they parked their cars down the Hall lane is anything to go by. Terrible ruts they made in the grass verges and that sort of rut never comes out, it's there for good, a blot on the landscape . . .'

'And you could hear them shouting and yelling, Rick,' said Julie. 'You know you could. We were going to complain . . .'

'Not to Mr Shand-Gibb, mind. He'd gone by then. We had serious thoughts of putting in a complaint to Buxton. Didn't bother him, did it? He wasn't here when they were. Oh, no, he was up in London living it up, no doubt.'

'It didn't sound English, what they were shouting,' said Julie. 'I C, I C, it sounded like.'

'What, the letters I and C?' Vine asked.

'That's what it *sounded* like but it's not English, is it?'

This emphasis on Englishness must have aroused some vestige of conscience in Mitchell, for, as they were leaving, he remarked in a kindly tone to the Kent DC, 'You OK then, are you?'

Wexford went back to Kingsmarkham, leaving the other two to pursue enquiries in the village. He was going to a funeral, Joanna Troy's. She hadn't driven the car over the edge of the quarry, she had been dead before she was put into the car. 'Murdered?' he had asked Tremlett on the phone.

'No reason to think so, no reason at all.'

Except that her body had been removed from wherever death took place. Pains had been taken to conceal that body. And where were the Dade children in all this?

The parents, at any rate, were at the funeral in St Peter's, Kingsmarkham, Roger Dade as well as his wife, and Katrina's parents too, if he was right in thinking the elderly man was her father. Now might be his chance to carry out his resolve of talking to the grandparents. Never mind that they wouldn't be in their own home. The Dades were feeling better, Wexford thought, they *look* better. They believe that because Joanna is dead and no other bodies were in the car, no other bodies have been found, Giles and Sophie are alive. Do I believe that, he asked himself. He couldn't find the slightest reason to think so and he knew those parents were relying on instinct and intuition rather than on reason.

It was a cold, wet day, icy inside a church the size of a cathedral. How many people know you don't have to have a funeral? How many know it's not necessary or prescribed by legislation to have voluntaries and glumly intoned prayers and hymns – invariably 'Abide with Me' or 'The Lord is my Shepherd' – if you don't believe and the dead person didn't believe? None of this lot had been inside a church for years, he thought. How much better it would have been for all of them to have had Joanna Troy's body cremated and afterwards held a quiet gathering of friends and family to remember her. At least there were only family flowers, a simple wreath of forced daffodils from Joanna's father and stepmother.

Ralph Jennings, the ex-husband, hadn't come but the neighbour, Yvonne Moody, was there, the woman who had told him she suspected Joanna's passion for Roger Dade. On her knees when everyone else was sitting or standing, weeping quietly. He noticed that Joanna's father didn't cry. His grief he showed otherwise, in an ageing that added a decade to his years. People hadn't yet discarded the habit of wearing black to funerals. All these mourners were in black but only Yvonne Moody and Doreen Bruce wore hats. They filed out of the church, George Troy clinging to his wife's arm, Katrina Dade holding her husband's unwilling hand, and got into the cars which would take them to the crematorium miles out in the country at Myfleet Tye. Katrina's parents weren't going. Wexford had been surprised to see them there at all but supposed they had come simply to support their daughter. The Bruces had their own car with them. As Mrs Bruce helped her husband into it and started the engine, Wexford got into his and followed them back to Lyndhurst Drive. He was on the doorstep before they had let themselves in.

Doreen Bruce failed to recognise him and assumed, for no reason, that he must be selling something. Even after he had explained, she wasn't forthcoming but announced that her husband had to rest, he had a bad heart, it was essential he lie down. She hadn't wanted him to come this morning. It wasn't as if they'd known Joanna Troy. Eric had had a coronary in October and since then had had to take things easy. Not that you'd know it the way he was always dashing about. To Wexford Eric Bruce looked far from 'dashing' anywhere. He was a thin little old man, pale and pinched, the last you would imagine to have a heart condition. He wasn't to be allowed to go upstairs but was led to the sofa in the living room and covered with a blanket. The black cat, lying on the shelf above a radiator, watched the fussy movements with feline scorn and stretched out one fore-leg as far as it would go as if admiring its pointed claws.

Wexford was shown into the dining room, a not-much-used place made dark by the small diamond panes of its windows and the heavy ruby velvet curtains. Doreen Bruce sat opposite him, nervously drumming her fingers on the table. 'Sometimes,' he said, 'grandparents have a better knowledge of their grandchildren than those children's parents have. I know Giles and Sophie enjoyed staying with you – in Suffolk, is it?'

She probably called everyone 'dear'. It wasn't a sign of affection or intimacy. 'That's right, dear. Berningham. Where the American Air Force used to be but it's much prettier now all those ugly buildings have gone. You hear about these teenagers wanting nothing but clubs and amusements and worse but our two weren't like that. They love nature and the countryside, being out in the open air. Sophie used to cry when she had to go home. Not Giles, of course, dear, a boy wouldn't.'

'What did they do all day?'

She was puzzled. To her, obviously, the mystery was what they did at home in Kingsmarkham. 'Went for walks, dear. We take them to the beach. Eric and I don't think they're old enough yet to go alone. Well, Eric does, but you know what men are, said I babied them. Mind you, he liked their company all right, always wanted to be with Giles whatever he did. Of course that was before his coronary, dear.'

'When did they last stay with you, Mrs Bruce?'

'In August.' She came back with her answer very promptly. 'In their school holidays, dear. They wouldn't have been allowed to come for a weekend in term-time. Roger keeps their noses to the grindstone, you know.' An aggrieved note had crept into her voice. 'Homework, homework, homework night after night. I don't know why they don't rebel. Most teenagers would, from what I hear. Mind you, it's my belief they'd work hard without his lordship cracking the whip over them. They like their school work. At any rate, Giles does. He's a clever boy, is Giles, he'll go far.'

One point Doreen Bruce had made Wexford hit on. He asked curiously, 'Did you say Sophie cried when she had to go home?'

'That's right, dear. Cried like her heart would break.'

'A thirteen-year-old?' he said. 'Would you call her young for her age?'

'Oh, no, dear. Not really. It's not that.' Mrs Bruce's voice dropped and she looked cautiously in the direction of the closed door. Then she seemed to remember that her son-in-law wasn't in the house. 'It's more that she doesn't get on with her father. Giles is afraid of him but Sophie – well, she just hates being near him. Shame, isn't it?'

And this woman had described the Dades as 'not one of those dysfunctional families' . . .

CHAPTER 16

The Bruces' home was to remain unseen but Wexford's reaction on contemplating Matilda Carrish's was that theirs had to be a more congenial place for teenagers to stay in. But perhaps Giles and Sophie seldom had stayed there. Situated in an exquisite Cotswold village of grey-gold houses and cottages, hers was of the same stone as the rest of the dwellings in Trinity Lacy but apparently built in the eighties, stark, flat-fronted and with a low-pitched slate roof. Rather forbidding at first sight. It was possible Katrina Dade had vetoed the children's staying with their paternal grandmother. She seemed particularly to dislike her mother-in-law. What a lot of disliking went on in that family!

'Were they frequent visitors?' Burden asked when they were shown into a chilly, sparsely furnished living area.

'Depends what you mean by "frequent". They came occasionally. When I had the time. When they were allowed.'

Discreetly, Wexford eyed the room where they were. Its redeeming feature was the number of bookshelves filled with books which lined three of the four walls. He noted the sophisticated means of playing music, the computer stand with screen, obvious Internet access, printer and other unidentifiable accessories. Every piece of furniture, apart from the white or black chairs and sofa, was of pale wood, chrome and black melamine.

On the bookless wall strange abstracts in aluminium frames hung side by side with photographs of inner-city squalor and industrial decay, which Wexford recognised as Matilda Carrish's own. She looked as chilly and as stark as her artwork, a long, lean woman with a flat back and etiolated legs in grey trousers and black tunic, round her neck and hanging to her waist a single strand of grey and white pebbles strung on silver.

She must be well into her seventies, he thought, and yet the last thing you think about when you look at her is that she's old. That in spite of the wrinkles, the white hair, the gnarled hands. 'You last saw them in October, I believe?'

She nodded.

'When you were together,' Burden put in, 'were you close? They were teenagers and this is hard to imagine, but did they confide in you?'

This time she smiled very slightly. 'They certainly couldn't be close to their parents, could they? My son's a bully and his wife's an hysteric.' She said it quite calmly as if she were talking about acquaintances whose behaviour she had occasionally observed. 'When she got the chance my granddaughter talked to me. Told me a little about her feelings. But it seldom happened. Her mother would have stamped on that.'

'Did they get on, Giles and Sophie? Were they good friends as well as brother and sister?'

'Oh, I think so. Sophie was rather under Giles's influence. She's inclined to do what he does. If he likes a piece of music, for instance, she'll like it.'

'What would you think of a theory that Joanna Troy was having an affair with your son? Or would have liked to have an affair with him?'

For the first time Wexford heard her laugh. 'One never never knows with people, does one? But I wouldn't have thought him such a good actor. Of course, I never met Miss Troy. Maybe she would have liked a relationship with my son. There's no accounting for tastes.'

A chilling woman. This was her own child she was talking about. '"Her feelings", you said, Mrs Carrish. What about Sophie's feelings?'

'That would be telling, wouldn't it? But this is a serious matter, as you'll tell me if I don't say it first. Not to put too fine a point on it, she told me she hated her father and disliked her mother. You see, Katrina lets her do as she likes, then flies into a rage when she does it, and my son forbids every pleasure and keeps noses to the grindstone. What Sophie would really like would be to come and live with me.'

There it was again, much the same as what Doreen Bruce had told him, only couched in different terms. 'What did you say to that?'

'Mr Wexford, I will be frank with you. I don't love my grandchildren. How could I? I only see them two or three times a year. I feel – how shall I put it? – benevolent towards them, that's all. I wish them well. I love my son, I can't help that, but I don't much like him. He's boorish and conventional, entirely without social graces. I don't have many of those myself but I hope I'm more honest about things. I make no pretence at being a conformist. I do as I like. Poor Roger is unhappy because he never does anything he likes, hasn't for years.'

Frank, indeed, Wexford thought. When, if ever, had he heard a mother and grandmother talk like this? 'Katrina would never even consider letting one of her children live with me,' she said. 'Why would she, come to that? I wouldn't have let my children live with a grandparent. Besides, I'm selfish, I like living alone, I want to go on living alone till I die. That's why I don't live with my husband, though we're on perfectly good terms.'

He was astonished. He had supposed she was a widow, that she had been twice widowed. Other people's mind-reading ability always amused him. It was gift he had himself. Matilda Carrish now demonstrated it. 'No, I divorced my first husband, Roger's father. He's dead now. My second husband teaches at a European university. He has his job and he prefers living abroad while I prefer living here, quite a simple and amicable arrangement. We spend some time together once or twice a year – oftener, incidentally, than I see Giles and Sophie.'

Burden had picked up on a word. 'You mentioned children, Mrs Carrish. You have another child besides Mr Dade?'

'A daughter,' she said indifferently. 'She's married, she lives in Northern Ireland. County Antrim.' Burden took this woman's name and address. He wondered if Matilda Carrish had a similar relationship with her daughter as that with her son, a gut feeling of love but without liking or respect or, probably, much desire ever to see her.

As they were leaving she indicated to them a colour print on the hall wall. A mezzotint, Wexford thought it would be called. It showed eighteenth-century buildings in some city that might have been anywhere in northern Europe. Matilda Carrish looked as if about to make some comment on it but she turned away, saying nothing.

On the phone Wexford said, 'Mr Buxton, I strongly advise you to do as I ask and come to Kingsmarkham Police Station tomorrow morning. I have already told you of the offence of obstructing the police in their enquiries. There is another, that of perverting the course of justice. You mustn't believe this is an empty threat. I shall see you here at twelve noon tomorrow.'

'I shouldn't mind coming down,' Buxton said in an aggrieved tone. 'There are a few things I have to see to. Can't you come to Passingham Hall?'

'No,' said Wexford. 'It's out of my way.' He paused. 'I shall expect you at twelve.'

If Buxton didn't come he would have a serious case against him. The idea of arresting the man rather appealed to him. The next phone call he made was to Charlotte MacAllister, née Dade. Her voice was uncannily like her mother's, crisp, cool and ironic.

'I don't know Roger's children very well. There's been no quarrel. I seldom go to England and they never come here. Katrina's afraid of bombs.' She paused to give a dry laugh. 'I say they never come here but Giles did come three or four years back when things were quiet. He came on his own and he seemed to enjoy being with my kids.'

Nothing there, Wexford thought. Then he remembered something. 'Do you know why they call their house Antrim, Mrs Macallister?'

'Do they? I've never noticed.'

'I don't think it's coincidence, do you? You live in County Antrim, your brother calls his house Antrim, yet you don't seem to be close.'

'Oh, that's easy. They lived here when they were first married. Giles was born here. Roger wasn't in real estate then. My husband and he had been at school together, best mates and all that, and my husband put him in the way of getting a job. That's why they came here, because of the job. He was a salesman for a computer supplier – computers were just becoming fashionable then – but apparently he wasn't very good at it. He hasn't inherited our mum's brains.' Implying that she had? Perhaps. 'Katrina was upset when he got the sack but she didn't want to leave. She loved the cottage they lived in, she wanted him to get work here. Then the pub in the village got an IRA bomb and she left fast enough after that.'

Buxton came. He looked ill. The whites of his eyes were pale yellow and his cheeks a network of broken veins. The suit he wore, a double-breasted pale-grey, seemed unsuitable for the time of year and his tie, too loosely knotted, was an inappropriate mélange of garden annuals, petunias, pansies and nasturtiums. Such cheerful, almost holiday, clothes contrasted ludicrously with the bags under his eyes and his thinning hair. In Wexford's pleasant office he seemed ill at ease.

'I've asked you to come here for two reasons, Mr Buxton,' Wexford began. 'The first involves a question you'll find easy enough to answer. The second may be more difficult for you – I mean difficult in the sense of awkward or embarrassing. But we'll leave that for now.' Buxton had turned his liverish eyes away and was looking at the pale chocolate-coloured telephone, studying it with fascination as if it were an example of radically innovative technology. 'You've already told us the names of various friends and acquaintances of yours who visit and know the lie of your land. Since then I've spoken to Mr Shand-Gibb, and he and his housekeeper mentioned various people and groups who borrowed what he calls the dancing floor for functions. There was, for instance, a couple who held their wedding reception there, and his housekeeper told me of a noisy group whose shouting and singing could be heard down at the house. Does this mean anything to you?'

Buxton's red face had gone redder. He gave the classic reply: 'It might do.'

'Yes, Mr Buxton, I know it might. It might mean something to me, such as for instance, that a bunch of people out in the open on a summer night usually do make a lot of noise. Let me rephrase the question. Do you know who these people were and were they there with your permission?'

Buxton seemed to speak unwillingly as if the words were dragged out of him. 'They used to use that clearing in the wood when the Shand-Gibbs owned the place. When I moved in the man – the boss, the organiser, I don't know – he wrote and said could they carry on with it. Twice a year they wanted it, July and January – must be bloody freezing in January.'

'So you agreed?'

'I couldn't see any reason to refuse. Sharonne and me, we wouldn't be there on a week night, so we weren't bothered about noise.'

'So they've used it four or five times since you moved in?'

'I suppose so.'

'And since it's now January they're due to use it again shortly?'

'They won't now. Not after – what was in the quarry.'

Why was the man so cautious, so evasive? Suddenly Wexford knew. 'You charge a fee? They pay a rent?'

'A nominal rent,' Buxton said unhappily.

'And how much might "nominal" be, Mr Buxton?'

'I don't have to tell you that.'

'You do,' said Wexford laconically.

Perhaps Buxton's thoughts strayed to the charge of perverting the course of justice, for he no longer hesitated. 'A hundred pounds a time.'

A nice little earner, Wexford thought. Especially if it came in twice a year and a similar sum from other organisations using the wood. A welcome addition to one's income but not, surely, to the income of a man like Buxton. But, of course. He wasn't declaring it, it was tax-free. And he'd insist on cash. Dropped through the letter box in an envelope, no doubt. That was the reason for the shame and the caution . . .

'Who are these people? What do they use the clearing for?'

Shifting in his seat as if his buttocks itched, Buxton said, 'They're religious. That singing is hymns. They shout out, "I see, I see!" meaning they've seen angels or spirits or something.'

'I thought you'd never been here when all this was going on?'

'The first year they used it after we moved in I came down. I wanted to know what I was letting myself in for.'

'Who *are* they, Mr Buxton?'

'They call themselves the Church of the Good Gospel.'

Of which Giles Dade was a fervent member. This meant that, having visited the wood on several occasions, he would know it and know about the quarry. And others would know about it too and know him. Know him enough to abduct him and his sister, and kill the woman who was looking after them? Perhaps. There seemed no point in enquiring about other parties who had used the place for here was a direct lead to the missing boy, the first link between him and Passingham Hall. 'The man, the boss, the organiser', as Buxton put it, would undoubtedly be Jashub Wright, pastor of the Good Gospel Church . . .

Buxton confirmed this, astonished that Wexford could identify him. But instead of reassuring him this evidence of the Chief Inspector's apparent omniscience only seemed to frighten him further. He pulled a mobile out of his pocket and asked if it would be all right to phone his wife. Wexford shrugged, smiling slightly. At least the man hadn't asked to use *his* phone.

Sharonne, it seemed, hadn't been given prior notice of her husband's visit to Kingsmarkham and interview at the police station. Wexford could gather quite a lot from Buxton's evasive replies and although he didn't actually say, 'I'm at Passingham' – that would have been too blatant in this company – the words 'Passingham Hall' were used. What would Buxton do if she called him back on the Hall phone? Perhaps say he'd had to pop over to Guildford. Buxton was getting a dressing-down. From where he sat Wexford could just hear the shrill reproving words of a scold. He couldn't blame her. Chronic mendacity seemed to come so naturally to Buxton that he told lies when the truth would surely have been perfectly acceptable to hearer as well as speaker. For instance, why on earth tell the woman, as he now did, 'I must go, darling, I've got a business lunch in five minutes'? When he ceased to be besotted with the 'divine Sharonne' and began on an adulterous spree he would have had plenty of practice at alibi-making.

'Then I suppose I should say I mustn't keep you,' Wexford said smoothly. For all his lying and prevarication, Buxton hadn't yet learned how not to blush. 'Unfortunately, I haven't done with you quite yet. I told you I had a second line of enquiry to pursue and I expect you know what that is.' A nod, an uncomfortable shrug. 'When did you first see the blue VW Golf in the quarry? No, don't tell me December the twenty-first. I know you were aware of it before that.'

'It would have been a bit before,' Buxton said, the words again wrenched out of him.

'Rather more than a bit, Mr Buxton. The weekend of the fifteenth perhaps? The eighth? Even before that? The *first*?'

Of course Wexford was enjoying himself. How could it be otherwise? Normally a compassionate and

considerate man, he felt no need to waste mercy on
Buxton. He watched the man squirming and watched
without compunction. Oh, what a tangled web we
weave, as his grandmother used to say, when first we
practise to deceive. The wretched Buxton said, 'I didn't
come down on the fifteenth or the eighth.'

'So it was the first of December and at the same time
the first weekend in December?'

'It must have been.'

'Well, Mr Buxton, you have wasted a lot of police
time. You've wasted public money. But if you tell me no
more lies and explain to me instead exactly what happened when you went up into the wood the first weekend in December, one week after Ms Troy and Giles and
Sophie Dade went missing –' he paused, looking search-
ingly at Buxton '– I think it's likely the Director of Public
Prosecutions will not decide to take this any further.'

He had taken pity on him but instead of relaxing
Buxton looked as if he was going to cry.

Nothing of what Buxton told him could set a precise
time on the arrival of the car in the quarry. But by
Saturday, 2 December the body inside the car was
decomposed enough to smell strongly. The weather
was far from cold but it was, after all, midwinter. The
air was moist and mild after that rain, and decay would
have happened quite quickly.

'I haven't even got a theory,' said Wexford when he
and Burden met in the Olive and Dove at the end of a
long day. 'Can you come up with anything?'

'We know now that Giles could have directed whoever killed Joanna to the wood and the quarry but I
don't think he and Sophie would have acquiesced in her
murder, do you? It's more likely he told the perpetrator
about Passingham Hall in all innocence. He didn't

know what the perpetrator wanted. He and Sophie didn't even know Joanna was dead. They may have been killed before they could find out. Or they may have been taken away while Joanna was still alive. Even taken by Joanna in the car with whoever it was.'

'So where do the Good Gospellers come in?'

'They don't. Their only function in all this is that of introducing Giles to Passingham Hall.'

'I shall still want to talk to them again. More of them. Not just the Reverend Jashub. I'd like to find out exactly what happens when they have their open-air carry-on at Passingham Hall, when they turn into Blue Domers.'

'What's a Blue Domer?'

'Someone who doesn't go to church but says he prefers to worship outside, under God's "blue dome". Mike, I don't know how, still less why, but I think Joanna Troy was killed in the hall of the Dades' house and on that Saturday night.'

Wexford had been staring out of the window, staring at nothing, but now the void was filled with three people he knew, all crossing the bridge and hand in hand. In the glaring yellow lamplight he had recognised his former son-in-law and his two grandsons. Of course. It was Friday, the evening Neil had access to his sons and took them out. If they were crossing the bridge towards the centre of town they were most likely heading for McDonald's, the boys' favoured venue for supper.

'What are you looking at?'

'Neil and Ben and Robin. I've just spotted them.'

'D'you want to go outside and say hello?'

'No.' Wexford suddenly felt deeply sad. Not angry or frustrated or regretful but just sad. 'Let the poor chap have some time alone with his children. You know, Mike, that's the insoluble problem today. The media are always on about how men should learn to be good fathers but they seldom say a word about the father who doesn't get the chance. His wife has left him and she's got his children, she's *always* got his children. But are they therefore to stay together and be miserable together for years and years so that he can be a good father? And suppose she won't? I don't know the answer. Do you?'

'Marriage partners should stay together for the sake of the children,' said Burden sententiously.

'Easy to say when you're happily married.' Neil and his children had passed on out of sight. Wexford sighed. 'D'you want another?'

'Only if you will.'

'No. I'd better get home.'

Outside it was raining harder than ever. The Kingsbrook, once more in spate, tumbled and foamed along towards the dark tunnel mouth. Wexford wondered if the floods would come back and he thought with dismay of his garden. Burden gave him a lift home but refused an invitation to come in. Wexford made his way up to the front door, noticing water gushing from the outfall pipe that drained the gutters. There was nothing to be done about it. He let himself in, found Dora in the living room with her glass of wine, first of the two she would have that evening. She got up, kissed him, said, 'Reg, I've just had a very odd phone call from Sylvia.'

'Odd in what way?'

'She sounded a bit wild. She said Cal was pressurising her to marry him. That was her word, "pressurising", And she'd said she'd think about it but she wasn't ready for remarriage yet. You know the ridiculous way they talk these days. She wasn't ready for remarriage.'

'Thank God for that, anyway.'

'The boys were going out with Neil, it being Friday, and she said that once she was alone in the house with Cal again he'd start and she didn't like the way he bullied her.'

'Why can't she just leave him?' Wexford said irritably. 'After all, she's left one man, she knows how it's done. I suppose I should say, why doesn't she chuck him out, she's done that too.'

'I'd no idea you felt as bitter as that.'

'Well, I do. About both of them, him for being a pig and a boor, and her for being such a fool. D'you think the garden's going to flood again?'

Calling in at Passingham Hall to check on the state of the heating – he couldn't trust Pauline's judgement – Buxton found the man called Colman standing on the gravel sweep at the front of the house, staring up at his bedroom window.

'What the hell are you doing? Get off my property and don't come back.'

'Keep your hair on,' said Colman, using a quaint old-fashioned expression Buxton vaguely remembered on his grandfather's lips. 'No need to get aerated.' Swiftly he plucked a card from his pocket and held it out to Buxton. 'It's more in your interest than anyone else's that we find those kids.'

Buxton supposed it might be, though he didn't say so. 'Who are you acting for?'

'Mrs Matilda Carrish. Now why don't we go up into the wood and you show me exactly where you found that car – when was it, now?'

'Just before Christmas.' Buxton was getting nervous.

'Come off it. Rumour has it you knew that vehicle was there weeks before you said a word. I wonder why you kept so stumm?'

Buxton took him up into the wood and recon-structed for him an itinerary for the car to have taken once it had left the road at the top of the lane. After a while he began to find Colman congenial company, particularly as the enquiry agent was carrying on him a hip flask of whisky which he passed several times to Buxton. By the time they parted, Colman to drive to the Cotswolds, Buxton to London, they had agreed to keep in touch.

Sharonne was out and no note had been left for him. Buxton wondered uneasily if after that call he had made to her from Kingsmarkham Police Station she had phoned Passingham Hall and, receiving no reply, absented herself in order to punish him. It wouldn't be untypical. The phone sat on its little table, silent and accusatory, a small white instrument whose invention and subsequent universal use had probably caused more trouble in the world than the internal combustion engine. For some reason he lifted its receiver and dialled 1471 to obtain the number of the last caller. He didn't recognise it but he knew it belonged to none of those he and Sharonne called their friends nor to any tradesman or shop that he could recall.

When he went to fetch himself a drink he noticed that he was holding between his fingers and turning it this way and that, the card given him by the representative of Search and Find.

CHAPTER 17

At Antrim they were taking the entrance hall to pieces.

'Everything will be put back exactly as it was,' Vine said to Katrina Dade, more in hope than certainty. Katrina moaned and wrung her hands, finally retreating to the living room where she lay on a sofa with a blanket over her and her face buried in cushions.

The carpet had come up and a couple of floorboards. A brownish patch was scraped off the skirting board and a section of flooring with a red-brown stain on it lifted away from between the bottom of the clothes cupboard and the uncarpeted floor. Vine knew what he had to do next and he didn't fancy it, but a policeman's lot, he sometimes thought, was a series of unpleasant tasks he didn't fancy. DC Lynn Fancourt said kindly to him, 'I'll ask her if you like, Sarge. I don't mind. Really.'

Vine sometimes thought that if he weren't a happily married man with kids and responsibilities he wouldn't have been averse to a runaround with Lynn. She was just his type, old-fashioned sort of figure and lovely golden-brown hair. 'No, I'll do it. Now. Get it over with.'

He went into the living room and coughed. Katrina lifted a tear-blotched face from the cushions. Vine cleared his throat. 'Mrs Dade, I'm sorry to have to ask you this. Believe me, it's just a precaution. Don't read anything into it. But do you happen to know which blood group your children belong to?'

Katrina read everything into it. She set up a loud
wailing. Vine looked at her in despair and called Lynn,
who came in calmly, sat down beside Katrina and murmured softly to her. No brisk admonitions, no slapping
of face. Katrina sobbed and gagged and stuck her fists in
her eyes, laid her head on Lynn's shoulder, but eventually gulped out that she didn't know, she never dealt
with that kind of thing.

'Would your husband be able to help us?'

'He's at the office. He doesn't care. Children are just
something a man in his position thinks he ought to
have. He's never *loved* them.' The emotive word set off
fresh wails and floods.

Lynn patted her shoulder, said gently, 'But would he
know about blood groups?'

'I suppose so. If there's anything to know.'

At this moment the front door was heard to open and
close, and Roger Dade came into the room. Katrina once
more buried her head in the cushions. As always on the
lookout for someone to blame, Dade said aggressively to
Vine, 'What have you been saying to her?'

Lynn answered, 'We need to know your children's
blood groups, Mr Dade.'

'Why didn't you come to me first? You know she's a
crazy hysteric. Look what you've done to her.' But he
lifted his wife – tenderly for him – and put his arms
round her. 'There, there, come on. You can't go on like
this.' He looked up at Lynn. 'Their groups are on file
upstairs. If I ask you what you want them for I suppose
you'll say it's just routine.'

Neither officer answered. Dade sighed, disengaged
himself from his wife's grip – she had locked both hands
round his neck – and went upstairs. Vine looked at
Lynn and cast up his eyes.

*

There was no reason to believe a triple murder hadn't been committed in that hall. Unless the absence of much blood might be a reason. The hall would be easy to clean, Wexford thought. No carpet, no rugs, the wood apparently coated with a hard stain-repellent lacquer that would resist blood as well as any other compound. He wondered if they even had enough on the samples to make comparison with Joanna Troy's group possible.

One of the Dade children, Sophie, had a blood group that matched hers, O Positive, the commonest. Giles Dade's group was A Positive. If the samples revealed only O Positive blood they still wouldn't know much, merely that Sophie might have been killed along with Joanna. On the other hand she might not. But if they showed A Positive as well there was a strong possibility it was Giles's. How about DNA comparisons? They already had hair from Sophie Dade's hairbrush. DNA would be discoverable on that if the hair had fallen out, not if it had been cut off . . .

He would be seeing Jashub Wright at midday. At his home, to ask him about the ritualistic meetings at the Dancing Floor. Lynn Fancourt, back from the Dades', went with him. This was his first visit to the semi-detached bungalow, its exterior coated with that most depressing of wall covers, grey pebble-dashing. No attention had been paid to the front garden until, apparently, someone had attacked grass, nettles and incipient saplings with a scythe. Presumably on one of the rare days when it wasn't raining. It was raining now, water staining the grey walls a deeper charcoal. Every time Wexford saw pebble-dashing he was reminded of long ago when he was seven and staying overnight for some reason with an aunt. The walls of her house had a similar surface. He had been put early to bed in a back bedroom while guests were entertained. The company sat under his window in deckchairs, his aunt and uncle, two old women – old to him then – and an old man with an entirely bald shiny head. Unbeknownst to them he watched them from his open window and, unable to resist the temptation, began picking bits of pebble-dashing off the wall and dropping them on to that bald pate. For a few moments he had the blissful satisfaction of seeing the old man brush what he thought was some insect off his head. Twice he did it, three times, and then he looked up. They all looked up. Auntie Freda came running up the stairs, grabbed her nephew and whacked him with a hairbrush, later the cause of much indignation to Wexford's mother. These days, he thought, as Lynn rang the doorbell and they waited, she'd have had her sister-in-law up before the European Court of Human Rights.

Thekla Wright answered the door. Wexford had never seen her before and was a little taken aback. She was blonde and very pretty but the way she was dressed – what did her clothes remind him of? It came to him when they were on the threshold of the living room. A photograph he'd once seen of the wives of a Mormon in Utah, polygamy long illegal but a blind eye turned to it. They had been dressed like Thekla Wright or she was dressed like them, her frock faded cotton print mid-calf length, her bare legs covered in fuzzy blonde hair, her feet in flat sandals of the Start-rite kind children had worn in his pebble-dashing days. Her long hair was looped up untidily with combs and grips.

He had expected to see Jashub Wright alone but the pastor's wife opened the door to disclose inside a gathering that made him think of a function he had never attended but only heard about, a prayer meeting. He had to stop himself staring. Probably most of the

chairs the Wrights possessed were arranged in a circle
and on each one, eight out of the ten, sat a man. They
weren't dressed in striped trousers and frock coats and
they weren't wearing stovepipe hats but for a moment
he had the illusion they were. All were in suits with
shirts and ties. All had very short hair. They rose to their
feet as one when he and Lynn came in and Lynn got
some very strange looks. He thought Mrs Wright had
left them because her baby was crying but perhaps not,
perhaps she had gone because they excluded women
from their counsels. But Jashub Wright stepped forward
with outstretched hand. Wexford ignored it – he was
practised in this – and introduced Lynn, expecting
verbal disapproval. But there was none, only a rather
oppressive silence.

Wexford sat down and Lynn did. Now all the chairs
were occupied. Before he could begin one of the men
spoke and he saw he had come to a conclusion too soon.

'I am an elder of the United Gospel Church. My
name is Hobab Winter.' He glanced quickly at Lynn
and away. In that glance a feminist would have detected
fear of women. 'It's my duty to point out that females are
not normally present at our meetings but we will make
an exception in this case.'

Wexford said nothing but Lynn spoke up, as he
was sure she would. 'Why not?' No one answered and
she repeated what she had said. 'I'd really like to know
why not.'

It was the pastor who replied, in a genial and friendly
tone, as if Lynn couldn't fail to appreciate what he was
saying. 'We must never forget that it was a woman who
brought about man's fall.'

Lynn was evidently too stunned for an immediate
riposte and when after a few seconds she opened her
mouth, Wexford whispered for no one's ears but hers,

'DC Fancourt, not now. Leave it.' She said nothing but
he was aware of the tremor of rage running through her.
He spoke quickly. 'May I have your names, please? So
that we know what we're doing.'

One by one the circle uttered them, preceded by
their titles, Elder, Reader, Officer, Deputy. Very odd, he
thought. 'Now would someone tell me about this cere-
mony that takes place in the wood at Passingham Hall
twice a year in January and July? Presumably this is the
cleansing ritual you once mentioned to me.'

'The ritual, as you call it, though we prefer another
name, will not be taking place there this January. Not in
view of the circumstances.'

'So if you don't call it that what do you call it?'

'It is our Confessional Congregation.'

They certainly weren't anxious to be forthcoming.
Wexford looked at the circle of men. Some of them
were vaguely familiar to him, he had seen them about in
Kingsmarkham. Each face was calm, enclosed, mild.
They were rather alike, not one could have been
described as good-looking, all had roundish faces, all
were clean-shaven with small eyes and small mouths,
though the noses varied in shape and size and the hair
colour varied where much hair could be seen. Every face
was curiously unlined, though somehow he could tell
the youngest was in his thirties and the oldest in his sixties. If he was still alive and if he stayed with them,
would Giles Dade come to look like this one day?

'What happens at the Confessional Congregation?'
he asked.

'Church members attend.' Jashub Wright was
laconic. 'New members confess their sins and are
absolved. Cleansed. Purified. As I said to you once
before, their bodies and spirits are cleared of toxins.
Afterwards biscuits and Coke and lemonade are served.

Women are involved in the catering arrangements, of course.' Once again he smiled gently at Lynn who looked away. 'Miss Moody is in charge of that. The people are very happy, they rejoice, they sing, they claim the new member as their own. Each new member has a mentor – one of the elders, of course – assigned to him. Or her. To prevent him sliding back into sin.'

'Who did you say was in charge of the catering?'

'Miss Yvonne Moody. She is one of our most deeply committed members.'

They left the room for a brief interval.

'She came to us of her own accord, sir, and she did admit to knowing Giles Dade,' Lynn said. 'You can't say she's tried to deceive us.'

'No, I dare say not. But it's interesting in various ways, isn't it? She knew Joanna Troy well, she lived next door to her, and she knew Giles through her church. Not only that. She knew about the clearing Shand-Gibb calls the Dancing Floor and therefore the existence of the quarry and the way through the wood to reach it. I revoke "I dare say not". She *did* deceive us. She came to us of her own accord because she saw that as the best way to project her innocence. Let's go back in there.'

The circle of members was as they had left it, the faces still serene, mild, inscrutable. Wexford noticed what he hadn't before, a faintly unpleasant smell pervading the small room. It took him a moment to realise this was the odour of eight lounge suits, worn daily but dry-cleaned seldom. He sat down again.

'How are you – maybe I should say, how *did* you – get to the site of the Confessional Congregation? By car?'

'Certainly by car,' Wright said. 'Occasionally some people went by train and station taxi but these means are difficult as well as costly. Our members in general are not well-off, Mr Wexford.' The circle indicated its approval by vigorous nods. 'Besides that, there was always limited parking space at Passingham Hall and Mr Buxton didn't care for us leaving cars outside his house. Add to that the limited incomes of our members and you will understand that we usually attended three or four to a car. That is the prudent way.'

'So any members of the United Gospel Church', said Burden, 'would know how to get to Passingham St John, the location of the drive to Passingham Hall, the way into the wood and the whereabouts of the quarry?'

'Broadly speaking, yes.' It was the man called Hobab Winter who replied. Where did they get these names? Not from their god-fathers and godmothers at their baptism, Wexford was sure. They must have adopted them later. 'Of course, as we've said, some would be passengers in other people's cars. Some can't drive. One or two come by train and take a taxi from Passingham Park station.'

If he had been going to say more, Jashub Wright cut him short. 'To what are these questions tending?'

Wexford spoke sharply, 'To finding, arresting and bringing to trial the murderer of Joanna Troy, Mr Wright. And to locating Giles and Sophie Dade.' He paused. 'Dead or alive,' he said.

Wright nodded silently but with an air of offence. His wife's voice from outside summoned him to the door and he held it open for her to pass through, carrying a tray. On it were ten tumblers of something pale-yellow and fizzy. Lynn took hers with an expression on her face that almost made Wexford laugh. The drink was lemonade but a surprisingly good home-made kind.

'I take it you are all present at Confessional Congregations? Yes. I'd like your full names and addresses and . . .' he dropped his bombshell '. . . I shall want to know where each of you were on Saturday, the twenty-fifth of November last, between ten a.m. and midnight.'

He expected a chorus of indignation but the faces remained impassive and only the pastor himself protested. 'Alibis? You're not serious.'

'Indeed I am, Mr Wright. Now perhaps you'll do as I ask and give your names to DC Fancourt.'

Wright made an attempt at a joke but his tone was sour. 'Round up the usual suspects,' he said.

Back in his office, Wexford regarded the list. The seven were called Hobab Winter, Pagiel Smith, Nun Plummer, Ev Taylor, Nemuel Morrison, Hanoch Crane and Zurishaddai Wilton. The first names were grotesque, the surnames uncompromisingly English. Not only were there no Asian names among them – he would have known that from the Good Gospellers' appearance – but none of Scots or Welsh origin, never mind any incomers from the continent of Europe. He wondered if all this meant they were subject to adult baptism when they joined the Gospel Church and received new names as people converted to Judaism did.

'Funny, isn't it?' he said to Burden. 'These odd Christian sects, they used to be called Dissenters, Nonconformists, I don't know what they are now, they all go on and on about the gospel but they're hooked on names out of the Old Testament, old Jewish names in fact, while Jews never are. You'd expect them to have names like John and Mark and Luke and whatever but they don't, they think those are Catholic names.'

'I know a Jewish chap who's called Moses, and you can't get more OT than that. And my sons are called John and Mark, but I'm not Catholic.'

'No, you're not anything and nor am I. Forget it. I know what I mean if you don't. Barry and Karen and

Lynn are checking on alibis and we are going to see Yvonne Moody but this time we'll go to her.'

There was one question he had failed to ask the elders and officers of the United Gospel Church but it was to be some time before he realised what it was.

The little town house where Joanna Troy had lived looked forlorn. Perhaps that was only because they knew it was empty and its owner gone for ever. A bay tree in a tub which, if Joanna had returned home on Monday, 27 November, would no doubt have been taken indoors for the winter out of the rain, snow and frost, had succumbed to one of these dire weather conditions and become a shivering pillar of brown leaves that rattled in the wind. The rain had given way to a whitish mist, not dense enough to be called a fog but obscuring the horizon.

Inside one of the panes in a downstairs window of Yvonne Moody's house was pasted a notice which announced that a 'Winter Fayre' would be held at the Good Gospel Church, York Street, Kingsmarkham on Saturday, 20 January. 'All welcome. Tea, cakes, stalls, games and bumper raffle.' She made no secret of her affiliation, Wexford thought. But really he had no justification for supposing she did, only the sneaking feeling that an honest woman when referring to Giles Dade would have said, 'I've only come across the son, he belongs to my church,' instead of leaving out reference to the church altogether. When they were inside, seated in a cluttered living room that smelt strongly of spring-time meadow air freshener, he asked her why not.

'It wasn't important,' she said and added, 'I didn't think it was your business, frankly.'

'But you thought it was our business to hear about a possible relationship between Roger Dade and Joanna?'

'It was useful information, wasn't it? Adultery contributes to murder. I know that. Not from experience, certainly not, but from what I've seen on TV. Half those serials and dramas are about that sort of thing. Of course I'm careful what I watch. Half those things I have to avoid, it wouldn't be suitable for a woman committed to Jesus as I am.'

She might be rather attractive, he thought, if she weren't bulging almost indecently out of her green jersey trouser suit. He looked, then out of politeness tried not to look, at the double bosom she seemed to have, her true breasts and the roll of fat underneath them and above her too tightly belted waist. Her dark frizzy hair was held back by an Alice band, the kind of headgear he believed no woman should wear after the age of twenty. She wore a lot of heavy make-up, so presumably the Gospellers hadn't latched on to biblical strictures against paint and adornment.

'Did you like your next-door neighbour, Ms Moody?'

'You can call me Miss. I'm not ashamed of my virginity.' Burden was blinking his eyes rapidly. '*Like* her? I didn't dislike her. I pitied her. We always pity sinners, don't we? I'd be sorry for anyone so lost to God and duty as to contemplate adultery with a married man. That poor boy Giles. I was sorry for *him*.'

'Why was that?' Burden asked her.

'Fifteen years old, on the threshhold of manhood, and subject to her influence. He was old enough to see what went on between her and his father if his sister wasn't. The corruption of the innocent makes you shiver.'

Did she always go on like this? Could her friends stand it? But perhaps she had none. 'When did you last attend one of the Good Gospel Church's Confessional Congregations, Ms Moody?'

She sighed, perhaps only because once again he had failed to pay tribute to her maidenhood. 'I couldn't go last July. I organised the food and drink but I didn't actually go. My mother was unwell. She lives in Aylesbury and she's very old, nearly ninety. Of course I realise this can't go on, she'll have to come and live here with me. These things are sent to try us, aren't they?'

Neither Wexford nor Burden had an opinion on this. 'So you haven't been for a year but you know the place pretty well? Passingham Hall grounds, I mean.'

Was she wary or was it his imagination? 'I don't know if I could find my way there if someone else wasn't taking me. Mr Morrison usually takes me, Mr Nemuel Morrison that is. And his wife, of course. I haven't a car of my own, I don't drive.'

'You don't or you can't?' Burden asked.

'I can but I don't. The traffic has become too heavy and too dangerous for me. I never go far except to my mother and I do that by train.' She began to tell them in detail the route she took from Kingsmarkham to Aylesbury, the train to Victoria, tube across London, train from Marylebone. 'I did once go to Passingham by train. All the cars were full, you see. It was an awful journey but worth it in such a good cause. It was Kingsmarkham to Toxborough, then the local train Toxborough to Passingham Park and then a taxi, but the taxi ride was only two miles. Mind you, I could afford a car. I've got a very good job in management.'

'We'd like to know where you were on the twenty-fifth of November of last year,' Wexford said. 'That was very likely the night on which Joanna Troy died. Can you account for your movements? The period we're interested in is from ten a.m. on Saturday until midnight.'

Questioning about alibis often elicited an angry response from people who were not necessarily suspects but simply had to be eliminated from enquiries. But seldom had either officer's simple query met with such a storm of indignation.

'You're accusing *me* of killing Joanna? You must be mad or very wicked. No one's ever said anything like that to me in all my life.'

'Ms Moody, you're accused of nothing. All we are doing is – well, crossing people off a list. Naturally, we have a list of the people who knew Joanna, that's all. *Knew* her. You're on that list just as her father and stepmother are and we would like to cross you off.'

She was mollified. Her face, which she had contorted into a grimace of fury and disgust, relaxed a little and her hands, closed into tight fists, loosened. 'You'd better cross me off here and now,' she said. 'I was in Aylesbury with my mother. I can tell you exactly when I went there and when I came back and I can do it without looking it up. I had a phone call from her neighbour on the twenty-third of November and went up there next day. Once again I had to get off work, take the rest of my annual leave. By the time I got to my mother's house she'd been taken into hospital. Anyone up there will tell you I was staying in her house that weekend and visiting the hospital twice a day – well, not the Saturday afternoon, she was having some procedures, had to be sedated, and there was no point in me going till next morning. The neighbours will all tell you I was in the house on my own all evening.'

'The neighbours', said Wexford as he and Burden enjoyed a quiet pint in the nearest pub, 'will tell us they didn't see her or hear her or hear any sounds from the house but they know she was there, where else would she be?'

'But we'll have to ask them. She could have got to Passingham Hall that evening and back probably but it would have taken a very long time. I'm sure she wasn't involved.'

'Maybe. Leave that for a moment and get back to Joanna herself. I think the contents of that overnight bag of hers point to the time they all three left, or perhaps I should say, were taken from, the Dades' house.'

'You mean it must have been late at night because Joanna was apparently wearing – well, a nightdress. That's what girls wear those oversize T-shirts for.'

'Do they, indeed?' said Wexford, grinning, 'And how would you know? But, no, that wasn't what I meant.'

'No, because she could just as easily have been killed on Sunday morning at that rate. She could still have been wearing that T-shirt.'

'Mike,' said Wexford, 'she was an early riser. Jennings told us so. Don't you remember? When he was talking about her energy? She always gets up at six thirty, he says, same at the weekends. Always gets showered and dressed, he said, or words to that effect. In that bag of hers she had two sets of underwear among the soiled clothes, one set for Friday, one set for Saturday, and one set *unworn*. Those were for Sunday. Therefore they were taken from the house on Saturday night and probably quite late at night.'

Burden nodded. 'You're right.'

'And now I'm going home,' said Wexford, 'to look up these loony names in the Old Testament and maybe the voters' list on the Internet too, find out what these Good Gospel people are really called.'

'What on earth for?' Burden asked as they began the walk back.

'For my own amusement. It's Friday night and I need a bit of hush.'

He wasn't himself capable of looking up the electoral register on the Internet but Dora was. In the past six months since this innovation came to their household she had learned computer skills.

'You don't want it downloaded, do you? It's miles long.'

'No, of course not. Just show it to me and tell me again how you scroll down or whatever it's called.'

There it was, on the screen before him. He had the addresses of the elders of the United Gospel Church and he viewed the register street by street. Just as he thought, not one of the elders bore the names their parents had given them. Hobab Winter had been – and in the register still was – Kenneth G. while Zurishaddai Wilton was George W. Only Jashub Wright of all the church hierarchy was still named as he had been at his baptism. Next Wexford turned to the Bible. This he could also have summoned on the Net but he had no idea how and didn't want to call Dora from her television serial.

He had told Burden he was doing this for his own amusement but there is nothing amusing about the Book of Numbers. All you could say for it was that it inspired awe and sent a shiver down the spine. It was something to do with the absolute obedience these people's God demanded from the Israelites. Had that too been handed down to these Good Gospellers along with their adopted names? He was looking these up, discovering that Hobab was the son of Raguel the Midianite and Nun the father of Joshua, when Dora came back into the room. She looked at the screen.

'Why are you interested in Ken Winter?'

'He's one of those Good Gospellers. An elder and he calls himself Hobab, not Ken. And he lives in this street, a long way down but this street.' The familiarity with which she had referred to the man suddenly struck him. 'Why, do you know him?'

'*You* know him, Reg.'

'I'm sure I don't.' said Wexford, who wasn't sure and now remembered how several faces at that meeting had seemed recognisable.

'He's our newsagent.' She was starting to sound exasperated. 'He keeps the paper shop in Queen Street. It's his daughter that delivers the evening paper, a girl about fifteen.'

'Ah, now I know.'

'I feel for that girl. Sometimes she's still in her school uniform when she starts that paper round. She goes to that private school in Sewingbury, the one where the children wear brown with gold braid. It's not right a girl of her age being out after dark and I really think . . .'

He was wondering whether all this was of any significance when the phone rang. Wexford picked up the receiver.

'Dad?'

The voice was unrecognisable. He thought whoever it was had a wrong number. 'What number do you want?'

'Dad, it's me.' Feeble, shaky, gasping. 'Dad, I'm on a mobile. It's so little, I hid it on me.'

'Sylvia, what's happened?'

'Cal – Cal beat me up and locked me in a cupboard. Please come, get someone to come . . .'

'Where are the children?'

'Out. Out with Neil. It's Friday. Please, please come . . .'

CHAPTER 18

To go himself would be wrong. The proper thing would be to send two officers, say Karen Malahyde, trained in dealing with domestic violence, and DC Hammond. But he couldn't have sat at home and waited. He phoned Donaldson for his car and he phoned Karen at home. She wasn't on duty but she didn't hesitate. By the time Donaldson got to his house she was there too.

'I must come,' Dora said.

'He may be violent,' Wexford didn't want to stop her but he had to. 'He *is* violent. I'll phone you when I find her. I won't leave you in the dark a moment. I promise.'

For the first ten minutes of the drive to the remote rural place where Sylvia – and once Neil too – had bought and converted the Old Rectory, Karen was silent. When she spoke it was to say she didn't understand, not *Sylvia*, Sylvia couldn't be a victim of this kind of thing.

'Not after all the time she's worked at The Hide. I mean, she's seen the results of it day after day. She *knows*.'

'When it's your personal life you see things from another perspective.' Wexford had been wondering the same thing. 'You say to yourself – and to others – "Yes, but this is different."'

The Old Rectory was a big house approached by a curving drive about a hundred yards long. The front garden, if such it could be called, for the house stood in its own grounds and was surrounded by garden, was

overgrown with shrubs and overhung by tall trees.
Maybe because of this Sylvia always kept the place a
blaze of light when dusk came, for her own comfort,
perhaps, or that of her sons. But tonight it was in darkness, total darkness, for not a glimmer showed or chink
between drawn curtains. If the curtains were drawn.
Even when Donaldson had driven up to the door it was
impossible to tell. Rain dripped from the branches of
trees and water lay in puddles on the paving stones.

The place looked as if no one lived there. When
was Neil due back with the boys? Nine? Ten, even?
They could lie in in the morning, they didn't have to
go to school. Wexford made his way to the front door
in the light from the car headlights and put his hand to
the bell. It is a peculiarity of the parent–child relationship that while children invariably have a key to their
parents' home the parents never have a key to theirs.
Wexford's sixth law, he thought wryly, half forgetting
what the others were. No one came to the door. He rang
again. As he turned round a great gust of wind blew rain
into his face.

What was he going to do if Callum Chapman refused
to let him in? Break in, of course, but not yet. Karen got
out of the car with a torch in her hand and shone the
beam over the front of the house. All the windows were
tight shut. Wexford went back to the door, pushed in
the letter box and called through the aperture, 'Police!
Let us in!' It was for Sylvia's benefit, not because he
thought it would have any other effect. He could make
his voice very loud and resonant, and projected it as
energetically as he could when he called again. Maybe
she could hear him, wherever she was.

He and Karen picked their way round the side of the
house. Doing this was impossible without getting very
wet. Untrimmed shrubs, most of them evergreens,

encroached on the path, their leaves laden with water. Rain dripped from the trees in large icy drops. Without the torch the darkness would have been impenetrable. As it was, its bulb cast a greenish-white beam, a shaft of foggy light to cut through the wet jungle and show equally wet long grass underneath. It lit up a red plastic football one of the boys must have kicked there in the summer and been unable to find.

'Does no one do any gardening round here?' Wexford grumbled, remembering as he'd said it that his own contribution to horticulture was sitting outside and admiring the flowers on a summer evening. Such a pursuit seemed unreal this evening, an illusory recall. 'The back door should be here somewhere, at the end of the extension.'

It was locked. Was it also bolted? The back of the house was as dark as the front. By the light of the torch he glanced at his watch. Just after eight thirty. What time would Neil bring the boys back and did he have a key? Very unlikely. Another one of Wexford's laws might be that the first thing an estranged wife does when turning her husband out of what had been their joint home is to take away his key.

Then he remembered. 'In the shed,' he said to Karen, 'in that outhouse place there, she used to keep a key to the back door. Neil made a kind of niche in a beam on the far side from the door. The theory was that no one could guess it was there.'

'The kind of person who might want to get in would guess all right,' Karen said. 'There's nowhere to hide a key and be sure it won't be found.'

'As I told her. She said she'd take it away but I wonder . . .'

At least the shed door wasn't locked. Inside it was a gloomy place, mediaeval-looking with its beamed walls and a ceiling where the timbering came down so low that Wexford couldn't stand upright. There was no interior light and never had been. Once a cottage and home to a family, it had last been lit by candles. The motor mower, unused garden tools, plastic sacks and cardboard crates were no more than bulky shapes in the darkness. He took the torch from Karen and directed its light on to the fifth beam from the door, revealing ropes of cobwebs and an irregular round fissure in the black oak that looked as if it might have been a knot-hole. His hands must be larger than Neil's for only his little finger was small enough to reach inside. But reach it did and when he wriggled it about and then withdrew it something metallic dropped out on to the floor. He bent down to pick up the key, straightened with a cry of triumph and gave his head a mighty whack on the beam.

'Are you OK, sir?' Karen was all concern.

'I'm fine,' he said, wincing and rubbing his head, still seeing stars and floaters and coloured flashes. 'Good thing she didn't take my advice.'

So long as the door wasn't bolted . . . It wasn't. He turned the key in the lock and let them in. Laundry room first, then kitchen. Karen felt for switches and put the lights on. A meal had been eaten at the kitchen table, begun but not finished. Wine had been drunk, half a bottle of it, and most of it, he guessed, consumed by Chapman, for the glass where he normally sat was empty and the other, Sylvia's, full. Wexford walked out into the hall, switched on more lights and called out, 'Sylvia? Where are you?'

A door opened at the top of the stairs. It was rather near the top of the stairs, only about a yard from the top step. Chapman came out of it. 'What are you doing here? How did you get in?'

'I have a key,' said Wexford who, in case he didn't know about its hiding place, wasn't going to tell him. 'I rang the bell twice and you didn't answer. Where's Sylvia?'

Chapman didn't answer. He looked at Karen. 'Who's that?'

'Detective Sergeant Malahyde,' she said. 'Tell us where we can find Sylvia, please.'

'Not your business. None of this is your business. We've simply had a row, normal enough, I should think, between partners.'

Suddenly Wexford knew where she would be. In the place she and Neil had called the dressing room, though it was really no more than a walk-in clothes cupboard. There was a lock on its door, he'd noticed that one day several years ago when Sylvia had the flu and he was visiting her. He set his foot on the bottom stair and when Chapman didn't move said, 'Come on, let me pass.'

'You're not coming up here,' Chapman said, and then, revealing he didn't know about the phone call, 'I don't know what's brought you here except maybe her usual whingeing but she doesn't want you and nor do I. It's between us, it's a private matter.'

'Like hell it is.'

Wexford went on up and tried to push past him. Chapman was shorter than he but a lot younger. He drew back his arm and struck Wexford a blow which failed to connect with his jaw but landed on his collar bone. Luckily, perhaps luckily for both of them – for Wexford was forced to think what the results of hitting him might be – the force Chapman had to bring to this made him stagger, lose his balance and tumble down the top stairs. He was up in a flash, his face red with rage. Wexford stood where he was, filling the square of carpet at the top, making a barrier which, to get past, Chapman would have had to make a fierce fight of it.

And he was on the stairs again, his fists up, when Karen called his name. She called it softly.

'Mr Chapman!'

He turned. He ran down the stairs. Perhaps he'd decided, Wexford thought afterwards, that if he attacked a woman, *another* woman, her superior officer would be down those stairs in a flash to defend her. As he would have done, as he was starting to do. It all happened very fast. One second Chapman was reaching for Karen's shoulders, reaching perhaps for her neck, the next she had taken him in some kind of hold, thrown him into the air and cast him with a smash on to the hall floor.

'Well done,' said Wexford. He had forgotten all about those karate classes she had regularly attended last year and the year before. It worked. He had seen it done in the past but never so effectively. Within a moment he was putting on lights, making for the dressing room. Karen followed him.

'Sylvia!'

It was ominous that the silence was maintained. Why, come to that, hadn't she heard him the first time? Her bedroom door wasn't locked and nor was the one to the dressing room. He opened it. It was empty but for the rows of clothes on hangers.

'Sylvia, where are you?'

Not a voice but the sound of feet drumming on something. There were a lot of bedrooms in this house and all had cupboards in them. But Chapman had come out of the one at the top of the stairs . . . It was Karen who found her, in that bedroom, in the place they called the airing cupboard, though nothing had been aired in it for decades. The heat inside was tremendous, pouring from the boiler and an ill-insulated immersion heater turned full on. It must have been close on 40 degrees Celsius. She was sitting on the floor, sweat streaming off her, surrounded by the clothes she had presumably been wearing but stripped down now to a thin skirt and a T-shirt. Her ankles were tied together with what looked like a dressing gown belt but her hands were nearly free. No doubt she was managing to ease herself out of whatever bound them. He saw why she hadn't answered. Presumably after she'd made that call, but for some other reason, Chapman had taped up her mouth with sticking plaster.

He picked her up in his arms and carried her out, laying her on the unmade bed. While Karen worked gently on her mouth to ease the plaster off, he phoned Dora, told her all was well and no longer to worry. Then he turned back to look at his daughter. Karen removed the last stubborn edge of the plaster with a swift and probably painful rip. Sylvia put her hand on her upper lip and whimpered through her fingers. She had two black eyes, a dark-red contusion down her cheek and a cut between upper lip and nose that the plaster had covered, though covering it had obviously not been its purpose.

'He did this to you?'

She nodded. The tears welled up in her eyes. Rage filled Wexford with a burning tremulous heat. He felt as if he might explode with it as he heard Chapman returning, coming up the stairs. The power of rational thought had left him when the overwhelming anger poured in, possible consequences were forgotten, prudence cast to the winds. He swung round and fetched Chapman a heavy well-aimed punch to the jaw. It was remarkable that he could do it, he thought afterwards, for he hadn't hit anyone since boxing at school, but he had done it all right, he had done it as to the manner well-taught. Sylvia's lover lay sprawled on the floor, apparently unconscious, his mouth open. My God, thought Wexford, suppose he's dead?

Of course he wasn't. He began to struggle into a sitting position.

'Don't let him come near me,' Sylvia screamed.

'You should be so lucky,' muttered Chapman, rubbing his jaw.

'I want him out of this house. Now.'

Wexford thanked God for it. What would he have done if she had decided to forgive him? It might happen yet . . . Karen said, 'Can you come downstairs, Sylvia? Are you up to that? I'm going to make you a hot drink with plenty of sugar in it.'

She nodded, eased herself up with difficulty like an old woman. 'My face must be a sight,' she said. 'My body will be worse only you can't see.' She looked at Chapman with loathing. 'You can pack your bags and go. I don't know how you'll get to Kingsmarkham. Walk, I suppose. It's only about seven miles.'

'I'm not fit to walk,' he grumbled. 'Your bloody father has nearly killed me.'

'Not near enough,' said Wexford, and then, because it was the only way he could think of to be sure of getting rid of him, 'We'll take him. I don't want to but he'll never do it on foot.' That remark of Chapman's in the Moonflower suddenly came back to him, something about skiving off on the taxpayers' money. 'I'd rather see him dead in a ditch but it's only the good die young.'

They got Sylvia downstairs. He could see the bruises on her legs now. Why hadn't he understood when he saw that red bracelet-like contusion on her wrist at Christmas? Because he couldn't believe a woman who worked in a refuge for victims of domestic violence would herself put up with abuse from a partner.

Oddly enough, Chapman came too. A hangdog air had replaced his truculence. He trailed behind them, silent, looking as if he might start crying. Karen put the kettle on and made tea for Sylvia, herself and Wexford. Sylvia's was very sweet and milky, the way she never took it normally but which seemed to comfort her now. Colour came back into her battered face and she began to talk. Wexford had believed she would have preferred to defer explaining until Chapman was out of the way but she seemed to take pleasure, as he confessed he would have done, in telling it all in her attacker's presence.

'He wants to marry me. Or he did. I don't suppose he does now. He kept on and on at me and once or twice he hit me.' She looked at her father and cast up her eyes. 'I'm a fool, aren't I? I of all women ought to know better. I can only say it's different when it happens to you. You believe them when they promise not to do it again . . .'

Chapman interrupted her. 'I do promise, Sylvia. I won't do it again. I'll swear on the Bible, if you like. I'll make a solemn vow that I never never will. And I still want to marry you. You know all this only came about because you wouldn't marry me.'

She laughed, a dry little laugh that stopped because it hurt her. 'We had a really big row this evening. I said I wouldn't marry him and I didn't want him living here any more. I told him to go and he started on me. He knocked me down and punched my face. I got away from him and ran upstairs. I thought I could lock myself in my bedroom but that was a fatal mistake. It was better for him having me up there. Easier to get hold of the sticking plaster, for one thing.' Chapman got a look of such viciousness Wexford was nearly shocked. 'This house is so cold it's a good thing I was wearing so many clothes – well, it is in one way. I nearly died of the heat in that cupboard but it meant I had my mobile with me, in the pocket of my cardigan.'

Chapman hadn't known. He shook his head, perhaps at his own lack of foresight in not searching her before making her prisoner. Sylvia said, 'He came back later and taped up my mouth and tied up my feet and hands and put me in that cupboard, the *hot* cupboard. That was deliberate torture. I don't know what he meant to do next, go out maybe in *my* car, or wait till Neil brought the boys back. . . . Where are the boys?'

As she asked that question the doorbell rang. Wexford went to answer it. Ben and Robin rushed in, making for the kitchen. Seeing their mother in that state wouldn't be pleasant for them but they would have to know some time. He told Neil as briefly as he could what had happened.

'Where is he? Let me get at him.'

'No, Neil. Not you too. As it is, I shouldn't have hit him and God knows what he'll do about it. He's going anyway. The best thing will be for Sylvia and the boys to come and stay with us. I'll get Karen to drive them in Sylvia's car.'

'I'll take them,' Neil said.

Sylvia had apparently told her sons she had fallen down the stairs. She had come out of the bedroom where the airing cupboard was, it was dark, she had missed her footing and crashed down the entire flight. Whether they believed that this would also account for her black eyes Wexford couldn't tell. But they seemed satisfied with the explanation and excited, as children mostly are, at the prospect of going away for the night. Chapman, the fight knocked out of him, had gone upstairs to pack suitcases.

'Why did he turn all the lights off?' Karen asked.

'I don't know. He was always saying I was extravagant with electricity but it's my house and I paid the bills. I don't know what he thought would happen when Robin and Ben came back. Maybe he was going to tell them I wasn't feeling well and had gone to bed and keep me in there all night. He's capable of it. Oh, I'm such a *fool*.'

So Neil drove his family to Wexford's house while Wexford and Karen took Chapman with them. He had brought so many cases, boxes and plastic carriers, filling up the car boot, that Wexford was driven to wonder how many of Sylvia's possessions the man had filched. It was worth almost anything to be rid of him. No one spoke. Donaldson at the wheel was consumed with curiosity, his ears on stalks for the hints of enlightenment that never came. He was directed to drive to a district of Stowerton he wouldn't normally have associated with the chief inspector's daughter or anyone belonging to her. There, in a street that ran along the back of a disused factory, he was told to drop their passenger outside a run-down block of flats with a nameplate from which several letters had fallen and never been replaced and where only one of the four globular lamps above the entrance was working. Donaldson was preparing to carry those cases and boxes up the steps to this entrance but Wexford said no, leave them on the pavement.

Chapman got out and stood there, surrounded by his, and possibly Sylvia's, property.

'Goodnight,' said Wexford, his head out of the window.

The last they saw of him was a weary figure humping inelegant luggage across the pavement, along the path and up the steps. There was so much of it that he would have to make several journeys. Maybe that would be the last they saw of him and maybe not, Wexford thought, his experience of life telling him that couples when they parted seldom made a clean break of it but drifted together again and apart again, the whole sorry process punctuated with rows, reconciliations and recriminations. Not this time, please, not when it was his injured daughter . . .

How about charging Chapman with causing Actual Bodily Harm, say, or even resisting arrest? He thought not. This was *his* daughter. Was he going to pre-empt any accusations which might come from Chapman by first telling Freeborn what he'd done? Chapman could be revenged by accusing Wexford of assault, but he was unlikely to do this when it meant admitting he'd been laid low by a man much older than himself. Wexford couldn't honestly say he regretted what he'd done, for the blow he had struck hadn't been for Chapman alone but for all the ghastly men who had been in and out of his daughters' lives over the past years. The weedy bore Sylvia had been running around with between Neil and Chapman, the awful literary prizewinner and poet Sheila had gone about with, and back, back to her drama school days, the idiot called Sebastian something who had dumped his dog on them and which Wexford had had to take walkies. I won't think about any of it now, he thought, I'll force it out of my mind.

He said goodnight to Karen and thanked her for her help. When she had gone he asked himself what it was, what had happened that evening, which kept teasing at the back of his mind. Something to do with that staircase it was, and the way the bedroom door opened only a couple of feet in from the top riser. Anyone coming out of that room could easily fall down the stairs, as Chapman had fallen part-way when he had overbalanced after hitting Wexford. He concentrated. He revisited the scene in his mind's eye.

The configuration of staircase and bedroom door was the same at Sylvia's as at Antrim. A matter of awkward and clumsy design in both cases but safe enough if caution was used. Imagine, though, someone coming to that bedroom door . . . No, not 'someone'; Joanna Troy. Because he was in that room doing that weary everlasting homework, the homework his father insisted on over and above the call of school duty, and Joanna came to the door and knocked, maybe to tell him it was time to put the light out and go to sleep. Possibly Roger or Katrina Dade had asked her to see the children didn't stay up too late. Perhaps she had come before, even two or three times, and, exasperated, he had flung open the door and pushed her away.

It was impossible. No fifteen-year-old boy would do that unless he were a criminal psychopath in the making . . .

CHAPTER 19

There comes a time in every case if it is a complex one, when the investigating officer reaches an impasse, when there seems no way forward and no unexplored paths to go along. This is what had happened to Wexford in the Missing Dade Children affair. He had thought he had a strong lead in the matter of the Good Gospellers, but not one of the enquiries his officers had made revealed anything suspicious beyond the fact that they knew Passingham Hall woods and Giles Dade had been one of them. Each one of the elders had been alibi'd by his wife and, in some cases, by his children. Joanna Troy's past had interested him but it had mostly been concerned with things she had done and not with things done to her. Now that she was dead, probably murdered, her own offences were of little account. Who cared any longer that she had been accused of stealing a schoolboy's money? That her marriage had been a failure? Or that another boy had been attacked by her and years later died by falling over a cliff? She was dead, dumped in her car in the bottom of a waterlogged quarry. As for all the teenagers closely or remotely connected with her, Giles and Sophie, Scott and Kerry Holloway, Hobab Winter's daughter, children *would* figure in her life. She was a teacher.

The Dade children were probably dead too. Wexford knew very well how simple it may be to find a body when it has been buried in its own back garden or in next door's, how almost insuperable when the killer has

disposed of it in some distant place, perhaps hundreds
of miles away, which even he has never visited before.
He knew he should be looking at the case from an
entirely different angle to those which he had explored
already. But which angle? Where to start?

Well, he could ask Lynn Fancourt about the Dade
children's school friends, though most had been dismissed from the case. It was Sewingbury Academy's
uniform that was brown and gold and which Dora said
she had seen the Winter girl wearing when she did her
father's paper round.

'What's her name?' he had asked her.

'One of those strange Bible names. Dorcas.'

'*Dorcas*?'

'I said it was strange. Come to think of it, it's not
really any stranger than Deborah only one's fashionable
and the other's not.'

Now he said to Lynn, 'Is she on the list?'

She scanned it. 'No. Was she Giles's or Sophie's friend?'

'I don't know. They're the same sort of age and they
go to the same school. She lives in my road and she's the
daughter of the Queen Street newsagent.'

'D'you want me to go round there and ask her if she
knows Giles, sir?'

Why? What on earth was the point? He shook his
head. 'If I decide to pursue it I'll go round there myself.'

Another disappointment. He consoled himself with his
relief that at least his garden hadn't flooded again, while
some low-lying properties in Kingsmarkham, especially
those near the river banks, were once more inundated.
Life at home now included Sylvia and her sons, for she
was afraid to go home lest Callum Chapman come back.
How could she tell whether he had a key or not? She had
taken his key which he had mislaid and she had found in
the bedroom they had shared. He might easily have had

another cut during one of their quarrelsome periods when he was pressing her 'to make things permanent' and she was telling him that if he went on like that he would have to leave. To her father and mother she continued endlessly to explain how it was possible she had endured him for even a day after he first struck her, she who had been the most ardent and the most vociferous campaigner against violence in the home, she who had almost daily advised women to leave abusive partners whatever promises they made or undertakings they gave.

'It's different when it's happening to you,' she repeatedly said. 'It's a real person with good qualities, it's someone who strikes you as deeply sincere whatever else he may be.'

'Strikes you is right,' said her father, who had scant sympathy with all this now time had passed and her wounds and bruises healed. At least Chapman hadn't attempted to have him charged with assault. 'You could leave off the rest of that sentence. You're a grown woman, Sylvia, you're a mother, you were married for God knows how long. Whatever Chapman did to you you've only yourself to blame.'

Dora thought him very harsh. 'Oh, *Reg.*'

'Oh, Reg, nothing. She's a social worker, for God's sake. She ought to know a lowlife when she sees one.'

Relations between him and his elder daughter were fast returning to what they were before Sylvia left her husband and miraculously became a nicer person. And he was back in the morass of guilt he struggled to be free of by repeating to himself a kind of mantra: You must not show favouritism of one child over the other. But Chapman was gone and that was something to rejoice about.

One of the difficulties was that they still had very little idea when Joanna and the Dade children left Antrim.

Let alone why. All of them had been there on Friday and overnight. Joanna had presumably still been there on Saturday morning and for part of the afternoon since her car was there. Giles was seen on Saturday afternoon, probably as late as half past two. On Sunday morning the car was gone. It was therefore reasonable to suppose that Giles and Joanna were alive and well by early evening on Saturday – but was it?

To Burden, over lunch in the Moonflower, he said, 'We know Giles went out at around half past two but we don't know when he came back. If he came back. We know Joanna was in the house because her car was seen on the driveway by Mrs Fowler and according to her father she never walked anywhere if she could help it. But we really have no idea where Sophie was. No contact was made with her, so far as we know, after she spoke on the phone to her mother in Paris on Friday evening at about seven thirty.'

Burden nodded abstractedly. He was ordering their meal with care. It had to be served fast, it had to be 'healthy food', to which he had lately become addicted, and it had to be as fat-free as possible for Wexford's somewhat raised cholesterol. Dragon's Eggs were still on the menu and another one, even worse, had been added: Flying Fleshpots.

'It sounds awful,' said Wexford, 'but I'm going to try it.'

'I shall ask Raffy about its fat content,' Burden warned, though he had little faith in an honest answer. And when this enquiry was put to him, Raffy, efficient and smart as ever, replied that it was lowest in fat levels of any dish they served.

'It's got Lo-chol in it, sir, which has actually been clinically proven to lower cholesterol.'

'You made that up.'

'I'd never tell a lie, Mr Burden. Especially to police officers.'

Making a face, Wexford drank some of the sparkling water Burden insisted on. 'To return to our ongoing problem,' he went on, 'did Giles ever come back from wherever he went? We've no reason to suppose he ever came back and none really to think he didn't. Come to that, where did he go?'

'To the shops? To visit a friend?'

'Those Lynn questioned say they didn't see him the entire weekend. Scott Holloway tried to speak to him on the phone but failed. He may or may not have gone round there, he says not and it's not much use saying I don't believe him. And where was Sophie?'

'In the house all the time with Joanna, surely?'

'Maybe. But we don't know that. All we can be sure of is that Joanna, Sophie and Giles left the house or were taken from it some time on Saturday night.'

Burden said carefully, 'There's a strong possibility someone else came to the house on Saturday after the rain began. Just because no one saw him it doesn't mean he didn't come. It's even possible Giles brought this person back with him.'

'Scott? If Giles had called on the Holloways and taken Scott back to his house, Mrs Holloway would know. No, if Scott went there he went alone and, I think, much later.'

'So you're saying', said Burden, 'this is someone we haven't included in our enquiries.'

'That's right. Because he or she has left the country. We know, for instance, that Giles's and Sophie's passports are here and Joanna's is here, but we know nothing about anyone else's. And it's not much use to us if we don't know who this person is. Was Joanna killed at Antrim and killed by this person? Did it take place in the hall and was it caused by her falling or being thrown downstairs? As far as we know she never left Antrim until Saturday night and when she did leave Giles and Sophie were with her. Was this caller driving her car? It must have been someone they or one of them knew, that they invited in.'

'As we know, the neighbours saw no one,' said Burden, 'after Mrs Fowler saw Giles leave the house. But I'm inclined to think there was a visitor to the house that night and that he came by prior arrangement. Or it could have been a chance visit.'

Wexford's Flying Fleshpots and Burden's Butterflies and Flowers arrived, the former indistinguishable from lemon chicken, the latter prawns, bamboo shoots, carrots and pineapple fancifully arranged. A large bowl of prettily coloured rice accompanied these dishes. At the next table a very affectionate couple, who contrived to link his right hand and her left while manipulating chopsticks with the other, were both eating Dragon's Eggs.

Burden pursued his theory. 'He'd want to get her body away. We'll say he had some sort of grudge to settle. We've heard about Joanna beating up Ludovic Brown while they were still at school and there may have been other instances of the same thing. She did coach children for their GCSEs. Suppose she attacked one of them and the child's father wanted revenge.'

'Then he'd have gone to her home, wouldn't he?' Wexford objected. 'Not to the Dades.'

'He may have enquired of the neighbours, Yvonne Moody, say, as to where Joanna was. No, he couldn't have. She was away at her mother's. Perhaps he followed Joanna or his child told him she might be at the Dades.'

'I don't know.' Wexford was dubious. 'The logistics are a bit funny. Your X finds out where Joanna is, though how is a moot point, and he goes up to Antrim on Saturday evening. He knows he's got the right place because her car is outside. He rings the bell and someone lets him in.'

'Joanna might not have done if she recognised him as antagonistic to her,' Burden put in quickly, 'but Giles or Sophie would have.'

'Right. Presumably he makes a row. I mean, you're not saying he sits down and has a cup of tea with them and watches telly, are you? No, he makes a row and blusters but he can't do much in front of the kids. So he somehow gets Joanna out into the hall – this is the sticky bit, Mike – and he gets her there alone. Twirling his moustaches, our villain hisses something like, "I'm going to get you for this, my proud beauty" and whacks her round the head. She screams, falls over and hits her head on the side of the clothes cupboard. Giles and Sophie come running out. "What have you done?" They find that Joanna is dead. The body must be removed and hidden. So X persuades the kids to go off with him in Joanna's car? It must have been persuasion, not force. They weren't babies, they were fifteen and thirteen. The boy will be quite strong. Remember how tall he is. They could easily have resisted. But they don't, they agree to go. They make their beds, they put Joanna's clothes into her case, but they don't take a change of clothes for themselves. Why do they go? In case they might be blamed along with X? I don't much like this part, do you?'

'I don't like it but I can't think of anything better.' Burden drank some water. 'How did X get to the Dades' house? It must have been on foot, maybe part of the way by public transport. If he or she came in their car that car would still have been there on the Monday. And they didn't leave in it, they left in Joanna's. Did he leave fingerprints? Maybe they were among the unidentifiable prints left about the house, many of them smudged by Mrs Bruce's fanatical dusting. Then there's the T-shirt with Sophie's face on it. Did X tell Sophie to bring the T-shirt so that he could drop it out of the window at the Kingsbrook Bridge as a red herring? That presupposes an intimate knowledge of the Dade family on his part.'

'It doesn't if he simply asked the children to bring something by which one of them could be immediately identified. But still . . . I don't know, Mike, there are so many holes in it and so many questions left un-answered.' Wexford looked at his watch. 'It's time I paid my visit to the Dades,' he said with a sigh.

'I'll come with you.'

It was more than two months since Joanna and the children had disappeared and in that time Wexford had made a point of calling on the Dades two or three times a week. Not to enlighten them, not to bring them news, but to show them they had his support. That their children weren't forgotten. Not that his calls were more warmly received now than at the beginning. Rather the reverse, for Katrina was more disturbed, terror-ridden and haunted than ever. Wexford thought that by the end of the first week she must have cried all the tears out of her but those weeping tanks behind her eyes still overflowed. Sometimes she was speechless, her face buried, throughout his visit, while her husband was either awesomely rude or else ignored him altogether. Strangely, though, he was out at work less often than when the children first went missing. He seemed to make a point of being at home when Wexford arrived, perhaps only to see how far he could go before the Chief Inspector rebelled and stopped coming. Wexford was determined this wouldn't happen. Until the children were found or the case was closed he would continue to pay his visits, however these parents chose to treat him.

The rain had stopped. It was cold and misty but already it was noticeable that the dusk came a little later and in spite of the wet, something in the air hinted at the dreadful sterility of winter left behind. The front door of Antrim was opened by Mrs Bruce. Never more than a week seemed to go by but she was back staying with her daughter, with or without her husband. The horror of his visits was lessened when she was there, simply because she behaved like a civilised human being, greeted them, offered them tea and even thanked them for coming. And she was old enough to say 'Good afternoon', instead of the habitual 'Hiya' or 'Hi, there', with which most householders met them.

Unfortunately, Dade was at home. He took no notice of Wexford beyond favouring him with a hard stare before returning to his paperwork, apparently a sheaf of estate agent's specifications. Katrina was in an armchair, sitting the way children sometimes do, her head and body facing into its back, her legs curled up under her. For a moment Wexford thought he was to be ostracised by both of them, left in silence but for Doreen Bruce's polite chatter. Burden, who came more rarely, stood looking incredulous. But then Katrina slowly turned round, her legs still up on the chair seat, and clasped her arms round her knees. In these two months she had got even thinner, her face gaunt, her elbows sharply pointed.

'Well?' she said.

'I'm afraid I've no news for you, Mrs Dade.'

In a crazy sing-song voice she intoned, 'If their bodies, their bodies, could be found, could be found, I'd have something, something, something, I'd have corpses to bury.'

'Oh, shut up,' said Dade.

'I'd have a stone to write their names on, their names on, their names on . . .' It was reminiscent of Ophelia and her mad dirge. 'I'd have a grave to put flowers on, flowers on . . .'

Dade got up and stood over her. 'Stop that. You're putting it on. You're acting. You think you're very clever.'

She began to sway from side to side, her eyes shut, tears trickling from between the half-closed lids. Doreen Bruce caught Wexford's glance and cast up her eyes. Wexford thought Dade was going to hit his wife and then he knew he wasn't, it was Sylvia's experience gone to his head. Dade's violence was all in his tongue. As Jennings had said Joanna Troy's was in hers. Mrs Bruce said, 'Would you like a cup of tea?'

She went away to make it. Dade began to walk about the room, stopping to look out of the window, giving a meaningless shrug. Katrina folded herself up, her head down on her knees, the tears gushing now and, because of her hunched and twisted position, running down her bare legs. Wexford could think of absolutely nothing to say. It seemed to him that he had extracted from these parents every detail of their children's lives that they were prepared to tell him. The rest he must deduce, they wouldn't help him.

The silence was the heaviest and the longest enduring he had known in that house. Katrina lay back with her eyes closed as if asleep, Dade had removed the cap from a ballpoint and was making notes on his property specification, Burden sat contemplating his own knees in immaculate grey broadcloth. Wexford tried to reconstruct what Roger Dade's own childhood might have been, using hints the man had dropped as to having been too much indulged when young. No doubt Matilda Carrish had allowed him and his sister the almost total freedom that was coming into fashion for children, free expression, liberty to do anything they liked without correction. And he had hated it. Perhaps he had disliked the unpopularity which resulted from the rudeness and ill manners it encouraged. If so, he hadn't done much to eradicate that aspect of things in his own character, only apparently determined that his own children should receive the reverse of this treatment, an old-fashioned severity and discipline. The result had been that one of them disliked him, the other feared him, which seemed to be constituent parts of the attitude he had to his own mother . . .

Mrs Bruce was taking a long time . . . His thoughts wandered to Callum Chapman. The man had over-balanced and fallen down the stairs. Not on account of his clumsiness or loss of control but simply due to that space at the top of the staircase being too narrow for safety. That's what happened here, he thought. Joanna fell down the stairs. Or someone pushed her. X pushed her. She would no more have died than Chapman had if she hadn't struck her head on the side of that clothes cabinet. There was a little blood and a dislodged tooth crown . . .

Katrina's mother came back, bearing a tray with a teapot on it and a large home-made simnel cake, marzi-panned and browned under a grill. It was years since he'd seen a simnel cake and it was irresistible. A look from Burden and a minuscule shake of the head he chose to ignore and allowed Mrs Bruce to lay a big slice on his plate. It was so delicious and its sweetness so comforting that Dade's glance of disgust passed over him and left him unscathed. Mrs Bruce made conversation about the weather, the nights drawing out, her husband's heart and the tedious journey here from Suffolk, while Burden replied to her in polite monosyllables. Wexford ate his slice of cake with huge enjoyment and saw to his surprise that Dade was doing the same thing. He thought about Joanna and the staircase. Did X push her down it or did she stumble and fall in the dark?

Perhaps neither. Perhaps X chased her along the passage at the end of which was Sophie's room, chased her and she fell down the stairs because she couldn't avoid them. And when was it? On the Saturday afternoon? No, later. In the evening? It must have been dark and maybe there were no lights on upstairs. But if she had been upstairs in the late evening or night and X with her, that must mean X was a lover . . .

Dade interrupted this reverie. He had finished his cake, shaken the crumbs off his lap on to the floor and turned to Wexford. 'Time you left. You're not doing any good here. Goodbye.'

Both officers got up, Wexford seriously wondering, in spite of his resolve, how much more of this he could stand. 'I will see you in a day or two, Mrs Dade,' he said.

It was Ken Winter's wife who admitted him to the house. Her first name was Priscilla, as he knew from the voters' list. Never having seen her before, he had expected an older and even dowdier version of Thekla Wright. Priscilla Winter was dowdy enough but the shabbiness of her clothes, the old slippers she wore and her rough red hands were not what was first noticeable about her. Wexford was struck, almost shocked, by her bent shoulders, the result possibly of repeatedly hunching them in a vain gesture of protecting face and chest, her withered look, the way her eyes peered fearfully at him.

Her husband wasn't yet home. Recognising him, she said this before he had uttered a word.

'It's your daughter I'd like to see, Mrs Winter.'

'My daughter?' To be the mother of a fifteen-year-old, she was very likely no more than in her late forties. Her wispy grey hair, uncut for years by the look of it, hung about her shoulders. No doubt the Good Gospellers banned hairdressers. 'You want Dorcas?'

The girl was good-looking, though there was something of her father in her oval face and regular features.
Her darkish hair was very long, tied back with a brown
ribbon, but to Wexford's surprise, the brown and gold
school uniform had been changed for the universal
teenagers' wear of jeans and sweatshirt. Dorcas looked
surprised that a grown-up had been asking for her.

'No paper round this evening?' Wexford said.

'I was late back from school. Dad's got one of the
boys on it or he's doing it himself.'

Priscilla Winter said, as if an attack had been intended
on her husband, 'It's not a big round.' She recited its
route like a child saying its tables. 'Chesham and this
road and Caversham and Martindale and Kingston to
the corner of Lyndhurst.'

She shuffled across the floor to open a door for
them. Dorcas could have done that but she left it to her
mother and, pushing past her, led Wexford into a sitting room. If not the most important person in the
household, she plainly ran her father a close second –
even though she was a girl. That spoke of a weakness in
Winter's religious principles in the face of paternal love.
There was television in this room, for the girl's benefit,
Wexford thought, but no books, no flowers, no house-
plants, no cushions or ornaments. Heavy curtains of a
nondescript colour shut out night and rain. The only
picture was a pale landscape, innocent of trees, animals, human figures or clouds in its sky. The room
reminded him of the lounge a third-rate hotel provides
for its guests when they complain of nowhere to sit but
their bedrooms.

Mrs Winter said timidly, as one making a daring
suggestion, 'Would you like a cup of tea?'

He had wondered if tea was included among banned
stimulants, but apparently not. 'I shan't be stopping

more than a minute or two,' he said, remembering the glories of the simnel cake, 'but thank you.'

'You will have heard about the missing young people,' he said to Dorcas. 'Giles and Sophie Dade. I've been wondering how well you knew them and what you can tell me about them. They're fairly near neighbours.'

'I don't know them. Well, I know what they look like but not to speak to.'

'You go to the same school and you and Giles are the same age.'

'I know,' the girl said. 'But we're in different forms at school. He's in the A form.'

'Where *you* should be,' said her mother. 'I'm sure you're clever enough.'

Dorcas cast her a glance of contempt. 'I really don't know them.'

Wexford had to accept it. 'And I don't suppose you've ever had private coaching from Miss Joanna Troy?'

'She doesn't need that,' said Priscilla Winter. 'I told you, she's clever. The only private teaching she has is her violin lesson. That reminds me, Dorcas, have you done your practice for your lesson tomorrow night?'

It seemed strange to him that Dorcas didn't know the Dades but he couldn't see why she should lie. He thanked her and said goodnight to Mrs Winter. The damp, dark night received him but he hadn't far to go. On the way home he met no one and no one passed him. He let himself into his own house, warm and well-lit and with a comforting smell of dinner in the air, and almost tripped over the evening paper which lay on the mat, damp and sodden at the edges as it always was these days.

CHAPTER 20

Sylvia remarked apropos of nothing that she thought of going home next day. Neil had promised to fetch her and the boys and take them home to the Old Rectory. The light in Dora's eyes was unmistakeable. Wexford could tell, as if he had read her mind like a book, that she was thinking there might be a reconciliation there, Sylvia and Neil reunite, remarry, live together as they once had, but this time it would be second time lucky and happiness ever after. Had she forgotten that Neil had at last found himself a new girlfriend? After Sylvia had gone to bed he said gently, 'It won't happen, you know, and if it did it would be a bad thing.'

'Would it, Reg?'

'When they got married it was sex and when that went there was nothing. It can't be revived, it's too late. But one day she will find someone to be happy with, you'll see.'

Brave words, but he was less sure himself. In the morning he said goodbye to his daughter and kissed her, and all was well again. More or less. He was sitting in his office, thinking more about her than the Dade case when the phone rang.

'Hello. Wexford.'

'I have Detective Superintendent Watts, of Gloucestershire Police for you, sir.'

'Right. Put him on.' Gloucestershire? No connection with the county came immediately to mind. Maybe another mistaken sighting of the Dade children. They still came in.

A voice with a pleasant burr said, 'Brian Watts here. I've got a piece of news for you. We've a young girl who says she's Sophie Dade at the station here . . .'

'You have?' A surge of excitement, then reason returned. 'We've had dozens of kids saying they're the Dades and dozens of people who've seen them.'

'No, this one is her all right. I'm as sure as can be. She got hold of the emergency services on a nine-nine-nine call at six this morning. Asked for an ambulance for her grandma. She reckoned the old lady had had a stroke and she was right. Pretty good for a thirteen-year-old, wouldn't you say? Anyway, she's here.'

'Any sign of the boy?'

'You're greedy, you are. No, it's just the girl and she won't say where she's been or how long she'd been with this Mrs Carrish. She's not said a word about her brother. Have you got someone who could come up here and fetch her home?'

'Sure. Yes, thanks. Thanks a lot.'

'You sound gobsmacked.'

'Yes, well, I am. That's exactly what I am. Has Roger Dade been told about his mother?'

'She's in hospital in Oxford. The hospital will have informed next of kin.'

'So he'll know *a* young girl was with her when she had her attack?'

'Maybe. Not necessarily.'

To say something to Roger and Katrina Dade? Better not, he thought. Not yet. The hospital wouldn't be interested in telling him who called them beyond saying it was a young girl.

It might not be Sophie. In spite of what his caller had said, there was more than a strong possibility it wasn't. The difficulty was that the rules said he couldn't question her without one of her parents or a responsible adult present. Waiting for Karen Malahyde and Lynn Fancourt to come back with the girl, he asked himself if he would recognise her. He got out her photograph and looked – really for the first time – at her face. The previous time he had seen it he had noted in passing that she was pretty and had elements of her mother in her expression, but not then having seen Matilda Carrish, hadn't observed the resemblance. By the time she was thirty this girl would also have hawk-like features, a Roman nose, thin lips. Her eyes were curiously large, their colour dark but otherwise unidentifiable, the fierce light of intelligence gleaming in their depths.

What was she doing in Matilda Carrish's house? Even more to the point, how long had she been there? She must be very cool and collected for one who was after all still a child. He imagined her awakened in the night, in the deep dark of a February morning, by the sound of a crash, made by her grandmother falling to the floor. Most people of her age, surely, would have run crying to a neighbour. She had phoned the emergency services. Once she knew they were coming and her grandmother would be looked after, had she contemplated running away again but decided it would be useless, that she hadn't a hope? Where would she go? Perhaps, too, though he hadn't suspected it, she loved her grandmother too much to leave her.

He ate lunch in the canteen, watched the rain falling. Karen phoned to say they were on their way back with the girl. He looked at the clock on the wall, looked at his watch, decided it would be wrong to put it off any longer and dialled the Dades' number. Mrs Bruce answered.

'Mr Dade or your daughter?'

'Katrina's asleep, dear, and Roger's gone to Oxford to visit his mother in hospital. She's had a stroke. He heard this morning.'

Wexford was at a loss, but he made a decision. 'There was a child with her when she was taken ill. It seems likely it's Sophie.'

The astonished silence and then the gasp told him no one in the Dade household had been alerted.

'Will you ask Mrs Dade to phone me when she wakes up?'

Doubts began as he put the phone down. Suppose it wasn't Sophie? He would have told Katrina Dade her daughter was coming home when it wasn't her daughter and he could just imagine Roger Dade's reaction to that when he found out, the enormous fuss he would make to the Chief Constable. Wexford went down in the lift. He wanted to be there when the two women officers came back with the girl. As the crow flew, or any other bird come to that, it wasn't all that far to Oxford, but in the current state of traffic it took a long time. And it was always worse when it was raining, which meant that these days it always was worse. Three o'clock, ten past. The swing doors opened and Burden came in, back from wherever he had been.

'D'you think it's her?'

'Don't know. I've told the mother it is. Who else would it be with Matilda Carrish at that hour of the morning?'

'She may have someone living in to look after her.'

'Sure,' Wexford said drily, forgetting that he too had doubted the girl's identity. 'Nothing more likely than that this someone is a thirteen-year-old paranoid schizophrenic who tells people she's her employer's granddaughter.'

The car came on to the forecourt, sending up a cloud of spray. Lynn was driving. He saw the girl get out, then Karen, Lynn last. It was still raining and they hurried in. He knew at once, there was no doubt. She wore the brown anorak missing from her home and shrugged herself out of it once she was inside the swing doors.

'Well, Sophie,' he said. 'We'll need to talk to you but not now. First you have to go home to your parents.'

She looked straight at him. Few people had eyes like hers, almond-shaped, slightly tilted, exceptionally large, as near dark- green as human eyes ever get. She was less pretty than in her photograph but more intelligent-looking, more formidable. The camera loved her; reality did not. 'I don't want to go home,' she said.

'I'm afraid you must,' Wexford said. 'You are thirteen years old and at thirteen you don't have a choice.'

'Karen says my father is at the hospital with Matilda.'

'That's right.'

'I'll go, then. At least *he* won't be there.'

She allowed herself to be helped back into her jacket and led back to the car by Lynn. 'A bit of a little madam, sir,' said Karen.

'You could say that. Will you tell Mrs Dade I shall want to talk to Sophie later? We'll say six o'clock. And one of them must be with her. If Mrs Dade isn't up to it Mr or Mrs Bruce will do.'

Now he was anxious to do everything by the book. First, he phoned Antrim again and this time spoke to a hysterical incoherent Katrina, managing at last to understand that she had phoned her husband on his mobile, or rather, her mother had, and told him. Wexford decided it would nevertheless be wise for him to do the same. Not having the mobile number and scarcely trusting Katrina to give it to him, he phoned the hospital where Matilda Carrish was and eventually was able to leave a message for Dade with someone who barely spoke English.

The temptation now was to indulge in speculation. How long had she been with Mrs Carrish? All the time or only part of it? Why had Matilda deceived them? And where, now, was Giles? Whatever he guessed would very likely be wrong. Imaginary solutions usually were. He must wait.

The rain had ceased and it had grown very cold, perhaps colder than it had been all winter. A sharp wind dried the pavements. In February it wasn't quite dark by five forty-five but the greyish-red sun was down and dusk had begun. The sky was dark-blue and jewel-bright, as yet starless. Karen drove him up to Lyndhurst Drive and, to his surprise, it was Dade who opened the door. He was considerably chastened and so forgot to be rude.

'There was no point staying up there. She's uncon-scious. It's my belief she won't survive this.'

A lay person's opinion is never of much value in these matters but Wexford said he was sorry to hear that and they went inside. 'I can't get a word out of my daughter,' Dade said, 'but that's par for the course. I never can.'

Wexford thought that boded better for him and Karen. They went into the living room where he had spent so much time in the past weeks. Katrina was there, looking madder than he had ever seen her. 'Like one of the witches from *Macbeth*,' whispered Karen, who wasn't usually given to a literary turn of phrase, and Wexford, normally only exasperated by Sophie's mother, felt a serious concern for this woman whose hair looked as if she had been tearing it out and whose mouth hung open as if she had seen and was seeing some dreadful vision. He said nothing to her because he didn't know what to say.

'You want someone with her when you question her, right?'

'I'm obliged to, Mr Dade. You or –' no, obviously not '– or one of your parents-in-law.'

'She won't talk at all if I'm there,' Dade said bitterly. He went back to the open door and called out in the sharp harsh voice all too familiar to Wexford, for it had been directed often enough at him, 'Doreen! Come here, will you?'

Doreen Bruce came in and went up to her daughter, giving her her arm. 'Now, dear, the best place for you is your bed. It's all been too much.'

Once more they waited. There was no sign of Sophie. Was Doreen Bruce putting Katrina to bed? Dade sat down in an armchair, or rather, lay down, his arms spread out over its arms, his legs apart, his head thrown back in the characteristic attitude of anguish. Wexford wondered what he had expected to see in this house. Relief and joy and sweetness and light? Something like that. He could no more tell how people would react in an extreme situation than he could predict the answers to the questions he would ask Sophie. If she ever came. At that thought, her grandmother brought her into the room. She looked at her recumbent father and immediately turned away her head, twisting her neck as far round as she could, as ostentatiously as she could.

'Where shall I sit?'

That was too much for Roger Dade and he bounced upright. 'Oh, for God's sake,' he yelled at her. 'You're not at the bloody dentist's.' He left the room and banged the door.

'You sit here, Sophie,' said Mrs Bruce, 'and I'll sit in this chair.'

Wexford noticed that the girl had changed her clothes since she got home. Under the anorak she had been wearing a pair of trousers that were a little, but not much, too large for her and a sweater that was wrong in some indefinable way for a girl of her age. He realised now that those must have been Matilda's clothes. She had taken nothing with her when she left except those, as people rather oddly put it, she stood up in. Now she was dressed in her own jeans and a T-shirt, unsuitable for anyone on such a cold evening, especially in a house where the central heating was inefficient. She didn't seem affected by it. Those disconcerting eyes gazed at him.

'You will have realised, Sophie, that I want to talk to you about what happened here the weekend of twenty-sixth of November?'

'Of course I have.'

'You're prepared for that?'

She nodded. 'I'm not hiding anything. I'll tell you all of it.'

'Good. You remember that weekend?'

'Of course I do.'

'Joanna Troy came here to look after you and your brother. She came on the Friday, is that right? Would I be correct in saying she arrived at about five?' A nod. 'What did you do that evening?'

'I had homework,' she said. 'I went to my bedroom and did my homework. My father's conditioned me to homework. I'm like one of that Russian guy's dogs. Come six and I'm doing my homework.' She sniffed. 'My mother phoned from Paris. I didn't speak to her, Giles did. He was downstairs with Joanna, watching TV, I guess. Joanna made us supper. Baked beans, it was. Baked beans and toast and bacon.' She made a face. 'It was skanky.'

Karen translated. 'That means "nasty", sir.'

Sophie looked incredulous, presumably because he hadn't understood what the whole world must understand. 'The bacon was skanky, it was soft. After that we watched some shit on TV. Joanna told us to go to bed when it got to ten. I didn't argue and Giles didn't.'

Karen said, 'Did you like Joanna, Sophie?'

As if three times her age, she said, 'Is that relevant?'

'We would like to know.'

'All right. I'm not my father, you know. I mean, rude and nasty to everyone. I'm mostly quite polite. No, I didn't much like Joanna and Giles didn't. He did for a bit and then he went off her. Not that that made any difference, we still had to have her here.'

'And next day?' Wexford asked.

'We got up. We had breakfast. It wasn't raining then. Joanna wanted to go to the Asda – you know, out on the bypass – and we went with her. Wicked way to spend a Saturday, wasn't it? She bought a lot of food and she bought wine, though there was plenty in the house. We all had lunch at the Three Towns Café in the High Street and she said she'd got a friend coming over for supper, that was why she'd bought the food.'

Wexford sat up straighter. 'A friend? What kind of friend?'

'A man.'

She was either a very good liar or all this was true. And it meant he had been right. She continued to look at him with that steady gaze and now she took hold of a lock of her long brown hair and twisted it into a spiral in her fingers. 'We went home and Giles went out. I don't know where so don't ask.'

'When did he come back?'

'I don't know. I was upstairs doing more homework, the stuff my tutor set me. When I came down Giles was there and Joanna was getting supper. Me and him, we just went cotch, he watched TV and I surfed the Net. Maybe it was six by then. Is this what you want?'

Karen nodded. 'Exactly what we want. "Going cotch" means relaxing, sir.'

'Considering what she'd given us, supper was going to be wicked,' said Sophie. 'Three courses. Avocados and grapefruit in something she called a coulis, some dumb-ass fish – I hate fish – and some sort of fruit tart with cream.'

'Did the friend come?'

A slow nod from Sophie. 'At around half-six. Peter, she called him.'

It was a common name. He must hear more before he jumped to conclusions. 'At around half-six' she had said.

'And his other name?'

'No one said. It was just Peter.'

'Had the evening paper come by then?' Wexford asked. He would ask Dorcas Winter but he wanted her version.

'I can't remember. I know it came. I suppose that girl brought it, the one that goes to our school. It was wet and we dried it on the radiator. God knows why, it's always full of shit.'

Doreen Bruce flinched but didn't interrupt.

'When we'd had the food Joanna wanted to know if Giles was going to church. "In this rain," she said. He must have told her in the morning he'd be going. He said he wouldn't because the service was on Sunday and that gamey Peter teased him a bit about church. Giles didn't like it, but he gets a lot of that. You know, "Going to be a vicar when you grow up, are you?" – that kind of crap.'

Once more Mrs Bruce drew in her breath. Probably Sophie had been more guarded in her speech when she stayed with her. Wexford said, 'What did he look like, this Peter?'

'A dumb-ass. Ordinary. Not in very good shape. Old.'

What did that mean from someone of thirteen? 'How old?' It was almost useless asking.

'I don't know. Not as old as my father.'

He left it. She hadn't given him much to go on but she hadn't eliminated the suspicion she'd raised either. 'Did Scott Holloway come?' he asked.

'Him? Yeah, I guess so. The bell rang but we never answered it.'

'Why not?'

'We just didn't.'

Perhaps that was standard practice in this house. 'Go on.'

'We had supper and watched *Jacob's Ladder* on TV. That guy Jacob got shot in a siege. Then Joanna and Peter said they were going to bed.'

She looked at Wexford, her head on one side. What he saw in her expression, in her eyes, shocked him more than if she had screamed obscenities at him. A wealth of knowledge was there, of adult experience, of a weary worldly wisdom. He wondered if he was imagining it or if he had guessed the reason, and when he looked at Karen he saw that she was thinking the same thing. There was no need to tell Sophie to continue. She needed no encouragement.

'They'd been feeling each other up, deep kissing and all that, you *know*. They didn't care about us being there. He was going to shag her, it was obvious. She didn't say anything about us going to bed, she'd forgotten us. That was when the doorbell rang.' She looked up and at him. 'I was too interested watching what they did to answer it. But when they were just kissing we did go to bed. It was about half past ten. I went to sleep. I don't know when it happened, maybe around midnight. The noise woke me, a scream and a crash, and footsteps running down the stairs. I didn't get up straight away. If you want to know the truth, I was scared, it was *scary*. I got up after a bit and went down the passage, and Giles was just standing there, outside his room. You know, it's right at the top of the stairs. He just stood there, looking down. Peter was down there, bending over Joanna, feeling her neck and her pulse and all that. He looked up and said, "She's dead."'

There was absolute silence for a moment and then that silence was shattered by the phone ringing. It rang only twice before someone in the hall picked it up. Wexford said, 'No one called the emergency services? You did that when your grandmother was taken ill but not when a woman fell downstairs. Why was that?'

'I wasn't the only one there, was I?' She had become aggressive. 'It wasn't for me to do anything. I'm only a child, like my father's always telling me. I haven't got any rights.' The same thought as he had had before came into Wexford's mind. Apparently unmoved, he shuddered inwardly. 'Peter tried to lift Joanna up but she was too heavy for him. He asked Giles to help him and they put her on the sofa. There was some blood, not much. Peter got a cloth and wiped it up and he asked me where there was a scrubbing brush. Always ask a woman, don't they?'

She was suddenly a forty-year-old feminist and her voice had grown strident. Doreen Bruce had gone quite white, her hands trembling on the arms of the chair. Karen asked her if she was all right. She nodded, the living symbol of an aghast older generation.

'I wasn't going to do it,' said Sophie. 'It was him pushed her down the stairs.'

'You didn't see that?'

'It was obvious. He said, was there any brandy? Giles got it for him and he drank it. Then he said he'd like another one but he'd better not, seeing as he was going to drive . . .'

The door opened and Roger Dade came in. Sophie stopped talking abruptly, fixed him with an insolent stare. He said, 'That was the hospital. My mother's dead. She died half an hour ago.'

Doreen was the first to speak. 'Oh, Roger, how sad. I *am* sorry.'

He took absolutely no notice of her, simply repeated, 'She died half an hour ago.' Then he turned with noisy violence on his daughter, shouting at her, 'That's your fault, you little bitch! She'd be alive now if you hadn't given her all that trouble. You've been a liar since you were born and you made her tell lies and turn against her nearest and dearest . . .'

Wexford got up. 'That's enough,' he said. 'You've had a shock, Mr Dade. You're not yourself.' He feared the man was only too much himself, but it was useless continuing now. Was the girl at risk? He thought not. Anyway, she had her grandmother, her *surviving* grandmother, for what that was worth. 'We'll go now. We'll see you tomorrow.'

Dade had calmed down into a disgruntled misery and laid himself in a chair in the attitude he had adopted earlier. Wexford thanked Sophie, told her she had been very helpful. After a fashion very unusual for him, he felt he had had about as much as he could take for one day. Mrs Bruce came up to him after the girl had gone, said apologetically, 'I don't know where they learn those words. They don't pick them up at home.'

Wexford wasn't so sure of that. He patted her on the arm. 'They all do it. It's a phase. Best ignore it, I think. Ten o'clock tomorrow morning?'

She nodded rather miserably.

Outside, the evening was colder, the sky clearer, a moon that looked as if it had been soaked in soapy water sailed above the trees. Against his face the air felt fresh and damp. He got into the car beside Karen.

'You were thinking what I was thinking, weren't you?'

'What would that be, sir?'

'That though Dade dislikes his daughter and she hates him, there has been more between them than there should have been.'

'You mean, *he's* done things *he* shouldn't have.' It was a reproof but he let it pass. 'Something has to account for her not wanting to go home while he's there. It makes me want to vomit.'

'Me too,' said Wexford.

The car turned into the street where he lived and she dropped him at his gate. He hadn't said anything about Peter. It was too soon.

CHAPTER 21

He hadn't asked the girl where her brother was. Because he knew she wouldn't tell him? Even supposing she knew herself. It was already clear to him that this Peter had driven them away in Joanna's car with Joanna's body in the boot.

'Why take the children with him?' Burden asked when they met in the morning.

'He couldn't trust them not to tell anyone what they'd seen,' Wexford said. 'But I think they went willingly. Sophie can't wait to get away from home. Her mother's crazy and I've a suspicion her father's been abusing her.'

'You're not serious.'

'It's not something I'd joke about, is it? I want a bit more to go on before I go to the Social Services. It could all be in my head.'

'How much of what she says do you believe? Is she a liar?'

Wexford thought about it. 'I don't know. In details perhaps, not in the essentials. For instance, the three of them didn't have lunch at the Three Towns Café. The staff there know the kids and no one saw them on the Saturday. The way Sophie talked about Peter at first sounded invented but when she said he and Joanna were feeling each other up . . .'

'She used those words?'

'Oh, yes, and then she said he was going to "shag" her. The obnoxious Dade says she's a liar but that's when

I knew she was telling the truth. That, too, is when I wondered if he'd been assaulting her. It's just what abusive fathers do say, that the child is a liar. And abuse is well-known to give children a precocious – well, sophistication. They have a knowledge inappropriate for their time of life, like those two in *The Turn of the Screw*.'

Burden's initiation into literature by his wife hadn't extended to Henry James. 'So you're going to see her again this morning?'

He nodded. 'Matilda Carrish died, you know. It's in the paper. Along with Sophie's reappearance, only there's no connection so far as they know. Better that way. Sad really, isn't it? If Sophie were dead it'd be the lead story, but she's alive and well, so it merits a paragraph. Matilda's obituaries will follow tomorrow, I suppose. Newspapers have them all prepared in advance of celebrities dropping off their perches. I wonder why she – well, harboured Sophie instead of doing the responsible thing.'

'Maybe Sophie told her what you suspect about her dad.'

'That would be quite something to hear about your own son. But I dare say she'd had enough shock-horror about ruthless Roger to take it in her stride.'

'I don't know if you've noticed,' said Burden, 'but those missing children posters are all over the place this morning. More than ever. No one's told Search and Find Limited that Sophie's turned up.'

'They'll know by now. Of course, there's no one *to* tell them now Matilda Carrish is dead.'

'Unless she's given them some payment in advance,' Burden said, 'they'll call their dogs off. They'd be daft to expect to recover what they're owed from Roger. Some hopes.'

When Wexford and Karen got to Antrim only Mr and Mrs Bruce and Sophie appeared to be at home. No

explanation for the absence of Roger and Katrina
Dade was offered and Wexford didn't ask. He didn't
want to know. The first question he put to Sophie was
unexpected. She had obviously hoped to be allowed to
proceed with the departure of the three of them from
the house, and for a moment she looked disconcerted.

'Where is Giles now?'

She shook her head slowly. 'I don't know. I *really*
don't know. I'm trying to be helpful but I can't be
because I just don't know.'

'Because your grandmother didn't tell you?'

'I asked. Matilda said it was better for me not to
know so that if anyone asked me like you're asking now
I wouldn't have to lie, I just wouldn't know.'

It made sense. Matilda Carrish had sent Giles somewhere to be safe. . . . But safe from what? And why had
she done it? Why had she done any of it? Why receive
the children in the first place? Now was the time to test
Sophie's truth-telling. 'Where were we? Ah, yes, you
heard a noise and a scream and came running out of
your room . . .'

'We'd got past that.'

'Maybe. I'd like to hear it again, though.'

She caught on where many three times her age
hadn't seen through his ruse. She knew quite well
what he was doing. 'Giles came out of his bedroom.
It's right at the top of the stairs. Peter was down in the
hall feeling Joanna's neck and her pulse. He looked up
at us and said, "She's dead." After a bit he tried to lift
her up but he couldn't and he had to get Giles to help
him. They put her on the sofa. Peter got a cloth and
wiped up the blood, there wasn't much, but he said he
needed a scrubbing brush and water. I told him where
it was and he fetched the brush. But before he started
on it he said he needed brandy and Giles gave him

some but he wouldn't have another because he was going to drive.'

'All right, Sophie, that's fine.' He wasn't imagining it, she looked triumphant.

'He scrubbed the carpet,' she said, 'and wiped the side of the cupboard and then he said we must pack up her stuff to take with us.'

'Take with you where?' Karen asked.

'He didn't say. He just said we had to get Joanna's body out of there. OK, I know what you're thinking – why didn't I just say no? I don't know why. I don't know why Giles didn't. I suppose we thought we'd helped him clear up and I'd packed Joanna's case and Giles had helped lift her, he helped carry her out to the car as well. We were sort of involved, you see. Look, I thought if we stayed I'd have to tell my father, I could imagine the questioning, all his shit, you don't know how he goes ballsing on. We'd get blamed, I knew that.

'It was pouring with rain; they got soaked out there. I put on my old anorak because Peter said the yellow one would attract attention, though there wasn't any attention, it was one in the morning and raining like the end of the world was coming . . .'

Karen interrupted. 'What were they wearing, Joanna and Peter? When she went down the stairs, however it was?'

'She had just a T-shirt on, a long one that sort of came to her knees. He was in pants, you know, underpants. Nothing else. But after he'd cleaned up in the hall he put on the clothes he'd been wearing, jeans and a shirt and a sweatshirt. We all went upstairs and Giles and me, we got dressed and we made our beds, we made them look the way they do when the cleaner does them.' She laughed. 'You can if you try. Then we shut all the bedroom doors. No, before that Peter said to take something with us to make it look as if we'd drowned. He said there'd be flooding and the river would – what do they call it? Burst its banks.'

'He said *that*?' Almost for the first time she had said something Wexford simply couldn't believe. The man was a prophet? That was before any of the floods began.

'Why not?' She sounded aggressively like her father. 'It was on the news at ten. There were flood warnings out all over the south.'

'All right. What did you take with you?'

'A T-shirt with my face on it and my name. It was cool but it got too tight. We had one done for me and one for Giles when we were in Florida.'

'So you left the house – at what time?'

'It was about two by then. He had to put the wind-screen wipers on at double speed or he wouldn't have been able to see, it was raining so hard . . .'

'Wait a minute,' said Karen. 'This was Joanna's car, right? What about his car? He arrived in the evening by car, didn't he?'

Sophie hadn't thought of that or she genuinely didn't know? Hard to tell. 'He never said. Maybe he didn't come in a car, he could have walked, or else he left his car out in the street.'

'Unless he came back for it on the Sunday – a risky thing to do – it would still be there if he had.'

'Well, I don't know. You can't expect me to know everything.' Wexford thought she was going to repeat that she was only a child but she didn't. 'The river *was* rising. You could still get over the Kingsbrook Bridge but it looked as if you soon wouldn't. Peter said to drop the T-shirt over the wall – what d'you call it? The parapet – and I did. Did anyone ever find it?'

'Oh, yes, it was found.'

'I want it back. It was groovy. Did they think we'd drowned?'

'Some did.'

'I bet my mother did. She's poop, you know. Two tracks short of a CD, Giles says. Or he did when he was skill. Before he got all Christian and good. D'you want to know what happened next?'

'Yes, please.'

'I hadn't a clue where we were going. I thought it didn't matter. I just thought Peter would look after us. He seemed sort of quite kind and friendly. I did notice when we went across the county boundary. There was a sign by the road said "Welcome to Kent".

'I was quite interested by then in where we were going. Peter knew. He wasn't just driving somewhere, anywhere. We left the main road and came to a village and there was another sign saying it was a place called Passingham St John.' Sophie pronounced it as it was spelt. 'Peter said that was wrong,' she said, 'it should be Passam Sinjen. You could tell he knew it well.

'He drove down a track – well, more a sort of lane. About halfway down was a track leading into a wood. It was quite wet and manky, and I thought the car might get stuck but it didn't. There was a big open space and on the other side of that was this quarry. All in among the trees. Peter stopped there. He said we were going to sit there for an hour because it was still only about three and once we'd got rid of the car we wouldn't have any shelter. It was still raining but not as much as it had been at home. I think I fell asleep for a bit. I don't know if Giles did. When I woke up it was still raining but not as much.

'Peter got Giles to help him carry Joanna into the driving seat. I sat in the back while this was going on, but he made me get out to help push. We all pushed as hard as we could till the car went over the edge. It didn't turn over, it just slid and bounced a bit and came to a stop when it got caught in bushes. You could still see it all right but only if you really looked.'

'All right,' he said. 'We'll break for ten minutes.'

'You could tell he knew it well,' she had said. He had driven there in the dark, in the rain, apparently without difficulty. He was called Peter . . . Yet Buxton had seemed such a fool. If all this were true – and how could it not be? – he must be a consummate actor.

They went back into the room and Mrs Bruce came in with Sophie. She brought three cups of tea on a tray and a glass of Coke. Her granddaughter looked at it and said, 'Real people drink it out of the can.'

'Just for once then, you'll have to be an unreal person, dear.'

Karen began the questioning. 'You and Giles and Peter were in the wood at – what? Four o'clock in the morning? – with no car and no future plan. Is that right?'

The girl nodded. She made a face over her Coke.

'There's a house at the bottom of the lane. Did you go to the house?'

'I didn't see any house. I didn't know there was one. We went to the station.'

Like some commuter on a routine journey to the office . . . 'What station?'

'I don't know. Passingham something. Passingham Park. There's not a park there. It means people can park their cars but there weren't any there. It was too early.'

'How did you get to Passingham Park?' Wexford asked.

'We walked. I suppose we had to. It was a long walk along a lot of lanes but Peter knew the way. They were just opening the station when we got there. We were very wet, soaked through. Then that dumb-ass Peter said he was leaving us, we were to stay away for a week and then we could go back home and say what we liked, he'd be out of the country by then. He wrote down an address and gave it to Giles and said we could stay there. The first train would be along a bit after five. We went into the station and he bought tickets for us. Out of the machine. We had to go over the bridge but he didn't come with us. He gave Giles some money and said goodbye and good luck or something like that. We waited on the platform and the train came along at around five fifteen.'

'That would be the Kingsmarkham–Toxborough–Victoria main line?' Karen said.

'I suppose. It did go to Victoria because that's where we got out. We were still thinking then that we'd go to the address Peter had given us but Giles said, no, we'll go to Matilda. It was a bit past six, too early to phone her, but we had to get across London to Paddington Station and we got into a muddle about that. We haven't been in the London tube much and when we changed from the first line we got into a train going the wrong way, so it was nearly seven when we got to Paddington. Giles had some money of his own and the money Peter had given him. The cafeteria was open and we bought rolls and cheese and bananas and ate them, and we had two cans of Sprite and then Giles went to find a phone box. He's got a wix phone but he'd left it at home.'

'A mobile,' said Karen.

'Matilda said to come straight away, she'd come to Kingham station and meet us. Kingham's the nearest station to where she lives. We bought two tickets to Kingham and got a train at seven thirty . . .'

'Wait a minute,' said Karen. 'Your grandmother just said to come straight away? Giles had presumably told her you'd left home and gave her some reason for that and she didn't want to know any more, she didn't question any of this, she just said to come? I don't believe you, Sophie.'

'I can't help that. That was what happened. She didn't like my parents, you know. She couldn't stand Mum.'

'Even so . . . Let it go for now. You went by train to Kingham, your grandmother met you there and you stayed at her house with her. No one thought of phoning your parents to say you were safe? Peter only told you to stay away for a week. Why didn't you go home after a week?'

She shrugged. 'I don't know. I hate it here and I liked it with Matilda. Matilda was deep . . .'

'Deep?' Wexford looked helplessly at Karen and Karen said, 'I think it just means "cool", sir.'

Sophie made a disgusted face. 'Giles had gone, anyway. He went away next day. I didn't want to be at home alone with *them*.'

'Giles went away?' Wexford said. 'Where did he go? Why did he?'

'Matilda said he ought to go. They didn't talk about it in front of me, so I don't know what she said or why. I told you. If I didn't know I couldn't tell, could I?'

'The police came – where were you then?'

She smiled, then laughed. 'The first time I just went up into one of the bedrooms. Matilda said they wouldn't search for us, not in the home of an old woman and a celebrity, she said. Then, when *you* came, I hid in the cupboard in the room where you were talking. I thought how manky it would be if I sneezed.'

'And all this', Wexford said, 'was set up by Matilda Carrish? She knew how anxious your parents were, she must have known every police force in the country was looking for you, she even came to us to complain we weren't doing enough.'

'She thought it was funny. She left me alone in the
house that day she went to London with strict instruc-
tions not to go out. I never did go out. I didn't mind, it
was raining all the time. I'd done enough walking that
night to last me my life.'

'How about these private investigators? These Search
and Find people? She took them on, she must have made
a down payment. Do you know anything about that?'

'She said it would make people think she couldn't be
to blame. It was cool, wasn't it? Really skill. She knew
they'd not search her place and they'd never find Giles,
she said.'

Wexford shook his head. Usually able to see the funny
side of almost everything (as his wife put it) he found
nothing in the least amusing here, in spite of the girl's
twitching lips and barely suppressed enjoyment of the
situation. For all that, his next words hadn't been
intended to bring her down to earth quite so violently.

'Well, she's dead now. She's beyond explaining to us.'

Sophie knew she was dead as well as anyone did, but
this reminder crushed her. She lifted a suddenly woeful
face. 'She was jammy, I loved her and she loved me.
That's more than anyone else does. Excepting Giles, she
was the only one I loved.' And she broke down in a
storm of tears.

At the beginning of this case, Wexford said to himself, I said they weren't the babes in the wood. Now I'm
not so sure.

In the afternoon they began again, but this time
Burden was with Wexford and her father with Sophie.
Wexford didn't like it and Sophie obviously loathed
him being there but there was nothing he could do.
Understandably, Doreen Bruce had had enough. But he
was sure Roger Dade's presence would make the girl clam

up. He hoped he wouldn't have to reprove him too often for interfering. Of Katrina there had been no sign all day.

As it happened, Dade hardly spoke and certainly he made no attempt to stop his daughter speaking, but sat with closed eyes in morose silence, seemingly indifferent to police questioning and Sophie's answers. Though he began by once more probing into Matilda Carrish's extraordinary willingness to take in and hide her grandchildren, Wexford's aim at this session was to discover as much as he could of Giles's possible whereabouts. He was disinclined to believe the girl when she insisted she didn't know. But he started with Matilda.

'I find it hard to believe your grandmother took you in without question. She simply agreed to take you in and lie to the police? Did she give you any explanation, tell you, for instance, why she was doing this?'

'She didn't say anything about it,' Sophie said. 'Giles told her what had happened to us and I told her. We told her in the car going back from the station. She just said she was glad we'd come to her.'

Dade opened his eyes and looked at his daughter. It was an unpleasant look but Sophie didn't flinch. Wexford persisted, 'You'd done nothing wrong.' Concealing a crime? Hiding a body? 'I'll correct that. You'd done nothing yourselves to Joanna. Why didn't she phone your parents? You'd told her about Peter. Why not phone the police and tell them what you'd told her?'

Sophie was beginning to look uncomfortable. 'She never even thought of that, I'm sure. She just wanted to look after us and see we didn't get into trouble.'

He left it. 'Your brother can't have left the country,' he said. 'His passport is here. When did he leave your grandmother's house?'

She had already told him but again he was testing her. 'It was early on the Sunday morning we got to

Matilda's. I slept a lot that day and so did Giles. We were tired, we'd been up all night. But in the evening Matilda said he ought to go first thing in the morning, she'd been making arrangements on the phone. He ought to go before our parents told the police we were missing. By the time I woke up it was all fixed. She drove him to the station. She said it was best for me not to know where he was going and then I couldn't tell anyone who asked.' She looked triumphantly at him. 'Like you,' she said.

The sheet of water that covered most of the road reminded him of the winter floods. Not again, *please*. The rain had stopped but it was obviously no more than a lull. He was putting out the recycling box on to the pavement, and thus breaking one of the local authority's rules. You weren't supposed to put the newspapers, cans and bottles out till the following morning but the rain might be torrential in the morning . . .

It was a funny thing, he thought, how you were always distracted from this task by reading whatever was on top of the pile. You wouldn't normally read it when you'd sat down with the newspaper it was in, you wouldn't dream of reading a piece about waterproof mascara or Burmese cats or the latest fifteen-year-old pop sensation, but somehow you couldn't resist it in these particular circumstances. The article that caught his eye was on a cookery page. It happened to be lying open on the top, although the date on it was a week ago. Its illustrations in full colour, it showed a starter of avocado and grapefruit in lime coulis, a monkfish confection and a *tarte tatin* with cream . . .

But wait a minute, wasn't that the menu Sophie had described as Joanna preparing for this dinner on the fateful Saturday night *three months ago*? He looked at it again, standing there in the road, under the street lamp. Coincidence? He didn't think so. More likely, it was proof of the extent to which the girl had lied. She had read that page while at her grandmother's and remembered its details when they were needed . . .

CHAPTER 22

Since he and Sharonne were detained there over Christmas, Peter Buxton had not been back to Passingham Hall. Events had given him a dislike of the place. He had even thought of selling it. But could he sell it while the discovery of a body in a car in the grounds was fresh in people's minds? He had tentatively suggested the possibility of selling to Sharonne but she had been adamant. She had been aghast, then furious.

'But we must have a country place, Pete.'

'Why must we? Sell it and we could buy a bigger house up here. Think about it. We haven't been there for two months. I don't suppose we'll go again before Easter, if then. The council tax still has to be paid, and Pauline. The house eats up fuel.'

'What am I going to say to people? That we don't have a country place? Oh, no. I should coco.' Incongruously, since she so obviously wanted to hold on to Passingham Hall, she added, 'Besides, nobody would buy it. Not since you advertised the fact there was a dead body in the grounds.'

The Warrens had invited them to their Silver Wedding party. The anniversary itself was on Valentine's Day but that happened to fall on a Wednesday that year so the party was fixed for Saturday the seventeenth. It was to be a big affair, half the county there. Sharonne was determined to go.

'Of course we're going, Pete. Why ever not?'

'You go,' Peter said daringly.

'What, and leave you here on your own?' As if he were a child or senile, as if he were likely to set the place on fire or invite other women in. 'Absolutely not. God knows what you'd get up to.'

What was that supposed to mean? What he'd get up to! Was she as pure as driven snow? That phone number was still hovering beneath the surface of his mind, he had long known it by heart. Every time he came home and found himself alone with the phone, he dialled 1471 but its records had never divulged that number again.

He would have to go to Passingham some time. It was obvious he must either go there or sell it, and Sharonne wouldn't let him sell it. Peter was beginning to think the unthinkable and wonder what exactly he got out of his marriage. He could see what he put into it – money, companionship, money, obedience, money, a continual yielding to pressure – but what did Sharonne put in? Herself, he supposed, herself. He felt most frightened and most like shying away from the whole subject when he began asking what that self amounted to. A caring – but deceitful? – bossy, clothes horse . . . Last week he had asked her about starting a family and she had reacted as if he had suggested she navigate the globe single-handed in an open boat or make her own clothes or something equally fantastic. They had never discussed it before. Naïvely, he had supposed all women wanted babies just as he had supposed they could all cook.

Of course, they went to Passingham. As they were leaving on the Friday evening the phone started ringing. After three rings it stopped and switched over to the answering service. It never crossed Peter's mind that this might be Kingsmarkham Police calling to fix a time to interview him. After all, he could check the message on Sunday night.

As they turned down the lane towards the Hall she began on the body in the car.

'They never would have found it if you hadn't phoned and told them.'

'Well, I did phone. It's too late now.'

'When all's said and done, I think we're very lucky the Warrens asked us. They must be very tolerant people to overlook a thing like that. Most people would give us the cold shoulder.'

'Don't be ridiculous,' said Peter in a rough tone. 'We didn't put that car there. We didn't put that woman in it. It was just our luck.'

'Well, *I* know that, but others don't. Others would say there was no smoke without fire and we must have had something to do with it.'

'You mean *you* would.'

It was in a state of mutual resentment that they entered the house, Peter lugging all his wife's three suitcases, one under his arm, two dragged behind him, a task she said was obviously his to perform. He reached for the light switch but the bulb was defunct and for a few moments they blundered about in the pitch dark. As Sharonne located the panel of switches in the drawing room but before the light came on, the phone began to ring. Peter felt for it, knocked the receiver off and was crawling about the floor feeling for it when light poured out from behind the half-open drawing room door. Kicking over the largest of Sharonne's suitcases in his haste, he gasped out, 'Hello?'

'I seem to have phoned at a bad time,' said a voice he recognised as belonging to Chief Inspector Wexford. 'Kingsmarkham Crime Management.'

'What do you want?' Sharonne was standing in the doorway, watching him intently. 'It is a bad time, very bad.'

'I'm sorry about that. I'm not at liberty to be tactful about these things. You'll be staying at Passingham for the weekend?'

'Why?'

'Because I'd like to talk to you tomorrow morning as a matter of urgency, Mr Buxton.'

Peter looked at Sharonne's stony face, thought with a disloyalty that amazed him, how anger reduced her to ugliness, and wondered how he could keep from her whatever it was this policeman wanted. He said a cautious, 'All right.'

'You have a car with you? I'd like you to come here. In the morning.'

The Warrens' lunch party . . . 'What time in the morning? Early preferably.'

'I was thinking of eleven.'

'Could you make it ten?' Sharonne was listening intently. 'Ten would suit me better.'

'It wouldn't suit me,' said Wexford. 'I'll see you at eleven.'

What could he say? In Sharonne's presence, he dared not ask what the police wanted this time. He thought only of the blamelessness of his life these past six weeks. Surely they hadn't found anything else on his land . . .? He dared not ask. Wexford said he would see him at eleven in the morning and rang off. Peter carried the suitcases upstairs and dumped them on the bedroom floor. The house felt damp and chill as the central heating began to cool. He went downstairs and after a good deal of grubbing about in the kitchen, dislodging stacks of heterogeneous rubbish, receipted bills, empty cardboard boxes, plastic bags, out-of-focus photographs, used matchbooks, triple A batteries, keys that locked no known doors, at last found a 100 watt light bulb in the back of a cupboard. Once he had managed with some difficulty to slot it into the socket, he went into the by now cold drawing room and poured himself a large Scotch.

'Did you take my cases upstairs?' said Sharonne. Getting a surly nod in response, she remarked that she was disappointed to see him lapsing back into his old drinking habits. 'You've been so good about it lately.'

Not all worms turn but some do. 'I haven't been good. I haven't cut down on my drinking, I've just done it when you weren't there. I'm a grown man, *Mummy*, I'm not a child. No one tells me what to do.' He picked up his whisky. 'I'm going to bed now. Goodnight.'

They had shared their bed but distantly, each one lying on an extreme edge. Peter woke up very early and got up. He couldn't lie there wondering if something else had turned up on his land, those children's bodies, for instance, or clothing or some weapon. He should have asked. But he couldn't, not with Sharonne looking at him so accusingly. So far she hadn't said a word about that telephone conversation.

It was still dark but dawn was coming. A fine precipitation, halfway between drizzle and mist, hung in the greyish air. In Barbour, rubber boots, country gentleman's tweed cap and gauntlets, he explored the wood, expecting at any moment to see blue and white crime tape showing brightly among the tree trunks. But there was nothing. The Dancing Floor lay passive within its encircling trees, a brighter green than he had ever seen it, quagmire green, bog green, in the increasing light waterdrops glittering on every blade of grass. No one could walk on it at present, still less dance. His search yielding nothing that might be construed as incriminating, he felt a little better and he returned to the house with a renewed appetite for breakfast.

He was making toast and, in some trepidation, boiling an egg, when Sharonne appeared unprecedentedly early. She had cleaned up her face before going to bed but not removed her eye make-up so that this morning she looked as if she had received a double whammy during the night. In her not very clean white dressing gown and with her hair sticking up in tufts, but not in a fashionable way, she was an unappetising sight.

'You never told me', she said, 'who that was on the phone last night.'

'The office,' he lied.

'You're never going into the office at eleven this morning?'

'Why not?'

'Well, for a start, what for? You never work on Saturdays. You once said it was a rule, no one in your firm worked on Saturdays or Sundays. Not ever.'

Peter didn't answer. He took the pan off the ring and rather clumsily cut the top off his egg. It had boiled hard, the way he disliked it. Sharonne sat down at the table and poured herself some coffee.

'You're not going to the office, are you? I can read you like a book, Pete. That wasn't the office on the phone, it was someone else.'

'If you say so.' He might say much the same to her concerning phone calls, but he didn't. He was afraid.

'Well, we're due at the Warrens by twelve thirty at the latest and I hope I don't need to remind you Trollfield Farm is fifteen miles away. So you'd better not be wherever you're going for more than half an hour.' She studied his face, reading him like a book. 'I know who it was,' she said. 'It was the police.'

He shrugged.

'You're going to Toxborough police station. Well, Trollfield Farm is between here and Toxborough, so

that's all right. What do they want? I thought all that
business was over. What have you been doing, Pete?'

'Me? I haven't done a thing. I never have done. All I
did was find a car with a body in it.'

She stood up, hands on hips. 'No, that wasn't all
you did. All you did was go and look at it, mess about
with something that was no business of yours. All you
did was go and tell the police and bring them here so
that this place has got a bad name and we'll never be
able to sell it.'

'But you don't want to sell it!'

'That's got nothing to do with it. It'd be all the same
if I did, you never take any notice of what I want. And
now they suspect you of something else. Putting that car
there, I expect, and maybe you did – how would I
know? I'd be the last to know.'

Peter picked a piece of toast out of the toaster and
hurled it across the room. He tipped the remains of
his egg into the sink. 'It's not Toxborough, it's
Kingsmarkham. And there's no way I can get back here
before half past one.' Like a child, he added, 'So there!'

She stared at him, gathering her rage for an outburst.

'And you can't have the car,' he said. 'I want it.'

'If you go to Kingsmarkham,' she shouted, 'and I
can't go to the Warrens, I'll never speak to you again.'

He found the nerve that had been in abeyance for
three years. 'Good,' he said.

The single sentence of that altercation that stayed in
his mind was the one she had uttered about the police
suspecting him of putting the car in the quarry. Maybe
they did, he thought as he began the drive to
Kingsmarkham, maybe that was what it was all about.
But they *couldn't*. On what grounds? He didn't know
the dead woman, he didn't know those missing kids. He

should have asked that policeman. But Wexford's tone had been so cold and repressive that he had sensed he'd get no more out of him on the phone.

At two minutes to eleven he drove on to the parking area outside Kingsmarkham Police Station. Before he had opened the driver's door, a young policeman was saying very respectfully to him, 'Sorry, sir, you can't park here.'

'Where can I park then?' Peter asked irritably.

'It'll have to be in the street, sir. On the "pay and display", sir, if you please, not the residents' parking.'

'I know that. I'm not a resident of this place, thank God.'

It took him more than ten minutes to find somewhere to park in a side street and walk back to the police station, so that when he was shown into Wexford's office the Chief Inspector was pointedly looking at his watch. But the interview, which he by now expected to be a gruelling interrogation, lasted no time at all. Wexford only wanted to know what he had been doing on the afternoon and evening of 25 November of the previous year. Of course he couldn't produce an alibi, though he could have done for almost every other Saturday night of the year, Sharonne enjoying such a very social lifestyle. In fact, that was why he remembered that Saturday without reference to his diary. Simply because, almost uniquely, they had been home alone together.

Wexford seemed not at all perturbed. He didn't even seem interested. He thanked Buxton for coming, made a few remarks on the weather and then said he'd escort him downstairs to the front entrance himself. They took the lift and crossed the black and white checkerboard floor towards the swing doors. He vaguely thought he recognised the girl of thirteen or fourteen who was sitting on an upright chair next to an elderly woman. Her picture had been in the news lately. For being murdered? For winning something? Having not yet seen a morning paper, he couldn't remember. She was gazing at him in a rude, brash sort of way but he soon forgot her.

He had been so short a time in the police station that he had a good chance of getting back to Passingham by noon. It was still only twenty-five past eleven when he got back into his car. Unfortunately for him (and for the victims of the accident) a container lorry had hit a car full of holidaymakers as the driver overtook a line of vehicles this side of the Toxborough turn-off. The traffic queue extended back from the crash site for two miles by the time Buxton reached the tail end of it. Eventually, when an ambulance had taken away the injured, when the broken and twisted metal that had been a people carrier was cleared from the road and the lorry towed away, the line of cars slowly proceeded towards Toxborough and London. The time was twelve twenty and it was ten to one when Buxton reached the Hall.

He knew Sharonne must be still there, however enraged and threatening, because he had the car and she no means of getting to Trollfield unless she'd called a taxi. If she'd done that she'd have had to explain to the driver she hadn't got a car. That wasn't Sharonne's way. But she wasn't there. He went round the house calling her name, a large whisky in his hand. Someone must have called for her, someone must have taken her to the Warrens. Well, she'd be back.

Later, on the news, he saw that Sophie Dade had been found or come home of her own accord. It wasn't clear which of these possibilities was the true one. So that was the girl he'd seen at the police station. There was a little whisky left in the bottle. He might as well drink it. It was wasteful leaving dregs. Reminding himself that what Sharonne had been to was a lunch party, he saw that it was after six. Soon afterwards he fell asleep and dreamed about the phone number disclosed to him when he dialled 1471. Once, just once. The chap had never phoned again. Because Sharonne had cautioned him not to? It was pitch dark and very cold when he woke up. Finding that it was four in the morning was a bit of a shock. Once again, though this time in a shaky state, he toured the house calling her name. She wasn't there, she hadn't come back. Maybe the phone number man, the lover, if he was a lover, had driven her back to London. After a hair of the dog and some work with an electric toothbrush to get the foul taste out of his mouth, he dialled his London number, got his own voice asking him to leave a message.

He slept again. He phoned his London home again, eventually phoned the number that had been haunting him. An answering service responded, only repeating the number he had dialled but giving no name and asking very tersely for the caller to leave a message. The only satisfaction he got, if satisfaction it was, was from the voice being male. By the middle of the morning it was plain to him that she had left him and instead of sadness, he felt a terrible rage. He took Colman's card out of his pocket and dialled not the main phone number but that of the man's mobile. Colman answered smartly.

'It's Peter Buxton. I want your people to act for me.'

'Sure. A pleasure. What might we be searching and finding?'

'Evidence for divorce,' said Buxton, and he explained.

'You're behind the times, Mr Buxton. Under the Matrimonial Causes Act, 1973, you can get a no-fault divorce in two years and the waiting time's since been reduced to one year.'

'I don't want a no-fault divorce. There's plenty of fault – on her side. And I want it fast.'

'Let me just give a rundown of our charges,' said Colman.

Thus the Buxton marriage was the first relationship to come to grief through the case of the Missing Dade Children.

CHAPTER 23

Matilda Carrish's funeral took place in the same church and the same crematorium as Joanna Troy's had a month or so before. There the resemblance almost ended. True, Roger Dade was at both and the same unfortunate clergyman officiated at both, intoning the same contemporary version of the funeral service to a similarly apathetic and vaguely agnostic group of mourners, but Katrina Dade was not there to see her mother-in-law laid to rest, nor were her parents. Attendance was poor. Perhaps, Wexford thought, more friends of Matilda, neighbours, fellow artists from the world in which she had moved for so long and with such distinction, might have come along if she had been buried in her local cemetery and the words of committal recited in her village church. It had obviously been Roger Dade's decision to do otherwise.

Dade sat in a front pew, looking sullen, beside a woman who looked not in the least like him nor like Matilda but who, Wexford nevertheless thought, must be his sister. She was a heavy woman with a full face and tightly curled hair. What was her name? Charlotte something. He had once spoken to her on the phone. Would talking to her face-to-face be of any use? Then he remembered the man Matilda Carrish had married, an old man who lived abroad and was now her widower. But there was no one in the front pews it could conceivably have been. Sophie had come into the church and seated herself as far from her father as it was possible to be. She had decked herself out in deepest unrelieved black – not difficult for any teenager these days. Matilda Carrish had sent her brother away and taken the secret of his hiding place with her to the grave. But why? Why? To keep him away from this Peter? If so, what was Peter's interest in the boy? Probably not a sexual interest at all but fear of Giles telling what he had seen at Antrim on that Saturday night. In that case, why had Matilda not sent Sophie away too? She had seen as much as he and possibly more.

He ought to be able to reason out *where* she had sent Giles. Was it possible he had gone to her daughter's house? If so, the daughter had left him behind to come here, but no doubt in the care of her husband and children. It was a place he could have gone to without a passport. As a kind of minor celebrity, Matilda most likely had friends everywhere, abroad as well as here. But he couldn't have gone abroad because he had no passport . . . Would a friend living in, say, northern Scotland harbour a boy who was involved in a murder inquiry and whom the police wanted to question? Matilda had and birds of a feather flock together . . .

The coffin was carried in. The sparse congregation rose as a dismal voluntary was played, and Wexford's earlier impression was confirmed. Very few people had come. There was no choir and no one with a strong voice among the mourners. They broke into a ragged version of – what else? – 'Abide with Me'. Just where could Giles Dade possibly be abiding at this moment?

All the members of Wexford's team that could be spared had spent the previous day questioning George and Effie Troy and Yvonne Moody about Peter. The results

weren't helpful. Only George Troy seemed to recall
Joanna mentioning a Peter but he had similar recollec-
tions of her talking about an Anthony, a Paul, a Tom
and a Barry. Effie interrupted to say that these weren't
boyfriends but children she had taught and this had
thrown George into confusion. Yvonne Moody's replies
were useless. She was obviously predisposed to a need
for Joanna to have no friends apart from herself and
possibly other women. Reluctantly, she had at last
admitted she had seen men – she called them boys –
going to Joanna's house for private coaching. One of
them might have been a Peter.

The coffin was removed and placed in the car that
would transport it to the crematorium. Only the officiating clergyman seemed to be accompanying Matilda
Carrish on her last journey. Wexford watched her driven
away. Dade had come down the steps from the church
with Charlotte something. He gave Wexford a sullen
glare, muttered to his sister. Wexford expected a putting
of heads together, a whispered colloquy, before both of
them ignoring him. But Dade's sister turned in his
direction, smiled and came over, hand extended.

'Charlotte Macallister. How do you do?'

'I was sorry to hear about your mother,' Wexford said
insincerely.

'Yes. What on earth was she doing, hiding those
children? I think she must have gone quite mad. Senile
dementia or something.'

She was the least likely victim of senile anything, he
thought. 'Giles is still missing, of course,' he said. 'But
he's alive . . .' A bellow from Dade momentarily took his
breath away.

'Sophie! *Sophie!*'

The girl was running out of the churchyard, running
as fast as only a thirteen-year-old can. Her father yelled

because he was powerless to stop her. He clenched his fist and stamped.

'Very bad for the blood pressure,' Charlotte Macallister said calmly. 'He won't make old bones if he goes on like that.'

'It occurred to me in there', said Wexford, 'that your mother might have sent Giles to you.'

'It did, did it? Well, I'm sorry to disappoint you but I'm not so much a chip off the old block as that. And if I fell in with her plots my husband wouldn't. He's a high-ranking officer in the Royal Ulster Constabulary and a pal of Sir Ronald Flanagan. Bye-bye. If you need me I'll be staying with Roger and Katrina for a couple of days.'

Wexford and Burden lunched together, not at the Moonflower, but in the police canteen. Burden sniffed his fish and made a face.

'Something wrong with it?'

'No. Not really. Cod ought to smell of something, it ought to smell nice. This smells of nothing, it might be cardboard – no, polystyrene. That's what it looks like.'

'Talking of fish,' said Wexford who was eating ravioli, 'this whole Peter story is fishy, don't you think? No one's heard of him. Katrina hasn't, Yvonne Moody hasn't, and they were apparently her closest friends. Her father and stepfather haven't. And I'll tell you something else. It may be coincidence but I had another look at that cooking piece I told you about and it was written by someone with Peter for a first name.'

Burden raised his eyebrows, nodded. 'None of the Dade neighbours saw anyone come to the house that Saturday evening except Dorcas Winter. They didn't even see her, only knew she'd been because the paper was there.'

'Why would Sophie invent him? Besides, *could* she invent him? A man called Peter she might, and the name she got from a magazine, but the things he did and said? His pushing Joanna downstairs, clearing up the blood, driving the car and knowing about Passingham? Knowing how it was pronounced?'

'He could be called something else,' Burden said. 'On the other hand, none of these people even knew of a man in Joanna's life. Why should she conceal him from her family and friends? She wasn't married.'

'Very likely he is, though. All we know is who he's not, and he's not Peter Buxton. Sophie was adamant about that. In fact, when I asked her after he'd gone she was so indignant that I might even think so for a moment that she was almost in tears. I'd say she passionately didn't want Buxton to be this Peter – and that in itself is odd.'

'It's not odd,' Burden said slowly, pushing fishbones to the side of his plate and the khaki-coloured peas to join them. 'It's not odd if she invented Peter and panicked when she saw we took it seriously, when she realised that here was a real person who could be accused of a crime he didn't commit.'

'Then, if she invented Peter, who *was* in the house and accidentally or purposely, killed Joanna Troy?'

'Someone she doesn't want us to know about. Someone she's protecting.'

'Then we'll have to talk to her again,' Wexford said. 'By the way, the Buxtons are splitting up. I met Colman in the High Street, taking down posters. He told me. Not very discreet of him, was it?'

There had been a funeral and, in other circumstances, he would have let a day pass, but no one except Sophie had shown much grief for Matilda Carrish. Even hers,

Wexford felt, was the grief of a child whose whole future, eagerly anticipated, is before her and who knows, anyway, that in the nature of things the old must die. What kind of a mother had Matilda been that Roger Dade seemed to regard her as one who caused almost less nuisance by dying than by remaining alive? Perhaps the kind he had imagined, well-intentioned, an ardent believer in free expression, but neglectful too, pursuing her own (lucrative) interests while leaving her children to pursue theirs. Or was it that Dade was simply a congenitally unpleasant man? And why, why, why had the woman taken those children in and defied the police forces of an entire country to find them?

He notified the family that he and Burden would return in the late afternoon to speak to Sophie once more. Fortunately it was Mrs Bruce he saw. Dade's reaction would have been less amiable. This time, surprisingly, it was her mother who chaperoned her at the interview, but she might as well have not been there, for she sat silent for almost the whole time, lying back in an armchair with her eyes closed. Also present was Karen Malahyde. 'I need you as interpreter,' Wexford said to her and then the girl came in. Once more she was all in black and a dancing devil with horns and trident had appeared on her forearm. It looked like a tattoo but was probably a transfer.

'Sophie,' he began, 'I'm going to be very frank with you in the hope that you'll be frank with me. Four hours ago when I was having my lunch with Mr Burden here we discussed the man you call Peter . . .'

She interrupted him. 'He *is* called Peter.'

'Fine. He's called Peter,' said Burden. 'I expressed my doubts about Peter's existence. None of your neighbours here had seen anyone come to this house that evening. Scott Holloway denies coming here. Only Dorcas Winter came, delivering the evening paper, and she didn't come in. But Mr Wexford thought Peter must exist because he doubted if you could have invented him. You might have invented a man called Peter but not the things he said and did. Above all, not the way he pronounced Passingham. What do you have to say about all that?'

Her eyelids flickered. She looked down. 'Nothing. It's all true.'

'Describe Peter,' Burden said.

'I did. I said he was ordinary, a dumb-ass.'

'What did he looked like, Sophie?'

'Tall. Not in good shape, quite ugly. His face was starting to go red. Dark hair but going bald.' She screwed up her eyes, apparently in an effort to think. 'One of his front teeth crossed a bit over the one next to it. Droopy mouth. Maybe forty-five.'

She had described her father. But even by the wildest stretch of imagination and the wildest manipulation of alibis, Peter couldn't be Roger Dade. At the relevant time he had been in Paris with his wife, as attested to by a hotel keeper, a travel agent, an airline and the Paris police. A psychologist would say she didn't know many men (as against boys) and had described her father as the one she knew best and most strongly disliked and feared – in other words, a man she thought capable of violent crime.

'Sophie,' Wexford said, 'what became of the piece of paper Peter gave you with an address on it?'

He hadn't asked her that before. It had seemed unimportant. He was astonished to see her flush deeply. 'Giles threw it away,' she said.

He was more certain she was lying than he had been at any of her other replies. 'Did you look at it before you decided to go to your grandmother? Was it something about that address which made you decide going to your grandmother would be better?'

'Giles looked at it. I didn't.'

He nodded. He glanced at Katrina. She appeared to be fast asleep. 'Giles hadn't got his mobile with him. He made the call to your grandmother from a call box. How did he know the number?'

'She was *our* grandmother. Of course we knew her phone number.'

'I don't think there's any "of course" about it, Sophie. You only saw your grandmother once or twice a year. You had seldom been to her house before. No doubt you had her number in an address book at home. Your parents probably had it on a frequently used number directory in their phone at home but what you're saying is that you knew the number by heart, you had it in your memory or Giles's.'

The girl shrugged. 'Why not?'

'I think you decided to make for your grandmother's *before you left this house*. I think you knew where you were going from the start.'

She made no answer.

'Who spoke to her, you or Giles?'

'It was me.'

'All right,' Wexford said, 'that will do for today. I'd like to speak to Mr and Mrs Bruce, please. Where are they?'

That awoke or at least stirred Katrina. She sat up. 'My parents are sitting up in their room. They went up there because they've had a row with Roger. They're going home tomorrow, anyway.' Her voice rose until it became somehow frighteningly high-pitched. 'And I'm going with them. I'm going with them for ever.'

Sophie said, 'Take my father with you.'

'Don't be more stupid than you can help. I'm going with them because I'm leaving him. D'you understand now?'

'You're poop.' The girl spoke roughly but she sounded afraid. 'What about me? I can't be left alone with him.'

Katrina looked at her and tears of self-pity welled. 'Why should I care about you? You didn't care about me when you took yourself off, you and your brother, when I thought you were both lying dead somewhere. It's time I started thinking of *me*.' She addressed Wexford. 'Having your child murdered or disappeared or thinking they have mostly leads to the mother and father splitting up. It's quite common. Haven't you noticed?'

He didn't answer this. He was thinking of Sophie, thinking fast and wondering.

'We'll be leaving in the morning. Early. If you want my parents they're in Giles's room. Just go up and knock on the door. I had to put that bitch Charlotte in the one they'd been using. Apparently she can only sleep in a room where the bedhead is to the north. I'll put it all behind me tomorrow, thank God.'

Wexford motioned to Burden to come outside into the hall with him. The house was very silent and seemed otherwise empty. Probably Roger had taken his sister out somewhere. Wexford said, 'No time like the present. We'll take Sophie into that other room, the dining room or whatever, and you ask her. Ask her outright. I can't leave it another day.'

'You can't do that, Reg. She's thirteen.'

'Oh God, so I can't. Then it'll have to be in the mother's presence.'

But when they went back Katrina had fallen asleep or was giving a very good imitation of someone who had. She lay curled up like a cat, her knees under her chin, her head buried in her arms. Sophie sat staring at her fixedly like someone watching a wild animal, wondering what it would do next.

Wexford said, 'Why do you dislike your father so, Sophie?'

She turned towards him, it seemed reluctantly. 'I just do.'

'Sophie, you seem very well-informed about sex. I'm going to ask you outright. Has he ever touched you or tried to touch you in a sexual way?'

Her reaction was the last either police officer expected. She started to laugh. It wasn't dry or cynical laughter but true merriment, peal on peal of it. 'You're all poop, the lot of you. That's what Matilda thought, that's why she let us come. Her own dad did it to her when she was a kid. So she let us come and said she'd hide us. But I put her right, though I don't think she believed me. He's skanky but he's not that bad.'

Burden glanced at Katrina. She hadn't moved. 'So fear of your father's, er, attentions isn't what makes you dislike him?'

'I get pissed off at him because he's just never never nice to me. He shouts at me and he's skanky. And he's always nagging me to go to my room and work. I can't have my friends here because it's a waste of time, *he* says. I'm supposed to work, work, work. I only like get books and CDs and gear as presents for working. It's the same for Giles. Is that enough for you?'

'Yes, Sophie,' said Wexford. 'Yes, thank you. Tell me something else, then. When did you set your grand-mother straight about your relationship with your father? As soon as you got to her house? The same day, the Sunday?'

'I don't remember exactly when but it was before Giles went away. We were all three there, Matilda and Giles and me, and Matilda asked me why we'd left and I told her and she said was it really more about something my father did to me. I'd heard about that stuff, it's always on the TV, but it never happened to me and I told her so.'

'In that case, if she was satisfied that your father was no more than strict and a bit bullying with you, why didn't she then call your parents or the police to say where you were or that you were safe?'

With a shake of her head and a brandishing of arms, Katrina woke up. Or came out of her self-induced trance. She put her feet to the ground. 'I can answer that.' As seemed to happen almost every time she opened her mouth, the tears started. But instead of constricting her speech or causing her to gag, they simply rolled down her thin cheeks. 'I can tell you why she didn't. She took my children in to get revenge on me. Because I told her when she was here in October that I wouldn't let them see her again. Not ever. Well, when they were grown-up I couldn't stop them but while they lived here with us I'd keep them apart if it took the last breath in my body.'

'Do you mind telling us why you wouldn't let their grandmother see them again?'

'*She* knows.' Katrina pointed a shaking forefinger at her daughter. 'Ask her.'

Wexford raised an enquiring eyebrow at Sophie. The girl said nastily, 'You tell them if you want. I'm not going to do your dirty work for you.'

Katrina pulled her sleeve down over her hand and used it like a handkerchief to wipe her streaming eyes. 'She was going to stay a week. My husband –' she put extreme scorn into the word '– said we ought to have her for a week. I didn't want that. She looked down on me, always did, because I'm not supposed to be clever like her. Well, the third day she was here I went up to Sophie's room to tell her her tutor had phoned to say he couldn't give her a lesson next day and when I opened the door she wasn't there and she wasn't in Giles's room, and I found all three of them in Matilda's room. They were all in there and Matilda was sitting on the bed smoking *pot.*'

'Mrs Carrish was smoking cannabis?'

'That's what I said. I started screaming – well, anyone would. I told Roger and he was *incandescent.* But I didn't wait to see what he'd do, I told her she'd have to go, there and then. It was evening but I wasn't going to have her in my house a minute longer . . .'

'You'd better tell what Matilda said, not just you,' Sophie said scornfully. 'She said she was doing what she always did to relax. If we didn't ever relax, she said, we'd get sick and be too ill to pass exams. It was harmless if we wanted to give it a go, she said, but she wouldn't give us any, she was sure we had plenty of chances to get it. Oh, and said my father was full of shit and he'd make us full of shit too.'

'Stop using that filthy language,' Katrina said at the top of her voice, and to Wexford in a more subdued tone, 'I even packed her bags for her, threw all her fancy clothes, all her black designer stuff, I threw it into her cases and put them outside on the doorstep. My husband fetched her downstairs – for once he asserted himself with *her.* I'd never seen that before. It was nine at night. I don't know where she stayed, some hotel, I suppose.' Suddenly she screamed at him, 'Don't look at me like that! She was an old woman, I know that. But she didn't act like one, she acted like a fiend, getting my children on to drugs . . .'

Sophie cocked a thumb at her mother. 'What she means is she thinks Matilda hid us to get back at her and I reckon she's right.'

'It was her revenge,' said Katrina, sobbing now. 'It was her way of getting revenge.'

*

Not for the first time, Wexford wondered what the people who talked so glibly about 'family values' would say to a scene such as the one he had just witnessed and the revelations he had heard. But come to that, wouldn't he, if in Katrina's place, have done just what Katrina had done, if more calmly? What had possessed Matilda Carrish to do something more readily associated with pushers a quarter of her age? No doubt it was because she had used cannabis herself, perhaps regularly for years, and she genuinely believed it a harmless relaxant.

He and Burden went upstairs. Wexford thought he had known who 'Peter' was and, broadly speaking, what had happened that night from the point when Sophie had described her father. But he had truly seen the light when she insisted they had memorised Matilda's phone number, when he knew the whole operation had been planned before they left Antrim.

He knocked at the door of Giles's bedroom and Doreen Bruce's voice asked who it was. Wexford told her and she came to open it. Her husband was sitting in a small armchair he recognised as having been brought there from the living room, the book he had been reading lying face-downwards on the bed. Giles's religious artefacts and posters had disappeared.

Wexford came straight to the point. 'Mr Bruce, can Giles drive a car?'

Afraid of the law, as many people of her generation are, his wife immediately plunged into excuses. 'We told him he must never try to drive before he'd got a licence and insurance and all that. We explained it was fine for him to practise on the old airfield but he couldn't take his test till he was seventeen. And he understood, didn't he, Eric? He knew it was all right for Eric to teach him on the old runway when he came to stay with us and he had to save driving for when he was with us, that was his treat here, something to look forward to.'

Yes, of course, the airstrip at Berningham, once a United States base . . .

'You took him out in your car, did you, Mr Bruce?'

'It was something for him to do. And I enjoyed it. We all enjoy teaching, don't we? Be a different matter if we had to do it for our livings, I dare say.'

'We'd have taught Sophie too, dear,' said Mrs Bruce, 'but she wasn't keen to learn. I think the truth was she wasn't keen to learn from a couple of oldies. Well, you can understand it, can't you?'

'Mind you, he was a good student,' said Mr Bruce. 'They are at that age. Giles can drive as well as I can – better probably.'

'Talk about reversing into a marked space,' said his wife. 'I've never seen it done so well. You could drive a cab in London, I said to him, though of course he'll do something a lot superior to that, won't he?' She looked up into Wexford's face. 'He will, won't he, dear?'

He understood. 'I'm sure he will.'

'We're leaving tomorrow and – and Katrina's coming too. I hope it's only temporary. Frankly, I've never cared for Roger but still I hope it's not a permanent break. I hope it won't come to divorce for the children's sake.'

That would make the second partnership to come to grief as a result of this case, Wexford remarked as he and Burden went down the stairs. Sophie and her mother were still where he had left them. Katrina had lapsed back into sleep, the place and condition she escaped to. Sophie's eyes were fixed inscrutably on her.

'You said Matilda drove Giles to the station,' Wexford said. 'That would be Kingham station?'

'She drove him to Oxford.'

'And was he going to Heathrow from Oxford? Was he going to catch a domestic flight?'

For a moment she was perfectly silent. Then she screamed at the top of her voice, waking her mother, 'I don't know!'

It was wet and by now very dark, a starless, moonless night, though not yet six in the evening. Wexford and Burden stood under a lamp-post, in its brassy yellow light.

'Scott Holloway's father is called Peter,' said Wexford.

'How do you know?'

'I don't remember how. I just know.'

'He can't be *the* Peter. Sophie would have recognised him. For God's sake, he lives practically next door.'

'Nevertheless, let's go and find out a bit more about those Holloways.'

CHAPTER 24

Peter Holloway no more fitted the generally accepted image of a lover than his son would in a few years' time. He was tall enough but stout with it and moon-faced. Sitting very comfortably by a fire of real logs, a cup of some warm milky drink beside him, the newspaper on his knee, he looked as if this was his natural role and habitat. For no other occupation could he be so well adapted. Scott and his sisters were also in the room, all seated at a table playing Monopoly, and when Mrs Holloway sat down in an armchair next to a small table on which lay pale-blue knitting, Wexford felt he had strayed into a 1940s advertisement for some cosy aspect of family life.

Burden rushed straight into the middle of things. 'Did you know Joanna Troy personally, Mr Holloway?'

The man sat up a little, startled and defensive. 'I never met her. My wife sees to that sort of thing.'

'What sort of thing? The children's education?'

'All that sort of thing, yes.'

Wexford had his eyes on the boy. The Monopoly game had been suspended, apparently at Scott's wish, for one of his sisters still held the cup with the dice in it in her hand while the other's face had taken on a look of exasperation. Now the boy turned round and looked at his father.

Wexford said sharply, 'What time did you go to the Dades' house, Scott?'

It was a good thing the police weren't armed. He could cheerfully have shot Mrs Holloway. 'He told you, he didn't go there.' She had picked up her knitting and her fingers worked frenetically. 'How many times does he have to tell you?'

'Scott?' said Wexford.

He had been made in his father's image. He wasn't quite as fat – yet. His face was as round and his eyes as small. Piggy eyes, they used to be called, Wexford remembered.

'I know you did go there, Scott.'

The boy got up. He stood in front of Wexford. It was possible that at that school he went to they taught children to stand when they were addressed by a teacher. 'I didn't go in.'

'What did you do?'

'I went round there. In the evening. It was – I don't know what time, maybe nine or a bit earlier.' He said to his mother, 'You and Dad were watching TV. I went up the road to their house. There were lights on, I knew they were in. *Her* car was there.'

'Whose car, Scott?' said Burden.

'Miss Troy's, Joanna's.'

'And you changed your mind about going in when you saw her car? Why was that? She'd been your teacher too, hadn't she?'

He gave no answer, but he blushed. The dark-red spread all over his face until it was the colour of raw beef. Like a child half his age, he muttered, 'Because I hated her. I'm glad she's dead,' and before the tears gathering in his eyes could fall, he rushed from the room.

'She's got a new one.'

Dora's words greeted him as he walked in the door.

'Who's got a new what?'

'Sorry, that wasn't very clear, was it? Sylvia's got a new man. She brought him in here for a drink. They were on their way to a – well, a political meeting. There was to be a lecture. "The Way Forward to a New Left" or something like that.'

Wexford groaned. He sat down heavily in the middle of the sofa. 'I suppose he's tall and handsome and thick and deeply boring, is he? Or weedy and buck-toothed and brilliant and rude?'

'Not any of those. He looks a bit like Neil. He's quiet. Sizing up the situation, I imagine. Oh, and he teaches politics at the University of the South.'

'What's his name?'

'John Jackson.'

'Well, it's different. He's not a Marxist, is he? Not these days? Not in the twenty-first century?'

'I don't know? How am I supposed to know?'

'I wonder what Neil will say,' said Wexford rather sadly. He hoped the man would be good company, not a bore, kind to the children. But he strove always – though not always with success – not to worry about things he couldn't change. He believed his daughters loved him but nothing he could say or do carried much weight with them any more. Their contention was the usual one in any family disagreement, that a parent can't understand, and who was to say they weren't right?

Dora went back to her book. He switched his thoughts back to the Dades. Their family disagreement had been far from usual. Examining it while alone, he wondered if it was the world's first instance of a grandmother introducing her teenage grandchildren to drugs. He was prepared to give Matilda – dead Matilda – the benefit of the doubt and concede that it was probably done because she really believed cannabis would be therapeutic to these over-stressed children. She had been using it for so long herself, she might even have a medical reason, arthritis for instance, and rather than harming her it had taken away pain. Now he remembered the faint scent of it, no more than a hint, a breath, he had noticed when she passed him in his office.

In any case, those children would have been offered harder and more dangerous drugs every day at their school gates. Of course, that didn't in any way exculpate Matilda, and it was no wonder the parents were enraged. Katrina had turned her out of the house and her own son had supported his wife. No doubt it was dark. Very probably it was raining. No taxis were ever to be found in the Lyndhurst Drive–Kingston Gardens area. She would have had to walk, carrying those cases, as far as the station taxi rank or, instead, to the nearest hotel. Most old women would have been seriously distressed but Matilda wasn't most old women. She would have been angry, furious, or, as Katrina might put it, *incandescent*. Well, she had had her revenge.

Had Scott Holloway had his? Almost certainly not. As far as Wexford could see at present, all he had said established that Joanna and the Dade children were still in the house at nine and the only Peter in the case, apart from Buxton, had been watching television with his wife.

Before he got the chance to talk to Burden next day, something else happened. He had a visitor. How she ever got past the front desk he didn't know but guessed it was because they were short-staffed. Experienced people were all away with flu and temps were taking their place in the network that separated him from the public. She walked in and the girl who showed her up presented her as Ms Virginia Pascall.

Wexford had never heard of her. He noticed – he couldn't help it – that she was young, still in her twenties, and quite startlingly beautiful. Apart from all that, the exquisite features, the long red-gold hair, the spectacular legs and stunning figure, he saw something else, stark madness in her blank blue stare and twisting, writhing hands.

'What can I do for you, Ms Pascall?'

Send for the attendants in white coats with the tranquillising syringes? She sat down on the edge of the chair, immediately jumped up again, put her hands on his desk, leant towards him. He could smell something on her breath, the scent of nail varnish perhaps or some sweet but non-alcoholic drink. Her voice was sweet, like the smell, but jerky and brittle.

'You have to know, he wants you to know, he killed her.'

'Who did he kill, Ms Pascall, and who is "he"?'

'Ralph. Ralph Jennings, the man I'm engaged to. The man I *was* engaged to.'

'Ah.'

'He's had secret meetings with her. It was a conspiracy. They were plotting to kill me.' She began to shudder. 'But they quarrelled over how to do it and he killed her.'

'Joanna Troy?'

Once he'd uttered the name, Wexford wished he hadn't. Virginia Pascall made a noise midway between an animal's roar and a human scream, then it was all screaming. For a moment he had no idea what to do. No one came. He'd have something to say about that once he'd got rid of her. But she stopped as abruptly as she'd begun and fell into the chair. It was as if the paroxysm had released something and for a while she was at peace. She leant across the desk and he looked into eyes which, in colour only, were normal human eyes.

'That night he killed her, I can prove he wasn't with me. I can prove anything. He ran her down in his car, you know. Her blood was on the wheels. I wiped it off and smelt it. That's how I know it was hers, it smelt of her, foul, stinking, disgusting.'

You were supposed to humour people like this. Or you were once. Perhaps in these psychiatric times that was no longer true. On the other hand, it couldn't do any harm. 'Where is he now? Is he at your home?'

'He's gone. He's left. He knew I'd kill him if he stayed. He ran her down outside our house. She was on her way to see me. Me!' The unsteady, sweet voice leapt an octave. 'He killed her to stop her coming to me. He drove backwards and forwards over the body till the car was all over blood. Blood, blood, blood!' She sang it, her voice reaching scream level. 'Blood, blood, blood!'

It was at this point that Wexford pressed the alarm bell on the floor under his desk.

'What happened then?' Burden asked over their coffee.

'Lynn came running and a couple of uniforms I've never seen before. One of them was a woman. This woman didn't fight them, though she spat at Lynn. I said to send for Crocker but they were already on the phone to Dr Akande.'

'Was she always like that or has the Joanna business driven her over the top?'

'I don't know. The main thing is for poor old Jennings that he's left her at last. That makes the third couple to split up through the Dade affair.'

'I'll be very surprised if George and Effie Troy make a fourth or Jashub and Thekla Wright, for that matter.'

Wexford managed a smile. 'Odd, though, isn't it? I think that's the only wise thing I've ever heard Katrina

Dade say, that it's common for couples to split up when their child is missing or killed.'

'You'd expect a loss like that to bring them closer together,' Burden said.

'I don't know. Would you? Isn't it likely that they depend on the other one in ways they never have had to before? And that other, who has always seemed strong or comforting or optimistic, suddenly shows they're none of those things. They're just as weak and helpless as the other one and that seems to show they've been living for years under an illusion.'

'Maybe, but that wasn't what you wanted to talk about, was it?'

'No, I want to talk about Giles. Now it's pretty obvious Sophie invented Peter. She probably thought him up on the journey here from Gloucestershire. I'm sure Matilda was never told about him. So who did Matilda think had killed Joanna?'

'Whoever it was drove the car. Someone drove it.'

'Giles can drive.'

Burden said nothing, raised his eyebrows.

'You're looking astonished but you shouldn't be. You know what kids are, you've got three. I guarantee even that small one of yours is talking about the day he'll be allowed to drive a car. They're all mad to drive pretty well from the time they can walk. Giles might be a religious fanatic but he was no exception. His grandfather Bruce taught him on an old airfield.'

'I should have guessed,' Burden said ruefully.

Wexford shrugged. 'There were just the two of them escaping from Antrim, Giles and Sophie. Sophie and Giles. That's all. With a dead body in the car. Maybe in the boot. And they knew all the time they were eventually making for Trinity Lacy and Matilda. They knew she was "cool". Remember the pot-smoking.'

Burden gave a dry laugh. 'I must say that boy's religious faith doesn't seem to have had much effect on his moral character. As for the girl . . .'

'You see them like that, do you? I see them as victims, truly as babes in the wood.'

'None of this is getting us any further with what Matilda did with Giles.' This was one of the times when Burden almost lost patience with Wexford. 'Where he is now, I mean. Where did she get him away to? Some friend we don't know about? What friend would consent to shelter a boy who'd just killed a woman . . .'

'Hold hard a minute. Is that what you're saying, that Matilda *knew* Giles killed Joanna Troy?'

'Or that Sophie did. But it wasn't Sophie she sent away. And if this friend wasn't told Giles was a killer, what were they told?'

'God knows,' said Wexford. 'This was Monday and Giles's picture was all over the papers by the following Wednesday. He would have been quickly recognised.'

Burden shrugged. 'Nevertheless, their friendship for or relationship to Matilda was such that they agreed to shelter him. It must be so and he has to be here. He couldn't get out of the country. Well, he could get to Shetland or the Channel Islands or Ireland but his aunt in Ulster hasn't got him, so who else is there in Ireland?'

Wexford turned to him, staring but at the same as if he were not seeing him. 'What did you say? About Ireland. Say it again.'

'I just said "Ireland". No, "Ulster".'

'Stay a minute. Don't go away. Something has just occurred to me. Suppose a British citizen born in Northern Ireland has a sort of dual citizenship . . . I'm going to phone the Irish embassy.'

*

He phoned Dade and sprang a surprise, one he'd sprung on Burden half an hour before. 'Giles,' he said, 'has he an Irish passport?'

Dade had groaned when he heard Wexford's voice. 'I suppose it's slipped your mind that this is Saturday?' Now he answered grudgingly, 'Well, yes, he has. Seeing he was born in Northern Ireland, he was eligible, and when he passed the Common Entrance to get into his school – did spectacularly well, in fact – well, I applied for an Irish passport for him. It was what he wanted. God knows why. Look, you're not saying he was planning this four years ago, are you?'

'Very unlikely, Mr Dade. I expect he thought it might come in useful. I wish you'd told me about this passport before. Why didn't you?'

'Because (a) I forgot about it and (b) I didn't suppose a son of mine could act the way he has done and do the things he's done. You'll be telling me next he killed that bitch Joanna Troy.'

Wexford didn't answer. 'Mr Dade, I'd like your permission to search your mother's house. With the cooperation of the Gloucestershire police.'

To his surprise Sophie came on an extension. He heard a soft click and then her breathing. 'Search all you like, as far as I'm concerned,' Dade said. 'The place won't be mine till we've got probate. You want me to ask my mother's solicitors?'

He had never been so willing to meet them halfway. Perhaps misery had sweetened his nature, though in Wexford's experience it seldom did improve anyone's.

'If you'd be so kind.'

'May I know what you're searching for?' A sarcastic edge to the question deprived it of its apparent politeness.

'I will be frank with you,' Wexford said. 'I want to find the whereabouts of your son. And that's as good a way as any of making a start.'

'She knows.' He too had heard the breathing. 'She knows where he is.'

'I do not!' Sophie shouted it at the top of her voice.

'I'd fetch it out of her only I know you people would be down on me like a ton of bricks if I laid a finger on her.'

On the way there, and accompanied by two officers of the Gloucestershire Constabulary, Wexford sat silent in the car, his thoughts turned to his last visit there. All the time he had talked to Matilda Sophie had been in the house, concealed and laughing. Could anyone be blamed for taking it for granted no grandmother would give sanctuary to a child in opposition to that child's parents, to her own son? That was what he had done. By now he ought to know better than to take anything for granted. Yet only a few days ago he was assuming that no social worker who spent her time witnessing domestic violence and its results would willingly continue to live with a man who beat her.

His heavy sigh fetched a glance and bracing words from Burden. 'Cheer up, it may not be true. We're nearly there.'

Already Matilda's house had an unlived-in look and a stuffy, airless atmosphere. It was very cold. Regardless of the possibility of frozen pipes and subsequent water damage, the heating had been turned off. Wexford suggested that Burden and one of the Gloucestershire officers should begin the downstairs search while he and the other officer started on the upper floor.

The difficulty was that he had no idea what they were looking for. Perhaps he had simply supposed that this would suggest itself when they began. One thing would lead to another. He found himself rather

distracted by Matilda's photographs, which proliferated
up here even more than on the ground floor. At least, he
assumed they were Matilda's, though they were unlike
any of those he particularly associated with her and
which her reputation rested on. These, on the staircase
wall and following its angle, seemed to be views of a city
with a large Gothic cathedral surmounted by twin
spires, the same city pictured on the wall by the door
that he had noticed last time. Between them was a print
in sepia of what might have been the same city except
that the cathedral had onion domes.

He was wasting time. He went into the principal
bedroom, the one that had been Matilda's. He turned
his attention first to the wardrobe and the pockets of
coats and jackets, and when this yielded nothing, to the
drawers of a desk and those of a tall chest. Matilda
Carrish had kept no letters. What unpaid bills there had
been, what bank statements, chequebooks, insurance
policies and all the rest of the paraphernalia of modern
paperwork, had been removed, no doubt by the firm of
solicitors and executors of the will Roger Dade had
spoken of. Wexford thought he had never before investigated such a barren desk. In the pigeonholes were four
ballpoints and a fountain pen as well as that outdated
substance, ink in a dark-blue bottle.

Inside the two clothes cupboards and the two chests
of drawers all was neat and orderly, hanging garments,
folded garments, black silk socks, no frivolities in the
shape of old lady's lavender sachets or dried rose leaves.
Creams and lotions in a top drawer but no make-up.
Matilda Carrish had no doubt decided that at her age
she must leave lipstick and eye shadow behind for ever.
He never quite knew what made him open a particular
jar labelled 'moisturiser'. Perhaps it was only because it
looked, from the scratched lid and partly worn-off label,

as if it had been long in use. He unscrewed the top and
found himself looking at a brownish, rather fibrous,
powder. The smell was unmistakeable. There is no more
unique and distinctive scent. Cannabis sativa.

Well, there was bound to be some. All his find did
was help confirm what the Dades had already told him.
He found one thing in the bottom drawer that told
him, along with the cannabis, that Matilda had been
human after all: a thick pigtail of black silky hair, apparently cut off while still in its plait. Whose was it?
Sophie's? Charlotte's? But Sophie's hair was brown and
Charlotte's fairish. Wexford decided, and this made him
smile to himself, that it must have been Matilda's own.
Cut off, perhaps, sixty or seventy years ago and kept all
that time. But hair never decayed, never dis-integrated,
lasted while teeth crumbled and nails fell to dust . . .

He turned his attention to her books, and found himself immediately diverted by their contents. It always
amazed him that an officer could conduct this kind of
search and, once he or she had flipped a book open and
shaken it, give it no further attention and show no
curiosity as to what it was about or who had written it.
But it often happened and he had often wondered at
it. These books held no revealing or incriminating
documents. As well as the contemporary ones he came
upon Cobbett's *Rural Rides* and Gilbert White's *The
Natural History of Selborne*. There was some Thesiger,
Kinglake's *Eothen* and T. E. Lawrence's *Seven Pillars of
Wisdom*. Incongruously, a child's book was beside it, a
book with a picture of a cartoon cat on its jacket and the
title in some incomprehensible language.

He passed on to the spare bedrooms. In one the
Gloucestershire officer was carefully removing small
objects from a drawer, a comb, a couple of postcards, a
music cassette, a tube of some cream a cosmetic company

gave away as a 'free' gift, and laying them on top of a chest. Like those in the main bedroom, the books on the shelves here held no revealing or incriminating documents or photographs; they were travel books, mostly. He began taking them out in quest of some paper or card that might have been laid between the pages but also found himself, as he always did find himself in this situation, looking closely at them and reading extracts.

The cameras were no doubt downstairs along with rolls of film. If she had still worked, Matilda had by this time probably acquired a digital camera as well as the trusted conventional sort – or whatever the term was. What had he expected from this chest? The kind of treasure trove he hadn't found in the desk, presumably. But there was nothing. Underclothes, three pairs of tights, unworn and still in their transparent wrapping. The trouser-suited Matilda would have worn socks. And here they were, many pairs, nearly all of them fine black silk. Downstairs Burden had found the cameras. They had a cupboard to themselves along with tripods. But that was really all which had come to light apart from an address book in which a lot of the pages were quite blank. He looked curiously at the many phone numbers whose codes proclaimed them to be in foreign countries. Matilda had more friends abroad than here but there might be an easier way than by calling every one of those numbers . . .

This time, tired as he was, he had to go to the house. A phone call wouldn't do. Signs of the absence of women – Sophie hardly counted – were already apparent. Takeaway had been eaten by the two sole occupants and its remains, foil containers, greaseproof paper, plastic carriers, as well as a pungent spicy smell, lingered in the dusty living room. Roger Dade's breath smelt of garlic and tikka marsala.

Retreating a little, Wexford said to Sophie, 'In your grandmother's house is a children's book in a Scandinavian language and there are some photographs, apparently taken by her, of a city that looks as if it might be somewhere in northern Europe. Can you tell me anything about that?'

'I didn't know,' Sophie said, and he believed her. 'I've never seen the book and I never noticed the pictures.'

'The language', Dade said, 'is probably Swedish. My stepfather, as I suppose I'm bound to call him, lives in Sweden. I hardly know the man. I've only met him once. They were married over there and my mother used to go over a couple of times a year but that all stopped when she got past seventy-five. They may have divorced for all I know.'

Wexford tried to imagine a situation in which one didn't know one's mother's husband and didn't know whether she was divorced or not, tried and failed. But he believed Dade. It was typical. Probably it would be equally useless asking the man where in Sweden but he could lose nothing by trying.

'I told you. I thought I made myself clear. I only met the man once. All I know is he's called Philip Trent – Carrish was my mother's maiden name – and at one time he was a university lecturer or whatever the term is.'

'He wasn't at your mother's funeral.'

'If you're implying no one told him you're wrong – as usual. My sister tried to phone him and then she sent an e-mail. Whether or not it got there I wouldn't know. Probably he just couldn't be bothered to come. Maybe he's dead himself.'

All he could get from Charlotte MacAllister was a message on her answering machine. He thought of trying to find her husband, the 'high-ranking officer' in the Royal

Ulster Constabulary, and then he decided the Internet might be easier. Some clever operator at work could find Philip Trent. He knew he was himself incapable of it. He could manage to name the universities of Sweden from an encyclopaedia and that was all. Stockholm, Uppsala, Lund . . . A young woman with a degree in computer studies, saying this was easy and implying, just, that with her talents she was capable of better things, got down to sorting out websites.

He began to walk home. He would have his dinner, hear the latest on Sylvia's new man – and please let it be cheerful encouraging news this time – and then come back for the search results. A fine, almost smoky, rain was falling, the kind of rain that is nearly mist, damp rather than wet, a mild hindrance to breathing. He saw Dorcas Winter, parcelled up in rainproof layers, delivering evening papers ahead, just turning out of Kingston Gardens into his own street. The large red plastic bag of papers she pushed along on what looked like a supermarket trolley. The rain was nearly as bad as fog, obscuring figures, turning them into ghostly shapes on a worn-out TV screen.

Wexford was quite close to the delivery girl before he saw it wasn't a girl at all but the newsagent himself. 'Good evening,' he said. At first the man failed to recognise him, then he did. 'Oh, good evening. Not a very good one, is it?'

'What's happened to Dorcas?'

'Gone to her violin lesson. I couldn't find anyone else to do the round.'

'If you've got a minute,' said Wexford, 'I'd like to ask you something. You remember the Confessional Congregation last July? You were there?'

'Certainly I was there.' It was interesting how, as soon as the subject was changed from the mundane to matters of the Good Gospel Church, from being an ordinary pleasant tradesman Kenneth 'Hobab' Winter became pompous and self-important. 'I am always present at significant church functions. I am an elder, remember.'

'Yes, well, can you tell me how Giles Dade went to Passingham St John that night and how he returned to Kingsmarkham?'

'By what means of transport, do you mean? As a matter of fact, I can, as I was closely involved. There was no car available to take the boy. Many of our members, you must understand, came straight to the Congregation from their places of work. Mrs Zurishaddai Wilton escorted him on the train from Kingsmarkham to Passingham Park and thence by taxi to Passingham Hall. The return journey was made in my car, driven by me and accompanied by my wife and Mr and Mrs Nun Plummer.'

'Was he upset? Distressed?'

'Who? Giles Dade? Not at all. He was happy and relieved. "Bubbly", I think one could say.'

'Really? He had just confessed what sins he had to confess. It must have been embarrassing, not to say – well, disturbing, with the congregation all chanting.'

'Not at all,' said Winter again, urbanely this time. 'People feel cleansed and liberated. It's a kind of God-given psychoanalysis. Giles felt free for the first time in his life as people do when they confront God after cleansing.'

'Thank you,' said Wexford. 'That's very helpful. I may as well take my paper. Save you delivering it.'

Smiling, Winter passed over the *Kingsmarkham Evening Courier* with a hand in a wet woollen glove. 'Well, goodnight, then.' He was a normal man again.

Wexford walked to his house, imagining the feelings of Giles Dade on that car journey. He must have made

some kind of confession, perhaps of the kind of clumsy
and unsatisfying sexual adventures a boy of fifteen
would have had, confessed too to teenage shoplifting
indulged in for bravado and the occasional pre-Matilda
spliff. Then, fresh from the howling mob 'shouting and
singing', he had to travel home sandwiched no doubt
between the Plummers and facing the uncompromising
backs of Mr and Mrs Winter. Yet he had been 'bubbly'?
It was a word in popular use which Wexford loathed
and here it seemed singularly inapt. Perhaps the other
passengers in the car had congratulated him, inducing
in him a kind of mad euphoria. That was the only
explanation that seemed reasonable.

He was back in his office by eight and had been there
only five minutes when the computer studies woman
walked in with a couple of sheets of A4 on which he
could see text in unmistakable Internet type.

Philip Trent wasn't dead, but very much alive and
living in Uppsala. His name hadn't been in the address
book. Perhaps no one would enter a husband's name
and phone number into a personal directory, however
apart or estranged they might be. She would have
known it by heart.

CHAPTER 25

Ice and snow were to be expected, a kind of Ultima Thule on the northern edge of the world. He supposed he was lucky to be sent. Police officers normally looked on it as a perk to be sent abroad – only he was ungrateful enough to wish that, in March, it could have been Italy or Greece. Maybe where Burden would be going next day on his fortnight's leave, the south of Spain.

But it was Sweden. He had managed, at last, to speak to Philip Trent. And after one short phone conversation he knew, in Vine's words, that he had 'a right one here'. The old man spoke much the same kind of English as Mr Shand-Gibb, former owner of Passingham Hall, but Trent's had a faintly alien intonation to it, not an accent – he was plainly a native English speaker – but the slight lilt that comes from habitually speaking a Scandinavian language. He admitted, without shame or apparent guilt of any kind, that Giles Dade was staying with him in his house in Fjärdingen, a district of Uppsala. A quarter or 'farthing' in mediaeval times, he explained kindly, though he hadn't been asked, and Wexford thought of *The Lord of the Rings* and hobbit country where counties were similarly named.

'Oh, yes, Mr Wexford, he's been here since early December. We spent a pleasant Christmas together. A nice boy. Pity about the fanaticism but I don't think we shall hear much more of it.'

Indeed? 'He must he fetched home, Professor Trent.'

An efficient young woman who spoke perfect English had revealed Trent's rank to him and that he formerly held the Chair of Austro-Asiatic Languages (whatever they might be) at the University of Uppsala and that now, although well past the retire-ment age of sixty-five, he retained his own office for research purposes at the university as one of its distinguished former faculty members.

'I am not up to travelling, as you will appreciate. Besides, I am too busy, I have my research to do here. Investigation of Khmer, Pear and Stieng, for instance, is still in its infancy, a situation not helpful to linguisticians and brought about by the warfare which raged for such an extended period over Cambodia.' He spoke as if the only consequence of that war was its effect on the languages spoken by the people. 'Perhaps you could send someone?'

'I thought of coming over myself,' said Wexford tentatively.

'Did you? We're enjoying rather pleasant weather at present. Cool and fresh. I suggest you put up at the Hotel Linné. It enjoys very attractive views across the Linnaean gardens.'

When he had rung off Wexford looked up Austro-Asiatic Languages in the encyclopaedia and found there were dozens if not hundreds of them, mostly spoken in south-east Asia and eastern India. He wasn't much wiser, though he managed to connect 'Khmer' with the Khmer Rouge. The section on Uppsala was more rewarding. Not only the botanist Linnaeus came from there, but also Celsius, the temperature man, Ingmar Bergman and Dag Hammarskjöld, second secretary-general of the United Nations, while Strindberg had attended Trent's university. He wondered what Trent had meant by 'rather pleasant weather'. At least, it wouldn't be raining . . .

*

At Heathrow he went into a bookshop and searched the shelves for something to read on the flight. A guide to Sweden he already had. Besides, he wasn't looking for a travel book but anything, fiction or non-fiction, which might spontaneously take his fancy. Much to his surprise, among the 'classics', he found a little slender book he had never before heard of: *A Short Residence In Sweden, Norway and Denmark* by Mary Wollstonecraft. Confessing to himself that he had never come across any work by Mary Shelley's mother apart from *A Vindication of the Rights of Woman*, he bought it.

The flight went at five. It was a mild day, very damp and misty, though no rain had fallen since the previous evening, but Wexford had rooted out his winter coat, a very old tweed affair, unworn for several years and superseded by raincoats. He laid it across his lap, settled down in his seat and opened his book. Unfortunately, Mary Wollstonecraft had spent more time in Norway and Denmark than in Sweden and while in that country had visited no more than Gothenburg and the extreme west. Wexford's hope that she might have given him a picture of Uppsala in the last years of the eighteenth century faded fast. It would, anyway, be very different today, as would the diet of smoked meat and salt fish denounced by the author, and the pallid, heavy appearance of the people. Certainly the poverty would be past and gone but the 'degree of politeness in their address' might, he hoped, remain.

He had decided to proceed straight to the Hotel Linné and meet Giles and Professor Trent first thing next morning. By now the Uppsala police knew all about Giles and the possibility of further spiriting him away was gone. Wexford had written 'Hotel Linné, Uppsala' on a piece of paper but the taxi driver at

Arlanda Airport spoke enough English to understand
his directions.

It was dark. The drive took them along a wide,
straight road through what seemed to be forests of fir
and birch. The houses he saw, or made out through the
fairly well-lit darkness, looked modern, uniform in
materials – red-painted weatherboarding, leaded roofs –
if varied in design. Then the lights of the city in the distance showed him with dramatic impact a huge cathedral standing on an eminence, a black silhouette, its
twin spires pointing at the jewel-blue starlit sky. In
Matilda's mezzotint it had onion domes. Only in the
very old pictures were there Gothic spires. He didn't
understand, unless the images weren't of Uppsala at all
but of some other north-European city.

A formidable castle on another hill, serene buildings
he thought might be baroque, a fast-flowing black river.
He got out of the taxi and the driver patiently sorted
out his kronor for him. Oddly enough, he felt he could
trust the man not to swindle him, something that
wouldn't be true everywhere. Outdoors only briefly, he
was chilled to the bone by the bitter cold. But inside the
Hotel Linné it was cheeringly warm. Everyone spoke
English, everyone was polite, pleasant, efficient. He
found himself in an austere room, pale, rather bare but
with everything he could possibly need. Boiling hot
water gushed out of the taps. He had eaten on the plane
and wasn't hungry now. In some trepidation he followed
the hotel's telephone directions and dialled Philip
Trent's number. Instead of a flood of Swedish, Trent's
voice said, 'Hello?'

Wexford told him he had arrived, would see him in
the morning at nine thirty, according to their prior
arrangement. Trent, who conformed uncomfortably to
clichéd images of the absent-minded professor, so much

so that his manner seemed assumed, had apparently forgotten who he was. Wexford wouldn't have been surprised to have been greeted in Wa, Tin or Ho, some of
the Austro-Asiatic languages he had discovered existed.
But Trent, saying vaguely that he must 'come back to
earth', agreed that nine thirty 'would do'. Coffee was
generally available at that time. He managed to imply
that he was living in a restaurant.

'My house is on the corner of Östraågatan and
Gamla Torget. That is "East Street" and "Old Square" to
you. More or less.' That was more or less the meaning
or was the house more or less there? 'It's on the river.
You can ask the hotel for a plan.'

Philip Trent sounded profoundly uninterested in his
visit. Wexford had a long hot shower and went to bed.
But the street outside was noisier than he had expected.
Just as the place was clean and cold, austere and not
very populous, so he had anticipated utter silence.
Instead, the voices of young people and their music
reached him, the sound of something being kicked into
the gutter, a motor bike noisily started up, and he
remembered that this was a university city, Sweden's
oldest, its Oxford, and one of the oldest in Europe, but
nevertheless full of modern youth. He sat up in bed
reading Mary Wollstonecraft on the ease of Swedish
divorce and the superiority of the little towns to similar
places in Wales and western France. Eventually quiet
came and he slept.

The morning was bright and cold. But where was the
snow? 'We haven't had much for many years,' said a
multilingual girl serving breakfast, or rather, directing
guests to the buffet tables. 'Like all the world, we are
affected with global warming.' She added severely, looking into Wexford's eyes, 'Are you knowing Sweden has
the best environmental record in the earth?'

Humbly, he said he was glad to hear it. She returned to his table with a plan of the city she had procured for him from reception. 'There. Fjärdingen. Not very large, all things are very easy for you to find.'

It was early still. He went out into the 'Farthing' and found himself in a place the like of which he had never seen before. It wasn't that it lacked the modern appurtenances of the west. Far from it. He suddenly realised how odd it was, how refreshing in more senses than one, to see the latest models of cars, an Internet café, a CD shop, fashionably dressed women, a smart policeman directing traffic, yet at the same time smell pure crystalline air, unpolluted and clean. The sky was a pale sharp blue, scrawled over with wind-torn shreds of cloud. Some of the buildings were modern but most eighteenth-century, yellow and white and sepia, Swedish baroque. They would already have been here if Mary Wollstonecraft had passed this way. Not many cars were about, not many people. Walking towards the Linnaean gardens, he recalled that the entire population of this large country was only eight million, less than three million in Wollstonecraft's time.

He really only wanted to step into the gardens or look into them over the wall because the night before he had started out he had quickly read up on Linnaeus and his earth-wandering journeys to find new species. It wasn't the best time of the year unless you were a plant enthusiast and expert, everything was still asleep, waiting for a later spring than England enjoyed. He thought of his own poor garden, swamped by unnatural rains. If it was true that this nation had the world's best environmental record, would their thoughtful prudence save them from coming catastrophes?

It was nine o'clock. He heard the chimes begin and, as if it were immediately above him, the deep-throated tolling of a clock striking the hour. Quickening his pace, he began to walk in the direction of that sound and, as buildings opened and parted to afford him a panorama, saw the great cathedral standing before him on an eminence. A line of prose came back to him, he had read it years ago, he couldn't remember when or where, but it was from the writings of Hans Andersen who, visiting this city, spoke of the cathedral 'lifting its stone arms to heaven'. It was exactly like that, he thought, as the final stroke of nine died away. The Domkyrka was crimson and grey, clerical grey, dark and austere, huge, formidable and as unlike any cathedral he knew as could be imagined. Only its straight lines and pointed arches recalled English Gothic. It made cathedrals at home look cosy. Below and beside it hung the buildings of the university, Odins lund and high above, the vast bastion of the castle with its two cylinder towers capped in round lids of lead. He was looking at the picture Matilda Carrish had hung on her staircase, even the sky was the same, pale, ruffled, a north-edge-of-the-world backdrop, but the cathedral's spires in her mezzotint had been onion domes . . .

Too early yet to make his way to the man who had been her husband. He came to a modern, rather ugly street of the kind of shops he most hated in English cities, the kind of architecture everyone dislikes but which goes on being used; then, turning his back on it, to the river. Called the Fyris, it scurried along to divide the town. Ice-cold and glittering dark-blue its little waves looked as they rushed and tumbled towards the bridge and the next bridge and the next. Standing on this one, he was glad of his old tweed coat and he noticed everyone was more warmly wrapped than they would have been in Kingsmarkham. Scarves and hats and boots protected them from the knife-blade wind and the icy bite of the air. He watched his own breath make a beam of mist.

It would be pleasant walking along this river bank in summer, past the little shops and cafés, watching the boats. When would summer come? May or June, he supposed. On the western side he walked to the next bridge and, looking across the river, realised he had reached his destination. According to the map, that was Gamla Torget on the other side and the river bank street that ran into it, Östraågatan. So the ochre-coloured house, three floors high, its plain windows in its plain façade each with its pair of useful shutters, must be Trent's. The shutters were open now, the panes of glass gleaming in the thin sunlight. Like them, the front door was painted white. No Swedish architect, he thought, had wasted time or money on spurious house adornment, and the result was peaceful, calming, serene, if a little stark. As the cathedral clock chimed the half-hour, he crossed the bridge and rang Professor Trent's doorbell.

Trent himself would answer it, he had supposed, or whatever might be this cool and progressive nation's idea of a servant, the maker of nine-thirty coffee perhaps, a young girl rather like the severe waitress at the Linné. Very unexpected was to come face-to-face with a boy of sixteen, dark, extremely tall, but with the almost fragile thinness of adolescence.

'Philip said I should let you in,' Giles Dade said. 'I mean he said *I* should and not anyone else.'

CHAPTER 26

The warmth he had come to expect but not the eighteenth-century interior and early-Victorian furniture, white and blue and gleaming gilt. Everything awesomely and most unacademically clean. The boy hadn't spoken again. He was a good-looking boy with regular features, dark-blue eyes and luxuriant dark hair, which Wexford fancied had been left to grow for three months, perhaps the first time such laxness had been permitted. He showed Wexford into a living room that spanned the ground floor of the house. Almost the first things he noticed were the books in a bookcase like the one Matilda had and with more pictures of a tailless cat on their jackets. *Pelle Svanslös*, he read on a spine, not attempting to pronounce it. More pale delicate furniture, a ceiling-high stove in one corner encased in white and gold porcelain tiles, and a view of the river from the front windows and of a small bare garden at the back.

The old man who joined them within a moment or two was tall and nearly as skinny as Giles. Perhaps once, half a century ago and more, he had looked like Giles, and he still had the copious hair, now quite white. His expression was not so much irritable as preoccupied, distrait. It was apparent he looked on this development as an intrusion on a largely unvarying scholarly life.

'Well, yes, good morning,' he said in his Shand-Gibb voice. 'Please don't trouble yourself about this. I shall not be going to the university this morning. Don't feel you have to, er, speed things up.' He brought out this phrase as if uttering an outrageous piece of recent slang. Wexford understood he was dealing with a man so self-absorbed that he genuinely believed others must be exclusively concerned with anxieties about his comfort. 'Take your time. Sit down. Oh, you are sitting down, yes.'

He turned to Giles, addressed him in what was presumably Swedish, to which Giles responded in the same tongue. Wexford had to stop himself gaping. Trent said, when the boy had gone, 'A very simple language to learn, Swedish. All the Scandinavian languages are. Nothing to it. Inflected, of course, but in an entirely logical way – unlike some I could name.' Wexford was afraid he might but do so and with examples, but he continued on the subject of Swedish. 'I picked it up myself – oh, a hundred years ago – in a month or so. Giles is taking a little longer. I thought he should occupy himself usefully while here. Naturally, I have seen to the continuance of his education – and not only in that particular respect.'

He spoke as if Giles's missed schooling was the only aspect of his flight likely to give anyone much concern. Wexford was for a moment struck dumb. But when Giles returned with coffee pot and cups and saucers on a tray, he addressed the boy.

'Giles, I intend to return to the United Kingdom this afternoon on the two thirty p.m. flight to Heathrow and I have a ticket for you as well. I expect you to return with me.'

He also expected resistance from one or both of them. But Giles said only, 'Oh, I'll come.' He poured coffee, handed Wexford a cup and the milk jug. 'I know I have to go back. I always knew I'd have to some time.'

The old man was looking out of the window, not as if pretending tact or insouciance but surely because he really was thinking of something quite other, Palaungic syntax perhaps. The boy looked up, looked straight at Wexford, his face taking on that curious collapsing look, a crumbling or melting, that precedes tears. 'I'll come with you,' he said. An effort was made, his face set and there were no tears. 'How is my sister?'

'She's fine.' She wasn't but what else could he say? Certainly not at this stage that she had been abandoned by their mother. The scalding coffee alerting him and waking him in a bracing way, he turned his attention to the owner of this house. 'May I know what possessed you, Professor Trent, when you gave shelter to Giles? What were you thinking of, a responsible man, a respected scholar of your age? Didn't you consider your civic duty if nothing else?'

'"Possessed" me,' said Trent, smiling. 'I like that. I used to think, when I was young, how amazing it would be to be actually possessed. By some kind of spirit, I mean. Would it bring with it the gift of tongues, for instance? Imagine being suddenly endowed with the ability to speak Hittite?' Giles's shocked expression halted him. 'Oh, come on, Giles, you've given up all that fundamentalist nonsense, you know you have. You've told me so often enough. You know very well it's not possible to be possessed by a demon, gift of tongues or not.'

'I used to think', said Giles, 'that Joanna was possessed by one. They said a demon was what made people behave like that.' He didn't specify who 'they' were but it was apparent he meant the Good Gospellers. 'They said *I* had a demon that made me do what I did.'

'You know better now, an enlightened young person like you.'

Wexford thought it time to put a stop to this.
Professor Trent, you haven't answered my questions.'

'Have I not? What were they? Oh, yes, something
about my civic duty not to harbour fugitive criminals.
Well, I've never supposed I had a civic duty and Giles
isn't a criminal. You've just said that yourself.' He broke
into a flood of Swedish and Giles nodded. 'I'm not particularly responsible either, I've never had the least interest in law or politics or, come to that, religion. I've
always considered I had quite enough to do elucidating
the knotty problems of the languages spoken by seventy
million people.'

More incomprehensible asides to Giles prompted
Wexford to say testily, 'Please don't speak in Swedish. If
you persist I must ask to talk to Giles alone. I may do
that, he is over sixteen now. I take it that your late wife
telephoned you and asked you to receive Giles?'

'That is correct,' said Trent slightly more affably.
Poor Matilda. She knew I would do anything for her
except live in the United Kingdom of Great Britain and
Northern Ireland.' He shuddered artificially. 'She knew
I was exactly the man to give sanctuary to someone flee-
ing its justice. Besides, my housekeeper had moved up
to Umea and it seemed to me Giles might be an ade-
quate substitute for a while. I am, oddly enough, quite
a domesticated man, but I need some assistance. I must
tell you, I've grown quite attached to this boy. He performed a few tasks about the house, running errands,
making the beds and the coffee – now is that an example of zeugma, Giles?'

Giles grinned. 'No. It would be if you'd said, "making haste and the coffee". Yours is syllepsis.'

'Not quite but we won't go into it now,' said Trent.
I would have been a good deal less happy, Inspector,
if Matilda had sent me a fool. The housework

accomplished would hardly have been a compensation
for lack of mental ability. Am I coming close to solv-
ing your problems?'

Wexford didn't answer. He saw that pursuing this
was useless. And what did he intend to do if he got
some sort of admission out of Trent? Have him extra-
dited? The whole notion was ludicrous. Perhaps all he
was after was that rather contemptible goal, revenge.
Not quite abandoning the idea of it, he said, 'You are
aware, Mr Trent, that your wife is dead?'

At that Giles turned away his face but Trent said only,
'Oh, yes, I knew. Matilda's daughter told me. I might
have gone to the funeral – not that I approve of funerals
– and even if it had meant passing the time of day with
Giles's appalling parents, but I could hardly leave Giles
here alone. Apart from all that, I had just reached a crucial point in my research into the early proliferation of
Pear, what I believe is called a breakthrough.'

'I won't ask you what Ms Carrish's motive was. In
asking you to receive Giles, I mean. I know what it was.'

Giles looked at him enquiringly but he didn't eluci-
date. 'You travelled on your Irish passport,' he said.
'Before you left your home with Sophie you phoned
Matilda, knowing she would help you, and she suggested you bring your Irish passport with you but leave
the British one behind – to fool the police. Am I right?'

Giles nodded. 'What happened to Matilda?'

'She had a stroke,' Wexford said. 'Sophie was with
her. She'd been with her all the time. She phoned the
emergency services and then, of course, she had to give
herself up. There was nothing else for it.'

'We should have done that in the first place, shouldn't
we? Phoned the emergency services, I mean.' He didn't
need an answer. He knew what Wexford would say,
what everyone would say. 'I thought no one would

believe me. They'd think what Matilda thought and they wouldn't be so – so understanding.'

'You can tell me about it on the flight,' Wexford said. 'And now you'd better get your things together. We'll take ourselves to the airport, have some lunch first.'

Trent had been silent through most of this. Now he turned round and fixed his eyes, cold and blue as the Fyris, first on Wexford, then on the boy, and there they lingered. 'If I'd known it was going to take such a short time I wouldn't have rearranged my schedule.' You could hear the quotation marks clanging into place on either side of the final word. 'I suppose I can get up to the university now before any more time is wasted.'

'I'll come back,' the boy said eagerly. 'You know what we said. In two years' time I'll come back here to the university.' In the silence which followed he looked at Wexford. 'I will, won't I?'

'Let's hope so,' Wexford said. He turned to Trent. 'Tell me something. The cathedral here has two Gothic spires. When it was built in the fourteenth century it must have had Gothic spires. But in the prints I saw in Ms Carrish's house from the eighteenth and nineteenth centuries it's the same cathedral but it's got onion domes. Why?'

Trent looked deeply bored and at the same time harassed. 'Oh, there was an enormous fire here and the towers fell down or something like that and they put those onion things there and then at the end of the nineteenth *they* were out of fashion so they tore them down and put Gothic spires up again. Ridiculous.'

'Could I . . .' Giles said to him, 'could I have a copy of *Pelle*? Kind of as a souvenir?'

'Oh, take it, take it,' said Trent testily. 'And now if you'll excuse me . . .'

At the duty-free Wexford bought perfume for Dora,
bearing in mind Burden's pre-Christmas advice on this
subject. Giles drank a can of Coke and Wexford, without much enthusiasm, a small and very expensive bottle
of sparkling water. The boy was subdued and quiet,
evidently fearful of this return home and reluctant to
leave the country that had received him. He still stared
nostalgically out of the airport windows towards where
the flat plain of Upplands lay.

The flight was delayed but only by twenty minutes.
Wexford gave Giles the window seat. As they took off
the woman in the seat across the aisle crossed herself,
a little shamefacedly it seemed to Wexford. The boy,
who had also witnessed this, speaking for the first
time since they fastened their seatbelts, said, 'I've
given up all that.'

'All what?' Wexford thought he knew but he needed
to ask.

'You'd call it fundamentalism.' Giles made a face.
'The Good Gospel, all that. What happened cured me.
I thought – I thought they were – well, what they said,
good. I wanted to be good. I mean, in the widest possible sense – d'you know what I mean?'

'I think so.'

'You see, the way people behave – I mean people my
age – makes me feel sick. My sister's getting that way.
The sex and the words they use and the way they – they
sort of mock anything religious or moral or whatever.
The foul stuff on TV, I mean comedy shows and that.
And I thought – I thought I wanted to keep myself
away from all that, keep myself *clean*.

'The church I went to wasn't any good. That was St
Peter's. They didn't seem to know what they believed or
what they wanted. The Good Gospel people seemed so
sure. There was just one way for them, you did all those

things they said and you'd be all right. That's what I liked. Do you see?'

'Maybe. Why did you want the book?'

'*Pelle Svanslös*? *Svanslös* means "the tailless one". They're children's books about a cat and his friends, and they all live in Fjärdingen, near where I was. I had to have something to remind me.'

'Yes. You liked it there, didn't you? Now why don't you tell me what happened that weekend when Joanna came to stay? I've heard your sister's version and most of it wasn't true.'

'She tells lies all the time. But it's not her fault.'

'Now I want to hear the truth, Giles.'

The aircraft had begun its journey along the runway, proceeding slowly at first, then faster as the captain called to cabin crews to take their seats for take-off. Smoothly they soared into the air, from blue sky into blue sky for there was no cloud barrier to break through.

'I'll tell you the truth,' the boy said. 'I've wanted to do that for a long time but I've been – I've been afraid.' His face had whitened and as he turned his head to look at Wexford his expression was desperate. 'You have to believe me. I didn't – kill Joanna. I didn't do anything to her, not anything at all.'

'I know *that*,' Wexford said. 'I knew that before I found out where you were.'

CHAPTER 27

'There seem to be a lot of people getting off scot-free,' grumbled the Assistant Chief Constable.

'I wouldn't say that, sir,' Wexford said robustly. 'We've a murder charge, one for concealing a death, another for wasting police time. Even if the boy gets no more than probation and a period of community service, his conviction will be on his record for ever. I very much doubt, for instance, if the Swedish authorities will let him enter the country to attend the University of Uppsala when the time comes, which is what he wants to do.'

'And you call that punishment?'

'For him it will be. His sister's punishment is to have to go on living with their father.'

He had submitted his report to James Freeborn and explained it in detail. Now he was due to meet Burden and enlighten him. It was, of course, a wet evening in April, the fields surrounding Kingsmarkham permanently waterlogged but not under water. From where Wexford walked down the High Street towards the Olive and Dove those meadows simply looked a brilliant fresh green in the yellow clouded sunset. At the Queen Street turning he made a detour. Curiosity impelled him and, sure enough, the newsagent's, normally open until 8 p.m., was closed 'until further notice'. Perhaps it was a sign, perhaps this was the moment to stop taking that absurd anachronism, a provincial evening paper. Who needed it? Who wanted it? Still, if it disappeared many would lose their jobs and there were other newsagents in the neighbourhood to distribute it . . .

His digression had made him a little late. Burden was already in their 'snug', the small room tucked away in a back region but still with access to the saloon bar, the only corner of the drinking areas of the hotel, as Wexford sometimes said, to be free of music, fruit machines, food and children. Nor were there posters asking who wanted to be a millionaire, the local and live version of the television programme, no advertisements for tugs-of-war or clairvoyant dog contests, attractions it had long been assumed at the Rat and Carrot, and was now assumed all over the town, to be demanded indiscriminately by everyone. The snug, where Burden stood with his back to an enormous coal fire in a small grate, was a very small room with brown woodwork and brown-papered walls on which hung very dark pictures of a vaguely hunting-print kind. At least, from what you could make out in the gloom, they were of animals on foot and men on horseback chasing things through bracken, bramble and briar. If no one had smoked much in this room for several years, time was when many had. As the bar rooms of the Olive and Dove were never decorated and probably never had been since the beginning of the twentieth century, the smoke of several million cigarettes had mounted to the once cream-coloured ceiling and stained it the dark mahogany of the furniture.

Two tables and six chairs were the snug's only furniture. On the table nearer the fire stood two tankards of beer, two packets of crisps and some cashew nuts in a dish. It was enormously, but not unpleasantly, hot. Burden, deeply tanned from his holiday, was dressed in one version of his weekend garb, a tweed suit with caramel shirt and tie that fortuitously matched the ceiling.

'Raining again,' Wexford said.

'I hope you've got more to say than that.'

Wexford sat down. 'Too much, I dare say you'll think. It's nice here, isn't it? Quiet. Peaceful. I wonder if this will be the end of the United Gospel Church. Probably, for a while.' He took a swig of his lager, thought of opening one of the crisp packets but changed his mind with a sigh. 'All the time we thought this case was about the Dade children but it wasn't. Not really. They were just pawns. It was about the conflict between the Good Gospellers and Joanna Troy – or, rather, people like Joanna Troy in the broadest sense.'

'What does that mean?'

'I'll explain. There was an aspect of the Good Gospellers we knew about but to which we neglected to give the importance it deserved: their keenness on "purity". I should have paid more attention to it because it was one of the first things about the church's aims that Jashub Wright mentioned to me. He talked about something he called "inner cleanliness" and all I could think of was Andrews Liver Salts, which, in case you're too young to know, was a constipation remedy when I was a child. "Inner cleanliness" was their slogan. I suppose that's why I didn't pay any attention to the fact that it was also the Good Gospellers' slogan. Only they didn't mean what today is called clearing the body of toxins, they meant sexual purity, *chastity*. Unchastity was the prime sin new converts were expected to be open about when they were brought to the Confessional Congregation.'

'I don't imagine', said Burden, sitting, 'that Giles Dade had much of that to confess. He was only fifteen.'

'Then there you'd be wrong. He had some revelations for that bunch of latter-day saints or however they think of themselves. But we'll leave him for the moment and get back to the Good Gospellers themselves. Like many such fundamentalists, they weren't much concerned with other sins, things that maybe you and I would call sins, if we were inclined that way. I mean violence, assault, bodily harm, cruelty, stealing, lying and simple unkindness, none of that bothered them. And I get the distinct impression from Giles that they would have been impatient with anyone who wasted their time confessing to hitting his wife or neglecting his children. It was sex they were concerned with, pre- and extramarital sex, fornication and adultery, most of it in their view caused by women and their tempting ways, rather in the way the early fathers of the Roman Catholic Church thought about it or some modern American cults. Sex, according to Giles, must in their view be confined exclusively within marriage and not too much of it there. Ideally, it should be restricted to the procreation of children.'

Burden nodded. 'Sure, but where does Giles come in?'

'Let's move on to Joanna Troy now. Joanna was apparently an entirely normal young woman, clever, gifted, nice-looking, a good teacher and potentially a successful person with a full life ahead of her. But she had already done a good deal to make that full life look unlikely.'

'What do you mean?'

Wexford looked up at the window, at the rain lashing against it and the dusk deepening outside. The curtains, of figured brown velvet, looked as if they had never been drawn since someone first hung them on their mahogany pole thirty or forty years before. He got up and tugged at them, releasing clouds of tobacco-smelling dust. As they met across the window the decay of years showed in the transparent ragged areas where they were coming apart. Both of them laughed.

'I only wanted to shut out the weather,' Wexford said and, after a pause, 'You asked me what I meant. When Joanna was a teenager she was attracted by her contemporaries, like most people of her age. At fifteen she lost her mother. What that meant to her we shall never know and I'm not a psychologist, but I'd guess she was very traumatised by that loss, especially as her sole parent then was that dreary old windbag George Troy with about as much understanding as a flea. Maybe an effect of it was to make her revert to childhood and to the companionship of children, though she was no longer a child. Maybe if she had had brothers none of this would have happened.

'The first thing to happen, or the first we know about, was the incident at school with Ludovic Brown. He was younger than she, probably prepubertal, and when Joanna made advances to him he was frightened and repelled her. She did all she knew how to do then – she fought him. He wouldn't, shall we say, love her? – so she beat him up. Revenge and anger and the misery of rejection all went into it. The consequences of that we know. His death, was an accident, quite separate from this case.

'Joanna must have had other relationships with boys, some of them satisfactory, but as she grew older and the ages of the boys remained the same, that is in their early or mid-teens, her tastes began to look unnatural. But she was trapped in adolescence by the trauma of her mother's death which happened when she was sixteen.'

Burden interrupted him. 'Are you saying Joanna Troy was a paedophile?'

'I suppose I am. We think of paedophiles as men and their victims as either girls or boys. Older women having a taste for young boys doesn't seem to come into the same category, largely, I think, because most men, when told about it, tend to make "Aarrgh" noises and say they should have been so lucky.'

Burden pulled a face that had a grin in it. 'I wasn't going to say that but they do have a point. You know me, you think I'm a bit of a prude, but even I can't imagine a boy of fifteen with all that testosterone slurping about inside him saying no to a good-looking woman ten or twelve years older than himself.'

'You'd better imagine it, Mike, because it happened. Only say seventeen years older. But first came Joanna's marriage. Ralph Jennings was in his early twenties when she met him but he looked years younger. Those very fair people do. Unfortunately, they also age correspondingly faster. I think Joanna believed Jennings might be her salvation. He was a passive yes-man but quite bright, a potential high earner, they had plenty in common. Perhaps if she was with him she'd stop fancying boys ten years her junior. This proclivity of hers, after all, wasn't just a nuisance, it was as much against the law as if she'd been a middle-aged man and the boys girls in their teens.

'But, sadly for her, Jennings started to go bald. His face reddened. Domestic life ruined his boyish figure. Sex was not only no longer the fun it had been, it was becoming distasteful. The marriage broke up. But Joanna remained in Kingsmarkham and in her prestigious job teaching at Haldon Finch. Instead of controlling her impulses towards boys of fourteen or fifteen, she let rip, as people so often do when some long-term relationship comes to an end.' Wexford paused, thinking of Sylvia, wondering how many more there would be before things worked out for her. 'She was in exactly the right place for a female paedophile, wasn't she?' he went on. 'A mixed school where she taught students of the age she most fancied. And in a much better position than her male counterparts, for young girls who may often have been raped or at least seduced are far more likely to complain than boys enjoying sex for the first time.

'Damon Wimborne didn't complain. He would happily have continued his relationship with Joanna for months if not years. You talk of testosterone but we forget the idealistic aspect; we forget how prone young boys are to worship and put the adored one on a pedestal. Damon was in love with Joanna, "whatever that may mean", as Jennings and a more eminent person put it. But it's a sad fact that for some people, having a sexual partner in love with them is the most off-putting thing. It put Joanna off and her feelings for Damon cooled to a point of – nothing. But in a way, she was still a teenager and always would be. Teenagers are rude to their contemporaries – and others – and they say bluntly what they think. She told him she was no longer interested in no uncertain terms, probably brutal terms. We misquote that most popular of aphorisms and say, "Hell hath no fury like a woman scorned." But the lines are: "Heaven hath no rage like love to hatred turned, nor hell a fury like a woman scorned." Love can turn to hatred in men as well as women and that's what Damon's did. He was scorned and he needed to lash back. Physically, he was a mature man but he was only fifteen, his mind was fifteen. He said he'd seen her steal a twenty-pound note from his backpack . . .'

'Yes. It fits.' Burden tapped Wexford's tankard. 'Another?'

'In a minute. The head teacher couldn't understand why Joanna didn't fight it and clear her name. But Joanna dared not do that. Everything would come out if she did. She knew her career as a teacher was over, there was no help for it. Resign now and make a new career for herself, be self-employed so that within reason she could do as she liked. She owned her house without encumbrances, she had the use of her father's car, she had her qualifications and the opportunity was there . . .'

He was interrupted by the arrival of the barman. 'Another round, gentlemen? I thought I'd pop in because we've a coach party and we may be a bit busy over the next half-hour.'

Wexford asked for two more halves, glancing complacently at the untouched crisps and nuts. 'Some months before she had made the acquaintance of Katrina Dade. I can't imagine Katrina was much company for a woman like her but she was a sycophant and people of Joanna's sort, clever, prickly, paranoid, immature, they like sycophants, they like to be buttered up all the time, flattered, told how brilliant they are.'

'This may be particularly true', put in Burden, 'when the flattered looks free and independent, self-supporting and successfully feminist, and the flatterer is disturbed, dependent, always seeking role models and someone to adore.'

'I see evidence of that psychology course Freeborn made you take.'

'Maybe, and why not?'

The barman came back with their order and two packets of a different variety of crisps. 'On the house, gentlemen,' he said kindly. 'I see you've drawn the curtains. Shut out the floods, eh?'

'Floods?'

'The river's rising just like it did in the winter. Those old curtains haven't been drawn since they went up in nineteen seventy-two and it shows, doesn't it?'

Wexford shut his eyes. 'I just hope my garden's all right.' He waited till the barman had gone back to his coach party. 'Still, as far as I know we've still got the

sandbags. To return to Joanna, she didn't know o
Giles's existence at that time, just that Katrina had tw
children. Katrina gave up being school secretary and
now neither of them was at Haldon Finch but the
went on seeing each other and eventually Joanna wen
to Katrina's house.'

'I take it that all this time Joanna was managing t
indulge her sexual tastes with young boys? These wer
the "men" Yvonne Moody had seen going to the hous
and they had ostensibly come there for private tuition?

'That's right. Then, at Antrim, Joanna met Gile
Dade. He was fourteen at the time but that wasn't to
young for her. A stumbling block was his commitmen
to religion, first to the Anglicans, then to the Unite
Gospel Church. But Joanna had offered her services t
the Dades as a child-sitter, the best possible way sh
thought she could get to know Giles. Oddly, like a lo
of teachers, she wasn't very good with children. Sophi
disliked her from the first, Giles, in the grip of religiou
mania, simply wasn't much interested, and Joanna di
nothing to win their trust or their affection. I gather sh
just gazed at Giles and started touching him, his arm o
his shoulder or running a finger down his back, and h
didn't understand what on earth it meant.

'That was one of her problems. Another was tha
though the Dades occasionally went out in the evening
they never went away overnight. Joanna simply wasn'
getting anywhere and her suggestion to Roger Dad
that his son might like to come to her for private tuitio
also failed. Dade might be a bully and a tyrant but h
recognised a good brain when he came across one. I
this case, two. He knew both his children were academ
ically clever – in a way he never had been – and perhap
he was even stricter because of this, he was determine
their talents wouldn't be wasted, they must be encourage

to get on. But not with Joanna Troy. Her services simply weren't called for. Giles had taken a French GCSE when he was only fourteen and got an A star. German wasn't on his curriculum. What could Joanna teach him?

'French conversation. Or so she thought. She began coming round – at her own invitation – to instigate French conversation with him, to watch videos in French and encourage him to read French classics. It wasn't a very successful move because Giles had changed courses since then and was working hard at Russian along with history and politics. French he had done with for the time being. That Giles is very quick at languages was shown, I think, by his picking up Swedish in a matter of weeks, and at that time it was Russian – a very difficult language – he was concentrating on. His spare time, such as it was, he devoted to the United Gospel Church. In a few months' time he was due to be received into that church after he had attended the Congregation in Passingham woods and made his confession.'

Burden said ruefully, 'He had very little to confess then, I suppose.'

'Nothing more than a bit of backsliding about going to church and possibly lack of respect to his parents, something else the Good Gospellers were very hot on. But in the spring the Dades went away for the night. It was the annual dinner and dance of Roger's firm's parent company and, for a change, it wasn't held in Brighton but in London. They would have to stay overnight. I don't know if Joanna overheard them discussing this and offered her services or if Katrina asked her. The only thing that matters is that Roger and Katrina went to this function and Joanna stayed the night with Giles and Sophie.

'It was a Saturday and one of those Saturday evenings rather than Sunday mornings when the Good Gospellers held their weekly service. Giles told me that Joanna, who arrived at about five, tried to stop him going. She insisted on speaking French to him in order to stop Sophie understanding, a stratagem you can imagine maddened the volatile Sophie who also has a very good brain, only her talents lie in the areas of maths and science, not languages.

'Giles, who is considerably more sophisticated now, had very little idea of why Joanna insisted on sitting close up to him and talking to him – in French – in what he describes as "a wheedling way". He's quite open and frank, and he says the way she behaved reminded him of actresses flirting on television, "making up to men", as he puts it. In real life he had known nothing like it but it made him uneasy. Still, he went to church but he had to come home again.

'It was only half past nine but apparently both Joanna and Sophie had gone to bed. He went up to his bedroom, relieved not to have to talk to Joanna any more. Much as he dislikes his parents, he found them infinitely preferable to Joanna Troy. He undressed, went to bed and sat up memorising grammar from a Russian textbook in preparation for a lesson on the Monday morning. Joanna came in without knocking. She was wearing a dressing gown which she undid without a word and dropped to the floor. He says he sat there, staring blankly at her. But something happened which he describes as "horrible". He doesn't know, I quote, "how it could have happened". He was aroused, and violently so. Things were utterly beyond his control. He hated Joanna then but he wanted her more than he had ever wanted anything in his life. I think we both know what he meant and further explanation isn't necessary. He was only fifteen and this was his first experience.

'He held out his arms to her, he couldn't help himself. He wasn't himself, he says, and for a while he really
believed he'd been possessed by a demon – to use Good
Gospellers' language. Joanna got into bed with him and
the rest is obvious – in the circumstances inescapable.'

CHAPTER 28

Wexford drew back a corner of curtain and they
watched the coach party leave, stumbling towards their
single-decker through deepening puddles, through
stair-rod-straight rain, coats protecting hairdos,
umbrellas up, one man with a newspaper over his head.
It was a copy of the *Evening Courier*.

'I'm going to phone Dora.'

The message service was switched on. He cursed
modern innovations, thinking how extremely mystified
his own parents would have been by a man's ability to
phone home, be spoken to by his own self and then
address that self with an abusive expletive which would
be recorded for himself to hear whenever he chose.
Burden listened with an impassive face while he spoke
these thoughts aloud, then said, 'Go on with all that
sexy stuff about Giles and Joanna.'

'Ah, yes. I think Giles felt at first as most boys of his
age would: astonishment, a certain amount of fear,
gratification that things had – well, worked, and even
pride. He was still enjoying the situation when Joanna
came back early next morning and a couple of weeks
later when Joanna came for the evening while the Dade
parents went out. Sophie was in the house but in her
room. However, in the following week she challenged
Giles about it and he told her. There was no risk, she'd
have been no more likely to tell Roger or Katrina than
he would.

'But her knowledge of the affair, if we can call it that, eventually gave her that daunting sexual sophistication which made me believe for a while that she must have been abused and that her father was abusing her. No one was. She was just privy to Giles's activities then and his changed attitude later.'

'His changed attitude?'

'Oh, yes. You see, at first he made no connection between what was going on between him and Joanna and his religious affiliation. Or so he tells me. They were in separate compartments of his life. Then, one Sunday morning, he was in church when brother Jashub preached a sermon on sexual purity. That was in early June. You might say if you were a Good Gospeller and given to biblical metaphor, that the scales fell from his eyes. Moreover, he had been told that he must make his public confession at the Confessional Congregation in July. Suddenly he saw that what had seemed a wonderful enhancement of his life, great fun at its lowest and sublime at its highest, was just a squalid sin. He would have to end it and make Joanna understand.

'He was only fifteen. He began by cancelling an appointment he had to go to Joanna's house. He never had been there, this was to be a first, and he told her it was too risky for him. His mother would find out. As luck would have it, the Dade parents weren't going anywhere in the evenings so Joanna's services wouldn't be called for. The Congregation date came and he was taken to Passingham Hall woods. There was a shortage of cars and various participants were starting from their places of work, not from home, so he was escorted to Passingham by train and thence by taxi, from which he acquired his knowledge of how to get to Passingham Park station. For the return journey there were plenty of cars and drivers willing to take him back. He came back in a car with four Good Gospellers. It must have been a right squeeze.'

Burden interposed, 'Do you feel like eating something? I don't mean these so-called nibbles. Shall I see if this place can rustle up a sandwich?'

While he consulted a menu the barman had brought, Wexford went out into the porch. The rain had eased a little. He picked someone's umbrella out of the stand, thinking how awkward it would be if the owner panicked and accused him of stealing it. But he would only be a minute. He stepped out on to the forecourt, avoiding puddles.

What had he expected? That the Kingsbrook Bridge would be under water? Certainly the river had risen and become once more a rushing torrent. This was the point at which Sophie had thrown her T-shirt over the parapet. Conditions must have been very much the same as now, the water rising but the bridge still passable, rain descending so steadily it seemed it must never cease. Giles had driven on, gaining confidence with every mile, Joanna's body in the boot of the car. Did he think, when he was on his way to dispose of it in Passingham woods, of the journey he had made home from there on that previous occasion? Had they, that sententious bunch in Nun Plummer's car, cited for him the example of the virginal Joseph resisting with iron chastity Potiphar's wife? I bet they did, Wexford thought. They weren't Catholics, so the temptation of St Anthony wouldn't have come into it . . .

He ran back into the hotel, opened and shut the umbrella to shake off the raindrops and replaced it in the stand.

Burden was back in the snug with more lager – time to watch it now – and toasted sandwiches ordered. 'So he confessed all that in public, did he?' he said.

'In front of a howling mob, you might say,' Wexford said. 'Singing and dancing, as Shand-Gibb's housekeeper put it. His only comfort must have been that no names were mentioned. They had allowed that. He was absolved, of course, on the usual grounds that his behaviour mustn't be repeated. And he was assigned a mentor to guide and watch over him. One of the elders to see he didn't sin again.

'He didn't intend to. That congregation had shaken him, as it might have shaken someone three times his age. Once again he told his sister about it but he said nothing to Joanna, he just did his best to avoid her and he was successful. At what cost to himself we don't know but I can guess at. In September his grandmother Matilda Carrish came to stay. An uncomfortable visit, I imagine, owing to the dislike of Katrina for her mother-in-law and Matilda's contempt for Katrina. I think she only went there because she was worried about Sophie. Why she thought she had any grounds for worry I don't know and now we never shall know. Perhaps it was only that as a child she herself had been sexually abused by her own father and she suspected Roger of having the same proclivities. She was wrong but we suspected the same and we were wrong too.

'Was the subject discussed between her and Sophie? Sophie is such an accomplished liar that it may be impossible to find out. I think of myself –' Wexford looked rueful, raising his eyebrows '– as a good lie detector but that child runs rings round some of the worst villains in that department I've ever interrogated. Pity you can't do GCSEs in mendacity, she'd be in the A star category. Maybe she inherited her talent from her paternal grandma who's no slouch at lying herself.

'Anyway, what Matilda did succeed in doing was establish a strong bond between herself and her son's

children. It wouldn't be an exaggeration to say that in
those three days they came to love her. Here was a
grown-up person who took them seriously, who wasn't
always yelling at them or weeping over them, and who
perhaps said before she left that if they ever needed her
she'd be there. They only had to phone. One phone call
would fetch her. Needless to say maybe, Giles said nothing to her about the Joanna business. Why would he?
He was trying to put it behind him.'

Wexford ate a sandwich and then another. As he
savoured the hot melted butter, the rare but not too rare
roast beef, the capers and raw red onion, he felt he could
see his waistline expanding. Few writers on the subject
seemed to point out that delicious food makes you fat
and the kind no one wants to eat doesn't. There must be
a reason for this but he didn't know what it was.

'Get to the crucial weekend, Reg,' said Burden.

'The crucial weekend, yes. When his mother told
him Joanna would be coming while she and his father
were away, Giles was seriously worried. Since the
Congregation he had become far more conscious of
the need for chastity than he ever had been before.
Well, he had scarcely been at at all conscious of it
before. Now he agreed that continence must be a
good thing, something worth adhering to until he got
married. He had heard several more sermons on the
subject and the Good Gospel elders, starting with lec-
tures in the car home from Passingham, had taken it
upon themselves to keep him up to the mark.
Incredible as it sounds, they even instituted a couple
of one-to-one tutorials. One of these was conducted
by Pagiel Smith and the other by Hobab Winter.
Brother Jashub was also around quite a bit, dispensing
admonitions and threats. They all made extramarital

sex into a far worse sin than cruelty, untruthfulness, fraud and even murder.

'Up till that time Giles had never specifically named his sexual partner to any of them,' Wexford went on. 'But now he was growing more and more worried by the day. She was coming to stay in a fortnight's time, in a week, in a few days. After church on Sunday, the nineteenth of November, he spoke to the Rev. Mr Wright, and told him everything. Joanna would be coming to stay in his home in the absence of his parents on the following Friday. Jashub called a council of elders, all of them bent on keeping Giles pure.'

'That poor kid,' said Burden.

He passed Wexford the sandwiches. Taking one, Wexford thought how, as long as he could remember back in their relationship, when there had been four sandwiches, Burden had had one and he had had three and when there had been eight he had had six and Burden had had two. This happened now and it was no doubt the reason why he was always thinking of battling with his weight if not actually battling with it, while Burden remained thin as a teenager. He sighed.

'As we know, the Dade parents went away on Friday the twenty-fourth in the morning and Joanna came in the late afternoon. One part of Giles hoped she would have forgotten everything that had passed between them, but we won't be surprised to learn that the other part of him longed for her to remember. She remembered all right, came to his room on the Friday evening and the rest was inevitable. Not without a struggle on Giles's part, though. He told her what he now believed, that this was very wrong, and she laughed at him. In a couple of weeks he'd be sixteen and what they were doing would no longer be illegal. She had misunderstood.

'Sophie knew all about it. She had watched Joanna's advances to Giles throughout the evening and translated them neatly for my benefit into passages between Joanna and "Peter". His name, of course, was an invention, unconsciously adopted from the author of that recipe article. It didn't take much imagination as it must be one of the commonest names there are. She didn't know that two real Peters were connected with the case, and if she had I dare say she'd only have thought it funny.'

'What happened next day?'

'All that shopping and cooking described to me by Sophie was rubbish. She got the dinner menu out of a newspaper supplement that wasn't published until two weeks ago. Not quite clever enough, but still she's only thirteen, there's plenty of time for improvement and by the time she's twenty she'll be the most expert spinner of fictions we're ever likely to see. Far from accompanying Joanna and Sophie on this food-buying spree and having lunch out with them, Giles went round to Jashub Wright's, told him what had happened and that he was fearful of its happening again. What should he do? Resist, he was told, be strong. There's something ridiculous these days about the image of a young highly sexed man keeping himself chaste for what is a wholly imaginary concept of the man we call Jesus – who never said a word about sex outside marriage – but not to these people. Giles was to resist *in His name* and he would get help.

'By the time he got back to Antrim, the rain had begun. He looked forward with dread to the evening ahead of him. Remember there was no "Peter", there was no dinner guest and no elaborate meal. There were just the three of them, each in his or her way tense about what was to come: Sophie curious and excited, Joanna preparing to break down a resistance which only

dded spice to the whole affair, Giles struggling to keep
er at a distance, desperately wishing, he says, that he
ad the practical aid of a lock on his bedroom door.'

'But wait a minute,' said Burden, 'you've told me
Giles wasn't involved in Joanna's death, but there were
nly the three of them in the house?'

'At that time there were only the three of them in the
ouse. But the situation changed. By six it was raining
ery hard indeed, as you'll remember. The newspaper,
he *Evening Courier* was late on account of the rain
ut at just before six thirty it came. The person who
elivered it didn't ring the doorbell but Giles heard the
aper fall on to the mat and went out to fetch it.'

'Where does Scott Holloway come into all this?'

'Scott hated Joanna. I'll tell you why I think this was.
ophie wasn't the only one Giles told about his relation-
ip with Joanna. When it first began and the guilt hadn't
arted he told Scott too, let's say he boasted to him
bout his – well, his conquest, his experience. When
cott found himself booked to have private coaching
om Joanna he hoped for the same thing to happen but
oanna rejected him. The poor boy isn't exactly attrac-
ve, is he? No wonder he hated her, gave up his lessons
nd when he saw her car outside Antrim that Saturday
vening, went straight back home to avoid seeing her.

'The occupants of Antrim went to bed early, Giles
n two minds. He knew now that he was safe, though in
nany ways safety was the last thing he wanted. Joanna's
dvances to him while they sat on the sofa watching
elevision, advances she barely bothered to conceal from
ophie, had quite naturally excited him almost beyond
earing. Yet he knew he was safe. Knowing his dilemma,
ophie refused to go to bed and leave them until Giles
ad gone. She went upstairs at the same time as Joanna
nd watched her go to her bedroom.

'Half an hour later Joanna was lying dead at th
bottom of the stairs. She had been pushed down o
thrown down, and by someone who saw himself a
opposing the Great Dragon, the Antichrist. His mis
sion accomplished, he left Giles to clear up the mes
and, presumably, face the music. This, Giles think
wise after the event, was intended as his punishmen
for with these people confession and absolution are no
enough. There must be atonement. Besides, Giles ha
sinned again since he confessed at Congregation. H
had repeated his sin, the same sin. Only after he ha
left the house did Sophie come out of her room an
saw what had happened.

'The first thing they did was phone their grand
mother. They were in a blind panic and she had said sh
would always be there for them. She was. She was a roc
and a sanctuary. The children calmed down. She sav
their difficulty, she understood Giles's terror of his fathe
of the law, of the discovery of his behaviour with Joann
— but she thought he had killed Joanna. She didn
believe in the intervention of a third person and nor di
Sophie. They were liars, you see, and liars think the res
of the world lies like they do. Of course, a sensibl
woman would have advised them to phone us at once
waste no more time, but Matilda Carrish wasn't ver
sensible. Clever, even brilliant, talented, but neither sen
sible nor wise. Bring your Irish passport, she told Giles
Leave Joanna where she is and leave her car and com
here as soon as you can get here.

'They obeyed her to a certain extent. They would go
but why not go in Joanna's car and take her body witl
them? Sophie didn't believe Giles's story, so the polic
wouldn't. If Joanna's body was here and they weren't
wouldn't the police assume them guilty? But if there wa
no body . . . Giles was only fifteen and he had beer

enormously afraid but I think some spirit of adventure came into it now. He could drive and he wanted to drive. Freedom was what was in Sophie's mind. Get away from here, get away from those parents. Make it look, they both thought, as if Joanna is still alive and has abducted us . . .'

Wexford's phone was ringing. Dora's voice said, 'Have you been trying to get me? I'm at Sylvia's with her and Johnny.' *Johnny*? Things had been moving fast. 'Where are you, anyway?'

'In a pub.'

'I see. If you've been worrying about the rain, there's no water lying anywhere near our garden but we've still got the sandbags and if there's any sort of threat Johnny says he'll come and put them up against the wall. See you later.'

'Do you know what *Plus ça change plus c'est la même chose* means?'

'No,' said Burden.

'It's pretty well the only bit of French I do know,' Wexford said. He went on unfairly, 'It's just that Sylvia's new chap sounds just the same as the last one.'

Burden said in a nasty tone, his upper lip curled, 'You are a master of suspense, aren't you? You love it. You even get better at it. I reckon you've been working on it.'

'I don't know what you mean,' said Wexford.

'Who killed Joanna Troy, is what I mean.'

'I'm coming to that. Let's go back a few hours to the evening paper delivery.'

'The *what*?'

'Wait. It's important. We all have the same Queen Street newsagent round my neighbourhood and Lyndhurst Drive is my neighbourhood. As you know, Antrim is only a few streets away from me. The round begins, not in Queen Street itself, nor does it touch Godstone Road. Therefore it also fails to take in most of Lyndhurst Drive, but starts in Chesham Road, follows my road, Caversham Avenue, Martindale Gardens, the north side of Kingston Drive, back along the south side and ends on the corner of Lyndhurst Drive and Kingston Drive. The last house in Lyndhurst is covered by the round and is always the last house at which a paper is delivered. That house, as you know, is Antrim. The person who delivers the *Kingsmarkham Evening Courier* is usually but not invariably a girl much the same age as Giles Dade and Scott Holloway, Dorcas Winter. On Saturday the twenty-fifth of November she didn't deliver those papers. She *seldom did on a Saturday*, because she had a violin lesson. Her father took over.

'He delivered the papers on foot and got very wet in the process. When he came to the last house, which was of course Antrim, he didn't have to ring the doorbell because Giles heard the paper fall on to the mat and went to the door. But even if Joanna had heard it and gone to the door it wouldn't have worried him. He had his excuse ready. Seeing that he knew Giles, they were both members of the same church and, more than that, he was Giles's mentor, assigned to him and teacher and guide. Could he come in and dry himself before returning home?'

'Members of the Good Gospellers, you mean?'

'The newsagent', said Wexford, 'is Kenneth, alias Hobab, Winter.'

CHAPTER 29

'He has already appeared in court, as you know,' Wexford said, 'on a murder charge and been committed. Charging Giles with concealing a death can't be avoided, though I hope to drop a wasting police time charge. The good things that have come out of it are that he's turned his back on the Good Gospellers and they seem to be in the process of disbanding, he's learned another language which he's going to take along with other GCSEs in a couple of months' time and he seems to be on slightly better terms with his father. Sophie won't be charged with anything. Frankly, I think any court would take her word against police and expert witness evidence. We'd be wasting our time.'

'Get back to Hobab Winter,' said Burden.

'You'll remember that during the afternoon Giles had appeared before Jashub Wright and an emergency session of the elders. Hobab, of course, was present. Something we're working on now is whether they all knew what Hobab planned to do, whether they all planned it, or if he did it off his own bat. Giles doesn't know. They dismissed him with those cryptic words that he would "get help". He thought it likely help would come from his mentor and, as you can imagine, he half wanted it and half wanted anything but. When the paper came he saw he had guessed right.

'Hobab came into the living room and was introduced to Joanna and Sophie. He was even *given a cup*

of tea. I know. You may well laugh. Something lik
that was a possibility we'd thought of and dismissed a
ludicrous. His raincoat was hung up in the hall over
radiator, his shoes dried in the kitchen and the woolle
gloves he was wearing also put on a radiator to dry. Hi
other clothes weren't wet apart from his trouser bottom
and these he left to dry on him.

'Hobab intended to kill Joanna, of that I'm sure. I
he had left her injured but alive she would hold him
and therefore the Good Gospellers, responsible. Mark
were found on her, you'll remember, indicative of he
having been beaten about the face and head. Also h
took another step to conceal the fact that he'd been in
the house. Unknown to Joanna and Sophie, h
remained there. When his gloves were dry – this i
important – and his shoes wearable, Giles took him
upstairs to his own bedroom. As far as Sophie and
Joanna knew, this hadn't happened. According to Giles
they thought he had taken his raincoat from the hal
and left the house. In Giles's bedroom, with Giles'
Bible to read, he sat in a chair and waited. He intended
Giles says, to wait all night if necessary, to preven
further sin being committed.

'Joanna, presumably made confident by Giles'
succumbing to her the night before, repeated the
process downstairs. Giles says he didn't encourage he
and of course he must have been mindful all the time o
the presence of Hobab Winter upstairs. However, afte
he had gone into his bedroom for the night Joanna came
to the door and once again she didn't knock. Perhaps i
she had she might have saved her life, if she had been a
little more tentative and a little less presumptuous.

'As it was, Hobab leapt from his chair and man-
handled her from the room. Beat her with his fists and
banged her head against the wall. No doubt he used al

sorts of imprecations to her, calling her the Scarlet Woman and the Great Dragon, whatever. She screamed – it must have come as a great shock to her – and from the very top of the staircase, Hobab threw her down, more than satisfied to see her strike her head against a corner of that cupboard.'

'Ah,' said Burden. 'I see. And he just left the house? He left two children to deal with it.'

'I think he barely noticed Sophie's presence down-stairs. After all, she was a girl, maybe growing up into another Joanna. His own daughter he probably thinks of as the only female worth saving. Besides, Sophie didn't come out of her room until he had left. She's a sound sleeper. Yes, he left Giles to it and walked the short dis-tance to his home through the driving rain, very likely congratulating himself on a successful mission.'

'Did he really think he could get away with it? He didn't know Giles and Sophie would leave and take the body with them.'

'And would anyone have believed Giles if he said the man delivering the evening paper had pushed Joanna down the stairs? A man who left no traces behind him? Someone Joanna had never even met? Someone Sophie knew had gone home hours before? Remember that Sophie too thought Giles guilty. Any of the elders of the Good Gospel Church would have alibi'd Hobab. His wife had done so, as all their wives had alibi'd them. Look how the elders behaved after the disappearance of the three was known. They – Jashub Wright certainly – acted not only innocent, but indifferent. Unchastity is the most heinous of all sins to them. Violent death didn't matter much, especially if in a good cause, and lying in court would have been a mere peccadillo, easily excused.'

'So this respectable newsagent, this pillar of his church, having led a blameless life, suddenly ups and kills a young woman with savage violence. A bit way out, isn't it?'

'It would be if what you've said were true.'

'What do you mean?'

Wexford said thoughtfully, 'You know I don't talk about these things at home. No more than you do. Dora picked up something about this case, she was bound to, managing the Internet for me, but Sylvia knew nothing till she saw the very brief bit about Hobab appearing in the magistrates' court. Saw it in the *Evening Courier*, by the way, which pretty well justifies its existence for me. She came round – with that Johnny, of course – and told me about something that happened one night when she was on the helpline at that women's refuge of hers.

'It was a couple of years ago. The woman who phoned in wouldn't give her name. Not at first. She said her husband had beaten her up and she was afraid to be in the house when he came back from his prayer meeting. Sylvia thought that bizarre enough for a start but she told the woman to take a taxi and come to The Hide. As you've guessed it was Priscilla Winter, Mrs Hobab Winter. Her nose was broken, she had two black eyes, and bruises all over her.'

'And an elder of the Good Gospel Church had done that?'

'Oh, yes, and not for the first time. Though the first for a long while. He regularly knocked her about, once *knocked her downstairs*, when their daughter was little, but this was the first time for a couple of years. The reason for it was that he'd come home and found her having a cup of tea with a male neighbour. The pity was that she only stayed at The Hide two nights and then she went back home. She couldn't leave Dorcas, she said.'

'She'll be free of Hobab now,' said Burden. He took his raincoat from the dusty old wooden coat rack and helped Wexford into his. They went out into the High Street. The rain had lessened to a thin drizzle. 'But I still don't see how you can be sure it was murder. A savage attack, yes, a tragic accident, even manslaughter. But murder?'

'Oh, didn't I say?' Wexford put up the umbrella he was carrying. 'After he'd dried his gloves, Winter kept them on all the time. Not for warmth. It was a mild night and the heating was on. He meant to kill her and he kept his gloves on to avoid leaving fingerprints in Giles's room and on Giles's Bible. If it doesn't sound too psychodiagnostic, I'd say he was killing his wife at the same time and maybe a lot of other women too.'

'And I', said Burden, forgetting all about his psychology course, 'would say he was a total villain.'

'Do you know,' said Wexford, 'I've taken someone else's umbrella, one of the coach party and they've gone now. I think that's the first time in my life I've ever stolen anything.'

ABOUT THE AUTHOR

Since her first novel, *From Doon with Death*, published in 1964, Ruth Rendell has won many awards, including the Crime Writers' Association Gold Dagger for 1976's best crime novel with *A Demon in My View*, and the Arts Council National Book Award, genre fiction, for *The Lake of Darkness* in 1980.

In 1985 Ruth Rendell received the Silver Dagger for *The Tree of Hands*, and in 1987, writing as Barbara Vine, won her third Edgar from the Mystery Writers of America for *A Dark-Adapted Eye*.

She won the Gold Dagger for *Live Flesh* in 1986, for *King Solomon's Carpet* in 1991 and, as Barbara Vine, a Gold Dagger in 1987 for *A Fatal Inversion*.

Ruth Rendell won the *Sunday Times* Literary Award in 1990, and in 1991 she was awarded the Crime Writers' Association Cartier Diamond Dagger for outstanding contribution to the genre. In 1996 she was awarded the CBE, and in 1997 was made a Life Peer.

Her books have been translated into twenty-five languages and are also published to great acclaim in North America.

Ruth Rendell has a son and two grandsons, and lives in London.